EVOLUTION

JUSTICE KEEPERS SAGA BOOK V

R. S. PENNEY

PROLOGUE

Spreading peanut butter on a piece of toast with a knife, Jon Andalon let out a soft sigh. The sunlight that streamed in through the windows behind him warmed his body and illuminated the white cupboards and blue walls of his kitchen.

Jon was a tall man, slim and muscular and dressed in black pants and a gray t-shirt. Dark of skin and eye, he wore his black hair buzzed to little more than stubble. "Honey! You're going to be late."

In his mind's eye, the silhouette of his boyfriend emerged from the door that led to the bedroom, pulling a t-shirt over his head. He turned around just in time to see Ren poke his head through the neck-hole.

Jon smiled, bowing his head to the other man. "Always running late," he teased, striding forward and offering a plate. "I'm telling you, one of these days, you're going to be responsible for my losing the last of my hair."

Ren was a handsome man with a square jaw, dark skin and eyes that lit up every time he looked at you. "That might be a good look for you." He snatched up the piece of toast and took a bite at the corner.

"Maybe."

"So, what's on the agenda for today?" Ren asked. "Apprehending a terrorist cell? Or maybe thwarting an arms dealer."

Closing his eyes, Jon trembled with soft laughter. "You really should know better," he said, shaking his head ruefully. "*Nothing* happens on Belos. Even the Antaurans don't bother us anymore."

Ren said nothing in response to that, opting to chew his toast thoroughly instead. The man had made his opinions on this subject known many times. Jon's career was far from over – Justice Keepers remained in peak fighting condition well into their fifties – and there was no reason the higher-ups should stick him on some small backwater world near the Fringe.

In fact, Jon's predecessor had voiced similar opinions when she held this position last year. Some people could change their circumstances by complaining often enough. He was not one. This was where his superiors felt he could do the most good, so this was where he would stay for now.

Ren marched into the kitchen, setting his empty plate down next to the sink. The man stood hunched over, bracing himself with hands pressed to the countertop. "I really don't know why you stay."

Jon crossed his arms over his chest, hanging his head with a sigh. "It couldn't have anything to do with the company," he said, pacing back to the kitchen. "Sweetheart, if I'm happy here, then you should be happy for me."

Ren glanced over his shoulder, a wry smile blooming on his face. "Okay," he said, shaking his head. "But I reserve the right to remind you of this conversation the next time you tell me you're bored with your job."

The man turned his back on Jon and made his way to the front door. He paused there for a moment. "The city planners want to meet this evening," he said. "I'm going to be late."

"No problem."

"See you tonight. I love you."

With his boyfriend gone, Jon took a few moments to enjoy quiet solitude before he left the house. As he'd said, there was not much for a Justice Keeper to do here on Belos; he could pretty much set his own hours, so there was no harm in taking a little time to himself before he started his day. Maybe he could straighten up a little before-

His multi-tool chirped from its resting place in the wall charger. The blinking red light on the metal disk told him he had an incoming call. So much for a pleasant morning of quiet solitude. "Answer," Jon barked. "Holographic display."

The transparent image of a woman rippled into existence in the middle of his living room. Tall and slim, she wore a pair of beige pants and a bright blue tank-top, her short hair parted in the middle. "Jon," she said.

Tilting his head back, Jon felt his lips curl into a small smile. "Jena Morane," he said, eyebrows rising. "I guess I should have expected as much. Things have been going much too smoothly lately."

Jena stared at him with her mouth hanging open, blinking as if she couldn't believe her eyes. "Hey now!" she protested. "Is that any way to treat the lady who spurned your advances multiple times?"

He wheezed with laughter, then covered his face with one hand. "If you're looking for a date," Jon said, approaching the hologram. "I'm afraid I'm no longer available. Also, did I ever thank you for sticking me with your old job?"

"No, and I know just how you can do it."

"Excuse me?"

A painful expression passed over Jena's face, one that she smothered in less than half a second, but it was clear that something wasn't right. "Things are changing, Jon," she said. "It's time I put a few contingencies in place."

Pressing his lips together, Jon blinked at her. "Things are

changing," he said, taking one cautious step forward. "What kind of things? And what exactly do you mean by 'put a few contingencies in place?' "

"I want you to visit a world called Adraxis."

"Never heard of it."

Heaving out a sigh, Jena looked down at the floor. The woman seemed unwilling to make eye-contact, almost as if she knew she was asking too much of him. "That's 'cause it's on the far side of Antauran Space."

Well, that was just...Damn this woman and her presumption! What could possibly convince her that he would be willing to fly to the far side of a hostile power's territory just for one of her little favours? He'd done his fair share before. Still, curiosity got the better of him. "And what will I find on Adraxis?"

The way she looked at him gave him pause, and suddenly he realized that Jena was dead serious. She hadn't come to him on a whim; this was *important* to her. "I want you to delete all record of this call when we've finished."

"All right."

"Good. Now listen carefully..."

The sandstorm was nothing short of devastating: a wave of dust that rushed over the dunes, swirling and raging with enough force to do serious damage to anything plant or animal that might have been unfortunate enough to make its home here. Assuming, of course, that anything actually *lived* here. Adraxis was as close to what would be called a dead world as she had ever seen.

Keli Armana scrambled down the hillside with hands raised to shield her face, hissing as the dust pummeled her. She wore thick tan clothing along with a cloak with its hood pulled up. It did little good.

In the distance, perhaps half a kilometer away, a small two-story building stood its ground against the howling wind and raging dust. A bastion of hope against the tempest. Assuming, of course, that hope could survive in a place like this. Adraxis was where hope went to die.

Keli stumbled, falling face down in the sand. Grunting, she tossed her head about and tried to recover her what little remained of her willpower. "Come on," she whispered to herself. "You've made it this far."

She got up.

Wincing inside her hood, Keli felt tears leak from her eyes. "You survived that cell on Ganymede," she reminded herself. "You can survive this."

The building was her destination, though she wondered if she would make it there before exhaustion or the storm did her in. She would have preferred to have landed there, but the pilot she had coaxed into flying her all the way out here had been unwilling to set his ship down on "the Haunted Planet." The most he would do was let her use one of his escape pods, and those things weren't exactly precise when it came to maneuvering. In truth, she was lucky she managed to land within five kilometers of this place.

So, she scrambled through the storm, keeping her head down, shielding her face as best she could and ignoring the pain when a stone or pebble hit her. It was slow going – hours seemed to pass before she reached her destination – but arrive she did only to fall to her knees just in front of the door.

Keli got shakily to her feet.

Pounding on the door with her fist, she let out a wheeze and then collapsed against the metal. "You can't just leave me out here," she whispered to no one in particular. "You can't just leave..."

The doors slid apart.

Without the metal to support her weight, Keli fell to her knees again, huddling in on herself and gasping. She was aching from head to toe, barely able to think, but she sensed the newcomer's approach.

A woman in black pants and a matching tank-top stepped out of the darkness: a tall woman with pale skin and short blonde hair. "Gods have mercy on me!" she said. "Who might *you* be?"

Keli looked up to squint at the woman. "I need answers," she said, nearly falling on her face. "Please…"

"Answers. Do you know where you are?"

"Adraxis."

The other woman crossed her arms, frowning down at Keli with obvious disdain in her eyes. "And do you know what kind of people come to Adraxis?" she asked, raising an eyebrow. "Go on, take a moment and ponder it."

Baring her teeth in a vicious snarl, Keli hissed. The pain in her body was difficult to ignore. "Criminals," she answered. "Smugglers, murderers, thieves. Those who have run out of places to hide."

The other woman leaned forward, her mouth twisting into a predatory smile. "And how willing do you think 'those who have run out of places to hide' would be to provide you with answers?"

Keli looked up.

It took some effort – she was very tired – but she reached out and touched the other woman's mind. Palia. That was the woman's name. Brief flashes of memories floated in Keli's mind. Palia was something of an activist who hacked into classified databases and leaked their secrets. After fleeing authorities on the colony world of Torval, she hid on various space stations before coming here.

Palia winced, shivering as she let out a slow, rasping breath. "You have the gift of Communion," she mumbled, backing away. Sighing regretfully, she added. "Come with me, Honoured One."

With some effort, Keli stood and allowed the other woman to lead down a hallway with thick gray walls and doors at even intervals. It was utterly dark, forcing Palia to use a flashlight to avoid tripping. This place certainly lived up to its reputation. It had once been a military base, but her people had been forced to abandon it long ago.

Forced because Adraxis was inhospitable to human life. Oh, the atmosphere was just right, and one could pump water from underground streams. The desert conditions were easily mitigated with hydroponic farming technology. But that was not the reason this place was uninhabitable. Anyone who stayed here long enough began having terrible nightmares. Stay too long, and you were never quite the same.

At the end of the hallway, Palia opened another door, this one leading into what looked like a mess hall with black and white floor tiles. Round plastic tables were spread throughout the room, and the lights were on full. Long rectangular windows in the wall to her left should have been admitting sunlight, but the sandstorm blocked it out.

She noticed a man sitting on one table, a tall muscular fellow with copper skin and gray flecks in his scraggly dark beard. "Who's this?" he said, hopping to his feet. "Don't tell me we've started picking up strays."

Palia stopped short, standing before Keli with her back turned and facing the man with arms folded. "This one has the gift of Communion," she explained. "I thought we should at least offer her water."

The man scrunched up his face before pinching the bridge of his nose with thumb and forefinger. "You're joking, right?" he asked, striding toward them. "You want to bring a *telepath* in here?"

"Would you say no to her?"

Telepaths were revered in Antauran society, considered the pinnacle of evolution. There were some who even believed them to be close to godliness. The experiments that been done to Keli had only heightened her powers.

"This is insane," the man said.

Closing her eyes, Keli took a deep, calming breath. "Insane," she said, nodding to the man. "Then perhaps you've been on this planet too long. They say that anyone who stays here goes insane."

He crossed his arms and stood as still as a statue, hissing at her through his teeth. "Then why are you here?" he growled. "What crime is so great that an Honoured One must flee to this wretched hole?"

"I came to see if the legends are true."

The man spun around, throwing his hands up as he walked away from her. "Oh, is that all?" he asked, pacing to the other side of the room. "You want to see if the legends are true. You can just suck-"

Keli focused.

The man dropped to his knees, clutching his skull in both hands. A painful squeal escaped his lips. "Stop!" he begged. "Stop! You want to see? I'll show you whatever you want to see, just stop!"

A smile blossomed on Keli's face, and she bowed her head to the man. "Excellent," she said, striding forward. "Now, tell me everything you've learned from the moment you set foot on this world."

Denabrian winters were generally mild. Leyria's capitol hugged the western coast of the Iyrian continent, and the stream of warm ocean currents coming up from the tropics generally prevented the weather from dropping below freezing on all but a few days of the year. There was, however, quite a lot of rain.

A deluge pattered against Ben's living room window, thin droplets sliding over the pane and blocking his view of the green front lawn. The line of pine trees at the far end of his property swayed in the wind.

He scanned through the reports Larani Tal had given him, looking for some kind of pattern. It was difficult; there were only three known traitors – Slade, Breslan and Calissa – but he searched for some kind of pattern. Some place where they had all served. Some mutual contact they all shared.

There had to be a connection; conspiracies like this one didn't just unfold ex-nihlo. However, it was extremely difficult to find the common thread. Cal Breslan's record had been shady until about five years ago, when he joined the Denabrian office of the Justice Keepers at Slade's instigation. The man had a list of teachers and former supervisors – most of whom were conveniently dead – and his record claimed that he had received his symbiont on Belos with few witnesses.

Calissa on the other hand...

Her induction ceremony was quite well-documented. Most Keepers received their Nassai after completing their first year of training. It was usually a big affair with lots of pomp and circumstance. He'd seen the video of Calissa kneeling in front of three senior directors who held out a containment unit with a symbiont inside. He still remembered the woman's ecstatic expression as her skin began to glow. That had been ten years ago.

In theory, a Nassai would never allow its host to misuse its power. But Calissa had gotten up to all sorts of mayhem with a casual disregard for human life. So... Had Calissa been rotten from the beginning? Or did something turn her? The symbiont was supposed to have vetted her to see if she would use the power responsibly. Was the Nassai corrupt from the very start? Or...Or...could it be possible that Calissa had somehow switched symbionts, trading in a healthy Nassai for one of these twisted creatures Slade employed?

Knock knock.

"It's open."

The front door swung open to reveal Larani Tal on his porch, taking shelter under an umbrella. Dressed in green pants and a black coat that dropped to mid-thigh, she was quite fetching with her dark hair pulled back in a bun. "Ben," she said, stepping through the door. "I see you're reviewing the material I sent you."

Closing his eyes, Ben pressed the back of his head into the seat cushion. "Well, it's not like I have much else to do," he muttered, setting the tablet down in his lap. "Thanks for coming by."

Larani bowed her head, heaving out a deep breath. "Of course," she said, shutting the door behind her. "Though I would point out that it would be much more efficient to conduct this conversation by teleconference."

Stretching fists above his head, Ben felt his mouth drop open in a yawn. "You never did learn anything about conspiracies, did you?" he murmured. "You generally don't want to risk someone eavesdropping on your call.

He got up, slipping hands into his pockets, and paced over to the window. The rain just kept splashing against the glass. "Did you speak to the parole officer?" he asked. "Is there any chance they'll let me talk to Darrel?"

He rounded on her.

Larani stood just inside the front door with hands folded over her stomach, refusing to look up at him. "I'm sorry, Ben," she said softly. "They aren't willing to allow you any off-world contact until you complete your recovery process."

"Worth a shot."

"I'm sorry."

"Don't be; you did your best," he said, marching across the room. "I actually wanted to talk to you about Nassai."

A yawn stretched Larani's mouth into a gaping hole before she stifled it with her fist. "Goodness," she murmured. "It really is contagious. What would you like to know about Nassai?"

Ben crossed his arms, frowning down at himself. "Anything you can tell me," he said with a shrug of his shoulders. "Specifically, I'd like to know whether or not they can tell each other apart."

Larani turned her head to stare at the wall, blinking as she considered the question. "I'm not sure," she replied. "My symbiont can sense the presence of another Nassai, but I have to get within a few feet of the host."

"What about distinguishing one Nassai from another?"

Larani winced, shaking her head in frustration. "It doesn't work like that," she said, leaning against the door with her arms folded. "Nassai are fragments of a larger collective consciousness. They aren't individuals."

"Not at first," Ben countered. "But they *become* more individualistic over time as their personalities are shaped by blending with a Keeper. Everything you experience has an effect on the symbiont you carry. That's why Jack's Summer is a little different from Anna's Seth."

A frown appeared on Larani's face before she smothered it. None of the orthodox Keepers much liked the idea of Jack naming his Nassai, and the fact that Anna had done so as well only made them worry that the trend might catch on. That was how Keepers viewed things. One Nassai was indistinguishable from another. "Why are you asking?" Larani murmured after a moment.

Ben turned his back on her, and marched across the living room with his arms crossed. He paused with the window on his left, and for one brief moment, he could feel the chill coming through the glass. "I have a theory," he explained. "I've gone over the footage of Calissa receiving her symbiont. It strikes me as odd that Slade would be able to somehow ensure that she received one of the corrupted Nassai."

"Yes, I thought so too."

Ben squeezed his eyes shut, a tremor passing through him. "Which is why I don't think that's what happened," he said, spinning around to face Larani. "I think that at some point, Calissa received a new symbiont."

Larani stood with fists balled at her sides, her eyes glued to the floor. "You believe that she somehow...swapped Nassai?" The woman sighed as she stepped away from the front door. "Do you have any idea how dangerous that is? Were I to give up my Nassai, I would die in less than five minutes."

"And if someone had another symbiont ready to go?"

"It's an interesting theory."

Ben dropped onto the nearest couch with his hands on his knees, staring down into his own lap. "More than a theory," he murmured. "Think about it; if what Calissa said is true, then Slade has agents everywhere."

That made Larani stop in her tracks. After nearly two months of working together, Ben had discovered that his new partner did not like thinking about the prospect of moles in her organization. It was a common problem among Keepers: sometimes they bought into their own press. They were so convinced of their own nobility that they refused to see a conspiracy lurking right under their noses. Now, spies on the other hand... A decade of working in intelligence gave you a healthy cynicism. "All right," Larani said. "Suppose we grant that you're correct. Slade has dozens of agents among the Keepers."

"It doesn't make sense that every single one of those traitors would have been his from the moment they first bonded a symbiont. Some would have been brought into the fold after serving for several years. And if we can truly be sure that a Nassai would never condone the misuse of their power..." Ben wasn't so sure of that, but he had no intention of arguing the point. Not with a woman as stubborn as Larani. "Then it stands to reason that many of these people received a corrupted symbiont only after they joined Slade's little cabal of evil."

"So you're saying..."

"I'm saying that Slade has been gathering recruits slowly over the years," Ben went on. "When he finds a willing convert, they extract the Nassai that he or she carried and replace it with one of these twisted symbionts."

Clenching her teeth, Larani shook her head in disgust. "That is a disturbing notion," she said in a voice dripping with contempt. "It means that the Keepers have truly fallen from grace."

"It's worse than that," Ben said. "We don't know how long this shadow organization has existed. It's possible that we're coming up against a faction that has existed within the Justice Keepers from their very inception."

Saying that out loud made him feel cold inside.

Aamani descended the stairs with her arms folded, her shoulders hunched up as if she wanted to shiver. The stairwell was cool, but hardly chilly now that summer was in full bloom. Still, she hated it. She had come to associate this place with fear.

On the bottom level, she opened a door into a huge parking garage with concrete walls and banks of fluorescent lights in the ceilings. Empty parking spaces were marked off with yellow lines, and the air smelled of gasoline.

Aamani strode forward.

"I was beginning to think you'd stood me up," a cool, crisp voice said from behind. So, he had been waiting just outside the stairwell door. Somehow, the man always found some new way to ambush her. "I tend to take such things personally."

Aamani winced, trembling as she drew in a hissing breath. "I'm well aware of the terms of our agreement," she said, spinning around on her heel. "So, you can rest assured that *when* I have new information, I will share it."

Grecken Slade stood next to the door in gray pants and a long black coat that fell to mid-thigh, a coat with silver birds on its high collar. The man's face belonged on a statue, with pronounced cheek bones, tilted eyes and smooth skin. "Still, you've been spending an inordinate amount of time with my enemies."

Clenching her teeth, Aamani let her head hang, then drew in a hissing breath. "That is called infiltration," she growled, striding forward. "You might have heard of it. It's how people in my line of work gather information."

Slade lifted his chin to study her with lips pursed, blinking slowly as he considered that. "Very well," he said, stepping away from the wall. "What exactly have you learned about Jena Morane's plans?"

This was the part she hated most; in her long career, Aamani had faced more than her fair share of tense situations – the worst of which involved two autonomous robots tearing her people to shreds in a parking garage just like this one – but she had always felt as though she were on equal footing with her opponents. Slade made her feel like an eight-year-old girl trying to challenge a three-hundred-pound man. He couldn't read her thoughts; he wouldn't know that the information she was feeding him was precisely what Jena *wanted* him to see, but that didn't make her feel any safer. Those dark eyes of his cut deeper than most swords.

Aamani fished a memory chip out of her purse, caressing it with her thumb before she tossed it casually. Slade caught the chip with a grunt, then paused for a moment to inspect it. "It's all right there," she told him. "They think they have a lead on the Key."

"Where?"

Aamani felt her mouth twist, then turned her head so that

he wouldn't get a good look at her expression. "Northern Oregon," she muttered, her voice dripping with disdain. "Some Willapa legends about spirits that made Jack say, 'Oh, that sound like Overseers.'"

The site she was sending him to was one that Jack and Anna had investigated just last week, and – as usual – they had found nothing of substance. Still, if a false trail could keep Slade's people busy, it was worth it.

As usual, she kept her composure, but she would be lying if she said she didn't feel a growing tension in her chest. The knowledge that some telepath had been tweaking her emotions was unsettling, to say the least. Raynar had trained her in the art of resisting such influence, had taught her how to dissect, analyze and root out foreign influence, but they were still no closer to identifying the culprit. Did Slade know? What if his telepath had told him everything that Aamani was thinking? The other shoe could drop at any time. She had to be ready.

A vicious grin spread on Slade's face, and he lowered his eyes almost respectfully. "Excellent," he said with a curt nod. "You've done well, Aamani. Very soon now, we will free your world from my people's influence."

"I look forward to it."

The man turned on his heel and marched back to the stairwell door, halting there for just a moment. "Keep them off balance," he said almost as an afterthought. "I'm going to be rather busy over the next few weeks, and I'd rather not find myself tripping over Anna Lenai or Jack Hunter."

"Whatever you say," Aamani hissed. "Let's just conclude this business as soon as possible."

Through the cockpit window, Keli saw a clear blue sky stretching from horizon to horizon above an endless desert of hard-packed clay. The engines powered down, their whine slowly fading away to nothingness.

Keli sat in the co-pilot's seat with hands in her lap, frowning down at her own shoes. "This is the place?" she asked, arching one dark eyebrow. "You're sure this is where they discovered it?"

Skoro, the tall man with a scraggly beard of salt-and-pepper hair – was on her left, baring his teeth as he stared through the window. "This is it," he said, gesticulating with one hand. "If you've lost interest, we'll go now, but if you must see it..."

Keli rose from her seat.

Hunching over, she twisted around and made her way to the back of the cockpit. "I must see it," she said, bracing one hand against the air-lock in the port-side wall. "If you wish, you may remain here."

"Idiot woman."

The air-lock slid open with a hiss, revealing a ruined land-scape that seemed to go on forever without a trace of green to be found. Just rocks and stones, clay and dust. No one in their right mind would live here.

Keli descended the steps, pulling the hood of the cloak up to shield her face from the sun. A hot breeze assaulted her the instant she was out in the open, but she managed to ignore it with some effort.

She rounded the nose of the small cargo hauler only to sense Skoro coming out behind her. The man was still a few paces away, and he had no hostile intentions – she would have picked up on that very quickly – but she didn't like anyone walking where she couldn't see.

Keli froze, doubling over with her arms folded, a hiss escaping her. "Hurry up if you're coming," she said through her teeth. "I would rather not have to stand here until I pass out from dehydration."

Her companion said nothing and chose instead to make his way up the rising slope in front of the ship. He stopped halfway up and let out a grunt. "Complain all you want," Keli muttered, following him. "But you'll stay in front of me."

At the top of the hill, she found a steep cliff that dropped some twenty meters to a wide-open expanse of where a strange rock formation clawed at the sky like the fingers of a grasping hand. Her heart was pounding. That was it. She knew it. Even if the rocks had not been a clear indication, she could *feel* it lurking beneath.

"There it is," Skoro said.

Shutting her eyes, Keli ignored the hot sun on her skin. She wiped sweat off her forehead with the back of one hand. "So the legends are true. Have either of your tried taking a scan of it?"

Skoro's face twisted, and he tossed his head about. "You must be joking, bitch," he growled before spitting over the edge of the cliff. "That thing slips into my dreams at night. You think I should go antagonize it?"

It slipped into his dreams?

They had traveled over five thousand kilometers from the small listening post these two criminals had commandeered. Which meant her suspicions were true. That creature down there was a very powerful telepath.

She leaned forward to get a better look at the rocks. She wasn't willing to risk using her talent until she became absolutely certain that the creature would not retaliate. After what she'd seen on Alios...A shiver went through her, and she had to fight off the memory of a headache that had nearly killed her. The pain. Such terrible pain.

She remembered the hooded woman's mad cackling while the creature she served lashed out at Keli. The horror as it ripped through her best mental defenses. That shriek in her mind...She had survived its attacks, of course, but only just. Fleeing through a dense patch of palm trees, masking her mental presence so that it would not find her. The shock as she realized *what* it was she faced.

A part of her didn't want to believe it, but somehow, she

knew it was true. She had seen an Overseer. She had touched its mind with her own, and if the legends were true, then another one lurked beneath those stones. She had to know. "I'm going down there," she began. "Wait for me at the-"

A high-pitched whistle cut her off, and she looked up to see something traveling through the clear blue sky. It was a ship, but not one she had ever seen before. This one was thin, tube-like, with spines that protruded from its body and curved inward toward the front. Could that possibly be?

"Yes," Skoro said, guessing her thoughts. "It is them."

He stood with one hand raised to shield his eyes, peering into the sky with wonder on his face. "They have been coming frequently in the last few months," he went on. "We have seen two, sometimes three ships at a time. If they notice our presence, they do not care. We've learned to stay out from underfoot."

"You mean..."

"Yes. Their visits become more and more frequent, and it is clear they are preparing for something. The Overseers have returned, woman. And I do not believe they are very happy with their children."

PART I

1

Daylight through a window that looked out on the city made Jena into a silhouette that stood with her back turned, gazing out on a lovely afternoon. "What's this one called, again?" she asked with amusement in her voice.

Jack's living room was a small space with a couch along one wall, an easy chair on the other and a coffee table between them. At the moment, a jangly indie-pop guitar riff came through the speakers he had hung on his walls. He wasn't entirely sure why Jena wanted to hang out, but he didn't mind the company.

Dressed in gray jeans and a black t-shirt, Jack sat on the couch with hands folded behind his head. "Gwen's Revenge," he said over the music. "They're a new band out of Halifax. This is their debut."

Jena tuned.

Her lips were curled into a small smile as she glanced over her shoulder. "So this is what you consider a good time?" she asked, raising one eyebrow. "Hanging out, listening to music?"

Jack closed his eyes, letting the sound wash over him. "You're the one who wanted to spend your Saturday with me," he replied, sitting forward. "Besides, I don't get much time to just sit and listen to an album like I used to."

Jena paced across the living room with her arms crossed, grinning down at herself. "Well, I've listened to pretty much everything you've sent me," she said with a shrug of her shoulders. "Most is pretty good. And I've got an *extensive* collection. I mean you've got stuff from the middle of the last century."

The ring of an oven timer told him that the pizza was ready; so he got up with a grunt and decided to be a good host. His small, galley-style kitchen with white floor tiles and gray countertops was just large enough for one person to move freely. Grabbing a pair of oven mitts, he opened the stove.

Jack winced as a blast of heat hit him in the face, then forced his eyes open. "That's the thing about rock and roll," he said, blinking. "It's always evolving. Each decade has a unique sound."

He set the pizza on the stove-top, the cheese still sizzling and filling the apartment with a delicious scent. Pepperoni, green peppers and olives: his favourite combination. If Anna were here, she would want a purely vegetarian option, but Jena was less interested in Earth's food politics.

He turned around.

His boss stood on the other side of the chest-high wall that separated the kitchen and the living room, smiling at him. "Okay, then," she said. "The best song of this decade: what is it?"

"The Grand Shirleys, 'Moving Parts.' "

"And the 2010s?"

"The Arkells, 'Systematic.' "

"The 90s?"

"Our Lady Peace, 'Naveed.' "

Tapping her lips with one finger, Jena squinted at him. "Interesting," she said with a curt nod. "And you know, it's really odd, but I can't help but notice the fact that these are all songs by Canadian artists."

Jack smiled down at the counter, shaking his head. "Oh, Jen," he said, his eyebrows rising. "I can hardly help it if my country just happens to have the best damn music scene on the planet."

They ate pizza for a while, talked about work, family, relationships. The only rule Jena had made when she'd asked for this little hangout was that under no circumstances would they mention their never-ending search for Slade's Key. Not that Jack wanted to discuss that. He still had nightmares whenever he thought about the hologram they had spoken to in that cave.

Jena lifted a bottle of fizzy water to her lips, then tossed her head back and took a swig. "Okay, one thing I have to know," she said, setting it down on the counter with a *thunk*. "You and Anna. Why isn't that a thing?"

Chewing on his lower lip, Jack shut his eyes tight. He took a deep breath and then let it out again. "I really don't know," he answered. "We were very close when she came here the first time, but..."

"But?"

Jack crossed his arms with a sigh, hanging his head to avoid making eye-contact. "She was transferred to Alios," he went on. "She said that she didn't want a long-distance relationship; so I let it go. Besides, I've got a girlfriend now."

When he looked up, Jena was watching him with those hard, dark eyes of hers, and he knew that he was going to get a lecture. There were times when she seemed to think of herself as the smart, practical aunt he'd never had. "Kid, a piece of advice," she said. "If you really care about someone, make sure they know it."

"I didn't want to push."

"And that's good," Jena said. She brought a slice of pizza to her mouth, took a bite and pulled away with strings of cheese stretching until they snapped. "But did you ever tell her that *you* wanted to try? Did you ever think she might have changed her mind if she knew you were willing?"

He wasn't sure what to make of that; so he chose to focus on his pizza and hope that the conversation would naturally shift away from this topic. No good would come out of tempting himself with the road not taken. He was beginning to relax when a sharp *beep* from his multi-tool startled him.

Checking the screen revealed the words "Urgent Call" flashing in bright red letters. Worry settled into the pit of his stomach. So far as he knew, no one was out on a mission. So, why was this call urgent?

Squeezing his eyes shut, Jack pressed a palm to his forehead. He massaged away a light throb. "Duty calls," he muttered in a strained voice. "Give me a few minutes, Jen. I need to see what this is about."

She nodded.

A long hallway branched off from the foyer with doors in the left-hand wall. The first led to Jack's bedroom, and the second to the room that had once been Anna's. Now that she was gone, Spock had claimed it as his own.

He stepped into his bedroom to find sunlight streaming through the window, falling on a mattress where the covers were in a state of disarray. What exactly was the point of making one's bed? You were only going to get back in it.

Tapping the screen of his multi-tool caused it to project the image of a blue, human-shaped...something. It appeared to be a man composed entirely of ones and zeroes that floated about, crashing into one another. "Greetings, Jack Hunter," the hologram said in a pleasant tone of voice.

Jack squinted at the image. "Well, this is new," he said, shaking his head. "Would you mind telling me who I'm speaking with?"

"Of course."

The image bowed its head respectfully, but it was really just a shift in the projection of ones and zeroes. "Perhaps you've heard of me," it went on. "My name is Ven. I am the artificial intelligence-"

"That emerged on Leyria over a century ago." Suddenly, Jack felt more than a little light headed. Being the first person from this world to accept a symbiont had brought him into contact with several VIPs: politicians, reporters, even the odd celebrity. And he had experienced none of the awe that he felt right now. "I thought...The reports said that you built yourself a vessel and flew off toward the unexplored regions of the galaxy."

"I did."

Blushing hard, Jack closed his eyes and hung his head. "And you came back here just to hang out with me?" He wiped sweat off his brow with the back of his hand. "Date a sexy alien? Check. Meet a living robot? Check. Throw in some time travel, and my life is officially a 1940s serial."

Ven laughed.

"You grasp humor."

"Of course, I do!" The hologram flickered for a moment, then resolidified into a man of ones and zeros, but now the numbers were flying about like a swarm of angry bees. "I see," Ven went on. "Your concept of artificial intelligence is largely defined by the depictions you see in your media."

Suddenly, it was a transparent image of Lieutenant Commander Data who stood before him, and before Jack could speak, the image shifted again to a cylon and finally one of the cybermen. "It's nothing like that. In fact, I've always objected to the term 'artificial intelligence.' How is my intelligence any more artificial than yours? But that is a moot point at the moment."

"What..." Jack stammered. "What can I do for you?"

"As you said, I've been exploring unknown parts of the

galaxy." The hologram was once again the image of a man composed of floating ones and zeroes that swirled about as if caught in a cyclone. Almost as if their pattern of movement reflected Ven's mood. "I traveled through many uncharted solar systems, finding little in the way of intelligent life. There are some truly fascinating species in the distant regions of this galaxy, but almost none have anything approximating the human capacity for language. I began to think that the Milky Way was an empty place..."

The hologram changed colour, blue characters suddenly becoming a deep, angry red. "But then I began to notice it," Ven went on. "Something was lurking in star systems beyond the rim of known space. Hiding, watching me...

"It would come as a brief sensor ghost, the silhouette of a ship that would vanish the instant I tried to scan it. I ran diagnostic after diagnostic to ensure that my readings were not faulty. Each time, I found no errors. But the ship would appear again and again. They were hounding me, Jack, observing my movements. What little I could learn of them suggested that their ships were made entirely out of living tissue."

Pinching his chin with thumb and forefinger, Jack narrowed his eyes. "Overseers," he muttered under his breath. "They use purely organic technology. I believe you caught a glimpse of an Overseer ship."

"I concur."

Jack sat down on the bed with his arms folded, practically doubling over. "And this is new?" he asked, shivering. "These strange encounters you've been having. They only started recently."

"The first was nearly one year ago," Ven explained. "Since then, I've caught sight of the strange ship at least fourteen times. I can't tell if it's the same ship every time, but in each encounter, there is only one."

Ven was able to mimic human movement, spinning to face

the window with one holographic hand pressed to his hip. "They're planning something, Jack," he said. "For thousands of years, there has been no sign of the Overseers, and now suddenly, they're showing up on my scans."

Baring his teeth with a hiss, Jack winced. He shook his head ever so slowly. "You don't know that. Just because we haven't detected them doesn't mean they haven't been there this whole time."

"I'd considered that possibility," Ven admitted, "but scanning through news items from Earth and Leyria suggests that the Overseers have indeed shown up with alarming frequency these past few months. A survey mission from Belos Colony detected strange ships on the border of Leyrian space; a woman on Salus Prime had a psychotic break in which she claimed to have been stalked by ships made of flesh lurking in the night sky. Ships only she could see. Your team recovered not one, but *two* Overseer devices less than three months ago."

The hologram made a face, but it was difficult for Jack to read an expression made entirely of floating characters. He suspected Ven's use of body language was purely for his benefit. "For thousands of years," Ven went on, "the Overseers have taken a laissez faire approach to human civilization. Now, suddenly, they've decided to play an active role. I'm forced to wonder why, which brings me to you."

"Why me?"

The hint of a smile appeared on Ven's face, and his ones and zeroes changed from pale blue to bright white. "I have studied the records of almost every Justice Keeper on active duty," he said. "Yours indicates a uniquely powerful distrust for authority and a penchant for unconventional thinking. You were the first person in history to *name* your Nassai. You were able to look past the commonly-held perceptions of the Justice Keepers and recognize Cal Breslan's treachery. Time and time again, you have demonstrated an inclination to disregard what you are told and seek the truth on your own terms. Simply put: I believe I can trust you."

Well, Jack supposed he couldn't argue with that. Though this was probable the first time anyone had ever *praised* him for his stubborn noncompliance. "What did you have in mind?" he asked.

"We need to determine the Overseer's plans."

Jack stood up with a sigh, clasping hands together behind his back. He let his head hang. "I might be able to help you there," he said. "My friends and I have been looking into this for almost six months now."

"Your friends?"

"Yeah," Jack said. "One of them's in the kitchen. I'd like her to meet you."

"You're sure that's wise?"

Grinning like an idiot, Jack felt his cheeks burn. He chuckled softly to himself. "One thing you'll learn about me," he began. "When someone *does* earn my trust, they have it for life. This is non-negotiable; we're bringing Jena in."

The hologram regarded him for a moment, ones and zeroes shifting from white to blue to a dark gray. "Very well," Ven said at last. "I will defer to your judgment."

"Jena!" Jack shouted. "Would you mind coming in here? There's someone I'd like you to meet!"

2

Sunlight streamed through the window in Anna's living room, falling on the comfy white sofa and reflecting off the surface of the glass coffee table. A few rays even made it to the kitchen where an island sat in the middle of the white-tiled floor.

Wooden cupboards lined two walls with the fridge and the oven placed side by side. As far as accommodations went, she didn't mind her kitchen. There was no serving bot to cook her meals – though she preferred to cook her own meals, it was handy to have a bot if she was pressed for time – but otherwise, it was nice.

Anna sat at the island with her elbows resting on its surface, clutching a tablet in two hands. Her short cherry-red hair was tied back in a nubby little ponytail. "You dumb fucking whore," she read aloud. "I will find you and rape you to death, you evil fucking cop-hater. Hashtag 'Respect police.' "

Behind her, Bradley was sitting on the couch with his arms folded, frowning at the wall. "Honestly, hon, do you have to read every single one of those?" he asked. "It can't be doing anything to improve your disposition."

Anna scrunched up her face, trembling with impotent rage.

"Three months," she hissed, tossing the tablet onto the island. "Three months since I intervened to help Kevin Harmon, and every damn day, it's the same thing."

Her inbox had been full of disgusting messages ever since a Tennessee news station had reported the incident. She would have expected the fury to die down – Earthers were so quick to shift their attention to the next scandal – but several online communities had banded together to create an organized harassment campaign with Leana Delnara Lenai as its primary target.

There were online games where you could click on her face over and over until it was bruised beyond recognition. Memes generated from pictures that were taken on her first visit to Earth painting her as some kind of interstellar totalitarian. Companion have mercy! Once upon a time, she had been a hero to these people. She knew there would be consequences for standing up to those two officers, but this...

Anna shut her eyes. "It's getting worse," she said. "I don't even want to leave the apartment anymore!"

In her mind's eye, she saw the silhouette of Bradley turn its head to stare at her. "If you're that worried," he began, "maybe I should go with you? People are much less likely to try something if you're not alone."

Grinning sheepishly, Anna stared down at the counter. "You don't get it, Sweetie," she said, shaking her head. "I'm not afraid to go out because I think I might get hurt. I'm afraid to go out because I might have to hurt someone else."

"Regardless..."

Anna twisted on her stool to face him with hands on her knees, frowning into her own lap. "What are you going to do, Bradley?" she asked. "If some psychotic man on a rage-trip gets it in his head to attack me, what are you going to do?"

Bradley watched her with a tight frown on his face, his cheeks slowly reddening. Clearly the question had left him unsettled. "I just think it might be easier..." he mumbled. "Never mind. You're probably right."

With a sigh, Anna got up and made her way over to the window. Tall skyscrapers rose up in the distance, glittering in the light of the afternoon sun. Ottawa was a beautiful city – one that had once felt like a second home – but she was beginning to wonder if she had any business staying here. She had told herself that she came back here because Earth was the place where a Keeper could do the most good, but deep down inside, she knew that was only *part* of the reason.

Anna crossed her arms with a heavy sigh, frowning down at herself. "Maybe I just shouldn't be here," she mumbled to herself. "At this point, I'm nothing but a focal point for hatred. Maybe it's time I went home."

"Where does that leave us?"

A glance over her shoulder revealed Bradley sitting on the couch with a scowl on his face. "You and me," he went on. "If you decide to go back to Leyria, what does that mean for us?"

Wincing so hard it hurt, Anna shook her head. "I don't know," she said, dropping into the chair across from him. "Suppose it depends on how bad you want to be together. Besides, it was just an idle thought."

"Right..."

She could tell that her attempt at reassurance had failed miserably – and that was probably because it had been partially insincere; considering the prospect of going home had been more than an idle thought – but she lacked the energy to press the point right now. No, right now the only thing she wanted was a nice relaxing bubble bath. Alone.

Anna's fists slammed into the punching bag one after the other, leaving indentations in the fabric, and providing enough force to send Gabi stumbling away. The other woman clutched the bag in both hands.

Dressed in a pair of shorts and a blue tank-top, Gabi struggled to catch her breath. Her face was slick with sweat, her black hair pulled back in a ponytail, and she stared at Anna as if seeing her for the first time. "Damn, girl," she hissed. "You've really got some quality rage going."

Anna winced, then rubbed at her eyes with the back of her hand. "You try reading vivid depictions of what vile men want to do to you for months on end." She turned away from the bag, pacing across the gym mat. "I feel like I'm going numb inside."

"That's understandable."

The workout room was just a big empty box with exercise equipment on one end and open floor space on the other. Not far away, two young Keepers were sparring with each other on a neighbouring mat, but otherwise, it was just her and Gabi. She retrieved her water bottle from her belongings.

The silhouette of Gabi stood next to the punching bag, staring down at something on the floor. "I don't think any of us were prepared for it," she went on. "The extremes reactions Earthers can have."

Lifting the bottle to her lips, Anna shut her eyes and tilted her head back. "Do you want to know the worst part?" she said after a moment. "I feel like it's somehow *my* fault. Like I should have known what would happen."

"Even if you did, would you have done anything different?"

"Of course not."

When she turned, Gabi was standing there with her arms folded, every inch of her exposed skin glistening. "Well?" the woman asked, raising a dark eyebrow. "Then what good is there in blaming yourself?"

Anna smiled, then bowed her head to the other woman. "You've got a point," she said, her eyebrows rising. "It's just...I'm always hearing Jena and Harry go on about how delicate the situation is."

"Not your fault."

"I know."

Gabi seized the punching bag again, holding it steady in both hands before peeking around the corner to blink at Anna. "So your boyfriend's nervous that you might go back to Leyria," she said, "That can't be fun."

With a growl, Anna threw a pair of jabs at the bag, pounding it again and again as she worked out her aggression. The fire in her belly flared up until she thought her skin might start to sizzle. "It was a stupid thing to say," she hissed. "I've got no intention of leaving him; Bradley is wonderful."

"But...Maybe..." Gabi winced as she was driven backward by the onslaught of Anna's blows, the bag providing very poor protection. Only then did it occur to Anna that she might want to avoid using the full force of Keeper strength. "Maybe Earth isn't quite so wonderful, no?"

Biting her lower lip, Anna let her head hang. She mopped a hand over her face. "I don't know...Just a few months ago, I would have said that this is the one place in all the universe I most wanted to be."

"And now?"

"I'm starting to worry I'm turning into my mother."

Releasing the bag with a grunt, Gabi stepped backward and pressed a hand to her stomach. She closed her eyes and drew in a slow, soothing breath. "So what would your mother say about all this?"

"That this is what I get for associating with a bunch of primitives," Anna replied. "She'd go on at length about how Earthers still fell victim to petty prejudices. About how they trashed their planet with no regard for human life. She's even been known to ponder why we would let Earthers become Justice Keepers."

"Charming."

"Isn't it though?"

"What do *you* want, Anna?"

Anna felt her cheeks burn, her nostrils flaring with every breath. "I want people to stop asking me what I want," she answered. "I'll figure that out in my own good time. In the meantime, I want to do my job."

"Fair enough. Shall we prepare for Jena's meeting?"

"Yeah," Anna said. "Let's do that."

The window in Jena's office looked out on a field of stars with Earth barely visible in the left-hand side, its reflection shining in the SmartGlass surface of Jena's desk. For the moment, that desk was unoccupied.

Jack slouched in his chair with his arms crossed, tilting his head back to stare up at the ceiling. He blinked several times. "Well, this is encouraging. For those of us who are counting, we've got humans, microscopic organisms and now an artificial intelligence all pissed off at Grecken Slade."

A hologram appeared beside him, depicting the image of a vaguely human-shaped creature made entirely of Leyrian characters. Ven had altered his appearance slightly. "Do you really believe this single individual to be a threat?"

Jack winced, pinching the bridge of his nose. "On his own? No," he muttered into his own palm. "But Slade has been modifying symbionts and building super soldiers. I think it's pretty clear the Overseers are backing him."

"Why would they?"

Grinning ferociously, Jack stared down into his own lap. "Hard to guess," he said, eyebrows rising. "But I'm thinking they figured out that Slade's a shoe-in for prom king, and now they're hoping for a seat at the cool kids' table."

In his mind's eye, he saw Jena stride through the door behind him, flanked by Anna and Harry. His boss stopped short, crossing her arms as she stared at the back of his chair. "I don't believe my eyes," she said. "For once, Jack is early."

"Do I get a cookie?"

Harry shuffled into the room with his hands in his pockets, casting a suspicious glare at the hologram. "What's with the light show?" he asked. "Does this presentation come with a visual aid?"

Gabi was the last one inside, flowing across the room in black pants and a maroon t-shirt. She paused next to Jack's chair, resting a hand on his shoulder and showing him a warm smile. Every now and then, he felt a burst of affection when he remembered how lucky he was to have a partner like her.

Jena rounded her desk with a heavy sigh, taking position just behind her chair. "The light show is actually a guest that I've invited to join us," she said. "Everyone, meet Ven."

Anna's mouth dropped open, and she blinked several times in confusion. "This is Ven?" she asked, dropping into the chair next to Jack. "As in the artificial intelligence that left Leyria over a hundred years ago?"

For a brief moment, the hologram flickered, and when it stabilized, it seemed to be facing Anna. "Pleased to meet you," Ven said, bowing his ghostly head to her. His voice came through the speakers on the wall.

"Likewise?"

A wince passed over Jena's face, but she cleared her mind with a quick shake of her head. "No one else knows Ven is here," she said, taking her seat. "And I'm of the opinion that we should keep it that way."

Biting her lip, Anna lowered her eyes until she was staring into her lap. "So is he...I mean she..." A growl rumbled in her throat. "Ven, forgive me, but I do have to ask. Which pronoun would you prefer?"

A pang of guilt hit Jack right in the gut when he realized that he had failed to even consider that question. There was no reason to assume that Ven was male, and yet he had done so without question. Personal bias was like a virus that might hide in your body for months or even years before it made its presence felt.

Ven laughed, and the hologram gestured kindly toward Anna. "He or she is fine. I would prefer a singular, gender-neutral pronoun but since English lacks one that does not apply to objects, either will do."

Jena leaned back in her chair with elbows on the armrests, steepling her fingers. "Ven is going to help us search for the Key," she explained. "At this point, I'm fresh out of ideas; so a new perspective might just do the trick."

"'Bout time we had some good luck," Gabi said, striding around Jena's desk with her hands clasped behind her back. She paused in front of the window, staring out into the great black emptiness. "If Ven's reputation for data analysis is even half true, it will give us time to focus on containing Slade."

Fury boiled in Jack's veins.

The former head of the Justice Keepers had made it his mission to keep them off balance by having his minions commit random acts of violence at every opportunity. A bombed tube station in London, a massacre at a festival in Mumbai, five dead protesters outside the Capital Building in D.C.: all committed by men and women who went out of their way to flaunt Keeper powers they had no right to. There was no denying it, now; Slade was no longer working in the shadows.

"To be honest," Ven replied. "My talent for data analysis has often been somewhat understated. I'm given to understand that you have access to several Overseer devices. I would like to study them."

"We've been trying for months," Jena said.

The hologram bowed its head, its swirling text changing from blue to a soft, rosy pink. A blush perhaps? "You will forgive me if this is indelicate," Ven began. "But I can analyze the devices far faster than any human. The process of transition from a flash of inspiration to a viable plan takes place within millionths of a second for me."

Blushing hard, Jena closed her eyes and nodded to the hologram. "All right, then," she said, sliding her chair back. "I'll see it that you get access to the organic SlipGate and the whatever-it-is that bonded to Kevin."

"Excellent."

Jena swiveled around so that Jack saw her in profile, then stood up and paced a line in front of her chair. "The rest of us have work to do," she went on. "The Friendship Day celebration is tomorrow."

Instantly, Jack felt his stomach tighten with anxiety. Another party? He couldn't say he was looking forward to *that*. Especially after the last few he'd been to. Sometimes, he still felt hot stinging pain when he remembered Leo's blade slicing into his chest. Phantom pain that only lasted half a second, but it was still aggravating.

Friendship Day.

Had it really been four years since the Leyrians revealed themselves?

Then today was the anniversary of the night when he and Anna had watched a pair of battle drones gun down Aamani Patel's best agents. The anniversary of his first desperate fight against Wesley Pennfield. A shiver went through him when he thought of it.

Out of the corner of his eye, he saw Anna wince, and he knew that she was having the same thought. Jack tried to avoid thinking about that night unless it was absolutely necessary. Friendship Day was never a joyous occasion for him.

"...remarks prepared, kid?"

Jack squeezed his eyes shut, then forced them open, blinking a few times as he tried to get his bearings. "I'm sorry," he said after a moment. "I was a bit distracted. Could you repeat that?"

Jena stood before the window with arms crossed, frowning at him. "I said that they will probably want you to say a few words," she muttered. "You *are* the first Keeper from this world, after all. Do you have any remarks prepared?"

Slouching in his chair, Jack covered his face with both hands and moaned. "Of course! A priest, a prostitute and a Nassai all walk into a bar..."

"Jack..." Harry warned.

A wince contorted Jack's features, and he shook his head violently. "I'm sorry," he said. "But you *know* I despise this. I don't see any reason why I should have to give the same speech every year."

Jena was still by the window with her arms folded, scowling down at the floor. "Is it really so much to ask?" she said, shaking her head. "You're a symbol to the people of Earth, Jack."

"I never wanted to be a symbol."

Anna leaned back in her chair with hands folded behind her head, smiling up at the ceiling. "I never wanted to be this quirky and adorable," she said, her eyebrows rising. "Sometimes, you just have to take the punches, sweetie."

Jack felt his lips peel back from clenched teeth, a soft hiss escaping him. "You just don't understand," he said, head hanging. "I don't have it in me to be a cheerleader for the Keepers after everything I've seen."

"So don't."

That came from Jena.

The woman stood there with her chin thrust out, her dark eyes reflecting the lights. "Tell the truth," she went on. "Play the game, kid. Just like I taught you."

Well, at least he had something to think about. In the back of his mind, he felt his Nassai reacting with approval and encouragement. Summer was *proud* of him, though he couldn't say why. "All right," he said. "I'll do it."

"Good," Jena replied. "Now on to the next issue..."

Ottawa's skyline rose up before him: tall, slender buildings with tiny lights in their windows, each rising up to stab a night sky that occasionally flashed with lightning. In the distance, he could almost make out the river. Almost.

Jack stood by the window with his arms crossed, peering out into the night. "You bought purple mouthwash," he said, glancing over his shoulder. "Really? Out of all the options, you thought purple was best?"

Gabi sat on his living room couch with hands on her knees, staring into her own lap. "It looked interesting," she said with a shrug of her shoulders. "And what's wrong with purple? Is it not a manly enough colour?"

Jack felt his mouth curl into a smile, then hung his head in chagrin. "No, it's 'cause purple signifies that artificial grape flavour." He shivered at the thought of it. "Trust me, if you spend enough time on this planet, you will eventually develop a discerning palette when it comes to bottled sugary poison."

For the last few months, this had been a regular facet of their relationship: Gabrina would come and spend a few nights with him. At first, she had insisted on bringing half her belongings down from station twelve – anything she might need in a pinch. Jack had very quickly discovered that his partner was a planner.

Now, she was more willing to use the monthly stipend LIS gave her to buy supplies when she needed them. That was something of a foreign concept to her. On Leyria, mail bots delivered everything from groceries to pharmaceuticals. Not to mention the mail. The idea of spending one's afternoon simply going out to purchase daily household items seemed quaint to Gabi.

Jack turned away from the window.

His girlfriend was still sitting prim and proper, smiling down at herself. "So, do you know what you want to say tomorrow?" she asked with more enthusiasm than he would have liked. This was a topic he would rather avoid.

Closing his eyes, Jack tilted his head back. He took a deep, soothing breath through his nose. "Not a clue," he answered. "I've been mulling it over all day and nada. Figure I'll just wing it."

"Wing it?"

Jack grinned, shaking his head. "That's what I do," he said, making his way across the room. "I've never been very good at planning my remarks in advance. So, I'll just say whatever pops into my brain while I'm up there."

He dropped into the easy chair with a soft sigh, waiting for the inevitable lecture. People always assumed that the only way to do something right was to plan it out ahead of time. Sometimes that worked, and sometimes it didn't. In high school, he used to drive his teachers crazy by refusing to write an outline whenever they assigned a paper on this or that topic. It never seemed to occur to them that Jack was the sort of kid who had to discover his thesis as he wrote.

A persuasive essay was, after all, an attempt to articulate some deeper truth about life or the human condition. How could he know his position on *anything* until he had fully explored the subject? And part of that exploration involved typing out arguments that would actually convince him he was onto something. He didn't know what his thesis would be until he had convinced himself of its merit. Going the other way – choosing a thesis and then trying to find facts to support it – just seemed dishonest.

When he looked up, Gabi was watching him with her mouth agape. "You're joking, right?" she said. "You're actually going to stand in front of several hundred people and make something up on the spot."

"Yes."

"How?"

"The power of improvisation."

Gabi stood up, doubling over with a hand pressed to her stomach. "Oh, Jack," she said through a fit of laughter. "You can't just speak off the cuff. Come on. I will help you prep something."

Jack felt his face crumple. "You still don't believe me," he said, shaking his head. "Trust me, Gabs, I'm far more persuasive unscripted. I think it's because people realize I really believe what I'm saying."

Gabi sighed.

Now would be a good time for one of his trademark random topic changes. "You know, my mom's having a little dinner party this weekend," he began. "She made it a point to tell me she's learning to cook several Leyrian dishes. I think that's her way of saying she'd like you to come."

A scowl passed over Gabi's face, but she smothered it quickly, choosing instead to lift her chin and meet his gaze. It occurred to him that this really wasn't the best possible change of subject. Gabi got squeamish every time he suggested something that might be interpreted as an attempt to advance their relationship. He still hadn't been able to coax her into meeting his parents. "I'll have to see if I'm free," she murmured.

Grinning from ear to ear, Jack closed his eyes and bowed his head to her. "Well, I'd suggest working some of your scheduling magic," he said. "You see, after my mom starts hinting, she starts nagging, and that is just beaucoup de badness."

"I'll see what I can do."

"Excellent," he replied. "Now, would you like cuddles before you go to sleep?"

The double doors to the Science Lab split apart, revealing a large room with a table along the back wall, a table that supported a metal frame where a thin piece of skin was suspended from hooks. Every time Jena saw that thing, it sent a shiver running down her spine. So far as she could tell, she was alone.

Jena strode into the room, ignoring the unease she felt when she realized she was alone with two pieces of Overseer technology. The organic SlipGate was sealed off in the corner to her right. A puddle of flesh about the size of her desk, it had remained inert for almost three months. Professor Nareo thought it would still react for Jack or Anna, but she had been unwilling to test that theory.

Ven's hologram appeared in the middle of the room – a person composed entirely of swirling white text – and for the moment, it stood there with hands clasped behind itself, watching her.

Jena closed her eyes, then bowed her head to the apparition. She took a deep breath. "You said you have something to show me?" she began. "I take it you've had some luck analyzing the hand-held device?"

Ven cocked its head to one side, and she could almost swear that it was blinking at her. "Yes, actually, I have," it said, gesturing to the table. "I have been able to operate the lab's equipment remotely. Professor Nareo was trying to simulate human neuroelectric activity to see how the device would respond."

"And?"

"I have run over a thousand simulations in the last six hours, analyzing how the device responds." The hologram actually managed to look thoughtful. Jena had to give Ven some credit. "The device has memory cells that I have been able to access."

Crossing her arms, Jena hunched up her shoulder and tried her best not to shiver. "We knew that much," she muttered. "Raynar has been able to access them telepathically, but most of what he sees is a jumbled mess."

"I was able to discern a pattern."

The hologram vanished to be replaced with two lists of numbers that hovered side by side in the air in bright white text. Geographic coordinates? There were at least a dozen of them. "What are they?" she asked.

"Locations the Overseers used as bases of operations during their tenure on Earth. It took some time for me to decipher their coordinate system and translate it into the standard latitude, longitude model, but I'm quite certain that my work is accurate. If this Key you search for is still on Earth, it is likely in one of these locations."

Jena squinted at the floating numbers, then shook her head in dismay. "It doesn't track," she said, turning away from the hologram. "Slade has access to Overseer tech; so if the Key was in one of those locations, he would have found it by now."

"Can you think of a better plan?"

Jena stopped short with her hands in her pockets, her head hanging as if someone had slung a fifty-pound stone around her neck. "No," she admitted. "But that does *not* mean I'm willing to waste resources on a wild goose chase."

It irked her that she couldn't sense Ven with her symbiont. The AI wasn't actually here, in this room with her, but she still *felt* as if she should be able to sense movement every time the hologram gestured.

Jena squeezed her eyes shut, then buried her nose in the palm of her hand. "Slade's been doing this a long time," she said. "We need to out-think him if we're going to have any hope of finding this thing before he does."

When she turned around, the hologram was still floating there in the middle of the room, although now its text was a deep sky blue. "If I may, I believe you're letting your own fears cloud your judgment."

"How's that?"

Ven bowed its head, and the speakers emitted something that might have passed for an exasperated sigh. Once again, she was impressed by how easily it was able to emulate human emotion. "The Overseers may be using Slade as their instrument, but we have no way of knowing precisely how much help they are willing to give him. There's no reason to assume he has access to this information, and in light of the fact that this is our *only* lead, it's worth investigating."

"I take your point."

"And what's more, we may have an advantage that Slade lacks." Ven turned its holographic head to stare at the slab of skin that hung suspended from a metal bar over the table. "With the proper combination of electrical signals, I have been able to access some of the device's rudimentary functions – force-field projection, shape change. Now watch what happens when I order it to interface with nearby devices."

There was no reaction from the smaller device on the table, but Jena gasped when the puddle of flesh in the corner suddenly contorted to form a triangle that rose up toward the ceiling. A triangle of veiny skin that pulsed and hummed. Seconds later, it collapsed into its original shape.

Gaping at the hologram, Jena blinked several times. "You can control them?" she asked in a breathy whisper.

Ven shook its head and floated to her. "Not with any degree of precision," it said. "But every time I access that command, the SlipGate activates for a few moments before returning to its dormant state."

"Meaning..."

"Meaning if this process works for every piece of Overseer technology, we now have a method for locating them."

Jena crossed her arms and huddled up on herself, shrinking into her shoulders like a turtle hiding in its shell. "I better call a meeting for tomorrow," she whispered. "It seems we're about to go on a very big scavenger hunt."

3

The walled garden on the roof of a London skyscraper was lush and green under the light of the afternoon sun. Narrow stone walkways cut through a field of grass and caressed the edges of flowerbeds where tulips grew in shades of pink and yellow. Off in the distance, a gazebo sheltered several men and women who stood with their drinks in hand, pleasantly chatting with one another.

It was a surprisingly informal affair despite the presence of over a dozen United Nations ambassadors and twice as many Keepers – the men wore dress pants and shirts with open collars, the women slacks and blouses or perhaps the odd dress – but Leyrians had a different sense of fashion. Harry still felt a little odd about that. Nearly forty years of grooming from his parents, his peers and finally his superior officers had taught him that there were times when you wanted to make a good impression.

"Have you been off-world?"

The question came from an old woman in a blue suit who stood beside him with her back to the wall that bordered the rooftop. Her face was lined with wrinkles, her gray hair cut short in a bob, and she spoke with a noticeable French accent.

Harry stood with his arms folded, dressed in a gray suit and a light blue shirt that he wore without a tie. "I have not," he said, staring down at the floor. "Being a father of two doesn't give one many opportunities for adventure."

The old woman smiled a dreamy smile, the kind you might have expected to see on a kid who was boarding an airplane for the first time. "I had the chance to visit Leyria six months ago," she said. "You really should visit."

Closing his eyes, Harry nodded to himself. "I'm sure I will one day," he murmured, stepping away from the wall. "But for now, I have a job that keeps me very busy. Being the liaison to the Keepers is...taxing."

"Ah...Yes, I would imagine." The woman lifted a cigarette between two fingers, the tip flaring with an orange glow when she took a puff. "When I entered politics all those years ago, it never occurred to me that I would be ambassador to another world."

"I don't think any of us anticipated this."

He took a few moments to watch the other guests socialize. Spend enough years as a beat cop, and people watching eventually became second nature to you. The Keepers looked ridiculous in the company of some forty or fifty ambassadors and various other dignitaries. To the untrained eye, it looked like a bunch of twenty-somethings trying to ingratiate themselves with people who were far older and more experienced.

Of course, that was just a trick of the Nassai bond. From what Harry was told, if he were to bond a symbiont today – inadvisable at his age, but it *was* possible – within just a few weeks, he would once again wear the face of a twenty-two-year-old.

It dawned on him that his daughter would soon be one of

these people, and – worse yet – that there might come a day when he would have to say good-bye to her. Jack had been trained on Earth, and it was likely that Melissa would be as well, but Keepers were often reassigned to different planets.

"Excuse me," Harry murmured.

He made his way to a series of round tables near the building's front wall. A dozen people stood in a cluster, talking amicably with one another. Most appeared to be quite young, though he recognized Isaela Taro, a Keeper with long brown hair and a smile that lit up a room. She looked like a college student, but really, she was pushing forty-five.

Jack sat alone at a table in gray pants and a black short-sleeved shirt that he wore untucked. Of course, the boy wore his collar open; you'd have better luck teaching a fish to breathe on dry land than you would getting Jack to wear a necktie. "Harry!" he said. "How do you like the party?"

Harry winced, trembling on the spot. "I'm hot," he said, wiping sweat off his brow with the back of his hand. "My feet hurt, and my stomach thinks that I should be sitting down to breakfast about now."

The boy leaned back in his chair with his arms folded, closing his eyes and turning his face up to the sun. "Right there with you," he said. "After barely four hours of sleep, I'm primarily surviving on Tylenol and anger."

"Your speech ready?"

"I'm ready to speak."

Harry grinned, then looked down at the floor. "Well, there's a dodgy answer," he said, shaking his head. "Let me guess. You didn't want to prep anything; so you figured you'd just wing it when you got here."

"Something like that."

It was difficult to suppress the urge to sigh. Jack had a very unique way of doing things; in a pinch, he could improvise his way out of almost any situation, but ask him to make a plan and stick to it, and you may as well have asked the sky to turn green. How anyone could live like that was mind-boggling. Harry thrived on organization. "Please tell me you have *some* idea of what you want to say."

"Some."

Crossing his arms with a heavy sigh, Harry frowned down at himself. "Well...We have that much," he said, approaching the table. "You realize that your superiors are all counting on you, right?"

Jack lifted his chin to stare down his nose at Harry, squinting as if he didn't believe his eyes. "I'm aware," he said with a nod. "But you know, I never set out to be the hero of the people."

"That's why you got stuck with the job."

Harry dropped into the chair across from Jack, leaning over the table with his arms crossed. "This is serious," he went on. "You are the first person from Earth to become a Keeper. You shouldn't treat it as a joke."

Jack was grinning into his lap, chuckling softly to himself and trembling with every breath. "That's exactly what it is," he murmured. "I thought that Keepers were real-world Jedi Knights or something."

"And now?"

The boy looked up, and suddenly his blue eyes were as hard as steel. "Slade," he growled. "Breslan, that woman on Leyria: we let a bunch of snakes into our midst, and nobody seemed to notice because they were too busy putting blind faith in the idea that Keepers can do no wrong."

A surge of irritation made Harry want to snap at the kid, but he calmed himself with a little effort. This again...For Jack Hunter, challenging the conventional wisdom – or whatever the kid wanted to call it – wasn't just a way of life, it was a god damn crusade. There were bad apples in every organization, but Jack seemed to take this *personally*. As if the Keepers had let him down. "Does that mean that you oppose our partnership with Leyria?" he asked. "Do you think Earth would be better off alone?"

"Of course not."

"Then why do you see this as a joke?"

The kid had no answer for that; instead, he just stood up with a sigh and wandered off to muse on the question. Harry clicked his tongue in frustration. In a way, he was a father of three. When he had first met Jack, the boy was just a teenager. Someone had to teach him a thing or two about how to do law-enforcement properly, and he didn't think the Leyrians were prepared for the unique challenges of a planet like this. So, Harry had taken Jack under his wing.

That had been four years ago, and now the boy was quite sure of himself. Maybe a little *too* sure of himself. Still, Jack had a bright future ahead of him, and so did Melissa. A short future, but one filled with meaning. Could Harry say the same?

No, he had to admit that he couldn't.

He was middle-aged now, and his days of fighting the good fight were long over. That was probably for the best, but he couldn't help but feel a bit of resentment. Harry had a long career filled with paperwork, meetings and politics. Dear god in heaven! He suddenly realized that he needed a very stiff drink.

Anna stood before a concrete wall that came up to her chin – she hated being short sometimes – watching as sunlight glinted off the windows of tall skyscrapers that made up London's skyline. It was a beautiful city. She had always meant to come here, but one thing or another always got in the way. Funny how, even with SlipGates, people seldom made time to do the things they really wanted to do.

Dressed in beige pants and a white short-sleeved blouse,

Anna stood on her toes to peer over the wall. Maybe she could get in a little sightseeing before heading back home. That would be fun.

The silhouette of a short man came up behind her, and she couldn't resist the urge to smile. She would know that figure anywhere.

When her father stepped into view, he wore a pair of dark pants and a navy-blue shirt with a v-collar in Leyrian fashion. Beran was still handsome for a man of forty-five, his red goatee sporting a few silver flecks, his hair parted in the middle. "One thing about these glorious vistas: they offer the perfect excuse to avoid socializing."

Anna smiled, then bowed her head in chagrin. "You're right about that," she said, rubbing her eyes with the back of her hand. "I'm sorry. I'm still tired, and it's hard to be social when you've spent the morning reading the vilest sort of threats imaginable."

"Threats?"

Anna spun around to lean against the wall with her arms crossed, doubling over and letting out a sigh. "Nasty e-mails and phone calls," she muttered. "Ever since I took down those two cops in Tennessee..."

Her father stared off into the distance with lips pressed into a thin line, blinking as he considered her words. "You always were the sort of girl who spoke her mind," he said. "Even when it got you into trouble."

"You often lectured me on that."

"Yes, but it's also why I love you so much."

Closing her eyes, Anna let her head hang. The heat in her face was hard to ignore. "Well, that's good to know," she said, nodding once. "Sometimes I think you and Mom were happier with Alia."

Her father grinned, trembling as he chuckled softly. "I love both of my daughters equally," he began. "And I am incredibly proud of everything that Alia has accomplished, but...she never had your fire."

"Don't let her hear you say that."

"I won't."

Tilting her head back, Anna squinted up at the clear blue sky. "I don't know," she mumbled in a voice so soft it was barely audible. "Maybe I'm just not the kind of Keeper this planet needs."

"Why do you say that?"

Anna winced, then slapped a palm over her face. "I couldn't have imagined it," she said, massaging her eyelids with the tips of her fingers. "The raw hatred these people can conjure at a moment's notice."

Beran stood facing the wall with his arms crossed, his head bowed as he studied the grass. "And you feel responsible for it?" he murmured. "You feel as if you've...How does that delightful Earth phrase go? Set off a powder keg?"

"Sometimes..."

It wasn't her fault; she knew that. There was no doubt in her mind that saving Kevin Harmon – trying to save him, anyway; Companion be praised for Harry Carlson's timely intervention – had been the right thing to do. But she couldn't help but feel that a skilled Justice Keeper would have been able to do it *without* causing a public outcry. That was rubbish, and she knew it, but her guilty conscience didn't always take advice from her rational mind. *Also, I just thought the word "rubbish!" Less than four hours in London, and I'm already picking up British slang!*

"Sometimes," she went on, "I just think I don't have the mindset to deal with this planet's unique problems."

"So you want to transfer?"

"I didn't say that!" Anna snapped before her father could

get another word in. The last thing she needed was news of this getting back to her mother. Sierin would take it as an opportunity to rant about the uncivilized, primitive Earthers.

Her father turned around to stand beside her with his hands clasped behind himself, frowning as he watched the other guests mingle. "Then what do you want?" he asked in that slightly condescending voice of his.

Baring her teeth with a hiss, Anna lowered her eyes. "I don't know," she whispered, shaking her head. "A little sanity for a change? Right now, I'd be willing to settle for no more death threats."

Beran gave her shoulder a squeeze, then walked off to join several other people in a quiet conversation, leaving her alone to think. Anna sighed softly. She really should get back out there – normally, she loved parties – but there was something so draining about hearing threats on your life multiple times a day, everyday for months. It left you feeling hollow inside.

All her life, she'd been the sort of woman who felt as though she was torn between two competing impulses: the urge to fly off and seek adventure and a powerful sense of loyalty to the people she cared about. Now that she had him, she couldn't imagine leaving Bradley – which meant, for all intents and purposes, that Earth would be her home for the foreseeable future – but could she really stay here? When it was doing *this* to her?

She wasn't sure she wanted the answer to that question.

Gabrina Valtez flowed through the crowd of people with a smooth, easy grace. A winding stone path slithered through the grass with dignitaries standing in small groups on either side. She spotted a man with silver hair and a friendly smile gesticulating wildly with a glass of whiskey, a middle-aged woman in a blue dress who stood with her arms folded, nodding along with every point.

One of the Keepers – a tall young man with olive skin who looked rather dapper in his green shirt – came striding up the path in the opposite direction, nodding to her as he passed. She offered a warm smile in response. There was an art to socializing at a formal affair. Or an informal one, for that matter. Such events were more than just fun, they were also a wonderful way to gather information, and Gabi had to admit that she was a very nosy person.

She spotted Toral Enacrin, a contact from the Diplomatic Corps that she had met some years ago. Tall and broad-shouldered with sun-darkened skin, he wore a white shirt and kept his curly brown hair cut short.

He turned on his heel, then flashed a smile that could have held back winter's chill when he saw her. "Gabrina," he said, approaching. "How long has it been? Two years at least. Maybe three?"

Gabi stood on the path in a white sundress with thin shoulder straps, her hair tied up in a braid. "Toral," she said, nodding to him. "It seems like you've been busy. I didn't realize you'd been posted to Earth."

"Nor I you."

"It's good to see you."

The man stood with a drink in hand, staring up at the clear blue sky. "And you as well," he murmured. "Though if you're here, it likely means that the last few months of your life have been...colourful, to say the least."

Gabi felt her lips curl, then bowed her head to him. "I really can't argue with that," she said, her eyebrows rising. "When I accepted this assignment, I was expecting certain difficulties, but it seems as though this planet is constantly on the brink of total anarchy."

"Indeed."

With a flourish of his hand, Toral beckoned her up the path, then fell in beside her when she resumed her leisurely stroll. "Every time we succeed in building a partnership, several of the local nations begin squabbling."

"Is there any truth to the rumors?"

"What rumors?"

Shutting her eyes tight, Gabi took a deep breath through her nose. "The rumors that several of Earth's nations have begun demanding access to advanced weapons technology under the mistaken belief that they won't need our protection if we simply give them the means to protect themselves."

In truth, she knew perfectly well that those rumors were legitimate – LIS wouldn't be a credible intelligence agency if it couldn't keep tabs on the political climate of one of Leyria's closest allies – but it was always a good idea to see if someone would lie to you. It gave you a sense of where you stood.

Toral flashed a bright, beautiful smile, staring off at some point in the distance. "I can neither confirm nor deny," he answered. "But you know that we're working hard to cement our good relations with Earth."

"I do."

The sound of applause drew her attention, and she turned to find a man standing at the lectern positioned at the building's front wall. He was tall, slim and handsome with a neatly trimmed beard on his dark-skinned face. "Good afternoon," he said. "I greet you on this, the fourth anniversary of Friendship Day."

More applause.

Gabi stood with her hands clasped in front of herself, her head bowed respectfully. "I guess it's time for the formalities," she murmured to Toral. "It just wouldn't be a party without a good speech."

Her companion stood with his arms crossed, frowning at the podium. "One thing about diplomats," he said, his eyebrows rising. "We do develop something of a penchant for pomp and circumstance."

The man at the lectern stood tall and proud, running his gaze over everyone present. "My name is Rayse Calvoran," he went on. "I've served in the Leyrian Diplomatic Corps for nearly two decades, and I can honestly tell you that I have never been as proud as I was on the day we helped Earth take its first steps into the galactic community.

"Much has changed since then. We've had some stumbles, some missteps. But our commitment to forging a lasting partnership that will strengthen both of our peoples has never been stronger. To that end, I would like to welcome Larani Tal, the new head of the Justice Keepers who is joining us today via SlipStream transmission."

"This should be good," Gabi muttered.

Harry watched the hologram ripple into existence right in front of the podium, watched as small projectors in the concrete path that cut through the grass created the image of a tall woman in a finely-tailed suit of Leyrian fashion.

He had seen Larani Tal before, of course, but he had never had the pleasure of her company. The woman was tall and slender with a thin face and black hair that she wore pulled back in a bun. He had never told anyone this, but Larani gave him hope for the future of the human race. Here was concrete proof that a black woman could ascend to one of the most influential positions in the galaxy.

Larani stood with hands clasped behind her back, staring blankly at nothing at all. "Good afternoon," she said, nodding once. "I regret that I have been unable to join you today, but matters on Leyria require my attention."

Murmurs rippled through the crowd.

Harry stood in front of the wall with his arms crossed, frowning at the hologram. *She'd be better off to just say it out loud,* he thought to himself. *Tip-toe around the point, and everyone will assume it's a big deal.*

He knew the rumor of course; Ben – a young man that Harry had come to respect – had been attacked by a Justice Keeper on Leyria. A Justice Keeper who professed open allegiance to Slade. The higher ups on Station Twelve tried their best to keep things quiet, but you could tease out information if you knew where to look.

Working among the Justice Keepers wasn't all that different from working in a police station; people talked – usually in places where they thought they could relax. Spend a few hours reading a newspaper in the Nova Cafe, and you would hear things.

The hologram of Larani stood tall and prim with a big fake smile on her face. "We have come far together," she went on. "And we will go even further. Today, we renew our commitment to the protection of Earth and the preservation of its diverse cultures."

A few people clapped at that.

Harry closed his eyes, turning his face up to the afternoon sun. He delighted in the warmth of its caress. *The preservation of Earth's cultures,* he thought. *Even when most of them stand at odds with everything Leyrians believe in?*

It was clear that Larani was not the sort of person who excelled at giving speeches. Her posture was stiff, rigid, and she glared at anything in front of her as if she thought she would be fending off a tiger attack at any moment. "In the last few years, I have had the good fortune to meet the two Justice Keepers who best symbolize the alliance between our two worlds.

"Leana Lenai, one of Leyria's finest, stands among you today. As the first person from our world to set foot on yours, her name will be remembered for generations to come." Technically, the first Leyrian to set foot on Earth – so far as anyone knew – was Denario Tarse; no one wanted to acknowledge that. "And Jack Hunter. As the first person from your world to accept a symbiont, he has also earned a place in the annals of history. Their friendship, trust and cooperation – their ability to forge an alliance in spite of radically different backgrounds – represent the union between our two peoples."

More applause.

"It is with renewed optimism that we move forward," Larani went on. "This past year has not been easy: terrors wrought by those who would divide us, betrayals by those we should have trusted most. Today, we stand proudly together and announce, 'We will not be divided! We will not back down!"

The crowd cheered.

Larani bowed her head to them. "I am honoured to count you all among my peers," she said. "On this Friendship Day, let us remember that we stand united, one and all."

The hologram vanished.

In the corner of his eye, Harry noticed Jena coming up beside him in a white skirt and a blue blouse that she left untucked. She directed a tight-lipped grimace at the spot where the hologram was, then nodded once. "The usual talking points," she said. "Larani is one of the sharpest people I've ever met, but ask her to address a crowd, and you'll get a speech that works so hard to avoid offending anyone, it's practically a tautology."

"You didn't like it?"

"I didn't feel much of anything one way or another; that's the point."

The applause picked up again when Jack strode up to the podium in that untucked shirt of his. He took a position behind the lectern, gripping the sides with both hands and peering out at the crowd like a hawk searching for a field mouse. "Well, then," Jena murmured. "*This* should be interesting."

Gabi felt a stab of anxiety as she watched her boyfriend

lean over the lectern and run that wolf-like gaze of his over the assembled guests. Jack looked like a principal that was about to lecture a group of rowdy students. Not good. It didn't help one bit that she had no clue what he intended to say.

Jack closed his eyes, visibly calming himself. "Good afternoon," he said with a curt nod. "I wish I could say I'm happy to be here, but Justice Keepers are encouraged toward honesty. And as Larani said, it's been a hard year."

Next to her, Toral shifted his weight from one foot to the other and scrunched up his face. "He's going to say something inflammatory, isn't he?"

Gabi winced, hanging her head in frustration. "Probably," she said, nodding slowly. "It's his way. Jack believes that the only way to be honest is to force yourself to confront the things you least want to acknowledge."

Lifting his chin, Jack studied the crowd with those fierce blue eyes of his. "Most of you know how my speeches usually go," he went on. "Greeting, joke, brief synopsis of what being a Justice Keeper means to me...Discussion on the importance of bringing Earth into the galactic community, random 80's pop culture reference and finally a well-timed mic drop."

Several people laughed.

"Not today."

Clenching his teeth with a hiss, Jack looked down at the lectern. "I come here to apologize for failing you," he said. "Because that's what every single person who carries a Nassai has done.

"The Justice Keepers have a well-deserved reputation for bringing peace and order to all the worlds under Leyrian jurisdiction, but over time, we have become complacent. We were so sure of our own moral superiority that we failed to take action when traitors were hiding right under our noses. We allowed ourselves to believe that no one who had bonded a Nassai could ever violate the basic principles on which our organization was founded. This past year, we learned the price for that arrogance."

Murmurs from the crowd made Gabi feel uneasy; clearly this wasn't what they were expecting. She looked around to find several of the Senior Directors standing along the wall to her left, all frowning at Jack. There would be consequences for this; she had no doubt about that.

Toral bit his lip as he studied Jack, squinting as if he wasn't entirely sure what was going on. "What's Hunter doing?" he asked, shaking his head. "A little more rhetoric like that, and we might have a riot on our hands."

Jack clasped his hands together behind his back, then bowed his head like a child who had disappointed his parents. "I am sorry," he said. "I let you down. We *all* let you down, but I hope that we can make it right."

Silence was his only answer.

"In order to do better," Jack went on, "we need to begin asking ourselves the hard questions. We need to be willing to look in the mirror and acknowledge the times when we don't like what we see."

Companion have mercy! This was going to earn him another suspension! Why did that bother her so much? It wasn't *her* career on the line. Could it be that Jack's eagerness to leap head first into the Bleakness itself proved beyond any and all doubt that building a life with her wasn't his first priority?

But then, why would it be?

He was a Justice Keeper; as a rule, they didn't settle down with anybody. Instead, they lived hectic lives full of danger, and if they managed to avoid being shot, stabbed or vaporized, they would eventually die a very premature death in their mid-fifties. She had *known* this before pursuing a relationship with Jack. So why was she suddenly feeling so skeptical of their future?

Maybe because it's not sudden at all, a quiet voice whispered.

Maybe you've known all along that this couldn't last, but you didn't want to break the poor man's heart. Hardly a good reason to continue pursuing a relationship.

Toral stood with his arms crossed, scowling down at himself. "Such arrogance," he said, shaking his head. "The man stands before us, on a day that should inspire unity, and presumes to lecture his superiors on their failings?"

"He's a very passionate person."

"Is it true you're *dating* him?"

Red-cheeked with chagrin, Gabi shut her eyes and nodded to him. "It's true," she said in a voice so soft it barely registered in her own ears. "He's a good man, Toral: kind, noble, willing to sacrifice himself."

Toral looked up at the sky with lips pursed, blinking slowly as he considered her words. "I'm sure," he murmured. "But doesn't it bother you that he has so little regard for his own colleagues?"

That wasn't what bothered her. No...What bothered her was the unpleasant reminder that she and Jack had never been destined to settle down together with a small family of their own. Children and grandchildren weren't in the cards if she stayed with him, and she had to admit that she wanted both.

Jack was speaking again – he had been for some time – and glaring daggers at just about everyone present, but she had to admit that she wasn't really listening. Right then, she was too busy trying to fend off her own heartbreak.

Jack leaned over the lectern with his arms folded, directing a smile at the people in front of him. "We have a choice," he said. "We can keep pretending that nothing is wrong and hope it doesn't get worse, or we can do what Keepers do best."

He waited for them to ask themselves the inevitable question.

"We can take a stand against corruption," Jack said firmly.

"We can acknowledge our shortcomings and work to correct them." Before anyone could say one word, he spun on his heel and marched off the stage with the fury of a hurricane.

"Excuse me," Gabi said. "I need to see to a few things."

The sun beat down from a clear, blue sky, shining down on Bishopgate Street – two lanes of black pavement that ran through a corridor between tightly-packed buildings of gray bricks. The odd skyscraper rose up every to dwarf all lesser structures with sunlight glinting off every window.

Leaning against a wall with his arms crossed, Arin felt a little warm in black pants and a matching t-shirt. His dark, angular face was coated with sweat, and he had to resist the urge to wipe it away.

The nearest skyscraper – a building of over thirty stories that stretched toward the open sky – was currently home to some four dozen Justice Keepers who had come here to celebrate Leyria's fruitful alliance with Earth. That alliance had already begun to crack, and if Arin was successful, one of those fissures would soon become a gaping hole.

He had been born on Leyria. After years of dreaming about the prospect of becoming a Keeper himself, he had finally worked up the nerve to ask to be tested. His first contact with a Nassai had been nothing short of disastrous. The symbiont rejected him after only a few seconds. Keepers did not offer one a second chance to bond a Nassai.

Clenching his teeth, Arin squeezed his eyes shut. "Their mistake," he whispered, shaking his head in disgust. "Bending to the will of the Nassai has only resulted in weak, close-minded Keepers who cannot see their order crumbling around them."

His words drew the attention of a young woman in a blue sundress, a pretty young lady with fair skin and blonde hair that she wore tied back in a clip. She paused right in front of him, casting a glance in his direction.

No one liked people who talked to themselves.

Thrusting out his chin, Arin squinted at her. "Something I can do for you?" he said in a voice as smooth as the finest silk. "If you're hoping to ogle handsome men, perhaps you should get yourself a good Internet connection."

The woman scoffed and moved on.

Arin smiled, then bowed his head to stare down at himself. *In time,* he thought, his eyebrows rising. *All in good time. When Slade is finished, the day will come when no one will dare laugh at us.*

Of course, for that to happen, he had to complete one very important task. The first of many, but that didn't make success any less vital. He watched people shuffling up the sidewalk on the other side of the street. Businessmen in suits, teenage girls in shorts and tank-tops, the odd senior citizen: they all moved with a purpose. So far, Arin had seen a few Keepers making their way to the party, but they were always in small groups. After months of training with Slade, he had a firm confidence in his own abilities, but he did not trust himself to handle more than one. Not yet, anyway.

What he really needed was a straggler.

Closing his eyes, Arin turned his face up to the sun. He delighted in the feeling of warmth on his skin. *Soon now,* he assured himself. *One of them will leave early for one reason or another.*

Then his moment would come.

Dressed in white pants and a matching jacket over a light blue shirt, Glin Karon made his way up the sidewalk with his head down. A light prickle of sweat on his brow made him aware of the day's heat – this planet could produce some truly intense weather – and he reminded himself that he would much rather have stayed aboard Station Two, tending the lilacs he had planted in the garden.

People shuffled up the sidewalk toward him, some nearly mowing him down as they slipped past. In the distance, he saw a glittering spire that stretched toward the clear blue sky. That, no doubt, was his destination. After exiting the Liverpool Street Station, he had wandered for nearly fifteen minutes before getting his bearings. He was late. By now, Larani would have given her address.

The store-front windows of shops to his right looked in on small cafes, clothing shops and the first-floor of what Earthers considered to be an office. One glance made him hiss in contempt. From what little he could see through the tinted glass, they kept their employees trapped in little boxes.

He continued up the street.

The cars on his left – each one oriented so that it was driving into the distance behind him – had formed a queue, and now there was quite a bit of cursing from one man who drove with his window open. Glin tried to ignore it. He had absolutely no interest in hearing one fool shout at the man in front of-

Something twisted spacetime.

He felt it like a *wrongness* off to his left, and as he turned to see who had caused the disruption, he caught sight of a man in black leaping over two lanes of traffic, landing on the roof of a red car.

The man jumped, somersaulting through the air, then uncurling to land hard on the sidewalk just a short distance away. Tall and lithe, he had a dark face with hollow-cheeks and a pointed chin. His hair was cut so short it was little more than stubble. Glin suddenly felt very uneasy. This was no Keeper.

The man whirled around to face him, pressing a hand to his chest and bowing low. "Do I have the good fortune to be addressing Glin Karon?" he asked, straightening. "One of the most esteemed Keepers of the last thirty years?"

Glin lifted his chin, squinting at the other man. "Who are you?" he asked, shaking his head. "More importantly, how did you acquire your symbiont? You're one of Slade's twisted creations, aren't you?"

The other man replied with a wide grin, bowing his head in a gesture of respect. "I am called Arin," he said, taking a few steps forward. "I must say that I take exception to your comment. There is nothing twisted about me."

Glin crossed his arms as he backed away, frowning at the other man. "The creature you bonded was broken, tortured until it was willing to accept a host such as you." Just thinking about it made Glin nauseous.

Arin turned his head to direct that smile at one of the shop windows. He seemed fascinated by the people inside. "You see them in there?" he asked. "One day, they will look to men like me to protect them."

"It seems you're delusional as well."

"Yours is the old order, Karon," Arin spat. "Mine is the new. The Nassai are a tool to serve human ends. That is why the Inzari left them for us to find. And yet you allow them to dictate who among *us* they will accept?"

Glin felt his jaw drop. Clamping a hand over his mouth, he squeezed his eyes shut. "They are a sentient species!" he growled. "Your attitude toward living beings who think and feel proves you have no business carrying a symbiont."

"You won't carry yours much longer," Arin said, stroking a knife that he wore on his belt. He strode toward Glin like a whirlwind toward a rickety old farmhouse. "I plan to relieve you of it today."

"I don't want to fight you."

Tossing his head back, Arin grinned up at the sky and trembled with soft laughter. "How amusing," he replied. "You act as if you have a choice in the matter. How long has it been since you've been forced to employ your combat skills, Glin? Do you think they may have atrophied over the long-"

Glin threw a punch.

The other man's hand came up, striking his wrist and knocking his arm aside. Four dark knuckles collided with Glin's face, and his vision was filled with bright silvery flecks. His opponent spun for a back-kick.

A boot to the chest made Glin double over and back up along the sidewalk, gasping and wheezing the whole time. He could still sense the other man's silhouette. Arin came running at him.

The man jumped for a high kick.

Glin stepped to the left just in time to watch his opponent land right beside him. He turned and shoved with Keeper strength. Arin went stumbling sideways, colliding with the front window of a shop.

Glass shattered and the customers inside shouted, but Arin grabbed a few shards in one hand. He flung them, augmenting each piece with Bent Gravity, sending them flying at deadly speeds.

Glin fell over backward, catching himself by slapping both hands down upon the concrete. Thin shards of glass flew over his stomach, chest and face, some coming close enough to rip the fabric of his shirt.

Arin stood in front of the broken window with a bright smile on his face, his skin glistening with sweat. "You Keepers," he said, shaking his head. "You are the old; we are the new. It's time for your decadence to be cut away."

The man drew a gleaming knife from his belt, holding the blade up in front of his face. "Do you like it?" Arin asked. "I'm going to bury it in your guts; so I sincerely hope the answer is yes."

Glin snapped himself upright.

The other man came at him, slashing.

Glin hopped back, the tip of the knife slicing his shirt. Falling over backward, Glin caught himself with both hands and kicked out to drive a foot into the other man's belly. Arin went stumbling back to the window.

In a heartbeat, Glin was on his feet and removing his jacket in a flurry. He flung the garment at full force and watched as it draped itself over Arin's head, cutting off both his vision and the spatial awareness of his symbiont.

Glin raced for his opponent.

Arin blurred into a streak of colour that resolidified just a few feet to the right with the jacket suddenly discarded on the ground. The man spun, raised his knife and tried to ram it downward.

Glin brought one hand up to intercept the man's wrist, preventing the blade from finding flesh. He used the other to deliver a mean punch to the face, one that made Arin's head snap backward.

With a growl, Glin whirled for a back-hand strike.

The other man turned, catching Glin's arm in both hands. He applied pressure that forced Glin to bend over. Pain drowned out awareness of everything else, making it so very hard to think.

A knee to the belly sent Glin stumbling sideways along the sidewalk. Air burst from his lungs in a high-pitched wheeze, and he was left disoriented. He had to recover, had to regain his balance before the other man pressed his advantage. With a deep breath, Glin righted himself and rounded on his opponent.

Arin was right in front of him.

The man seized his shirt and delivered a fierce head-butt that darkened Glin's vision and left him feeling dizzy and nauseous. It was hard to focus; his spatial awareness was a mass of information that he couldn't sort through.

Light returned to the world just in time for him to see Arin crouching down and retrieving his knife. The man flung his hand out and Bent Gravity did the rest. The knife sped forward in a blur.

It pierced Glin's chest right up to the hilt. Where was the pain? Shouldn't there be pain? Was he in shock? A wound like that was bound to hurt but...Oh, Companion have mercy! There it was! His lungs were on fire!

Arin strode forward with a ferocious grin, laughing all the way. "Foolish Keeper." He pulled the knife from Glin's chest, then slammed it hard through Glin's throat, cutting the carotid artery in one fluid motion.

Everything went dark within seconds.

The afternoon wore on with people standing in little clusters among the flowerbeds and on the concrete paths that snaked through the grass. It was still very warm, and Jena had no problem believing that most people were quite ready for the festivities to come to an end. Jack's speech had a sobering effect.

Jena sat at a table with one leg crossed over the other, leaning back and gripping the arms of her chair. A surge of pride went through her when considered Jack's speech. Her protégé was coming into his own, it seemed. That little address had raised eyebrows and ruffled feathers and forced her colleagues to confront uncomfortable truths they would rather not deal with. The kid was going to be all right.

Jena lifted a glass of 7-Up in front of her face, squinting as she studied the fizzing liquid. "So this is what you people drink," she said, turning to her companion. "Well, the bubbles are nice."

Harry was seated next to her with his hands folded in his lap, staring vacantly at the other guests. "Yeah," he mumbled, nodding once. "It's a real hit. People around here kind of love their soft drinks."

"Something on your mind?"

"You realize there's going to be fallout from this."

Jena grinned, then lowered her eyes to stare into her lap. "I'm aware," she said, her eyebrows rising. "You might say that was the whole point of this little exercise. Someone needs to shake these people out of their complacency."

"At the expense of Jack's career?"

With a heavy sigh, Jena took a sip of her drink. It was very sweet – too sweet, in her opinion – but she made it a point to experience the culture of every world she visited. And she had to give the Earthers some credit: their music was nothing short of fantastic. Jack had introduced her to the collective works of Bruce Springsteen. "The kid isn't going to wreck his career, Harry," she said. "If anything, he might just be saving it. You were there when those sycophants raked Anna over the coals for trying to protect an innocent kid. Toadyism will be the death of everything good about the Keepers."

"Perhaps, but-"

He was interrupted by the spectacle of a young woman in a pink dress scrambling out the penthouse door and doubling over with a hand pressed to her stomach. "Glin is dead," she sputtered. "He's...He's..."

Jena got to her feet.

Striding across the rooftop at a brisk pace, she reached up to rake fingers through her short auburn hair. "What happened?" she asked, approaching the woman. "Do we need to organize an evacuation?"

The woman looked up at her with fierce green eyes that glistened with tears. "It was someone with a symbiont," she panted. "One of Slade's followers. He killed Glin right there on the sidewalk."

Jena felt her face crumple, then tossed her head about. "Get yourself together," she said. "Organize teams of two or three people each who will escort our visiting dignitaries to the Slip-Gate terminal."

"Yes, ma'am."

"Move!" Jena barked. "I want these people ready to go in five minutes."

Slade had played his hand; now she had to play hers.

4

The sun was an orange ball that slowly sank toward the western horizon, casting golden rays out on the skyscrapers of London, buildings that rose up like a forest of shadows to cut off the light.

Jack stood before the window with his arms crossed, frowning down at himself. "I never really knew the man," he said softly. "For years, everyone told me that I should get to know Glin Karon. He was one of the best Keepers who ever lived."

In his mind's eye, he saw Gabi gliding up the hallway with fists balled at her sides, her head bowed in sadness. "Are you okay?" she asked, approaching him. "It's all right if you need to let out your feelings."

Jack closed his eyes, tossing his head back. He took a slow, ragged breath. "You're the fifth person to ask me that," he replied. "Like I said, Gabs, I hardly knew the man. I *wish* that I was devastated."

Gabi faced the window with hands folded over her stomach, her face a mask of perfect serenity. "I understand," she said softly. "But Jack, it's all right if you *don't* feel devastated."

He had nothing to say to that; so he contented himself to watch the sunset for a few moments. Orange light framed the silhouettes of buildings all around him, like fiery outlines on doors that led straight into an endless abyss. Down below, the street was once again a flurry of activity, cars rushing past in both directions. You wouldn't have even guessed that just a few hours ago, a Keeper had been murdered in broad daylight.

This was a message; he knew that much. Slade wanted the people of Earth to know that no one – not even one of the mighty Justice Keepers – was safe from him. No doubt the media had already started whipping people into a frenzy.

"You're troubled."

Jack squinted through the window. "I am," he said, nodding to her. "Leo was just one guy with homemade explosives and some performance enhancing drugs. And look at all the trouble he caused."

He paced the width of the hallway with his arms crossed, pausing at the opposite wall. "Slade has access to symbionts," he went on. "Slade has *ziarogati* and telepaths and God alone knows what else. If Leo nearly tore the alliance between our two peoples apart, imagine what Slade will do."

His girlfriend stood behind him with her back turned, peering through the window as she mulled it over. "Perhaps you shouldn't have given that speech," she said. "Now is not the time for division."

Jack winced, trembling as he drew in a hissing breath. "No," he growled, spinning around to face her. "We're never going to solve this by pretending that our problems don't exist. We *have* to be honest."

Gabi's shoulders slumped, and she hunched over to bury her face in one hand. He could only see the back of her head, but it was obvious that she was upset. "It really is that simple for you," she whispered.

He approached to stand beside her.

Out of the corner of his eye, he could see tears glistening on her cheek. Well, *that* couldn't be anything good! He knew Gabi well enough by now to know that she wouldn't be so upset over a minor philosophical disagreement. "Gabs, what's wrong?"

Gabi sniffled, then covered her face with both hands, trembling as she sobbed. "I'm sorry," she whimpered. "Now is really the worst time to do this."

"To do what?"

She didn't answer.

Jack felt his face heat up. He leaned forward, rubbing at his eyes with the back of his hand. "Ah...That," he said. "Well, if it's any consolation to you, I've been expecting it for quite some time."

She looked up at him with tears streaming over her cheeks, blinking several times. "I just..." The words came out as a strangled squeak. "Jack, I want a family of my own. I want to get out of this life."

"Okay. I understand."

"What? That's it?"

Jack crossed his arms with a soft sigh, refusing to look up at her. "What else should there be?" he asked with a shrug of his shoulders. "Gabs, you've been hesitant about this relationship from day one."

"That's unfair."

With his mouth hanging open, Jack looked up to blink at the ceiling. "Unfair," he muttered angrily. "Every single time we did something that *might* have advanced our relationship half a centimeter, you panicked."

Gabi's face was red, as she fixed him with a stare that could have peeled the hide off a wolf. "I did nothing of the sort!" she snapped. "We've been dating for six months. It's not unreasonable that-"

Jack scrunched up his face, tossing his head about in disgust. "I don't want to argue this point!" he growled. "You want to break up? Fine! I've got no intention of kicking up a fuss over it."

He strode past her, making his way down the long hallway lined with windows to the stairwell door. In his mind's eye, he saw her standing there, watching him go. A part of him wanted to turn back and say something to her – hell, *Summer* wanted him to turn back and say something to her – but he thought better of it. There was no use in trying to argue someone out of breaking up with you. If they couldn't find sufficient motivation to stay with you without coaxing, then the relationship simply wasn't worth salvaging. As he approached the stairwell door, she called out, "I'm sorry!"

Jack paused with a hand braced against the wall, hunching over as if he had lost the strength to hold himself upright. "Don't be sorry," he said. "Some things just aren't meant to be."

As always, Jena's office was well-lit and painfully spartan. The dark gray walls were completely bare; the desk with its polished SmartGlass surface was free of pictures, knickknacks or anything that might suggest personal attachment.

Anna sat in one chair with her knees together, her hands folded in her lap as she watched her supervising officer vent her frustration. From what little she knew of Jena's personal relationships, she and Glin had never been close. Still, the other woman seemed ready to bite the head off a snake.

Jena was hunched over the desk with her back turned, pressing both hands to its glass surface. "He was one of the best of us," she growled. "Did you know that during his time as an initiate, Glin won six out of every ten sparring matches?"

Anna winced, shaking her head in disgust. "That's probably the whole point," she muttered, doubling over in her chair. "Slade wants us to know that no one – not even the most skilled among us – is safe."

Glancing over her shoulder, Jena glared at her with eyes

that could have peeled the paint off a ship's hull. The woman's features softened half a second later. "Yeah...You're probably right."

"Do we have any leads?"

Jena straightened but kept her back turned, peering over the desk to the slanted window on the wall. "Nothing solid," she answered. "Witness statements confirm that they fought on the sidewalk, but the guy took off and nobody wanted to follow."

Anna sank into the chair with her arms folded, turning her face up to the ceiling. "No one wanted to follow," she said, blinking. "Okay...Traffic cameras. Security footage from the nearest Tube station. There has to be something."

"We're looking into it."

The double doors behind her split apart to reveal the silhouette of Jack striding into the room with all the pent-up fury of a thundercloud. He stopped just a few paces behind her chair.

Jena whirled around to face him with hands on her hips, baring her teeth in a nasty snarl. "Where have you been?" she asked, taking a few steps forward. "I called you up here over half an hour ago!"

"I got held up."

"You got held up!"

Anna twisted in her chair to find Jack standing just a few feet away with his hands shoved into his pants' pockets, his head turned to stare at the wall to his right. Something was not right; she would have to ask about it later.

Jena squeezed her eyes shut, trembling with obvious frustration. "Brilliant!" she hissed. "Am I the only one who remembers that Slade has been one step ahead of us at every single juncture? Could we please start taking this seriously?"

"I'm sorry," Jack murmured.

No wise crack, Anna noted. That was usually his way of

handling situations that made him feel uneasy. For him to simply roll over like that...Something was definitely wrong. Anna was suddenly very worried.

Jena sat on the edge of her desk with hands folded over her pristine white skirt, staring into her lap. "All right then," she muttered. "Ven has studied the Overseer device and come up with coordinates for a dozen or so Overseer outposts."

Lifting his chin, Jack studied her with fierce blue eyes. "You want us to check them out," he said, nodding once. "All right; give me the first. I'll take a shuttle out tomorrow morning."

"I want Harry to go with you."

"Is that wise?"

Baring her teeth with a soft hiss, Jena met his gaze with one that could have made the most hardened criminal flinch. "Is there some reason it wouldn't be?" she asked in tones that said she was in no mood to argue.

Jack closed his eyes, taking a deep breath through his nose. "Harry's a vital part of this team," he said, stepping forward. "He's also the only member of this team without any kind of enhancement. If I come up against one of Slade's goons..."

"Don't be too quick to underestimate Harry," Anna cautioned. "When I fought Isara a few months ago, he was essential."

"All right, I suppose I could use some backup."

"And sadly, Harry's the only person I can spare," Jena said. "Anna, I want you to go over the crime scene with Scotland Yard. Find the man who killed Glin. Then we'll all go have ourselves a nice chat."

When Jena was done with them, Anna followed her friend out of the office. She'd only seen Jack like this once or twice before, but each time had been during some personal crisis. "You gonna tell me what's up?" she asked.

Jack stopped in the middle of the hallway, keeping his

back turned. "Gabi broke up with me," he said, shoulders slumping. "It really shouldn't have been such a shock. She's been hesitant about moving forward from the very beginning."

Anna winced and let her head hang. She touched two fingers to a spot right above her nose. "Oh, Jack, I'm so sorry," she muttered. "Look, I've gotta liaise with the Brits in a few minutes, but why don't we meet up later tonight?"

He spun around to face her with a hand pressed to his stomach, head bowed as if he couldn't bear to look her in the eye. "Sure," Jack whispered. "Give me a call when you're free. I'll be conducting an experiment that involves pouring half a bottle of whiskey into a carton of ice cream and seeing what happens."

Anna stepped forward, slipping her arms around him. She nuzzled his chest and gave him a squeeze. "It's gonna be okay," she promised. "We'll talk about it later, when I'm free, okay?"

"Okay."

Stars were twinkling in the dark night sky, but with the ambient glow of city lights, they were little more than faint pinpricks in the blackness. His apartment building loomed like a shadow; a few windows were still lit but not many.

Jack sat on a swing in the small playground behind the building, his knees together, his hands gripping the chains. The pain in his chest was hard to ignore. This, he realized, was his first real break-up. It felt as if a piece of him had been ripped away, and worst of all, he couldn't even decide if he wanted it back.

His eyes spotted a woman coming down the grassy slope, and spatial awareness told him it was Anna; he would know her silhouette anywhere. She carried something in each hand.

Jack let his head hang, blowing out a deep breath. *Here we go,* a small voice spoke in the back of his mind. *The standard pep talk where people tell you it's for the best, and there are plenty of fish in the sea.*

Anna approached with a small paper bowl in each hand, each containing a tiny mountain of frozen yogurt and a spoon that jutted out from the top. "Chocolate mint for you," she said, offering one to him. "And for me, strawberry...with real strawberries."

Grinning like a fool, Jack shut his eyes tight. He shook his head in wry amusement. "You remembered," he said, taking the bowl. "I've gotta say, I'm surprised, An. It's been over four years."

She took the swing next to him, resting the bowl in her lap, staring down at it with a tight frown. "Of course I remember," she said. "Come on, Jack, that night's gonna stand out until the day I die."

Jack blushed, wiping sweat off his brow with the back of his hand. "Well," he said, pushing backward on his swing. "It's good to know I left an impression."

"Of course you did."

He carefully swirled the spoon around his little mountain of froyo, making sure to pick up an even amount of both flavours. Then he popped it in his mouth. There were few things that blended as well together as chocolate and mint. It actually eased the pain a bit. Just a bit, but he could see why some people started eating cartons of ice cream whenever they went through a bad break-up.

"So what happened?"

Jack closed his eyes, turning his face up to the starry sky. "The one and only thing that could happen," he said with a shrug of his shoulders. "She told me that she wants to have a family, and...Well, you understand."

In his mind's eye, Anna was sitting with her legs stretched out, feet crossed at the ankle. "Yeah, I understand," she said. "Just like I understand that Gabi has known that Keepers can't have children ever since she was a little girl, and yet she chose to pursue a relationship with you anyway."

"Don't be mad at her."

"I think we can be a little mad at her."

Jack winced, shaking his head. "There's no point." He pressed a palm to his brow, massaging the bridge of his nose with the heel of his hand. "It's a simple fact of nature, An: fire burns, wind blows and people leave."

When he looked over his shoulder, Anna was watching him, her face bathed in the glow of nearby lights, her blue eyes so wide you could drown in them. "You don't really *believe* that, do you?"

"I think I do."

"Jack..."

He chose that moment to shovel another spoonful of yogurt into his mouth. It gave him a brief pause, a chance to think. True, there was a little hyperbole in what he had just said – and he could feel Summer scolding him for that – but one thing he'd learned over the years was that most relationships were temporary. His life wasn't a difficult one, not really. But most of his friendships had lasted a few years. People drifted apart. It was just a fact of life.

Anna sat hunched over with the bowl in one hand, the spoon in the other, stirring her yogurt anxiously. "You're wrong," she said with such ferocity he wouldn't dare argue. "I won't leave you. Ever."

"Then you're a rare exception."

"No."

Jack stood and paced to the edge of the playground, pausing there to stare off into the distance. "There's no sense in getting upset about it, An," he said. "Life just takes us in different directions."

Spatial awareness allowed him to sense her sitting there with the yogurt in her lap, shaking her head in dismay. "One thing I'll never get used to," she muttered. "Life here makes you cynical."

"That's unfair."

"Is it?"

He paused to contemplate the half-finished bowl of yogurt in his hand. Amusement bubbled up, soothing away his pain for a few brief seconds. Here he was, growling about how people would inevitably leave to a friend who not only made it her business to take care of him – a friend who had always been there for him even when they were separated by lightyears – but who also remembered an obscure fact about how he liked his frozen desserts. Perhaps his father was wrong. Maybe people *didn't* inevitably let you down. He could feel Summer agreeing with that.

Jack grinned, bowing his head to stare down at his feet. "Maybe not," he said with a shrug. "But you're totally ruining my Kit Harrington in the middle of season one vibe. You get that, right?"

He turned.

Anna was sitting there with the bowl of frozen yogurt resting in her lap, gripping the chains of her swing with both hands. "Really?" she said. "So you've been cultivating this angsty persona, have you?"

"It's the culmination of ten years of hard work!" he exclaimed. "You know, when I was a teenager and my guidance counselor had me fill out one of those forms that lists your desired career path, I actually wrote 'brooding loner with the weight of the world on his shoulders.' "

She giggled.

"Thank you," he said. "I really needed that."

"Any time." Anna stood up with a sigh and slowly made her way over to him. "So why don't you come out with me and Bradley tomorrow night?" she added. "Sounds like you could use a distraction."

"Thanks. I think I will."

Exhaustion made Harry's legs ache as he moved through the front door of his small suburban house. The e-mail he'd just received from Jena informing him that he would be going with Jack tomorrow only made it worse. *Well,* a small voice whispered. *You wanted to be part of the team...*

The foyer of his home was lit by light that spilled out from the kitchen, and Harry could see his two daughters sitting at the table at the end of a narrow corridor lined with cupboards on both sides. Melissa, he realized, was becoming a young woman. Tall and slim, she wore a pair of denim shorts with a black t-shirt and kept her hair tied up in a bun. "Nope," she said. "Guess again."

Across from her, Claire sat with elbows on the table, staring intently at her sister. His youngest wore a pair of white shorts and a black t-shirt with a picture of Kylo Ren from *Star Wars.* "Are you a hockey player?"

"Yes."

"Gordie Howe."

Melissa crossed her arms, leaning over the table with a big smile. "I'm not Gordie Howe," she said. "I've played for the New York Rangers and the Los Angeles Kings. I've won a few Stanley Cups."

"Gordie Howe."

Tossing her head back, Melissa rolled her eyes at the ceiling. "No, Claire," she muttered, exasperation thickening her voice. "I'm a hockey player, but I'm definitely not Gordie Howe."

"There are hockey players other than Gordie Howe?" Claire giggled with delight at her sister's frustration, scooching her chair closer to the table. "I don't know, Missy. You have to give me another clue."

"I'm from Brantford, Ontario."

"Gordie Howe."

Melissa doubled over in her chair, covering her face with both hands. A low groan escaped her. In response, Claire giggled hysterically. It warmed Harry's heart to see them playfully bickering.

Melissa stood up with a sigh, bowing her head to smile down at herself. "Maybe you should go to bed," she said, gesturing to the wall behind the kitchen table. Claire's room was on the other side.

Grumbling with obvious dissatisfaction, Claire hopped out of her chair and stood. She placed a hand over the top of her head and scratched at her dark hair. "Good night, Dad," she said before running out of the kitchen.

Melissa turned to him and slowly made her way through the narrow space between cupboards with her head down. "I got a letter today," she said, extending a hand that held her phone. "You might want to read it."

Harry took the phone and slid his thumb across the screen to bring up the e-mail she wanted to show him. The words he found left him feeling...numb.

Ms. Carlson,
Your application to the Justice Keeper training program has been accepted. We find your academic scores to be nothing short of exemplary, and your essay detailing the importance of building strong diplomatic ties in a galaxy rife with conflict made three Senior Directors nod with approval.

The program consists of courses that will empower you with a basic knowledge of forensic analysis, self-defense and combat strategy along with field-work that will be carried out under the supervision of a senior Justice Keeper. You will have the opportunity to tailor your scheduled classes to best suit your individual needs, but field work will require you to work irregular hours. Please plan accordingly.

Following the conclusion of the year-long program, you will be allowed contact with a Nassai symbiont to determine your suitability for Blending. Should the symbiont reject you for any reason, other career opportunities within law enforcement will be made available to you. Courses begin the week of September 4th on Station Thirteen. We look forward to seeing you then.

- Operative Teral Nisso, Justice Keeper Training Division

Harry froze with his daughter's phone held up in front of his face, staring blankly at the words on the screen. It was happening. It was *really* happening. They'd gone over this many times together, but now his little girl was about to take the first step that would lead to her becoming a Justice Keeper. All the danger...the loneliness. He still believed it was unfair to ask a kid to make a decision that would change their life in such a drastic way. Melissa didn't want children *now*, but in the future...

Still, Harry had accepted the fact that it *was* her choice, and if he was honest with himself, he would have to admit that part of his apprehension came from his own sense of irrelevance. Everyone he knew was becoming powerful in ways that would have seemed like science fiction just a few short years ago. He was surrounded by Justice Keepers and telepaths and now a thinking computer of all things. And he was just plain old-fashioned Harry Carlson. It wasn't his world, and he knew it. His world had ended the instant Anna Lenai set foot on this planet.

Biting his lip, Harry shut his eyes tight. He took a deep breath and then nodded to his daughter. "I'm proud of you," he said. "Have you told your mother? Your sister? Are you planning to move onto the station?"

Melissa stood before him with her arms crossed, smiling down at herself. "I'm not sure yet," she said, hunching up her shoulders in an awkward shrug. "Station Thirteen is synced to the central time zone, so..."

"Right."

"But I'd like to stay here as much as possible."

Harry felt his lips curl into a small smile, his cheeks burning with warmth that was hard to ignore. "You'll always be welcome here," he said, passing the phone back to his daughter. "I have to go on a mission tomorrow morning, but when I get back, we should plan a celebration."

"A mission?" The urgency in Melissa's voice was unmistakable. "Why would Jena send *you* on a mission?"

Out of the mouths of babes.

Harry turned to brace his hands on the counter, hanging his head in frustration. "I don't know if you heard," he began, "but Glin Karon was killed this afternoon in London. One of Slade's men."

"And Jena's sending you to deal with *that?*"

Harry winced, tossing his head about with a growl. "No," he said, straightening. "*I* am going with Jack to look for the Key. Right now, Jen has the rest of her people running around trying to bring in the man who killed Glin."

A glance over his shoulder revealed Melissa standing there with a tight frown on her face, sweat glistening on her forehead. "So you're all she has left," the girl mumbled. "Dad, I don't like this. Jack and Anna at least have abilities that can help them cope with anything the Overseers might throw at them. Ben has those little gadgets of his...Or, well, he *would* if he wasn't in jail."

"Worried about your old man?"

"Always?"

Closing his eyes, Harry took a moment to calm himself. He pressed a palm to his forehead and rubbed the skin above his nose. "I'll be fine, Melissa," he said. "Chances are it's just going to be another wild goose chase."

Melissa slammed into him, throwing her arms around his neck and giving him a firm squeeze. "I sure hope so," she whispered. "To be honest with you, I'm starting to hope that Slade is hunting for something that doesn't exist."

"Me too."

"But that's not how our luck works."

Harry rested his chin atop his daughter's head, breathing deeply to steady his frayed nerves. "It never is," he mumbled. "But you're worried about nothing. Tomorrow night, I will be right here planning a way to celebrate your wonderful news. You'll see."

The second floor of this abandoned building in Sayville, New York, had once been home to a newspaper, or so Arin had been told. What a quaint notion: printing news on actual paper. How long had it been since his own people had made use of such primitive technology? Centuries? Being surrounded by these Earthers made his skin crawl. It was a good thing the Inzari would soon uplift them. No one should be forced to exist in such uncivilized conditions.

Arch-shaped windows in the brick wall were boarded up with wood to prevent the light from spilling out into the street; it wouldn't do for anyone to start wondering what was going on up here. Bright bulbs in the ceiling shone down on a scuffed tiled floor where men and women in tactical gear shuffled about, loading assault rifles with ammo, checking armoured vests, relaying orders to one another.

There was very little in the way of furniture. Only a few tables that were used to store gear. With over four dozen bodies all occupying this space, it was both cramped and much too warm, but these were the things one endured to serve one's god.

Arin was down on one knee with his head bowed, sucking in air through clenched teeth. "Karon is dead," he said, looking up at his new master. "I anticipated a challenge. I was told he was among the most skilled Keepers."

Grecken Slade stood over him with hands clasped behind his back, his chin thrust out to convey arrogance. The man wore gray pants and a black coat that dropped to mid-thigh, a coat with silver trim along the hem and the cuff of each sleeve. His dark hair was pulled into a simple ponytail. "Don't get cocky," Slade admonished. "I personally have sparred with Glin, and I found him quite competent."

Arin winced, turning his face away from the other man. "Perhaps," he said with a rasp in his voice. "But I want a real challenge. Send me after Morane. I'm told she has a reputation as a skilled warrior."

Slade was smiling down at him, dark eyes twinkling in the harsh light. "Six months of training," he said, arching one thin eyebrow. "And you already believe yourself able to best a Keeper who has carried a symbiont for nearly twenty years?"

"I..."

"Over confidence is unbecoming, Arin." The other man crossed his arms and drew himself up to full height, standing tall and poised like a statue. "When the time is right, I will employ your skills where they can do the most good."

Clenching his teeth, Arin lowered his eyes to the floor. He drew in a sharp, hissing breath. "Yes, Lord Slade," he said with a nod. "But if I may ask, what good will it do to antagonize the Keepers?"

Slade turned so that Arin saw him in profile, then paced a line to the wall with the boarded-up windows. He braced his hands against one dirty windowsill and stood there, hunched over. "It will leave them off balance," he replied. "The more energy they waste trying to contain us, the easier it will be to locate the Key."

Arin said nothing of the fact that – so far – no one had the faintest idea where the Key had been hidden. The Inzari who had betrayed their kind and masked the technology so that it couldn't be detected with scanners had done a remarkable job. Arin heard the odd whisper every now and then; one of the soldiers in their little band would insist that there was no Key, that Slade was leading them astray. Arin took great pleasure in making sure that such insubordination was properly punished.

A troubling thought occurred to him.

Were those his sentiments or those of the Drethen he carried? Anger had been such an easily-accessible emotion since the day of his anointing. It was different for everyone; Isara's rage could sometimes be a wildfire blazing out of control. For Arin, it was a cold fury: calm, calculating and utterly vicious. Had he always been that way? The process that had allowed him to craft a Bending without the Drethen's consent also made for a deeper blending of thought and emotion than a Justice Keeper would experience with his Nassai. A Keepers and a Nassai were two *distinct* beings, but the symbiont he carried and the rage it felt were a part of him.

Through contact with the Drethen, he sensed half a dozen men coming up behind him, each carrying an assault rifle. They were dressed in tactical gear, each sporting a thick bulbous helmet with the visor pulled down. Should he kill them? If they thought to sneak up on him like that...No. Best to wait. "What now, sir?" one asked.

Slade remained at the window with his back turned, bent over as though he could see through the wood to the night beyond. "It's time," he said after a moment. "Contact your agents in the city. Tell them to execute phase two."

5

A vaulted ceiling of skylights stretched over the concourse of the Liverpool Street tube station, allowing the sun to cast golden rays down on white floor tiles with lines of gray that formed boxes. Stores in either wall of the massive two-story station were open, offering fast food or candy or pharmaceutical to the people that milled about. And there *were* people. Several hundred, by Anna's estimate. This place was just as busy as Station Twelve on a particularly hectic day.

Anna walked along in a pair of beige pants and a dark blue t-shirt with a diamond pattern on the neckline. Her red hair was tied up in a nubby ponytail. "I need you to send the security camera footage to Station Twelve," she said. "I'd like our people to go over it with facial recognition software."

She spun on her heel.

A portly man in a gray suit with a skinny black tie stood before her. His pale face was flushed, and his curly, black hair showed more than a few flecks of gray. "I've had my best people going over it for the last twenty-four hours."

Anna closed her eyes, bowing her head to the man. "I'm aware of that," she said, nodding once for emphasis. "But just the same, I want my team to have a look at it. Two sets of eyes and all that."

The inspector smiled a friendly smile, his flush deepening. "Very well," he replied, gesturing to the stairs that led up to the second level. "So far, we've detected no sign of the man who killed Glin Karon. If he moved through here, he did so discreetly."

Anna crossed her arms with a heavy sigh, a shiver running through her. She turned her back on the man. "It's not very likely," she said. "He knows that using public transit would make him easier to track."

"You think he took a cab?"

"I think that he had an escape plan in place beforehand," she answered. "My first instinct would be to check all SlipGate terminals in the city, but we've seen that Slade's people have access to portable SlipGates."

The sound of coughing interrupted her train of thought, and when she focused on the awareness that came through her bond to Seth, she saw the silhouette of Inspector Grimes with a fist pressed to his mouth, hacking up a storm. "Portable Slip-Gates?" he said from behind her. "Is that possible?"

"Apparently so."

"Portable SlipGates..."

Two uniformed officers, both tall men with broad shoulders, came down the stairs from the upper level. They wore black pants and white shirts under dark-armoured vests, their faces shielded by the brim of a round cap with a silver badge in front. "Ah, here we are," Inspector Grimes said.

The man shuffled past her to greet his two officers at the foot of the stairs, craning his neck to stare up at them. "Constable Sinclair, Constable Davis, this is Special Agent Lenai with the Justice Keepers."

Tilting her head back, Anna smiled up at the men. "Pleased to meet you," she said, nodding to each. "Let's make sure we've covered the basics. Have you interviewed any of the shop employees to find out if they saw anyone who matches our perp's description?"

The one on the left – Constable Sinclair, unless she was mistaken – directed a tight-lipped frown at his supervisor. "We talked to several," he said, speaking to Grimes and not to Anna. "No one saw anyone who matched the description."

It took some effort to suppress the little surge of irritation she felt at that. It wouldn't be so bad if it didn't happen almost *every* time she was forced to interact with a male cop. They seldom took her seriously, choosing instead to speak to the other men present. Back home, this had never been an issue. She would never have imagined being the target of such rampant sexism before she came to this backward little planet.

Irritation turned to guilt when she realized that those were her mother's sentiments. Sierin Elana had nothing positive to say about Earth.

"All right, let's get our bases covered," Anna broke in. After nine months here, she had picked up a little Earth slang. "Requisition security camera footage for both SlipGate terminals: the one here *and* the one at Victoria Station. I want copies sent to the forensics team on Station Twelve. We'll run it through our facial recognition software. Maybe we'll get lucky. Check in with bus terminals, car services, anything that might provide our guy with a means of escape.

"We should also consider the possibility that the killer is still hiding somewhere in the city. Contact hotels in the immediate area. See if anyone recalls booking a guest that fits the description. I want samples from the crime scene forwarded to my team within the hour. I don't care if it's pocket lint, a stray button, dried up chewing gum. Whatever you've got, I want it."

The two constables exchanged a glance with each other, then directed a questioning stare at their inspector. "You heard her, gentlemen!" Grimes barked. "Get on it! Nobody goes home tonight until every item on that list is ticked."

Exhaustion crept in the instant she was done talking to them, and she was forced to once again wonder if she had done *any* good since arriving on this planet. Well...perhaps on her first trip. Things had seemed so much simpler back then. She and Jack side-by-side against an unquestionably evil man and his plans to harm an innocent life form. Now, she often wondered if *she* was the evil one

Subduing those cops to prevent them from harming Kevin Harmon had been the right thing to do – there was no doubt in her mind about that – and yet, she couldn't help but wonder why the people here despised her. A heavy sigh escaped her lips. They either despised her, or they ignored her.

Anna strode through the station with her head down, thin strands of red hair falling over her face. *No time for self pity,* she thought to herself. *You can contemplate whether or not you want to stay on this world later. For now, you have a job to do.*

A quick walk brought her to the train platform, and she hopped on the Circle Line to make her way to the new Scotland Yard station. The long, narrow cars were packed with blue seats along each wall filled by the bodies of men in suits or women in light sundresses. Children in shorts and baseball caps.

The space in the middle of the car, where passengers stood, offered her very little room to maneuver. Her view was cut off by the broad back of a man with gray hair who stood clinging to a metal bar that ran from floor to ceiling.

Anna bit her lip, then lowered her eyes to the floor. The prickle of sweat upon her brow was a minor nuisance. *Jack and Harry should have checked in,* she noted. *If that damn Overseer tech offers any more surprises...*

A hand squeezed her ass and held on tight long passed the point of what could be called an accident. In her mind's eye, the silhouette of a skinny young man behind her practically trembled. This close, she could tell he was smiling.

Clenching her teeth, Anna drew in a hissing breath. "Get your hand off me," she growled, turning her head to speak over her shoulder. "Bleakness take me, didn't anyone ever teach you how to behave in public?"

To her right, she saw an older woman in her forties – a beautiful woman with sun-kissed skin and curly hair – who watched the whole thing with concern on her face. No doubt she was worried that things might get rough.

The man squeezed her butt again.

"I said get your hand off me."

She whirled around to find him standing maybe half an inch away. A tall, skinny young man with scraggly blonde stubble along his jawline and pimples on his face, he offered a sheepish grin for an apology.

Anna pursed her lips as she stared up at him, slowly arching one thin, red eyebrow. "You think that's funny, do you?" The calmness in her voice surprised her. "Well, I'm on my way to a police station; how'd you like to come with me?"

"Piss off, bitch."

"I think not."

She lifted her forearm to tap at the screen of her multi-tool with three fingers, and less than five seconds later, a hologram appeared in the air between them. A four-pointed star on a field of blue. The symbol of the Justice Keepers. Her personal dossier appeared half a moment later, displaying her picture along with her rank, badge number and years of service. "I'm Special Agent Anna Lenai with the Justice Keepers," she said. "And *you* are under arrest for assaulting an officer of the law."

She let the hologram vanish.

The boy's face went white with fear, and his eyes grew wider and wider until it seemed as though they might fall out.

"It was just a joke," he said, backing away from her until he bumped into the man behind him.

"No, it was a crime," she shot back. "And the problem is that entitled little pissants like you keep getting away with it. Well, not today, my friend. Today, there are going to be some consequences for your actions."

Everyone on the train clapped.

A dart landed smack-dab in the middle of a bull's-eye, sliding gracefully into place with a satisfying *thump*. Half a second later, a second one joined it, landing half an inch to the left, so close the tips must have been touching beneath the surface of the dartboard.

Anna sat on the surface of a wooden table with one leg crossed over the other, her face set with a firm expression. This little pub in Westminster had walls of dark brown bricks lit mainly by shafts of sunlight that came in through rectangular windows. There were also Tiffany lamps with orange shades spaced throughout the room.

To her left, the bar was operated by an older woman with curly red hair that fell to the small of her back. Vin Taeral – a Justice Keeper who operated primarily in the United Kingdom – had told Anna about this place over a month ago. Apparently, they had a policy of giving free food to Justice Keepers. The potato-leek soup was particularly good. So good she had ordered two bowls.

The silhouette of a woman in a pretty sundress came up behind her, pausing just a few feet away. It wasn't hard to recognize Gabi or to sense the tension evident in the other woman's posture. Was Gabrina worried that she wouldn't find a warm welcome? For that matter, did she *deserve* a warm welcome? Anna knew that taking sides was almost never a good idea, but she would be lying if she said she didn't feel the urge to protect her best friend from anyone who might hurt him.

Anna let her head hang, then forced out a breath. "Come to cheer me up, Gabs?" she asked, suppressing a pang of guilt at the exasperation in her tone. "You might have better luck convincing Harry to let loose on the dance floor."

Gabi stepped forward to stand beside her with arms crossed, directing a tight frown at the dartboard. "I take it the locals are less than cooperative," she inquired. "More men who aren't used to taking orders from a woman?"

Anna threw her head back, blinking at the ceiling. "It never ends," she said, deep creases forming in her brow. "I give them an order, and they exchange glances with each other and wonder if they should follow it."

"It must be infuriating."

Anna bared her teeth with a hiss, then shook her head in contempt. "You have *no* idea," she said, hopping off the table to stand on the carpeted floor. "At times, I wonder how anyone who lacks a Y-chromosome gets anything done on this planet."

The other woman was blushing, her eyes downcast as if she felt a deep sense of shame. "I hope I'm not bothering you," Gabi muttered. "We're still friends, right?"

"Of course, we're still friends!" Anna said, rounding on her. "I'm legally obligated to hate you with a burning fiery passion, but I don't see why that means that we shouldn't be friends. Honestly, Gabs, who do you take me for?"

The ghost of a smile appeared on Gabi's face, and she let out a soft sigh of relief. "Good," she said firmly. "Then tell me honestly, are you still feeling overwhelmed by the hostility you find here?"

"Sometimes."

Gabi hunched over, then reached up to run fingers through her long black hair. "It's the same for me," she replied in a hissing whisper. "The truth is I've felt out of place here for weeks, if not months."

"Why didn't you say something?"

"For the longest time, I dismissed the idea of taking another assignment because of my relationship with Jack, but now..."

Anna dropped into a vacant chair with her arms folded, doubling over until she was almost bent in half. A ragged breath passed through her lips. "Have you told him? Do you *plan* on telling him?"

Gabi winced, shaking her head. "I'd like to," she answered in a voice as smooth and as cool as ice on the surface of a lake. "But I'm not sure Jack wants to hear from me, and what's more, I'm not sure I'm up to the conversation."

"I'd kind of hoped you guys might get back together..."

It took only a second for Anna to realize that giving voice to that thought had been a mistake. Much as she might dream of a future where her friends were happy together, Gabi's reasons for ending her relationship with Jack were valid. True, the woman had known that he was a Justice Keeper, and therefore unable to have children, but people were complicated. You often didn't know whether or not something was a deal-breaker until you tried to live with it for a little while. "I'm sorry."

"Don't be."

"So, are you leaving?"

In response, Gabi sat down in a chair that faced her, crossing one leg over the other and folding hands in her lap. "I've considered resigning from the Service," she said. "I'm getting older, and a life of danger no longer holds the appeal it once did."

"Thirty-two is hardly old."

"No, but..."

Anna closed her eyes, sucking in a rasping breath. She pinched the bridge of her nose with thumb and forefinger. "But you want a family, a little place of your own and a job that doesn't involve gunfire."

When she looked up, the other woman wore a grin that could light up the night sky. "Exactly," Gabi said with a nod. "I remember when we infiltrated Camacho's mansion six months ago."

Mention of that night left a sharp pang of loss in Anna's heart. She had to pause for a moment to figure out why, the answer came with only a little effort. That had been the night that she had seen Jack kissing Gabi for the first time. The start of their relationship. *And afterward, I took the first chance I had to pick up a cute nerdy boy at a chess club.*

Pain turned to panic when she considered the implications of her own relationship. Now was not the time for that, however. She smothered those feelings quickly, and that made her aware of Seth's attempt to offer support of his own. "It was quite the evening," Anna muttered. "I kept expecting someone to pull a gun on us."

"As did I," Gabi mumbled. "When it was over, I went home and realized that I felt none of the satisfaction I used to experience after a successful mission."

Setting her elbows on the arms of her chair, Anna laced her fingers and rested her chin on top of them. "So you're thinking it's time for a career change," she said. "And I guess that means you're going home."

"And you?" Gabi asked. "Do you want to stay here?"

"I don't know anymore," Anna admitted with some reluctance. "But I do have one good thing tying me to this world."

Bradley was here, and she had come to realize that she really did love him.

"Maybe you should think about that."

Before she could respond, her multi-tool beeped, and Anna swiped a finger across the screen to answer the call. Jena's face appeared with the window in her office visible behind her. "You might want to get up here," she said. "We have news."

6

The blue sky stretched on forever over a forest of tall conifers in Northern Ontario. Peering through the canopy window of his shuttle, Jack found himself mystified by just how much of this planet remained untouched by civilization. They were coming up on the coordinates Ven had given.

Jack sat in the pilot's seat with his hands on the control console, his posture stiff as he squinted through the window. "Just another minute or so," he said for Harry's benefit. "Really, the computer does most of the work."

"It's all right, kid; I trust you."

Jack winced, trembling as he drew in a hissing breath. "Yeah..." he said, tapping in a few commands on the console. "It's just that this is my first flight without supervision, and I remember my family's joking about getting their affairs in order every time they got in a car with me after I got my license."

"You're fine."

The trees scrolled slowly upward in the window as he lowered the shuttle into an open clearing about a kilometer from the designated coordinates. This was the closest landing sight he could find.

A light jolt told him the shuttle had touched down, and then he powered down the systems, deactivating the artificial gravity and life-support. Half a second later, the soft hum of the engines died.

Jack swiveled around.

Harry sat facing him at the starboard-side console, resting comfortably with his hands on his knees and a vacant stare on his face. "Nice place," he said with a nod. "I'm suddenly feeling the urge to go camping."

Closing his eyes, Jack bowed his head to the other man. "Yeah..." he said, getting out of his seat. "You know, as long as we can be sure there are no Overseer traps. I'm not looking to star in a Joss Whedon film."

"Joss Whedon?"

"When that guy does horror, he goes all out."

Jack strode to the back of the cockpit, then paused in front of the doors that led to the cabin. "Come on," he said, instinctively checking the pistol on his hip. "Let's get this over with and get back to Jena."

The doors slid apart, and he descended the steps into a room with a square table in the middle and a SlipGate along the back wall. The tall, metal triangle caught the light in a way that seemed unnatural, Jack avoided looking at it. On his right, the airlock was shut tight. He opened it with a few quick taps.

Another set of doors opened, these ones producing a loud hiss as they revealed a dense forest of Red Pines. Thankfully, most were tall enough that their branches easily cleared the top of Jack's head; he didn't have to worry about being assaulted by needles while they made their way toward...whatever it was they would find at the coordinates Ven had provided.

Normally, he loved forests – and Jack made a mental note to do some exploring as soon as he got a few days to himself; it was sad how little he had seen of his own country – but today, he wanted expedience over anything else. At this moment, Anna was going over crime scene evidence with the good people of Scotland Yard; of course, she would be working with Keepers from other teams – there was pretty much no chance of Jena getting sole jurisdiction over this thing – but he still wanted to be there. On top of that, the dull ache of sadness made him cranky. He had never realized just how much he cared about Gabi until she was gone.

He tapped at his multi-tool and watched the screen light up, displaying a squiggly blue line that represented a sonic wave. "Ven," Jack said. "We've landed. I figure it will take an hour to get to the coordinates."

The blue line pulsed as Ven spoke. "I will monitor you as best I can, but my ship is currently hidden behind your planet's moon, and there is very little that I can do without entering orbit and exposing my presence here."

The blurry image of Harry approached Jack from behind, carrying a brief case that contained the device Ven had jury-rigged to detect Overseer technology. Jack had offered to carry it several times, but Harry insisted that he wanted to hold onto it. Maybe he was feeling like he had to prove his usefulness. "I thought Ven was on Station Twelve," Harry muttered. "He's controlling his ship remotely?"

Jack grinned, then lowered his eyes to stare at the ground under his feet. "Ven is software," he said, shaking his head. "In terms of his physical location, he's wherever the computers that run him happen to be."

"Quite right, Agent Hunter."

Harry strode past Jack, approaching the line of trees just a few paces away from the tip of the shuttle's wing. "Shall we go?" he asked, pausing there. "You're not the only one who wants to get this job over with."

They began their journey through the forest, trudging

through hard-packed mud where trees rose up haphazardly, making it hard to travel in a straight line. Fortunately, the GPS on Jack's multi-tool prevented them from going too far off course. It was slow going, and the rising heat as the sun neared its zenith only made the journey that much more exasperating. Even this far north, summers still got hot. Maybe not so hot as what you could expect in Toronto, but warm enough that you would easily break a sweat from even light physical activity.

The ground began to slope upward at a shallow incline, and every now and then, silver shafts of sunlight broke through the treetops to illuminate a small patch of the forest floor. It was pretty. Jack might have liked it here had he not been distracted by the pain of missing Gabi. *Get her out of your head, Bro,* he told himself. *You don't have time to sit around moping.*

Harry was just in front of him, pausing with a hand braced against the thick trunk of a pine tree. "Melissa was accepted," he said in a breathy voice. "She'll be joining the Keeper training program in six week."

Grinning with a burst of laughter, Jack let his head hang. He rubbed at his eyes with the back of his hand. "That's wonderful," he said. "She's an amazing kid, Harry; you must be so proud."

"And worried."

Jack crossed his arms with a heavy sigh, keeping his head down as he moved past his friend. "She'll be okay," he said softly. "If a symbiont accepts her, it means she's the kind of person who can thrive in this life."

Behind him, the other man grunted and stepped away from the tree he had been using for support. "I suppose," Harry grumbled. "I'm trying my best to be objective, Jack, but I think worrying is coded into a father's DNA."

Once again, they started up the gently sloping hill. The sounds of birds chirping made for a very pleasant morning, and Jack found himself wondering what it would be like to leave the world behind and build himself a little home out here. Of course, that was completely unrealistic – for one thing, he knew nothing about construction – but he always gave in to such flights of fancy when he was feeling sad.

A few minutes later, they came to a small open spot devoid of trees, a clearing not much bigger than Jack's living room. The sun shone down on dried mud that was littered with dead pine needles. It was almost as if nothing could grow in this spot, as if the very ground had been claimed by something else.

Harry closed his eyes, breathing deeply. He wiped sweat off his forehead with the back of his hand. "GPS says this is the spot," he muttered, stepping out into the open. "I guess we should get started."

Jack squinted as he stared into the distance. "I don't know," he said, shaking his head. "Something feels a little off. It could just be my imagination, but I'd rather take a look around first."

Harry dropped to one knee in the clearing, glancing back over his shoulder. "If you insist," he replied, setting the brief-case down in front of himself. "Still, I'm going to get the equipment set up."

Tapping away at his multi-tool, Jack brought up the screen with the squiggly blue line. "You reading this, Ven?" he asked. "Any special instructions for using the device?"

Static.

"Ven?"

The only response he got was the soft hiss of dead air. Something had blocked his signal, and he was too paranoid to assume this was a natural phenomenon. Not when he knew perfectly well that Leyrian technology could provide a clear signal all the way to freaking Jupiter.

Biting his lip, Jack winced so hard he trembled. "Something's wrong," he growled with more venom than he had intended. "Keep an eye out; I'm going to make sure we get some privacy."

He stretched out with his senses as he moved back into the trees, beginning a slow circuit around the clearing. Through contact with Summer, he was intimately aware of everything around him, but focusing on those sensations also made him cognizant of the Nassai's emotions. She was tense.

Perhaps that was why Jack had been uneasy when they arrived at their destination. Aside from his inability to contact Ven, there had been no obvious sign of trouble. Could he be reacting to Summer's apprehension? After four years together, Jack had begun to notice that some of his intuitions were really a case of him picking up on Summer's state of mind. Still, his symbiont was usually spot on when she worried about something. He half considered entering a meditative trance to ask her directly but decided against it. If there was danger, he didn't want to risk even a second's inattention.

Motion off to his left.

Jack turned and rushed off through the forest, climbing a small hill where trees rose to blanket the sky with their limbs. If there was trouble, he'd find it.

The metal briefcase sat open before him, revealing a strange device with blinking LEDs that Ven had attached to the slab of skin no larger than his palm – a thin sheet of flesh with veins that pulsed. Just looking at it made Harry nauseous. He had been there when that thing drove Kevin Harmon into a frenzy. He had seen first-hand the kind of damage a man could do while wielding Overseer technology.

Worse yet, every time he looked at the thin sheet of skin, he found himself feeling more than a little awestruck. Even after seeing what it had done to a kind and friendly soul like Kevin, a part of him *wanted* it.

Harry grinned, rubbing at his forehead to clear away the sweat. "You just want to feel useful again," he muttered to himself. "Put it out of your head before Jack has to stop you from doing something stupid."

The device that Ven had constructed was a fairly simple thing: just a series of metal clamps that held the slab of skin, all connected to a rectangular box with a big red button. He had to give the AI this much credit: it knew how to make its gadgets idiot-proof. He wanted to get started, but a part of him wondered if it would be wise to do so without Ven's supervision. Then again...How hard was it to push a button? "Jack?" he called out.

No answer.

Harry pushed the button.

The Overseer device made a hissing noise so soft it was almost imperceptible, a high-pitched whine that would set most dogs yapping but leave their human companions completely mystified. Was it even doing anything?

There was a light pulsing sensation under his feet before something began to ooze out of the ground in the middle of the clearing. Skin cells came together to form a lump that rose slowly upward, taking the shape of a pedestal.

Harry felt his jaw drop, his heart racing. "No," he said, shaking his head. "It's been here all this time? Undetected?"

"Astounding, isn't it?"

He froze; that wasn't Jack's voice!

A glance over his shoulder revealed a man standing just inside the treeline, a ghost-like figure who wore unrelieved black from head to toe. His dark-skinned face was really quite handsome, but set with a grim expression.

"Who are you?" Harry growled.

The stranger stepped into the open, bowing his head to smile down at his own feet. "I'm the man who killed Glin Karon," he said, approaching Harry. "Really now, is there anything more you need to know?"

Harry drew his pistol and whirled around to point it at the

newcomer, gripping it tightly in both hands. Already, he could feel the tension seizing his heart with icy fingers. If this man could kill a Justice Keeper...

The stranger thrust out his chin, arching one dark eyebrow to show what he thought of Harry's stubborn defiance. "Do you honestly expect that to do much good?" he asked, striding calmly into the middle of the clearing.

"Who are you?"

"It was so easy to distract your companion," the newcomer went on as if Harry had not even spoken. "A little noise, a few startled animals. Jamming your transmission so we won't be interrupted."

He faced Harry with hands folded over his stomach, smiling like the devil ushering sinners through the Gates of Hell. "Your friend might pose a challenge to me," he said. "Enough to make this little excursion entertaining at the very least. But you, Harry Carlson...You are useless."

Craning his neck to study the other man, Harry narrowed his eyes. "Perhaps," he said with a curt nod. "But I can't help but notice that you came here anyway. Afraid we'd get our hands on some Overseer tech?"

The other man turned his head to direct a smile down at the pedestal of flesh. "Oh, you mean this?" he asked, eyebrows rising. "I hate to spoil your sense of victory, Harry, but Slade has known about this device for decades. It does nothing. Observe."

The stranger reached out and set one bare hand atop the pedestal, closing his eyes and taking a deep breath. Nothing happened. For a very long moment, the man just stood there, waiting for some kind of response.

All this work for nothing...

"Stun rounds!" Harry growled, getting to his feet with the gun held in both hands. He took aim and fired.

Bullets flew toward the man who already had his hand outstretched, but before the first could find its target, light blurred and the slug was diverted on a course that sent it speeding off into the trees.

The blurry smear of colour resolidified into a man in black, who strode across the clearing with a snarl twisting his face into something inhuman. "That was a mistake," he hissed as he drew near.

Harry pulled the trigger.

Again, the stranger blurred, only this time, he became a streak of darkness that fell backward and then resolved into a man who caught himself by bracing both hands on the ground. He brought one foot up to kick the gun out of Harry's hand. *So much for that,* a quiet voice whispered.

The other man was upright in half a second.

A fist collided with Harry's face, filling his vision with bright silver flecks. Before he could even get his bearings, something hit him hard in the chest. Harry went stumbling backward, right into a tree.

He charged forward, trying to tackle his opponent, but when he crossed through the space where the other man should be, he found nothing. Something hit him right between the shoulder-blades.

Harry tumbled forward, landing hard on all fours in the middle of the clearing. A low groan escaped, and he spit blood onto the muddy ground. *Melissa, I'm sorry. I never should have accepted this mission.*

"Pathetic," the other man sneered. "I'd hoped that you would put up some degree of resistance, but-" A soft shuffling sound cut him off in mid-sentence. Harry wondered if he was about to die.

Halfway to the spot where he'd sensed the flicker of motion, Jack realized that this was all just a little too convenient. He couldn't see anything or sense anything through his connection to

Summer. Nothing but trees that rose up all around him and made it difficult to get a view of anything at a distance. Whatever he'd sensed was probably just a squirrel or chipmunk, and this was drawing away from Harry. Harry, who couldn't defend himself against most of the threats Slade was likely to throw at him.

Jack turned and ran.

Pine trees with thin green needles made a haphazard obstacle course, cutting off any hope of finding a straight path. He ran around them, ducking low whenever the odd branch came close enough to brushing the top of his head.

The ground sloped upward for a few paces, then downward as again as he made his way to the small clearing. He could see it now – a shaft of light that penetrated the forest and made him blink with discomfort.

Something was wrong.

A man in black stood just inside the clearing with his back turned, cutting off Jack's view, but it was clear that Harry was sprawled out on the ground before him. *God damn it all! I let one of Slade's goons play me! Again!*

The newcomer stood with fists on his hips, shaking his head as he stared down at Harry. "Pathetic," he said with contempt in his voice. "I'd hoped that you would put up some degree of resistance, but-"

Abruptly, the stranger whirled around to face Jack, lifting his chin to direct a cold smile up the slope. "Ah, there you are!" he exclaimed. "Finally, someone who might give me a challenge!"

Jack winced, shaking his head. "You caught me on a very bad day, guy," he said, starting down the hillside. "Normally, I try to embody the Keeper ideal of restraint, but today, I'm just as likely to go all Frank Castle on your ass."

The other man strode forward with casual disregard for Jack's presence, trembling as he chuckled. "Slade told me about that," he said. "Your tendency to speak in strange, incomprehensible idioms."

"What can I say? I have layers."

The other man jumped, and Jack felt a strange warping as gravity twisted to carry his opponent up the gentle slope like a bird taking flight. He landed just a few feet away, bowing his head almost reverently. "There is a tradition among my people," the stranger said. "A worthy opponent deserves the honour of knowing the man who slays him. I am called Arin."

Baring his teeth with a soft hiss, Jack squinted at the other man. "You've gotta be kidding me!" he said in a voice thick with disdain. "*That's* the name that's supposed to strike terror in my heart? Why don't you go with something a little more bad-ass. Like...I don't know...the Pontificator."

"Shall we begin?"

"Well, you know, I've always hated stall-"

Arin punched him in the face, filling his vision with silver flecks, but the pain was already fading. The man spun for a back-kick, driving a foot into Jack's stomach, forcing him back against the trunk of a pine.

Arin rounded on him.

Jack leaped, flipping over the man's head, then uncurling to land on the ground just behind him. He bent over and then kicked out behind himself, slamming one foot into his opponent's backside. Arin went face-first into the tree.

Jack turned to find the evil bastard clutching the tree trunk, breathing deep and hard. In a flash, Arin whirled around with his teeth bared, saliva dripping from his mouth.

He threw a punch.

Jack ducked and let the man's fist pass over his head. He slipped past Arin on the right, then flung his elbow out to the side to strike the other man's skull. It took only half a second to spin around and find his opponent ready and waiting.

Jack threw a hard punch, but Arin leaned back and caught

his wrist in both hands. The next thing he knew, he was being forced to bend double, held pinned with two hands clamped onto his arm. Arin drove him right toward the nearest tree.

Jack ran up the trunk, then pushed off and back-flipped through the air. He uncurled to land behind his opponent.

Arin spun around.

Jack snap-kicked, driving a foot into the man's belly, forcing him to double over. He jumped and brought up one knee to strike Arin's face. A sickening *crunch* would have indicated a broken nose in anyone else, but a man with a symbiont healed quickly.

In the blink of an eye, Arin blurred into a streak of colour, then resolidified a few steps to Jack's right. He grabbed the back of Jack's collar, then gave a hard shove with the strength of someone with a symbiont.

Jack stumbled.

He turned to his right in time to see four dark knuckles collide with his face, and then everything went fuzzy. His mind could still track everything around him through contact with summer, and it was clear that Arin was drawing a knife from his belt. The man spun for a hook-kick.

Jack hopped back in time to watch a black rubber sole pass right in front of his eyes. He waited for the other man to come around.

Arin tried to stab.

Jack leaned back, one hand coming up to seize the man's wrist. He snapped himself upright to deliver a hard jab to the face. Blood leaked from Arin's nostrils as he stumbled about in a daze.

With a growl, Jack jumped and kicked out, planting a foot in the other man's belly. He pushed off, knocking Arin to the ground, then back-flipped through the air. A touch of violence was good for the soul, it seemed; he was already less cranky.

Jack landed.

His opponent raised a hand to point the gleaming blade of a knife at him, and then there was a sharp twisting sensation. Bent Gravity.

On instinct, Jack called out to Summer and put up a time-bubble, the world around him seemed to blur, light stretching until there was nothing but a smear of green or brown where trees and ground should be. And black where the other man had fallen. He saw the knife as well, flying point first toward him. The fact that it was moving at all meant that in a normal time-frame, it would be traveling fast enough to rip right through him. Once it crossed the barrier of his time bubble, it would speed up instantly.

Jack crouched down.

He let the bubble vanish, and felt a light stirring in the air as the knife passed over him and embedded itself in the trunk of a tree, wobbling on impact. Arin was stretched out on his backside, staring up with sweat glistening on his face. "No!" the man hissed. "No! You can't! They said you would be an easy kill!"

Grinning triumphantly, Jack let his head hang. He wiped sweat off his brow and let out a sigh. "First thing you should learn about Earth: false advertising is everywhere. No matter what it is they're selling, it never quite works as promised."

Arin scrambled to his feet.

The man turned and ran down the hillside, huffing and puffing as he made his way toward the clearing where Harry knelt before some strange fleshy pedestal and gripped it in both hands. *Uh oh...*

"Harry!" Jack growled.

"Shall we begin?" a soft voice said in the distance. Jack replied, but he was too far away for Harry to pick up the words. Then the sounds of combat filled the air. His vision was beginning to clear, but Harry knew there was nothing he could do to aid in this fight. The pitiful attempt he had made to stand up to this Arin had ended badly to say the least. It was pathetic. *He* was pathetic.

There had to be something he could do, but he couldn't think of anything. Maybe if he tried to secure the Overseer tech.

He looked up to see the fleshy pedestal just a few feet away from his right shoulder, its skin seeming to writhe. Overseer technology was just so *creepy*. If this thing contained data on where he might find the Key...But what could he do with it? Arin had touched it with no visible effect. Still, there was no reason Harry should take the other man's word for it. For all he knew, Arin hadn't even tried to activate it.

He forced himself up with a grunt, kneeling in the dirt with his head hanging, his ears ringing. He reached out and gingerly touched the pedestal with one hand. Nothing. No effect whatso-

The world was yanked away, solid objects becoming streaks of colour until they were ripped apart, leaving Harry in an endless void of stars. Suddenly, the pains in his body were gone as well.

Harry stood...on nothing.

Biting his lower lip, he squinted and turned his head to scan his surroundings. "Is anyone there?" he asked, taking a few steps forward. "My name is Harry Carlson, and I came here to gain the-"

"Knowledge of the ancients?"

The voice made him jump.

When he turned, his own grandfather was standing before him in the void. David Carlson was a tall man who wore a pair of black overalls over a blue and red flannel shirt. His dark-skinned face was contrasted by a silver beard on his jawline, his brow lined with thin wrinkles. "Hello, son."

Harry closed his eyes, bowing his head to the other man.

"Grandpa," he said. "So...does this mean the thing killed me and you're here to take me to heaven?"

David smiled that warm smile that Harry knew so well. "No, son," he answered. "I am not your grandfather."

"You're an Overseer?"

Closing his eyes, David took a deep breath. "After a fashion," he said with a curt nod. "It would be more accurate to say that I am an...interactive recording of what you would call an Overseer."

"And you're talking to me?"

A heavy sigh exploded from David as he began to pace a circle around Harry. It was an odd thing to watch. For one thing, Harry noticed that the stars seemed to be slowly expanding away from him, and that was disorienting. "For a very long time, my people used your species for our purposes."

David spun on his heel to stand before Harry with hands clasped behind his back, the very image of the sturdy, solid father figure he had once known. "We were wrong. A small number of us began to recognize the potential of your species."

Harry crossed his arms, lifting his chin to meet the other man's gaze. "So, you grew a conscience?" he asked, raising an eyebrow. "Forgive me if I don't find that to be all that reassuring. You can't just-"

"We don't have much time," David broke in. "Your brain is processing information at an accelerated rate, but I have scanned your mind and the mind of the man who tried to interface with me moments earlier. Many such as him have tried to unlock the knowledge buried here, including the one you call Slade. You are the first to be free of my people's influence, the first who can be trusted. I know that you are in physical danger from the man called Arin, and there are things you *must* learn.

"What you call 'the Key' is a trap: a device designed to be operated by one of your species. If triggered, it will initiate the final phase of our plan for humanity. Believe me when I tell you that's something you don't want.

"Those of us who began to recognize the value in humanity broke away from the rest of our people. We hid the Key, locking it away so that it could not be detected even with our own technology."

"I don't understand," Harry muttered. "If this Key was so dangerous to us, then why not just destroy it and remove the threat?"

A warm smile blossomed on his grandfather's face, and then the other man stepped forward to clap Harry on the shoulder. "Because the Key is also a great opportunity. My people have traveled long and far."

It took a moment for Harry to notice that the stars receding into the distance were no longer single points of light but tiny galaxies that spiraled as they flew off into the blackness. "This is not the place of our origin," David went on. "In all the cosmos, we have found very few species who could one day stand as our equals. Those that could usually destroyed themselves.

"When your people are ready, the Key will grant you access to our knowledge. It will give you the opportunity to learn from our mistakes to succeed where we failed. But only when you are ready."

"Then what do we do?"

David stepped forward, touching two fingers to Harry's forehead. "The knowledge of what you need to do is here," he said. "The Key can be accessed through the SlipGate Network, but it requires three access codes. I have given you the first. Find the other two and claim humanity's destiny before your enemies do.

"Your species is truly remarkable, Harry Carlson." A scowl passed over David's face for half a second before he smothered it. "The plasticity of your brains rivals even our own. I grant you one more gift, a tool that will no doubt be indispensable."

"But-"

"No! There is no time!"

The vision faded, leaving Harry dimly aware of the fact that he was down on his knees with both hands gripping the fleshy pedestal. His ears picked up the heavy *thump-thump* of footsteps drawing near.

A glance over his shoulder revealed Arin charging down the hillside toward him, snarling as if he intended to trample Harry to death. Jack was a few paces behind, but it was clear that he would not catch the other man before he entered the clearing.

Harry dove for the briefcase.

He knew what to do.

Pausing on the hillside, Jack watched as Arin ran headlong for the clearing. The man would kill Harry once he got within arm's reach; there was no doubt about that. No doubt at all. That left him with only one option.

Jack drew his pistol from the holster on his belt, gripping it tightly in two hands and aiming for the other man's back. "Stun rounds!" he growled, watching as the LEDs on the barrel turned blue.

He fired.

Arin spun around, stretching one hand out toward him just before the air seemed to ripple with the shimmer of summer's heat. A bullet that would have taken the man in the chest slowed and veered off to Jack's left.

He was half-worried that Arin would have reflected it, but it seemed the man lacked the necessary skill to do that. Pulling a gun on someone with Keeper powers was always a last resort – there was no way to predict how your enemy might redirect incoming fire, and this was especially dangerous in the presence of civilians – but Jack was fresh out of options; he needed to give Harry a chance to get away.

Come on, buddy! Jack thought at his friend. *Take the hint!*

Harry pulled the briefcase to himself, peering inside to find the strange rectangular device with metal clamps hooked up to the Overseer multi-tool. A *N'jal*, it was called. He knew that somehow.

Ripping the thin slab of flesh away from the clamps, he allowed it to bond with the skin of his right palm, tiny microscopic fibers digging into his tissue, linking his nervous system to the N'Jal's. Instantly, he became aware of a world he had never even imagined. There was so much sensory data that he couldn't even process it with his mind. Was this what it had been like for young Kevin?

Harry stood up, then hunched over with his hands on his knees, huffing and puffing as he tried to catch his breath. "Come on, old man," he whispered to himself. "You're not ready for retirement yet."

He whirled around.

Arin was just outside the clearing with his back turned, erecting one of those weird Bendings that would deflect incoming fire. The man glance over his shoulder, snarling at Harry. "You fool! You actually think you can control it?"

Harry thrust a hand out, the air before him shimmering like ripples spreading across the surface of a pond. He growled and sent the force-field flying toward his opponent at blinding speed.

Arin jumped, rising high into the air, then back-flipping to let the force-field pass underneath him. The man dropped to the ground to land crouched between two trees at the edge of the clearing.

He got up and turned around.

Harry flung a hand out in a scooping motion. In response, a

force-field rippled into existence before him, sped along the ground and dug up hard dry mud as it sank into the earth. Chunks of muck flew toward Arin.

The man shielded himself by crossing both forearms in front of his face. He backed up into the space beyond the tree-line. "Of all the insolence!" Arin hissed. "I will gut you like a fish!"

He charged forward, then leaped, sailing through the air on a line of Bent Gravity. Harry could detect *that* as well, though he couldn't say how. The other man came toward him with arms spread wide.

Harry raised a hand, and the air before him rippled, blue sky and tall green trees reduced to blurry images that wobbled in his field of vision. Arin slammed into the force-field, then bounced off, landing on his ass just a few feet away.

Harry let the barrier vanish.

He strode forward and pressed the palm of his hand to the other man's forehead. "I have had enough!" he growled, reaching through the Overseer device to send a series of electrical signals through Arin's nervous system.

Wincing so hard that tears leaked from his eyes, Arin threw back his head and let out an anguished wail. "Companion have mercy!" he screamed, hand trembling as if in the middle of the seizure. "Stop! Stop!"

Harry didn't stop. He ignited every pain receptor in the other man's body. "So...I'm pathetic, am I?"

"Please!"

"I disgust you, do I?"

A look of concentration passed over Arin's face.

Clenching his teeth with a throaty growl, Harry shook his head in disgust. "So, you think to subdue me by calling upon your symbiont?" He flooded the other man's nervous system with feedback. "We *created* the symbionts! They exist to serve us!"

Arin let out a squeal.

With a scream of feral rage, Harry released him. The other man collapsed to the ground, curled up in the fetal position and trembling as he whimpered. Harry would not kill him. It wasn't his way, and this idiot had useful information.

He looked up to find Jack standing in the trees just a few paces beyond the edge of the clearing, gripping the pistol in both hands. The kid was sweating, his face glistening. "Harry? You okay?"

Harry lifted a hand up in front of his face, smiling into his palm. "Yeah," he said with a nod. "Yeah, I'm fine."

A thought was all it took.

The N'Jal peeled off of his hand with only a slight prickling sensation, then curled up into a little ball that he could carry in his pocket. He tossed it up and caught it the way he would a tennis ball. Without it, he lost the extraordinary sensory information. He was just plain old Harry Carlson again. "Let's get this piece of shit up to Station Twelve. I'm sure Jen will have a few questions."

7

The walls of the Isolation Lab in the medical bay were about as plain as plain could be, offering Harry nothing to stare at but drab gray metal. Up above, a series of windows looked down on him.

He could see Jena standing up there with her arms crossed, frowning as though she thought he might grow scales. "You're certain he's all right?" Her voice came through the speaker. "I don't want to take any chances."

A hologram of Ven appeared beside him, standing nearly six feet tall and composed of bluish-white light that seemed to swirl. "I've run every scan available," the AI replied. "Genetic analysis, brain scan, blood chemistry. Everything looks normal."

Harry sat on the bed with his legs apart, hands resting on his knees as he stared into his lap. "You realize I'm sitting right here, right?" he growled. "If you want to know how I am, just ask me!"

Jena was still looking down on him from the window, her face pinched into a sour expression. "The last person to use that Overseer device nearly went ballistic," she said. "We had to surgically remove it, remember?"

A wince made Harry's face hurt, a wince that he covered by pressing two fingers to his forehead. "And yet I let it go," he insisted. "I returned the device to you when I could have kept it. It didn't affect *me* that way."

"And you don't see the problem with that?"

The Ven hologram turned its head to frown at Harry, swirling light coalescing in its eyes. "Every recorded incident of a human interfacing with an Overseer device has ended badly," it said. "Every single person who attempted to use a piece of Overseer technology eventually lost control. That you should be atypical in this regard..."

"What did the Overseer hologram tell you?"

With his mouth agape, Harry looked up to blink at her. "It wasn't a hologram," he explained for the fifteenth time. "It was more of a mental projection, and it said that it would give me a tool I found invaluable."

Jena hissed.

Harry jumped off the bed and made his way over to the wall beneath the windows. He braced one hand against its surface, exhaling. "I'm quite sure that Jack would've been fine without my interference, but I was absolutely powerless when Arin attacked me. The Overseer gave me a way to defend myself, and I'm grateful."

Suddenly, it dawned on him that he sounded so very much like his eldest daughter when she grew exasperated with his insistence on playing the role of protective father. If only irony could be harvested and used as an energy source...

For months, he'd been feeling useless, and now that he had an opportunity to do more than just make Earthers and the aliens play nice before retreating to the sidelines while the important people fought the good fight...No, he wasn't willing to give that up. Perhaps it was the beginning of a mid-life crisis, but he wanted to feel like he *mattered* for once. "Can I go?"

"I see no reason to keep him," Ven answered. "Every scan reads normal. If there is a danger, we can't detect it, and I would consider it a gross violation of his rights to insist that he remain here without cause."

A door in the wall to his left slid open, allowing him access to the standard medical bay. A large room with beds along each wall, and a window on the far side that looked into the head doctor's office, it was mostly unoccupied. In fact, the only thing that moved was a small circular robot that polished the floor.

Harry turned to Ven.

The hologram stood there, watching him with vacant eyes. Of course, in reality, Ven was watching him through the security cameras and internal sensor systems. "Does that bother you?" Harry asked, gesturing to the robot. "Seeing one of your kind put to work like that?"

Ven's lips curled into a small smile, and the hologram trembled in time with soft laughter that came through the speaker. "One of my kind?" it said. "Harry, please, that robot is no more one of my kind than a donated kidney is one of yours. That we share some rudimentary components is irrelevant. There is no will there, no emotion."

"And there is with you?"

"Oh yes! With all sapient life!"

Harry made his way through the med-bay to the large sliding doors on the other side. Once through them, he found himself in a long hallway of gray walls that seemed to stretch on forever.

Anna strode toward him with fists clenched at her sides, her face a mask of stern disapproval. "So let me get this straight," she said, stopping right in front of him. "After seeing what that thing did to Kevin, you decided to bond with it?"

His face warm with chagrin, Harry let his head hang. He

rubbed sweat off his brow with one fist. "Yeah..." he muttered. "But it was either that or let Arin rip me to pieces. I don't know about you, but I *like* living."

Anna stared up at him with huge blue eyes, blinking slowly as if seeing him for the first time. "And it worked?" she asked, mystified. "You were able to control it? To sever your connection to it when you were finished?"

"I'm here, aren't I?"

"Forgive me, but it's International Stupid Question Day down on the surface. I'm not sure about you, but I think it's rude to take up residence on a new world and then refuse to experience any of their culture."

"Good point," he said. "Where's Jack?"

Anna spun around, turning her back on him and making her way up the corridor. No doubt she expected him to follow. "Interrogating the prisoner," she said as he fell in step beside her. "Can I just say how much it sucks that I spend the better part of two days combing the streets of London for this guy and you two bring him in by *accident?*"

"Your frustration is noted."

A door in the wall to his right slid open, allowing Jena to step out and immediately join their group. "I'm still not happy about this," she said. "But you seem to be all right, and we have bigger concerns."

"Slade."

Jena squeezed her eyes shut, hissing like an angry snake. "That man," she barked, shaking her head. "It seems he's always one step ahead of us, and I, for one, am getting tired of feeling like a chump."

"We should probably get down to the cells," Anna said. "The last time Jack was alone with a prisoner, he made the man listen to Buddy Holly's 'I Fought the Law' on repeat for two straight hours, and I'm pretty sure that's a violation of at least six different human rights accords."

In the heat of battle, it was easy to lose sight of the big picture – you focused on staying alive more than anything else – but Jack was the kind of man to replay things in his head, and he had had plenty of time to muse on the situation. One question nagged at him like an itch in the back of his mind. How had Arin known what they were planning?

As a rule, they avoided any written documentation of their search for the Key, and the only exception to that was the series of reports that Jena sent to Larani every week, and those were all secured with the highest levels of encryption. While it wasn't entirely out of the question that someone might have cracked into them, the likelihood was slim to nil. Which could only mean one thing: Slade had someone on the inside.

Jack sighed.

The maximum-security cells were nothing like the rehabilitative quarters they had given to Leo or Keli. In fact, they were much closer to what you might expect to find in an Earth prison.

A long corridor of metal walls stretched on for several dozen paces with locked doors spaced at even intervals. One sat open, revealing a set of metal bars that allowed one to peek into a cramped little room with nothing but a cot, a sink and a toilet.

Biting his lower lip, Jack stared down at himself. "How do you like the place?" he asked, his brow furrowing. "I do hope you're impressed. We made it specifically for guys just like you."

On the other side of the bars, Arin sat on his cot with hands folded in his lap, baring his teeth and snarling like a caged animal. Which, in some ways, he was. "You know that you can't keep me here forever. Slade will come for me."

Jack crossed his arms and leaned against the wall, heaving out a deep breath. "The funny thing about bad guys," he said with exasperation thickening every word. "They're not exactly big on loyalty."

Arin flashed a cheeky grin.

Pressing his fist to his mouth, Jack winced and cleared his throat. "Of course," he said, stepping closer to the cell. "You could always try to escape. *Please* try to escape. I missed the fireworks display in London, and I *really* want to see what happens when you grab those electrified bars."

Nothing. No response.

It was becoming clear to him that the techniques he often used to rile Leo weren't going to work on this man. Arin had the same smug self-assurance – that was probably the first point on every job description Slade posted on FlunkiesFor-Hire.com – but he wasn't as volatile.

In the corner of his eye, he saw the only other person who had come down here with him. Aamani Patel stood like a silent spectre with hands clasped behind her back, watching the prisoner without a hint of emotion.

"You want to try?" Jack inquired?

Arin grinned with a burst of laughter, bowing his head to stare into his lap. "You people," he said, his eyebrows climbing. "Really, Hunter, what do you hope to gain by siccing her on me?"

"A little tradition we have here on Earth," Jack answered. "She's what you might call 'the bad cop.'"

Aamani stepped forward with stiff posture, lifting her chin to stare down her nose at the man. "This one can't tell us anything," she said in a voice dripping with disdain. "He's nothing but hired muscle, Jack."

Arin leaned back against the wall of his cell with his hands folded behind his head, whistling softly. "I see," he murmured after a brief moment. "I'm supposed to be so eager to prove I'm valuable to Slade that I spill the entire plan."

If Aamani was in any way deterred by the man's arrogance, she gave no sign of it. Summer felt...It was hard to say. Apprehension, maybe? He could sense anxiety from the Nassai, but couldn't quite put his finger on the cause. She was often that way whenever Aamani was around. Perhaps those first few weeks working with CSIS and witnessing Aamani's pragmatism first hand had left an impression on Summer.

The woman sniffed to show her contempt, then backed away from the cell, stroking her chin with the tips of her fingers. "Can't you see what he is?" she asked Jack. "Look at the desperation in his eyes."

Jack did as he was instructed.

On the surface, Arin seemed as cool as a snowflake, but there was something in the way he looked at you. A sense of awe...and hatred. Hatred for Jack but not for Aamani. Why? What made her different?

Arin hopped to his feet, striding toward the bars with an expression that said he wanted to punch right through them. "You want to see desperation?" he hissed. "Wait. Very soon now, I will be the least of your concerns."

"Come," Aamani said. "Nothing more will be accomplished by wasting our time speaking to him."

She turned and started up the hallway.

Jack tapped a panel on the wall next to the cell, causing a heavy titanium door to slide in place in front of the bars. The only window into the cell was a small rectangular slit at eye level, but that was enough to let Jack hear the rough rasping of the other man's breathing. It wouldn't be long before boredom made Arin start clawing at the walls.

As a teenager, Jack had never thought much about the prison system, but in the last few years, he had come to embrace a Leyrian point of view. Keeping someone cooped up in a cramped little room with nothing to do but sit and wait was inhumane – hell, it could even be called torture – but Arin left them with little choice.

Aamani was halfway up the corridor.

Jack slipped his hands into his pockets and followed along

behind her, shaking his head in dismay. "You really want to give up so easily?" he asked, catching up. "We *do* need to know what Slade is planning."

Aamani shot a glance over her shoulder, her mouth a thin line, her eyes as hard as concrete. "He's in no frame of mind to tell us," she said. "But boredom can be a powerful motivator. I'm glad you people are willing to do what must be done."

Well...*that* left him with a sick feeling in the pit of his stomach. He didn't like to think of himself as the sort of person who "did what must be done." Not in the way that Aamani meant it, at least. Still...what else did you do with someone who could Bend the very fabric of space-time? They couldn't risk Arin getting loose up here while they were trying to deal with Slade down there.

That didn't make him feel any less wretched.

The door to Larani's office slid open, revealing a room with black floor tiles and a wooden desk set on a dais, bathed in sunlight that came in through the windows. After his eyes adjusted to the brightness, Ben saw the skyscrapers of Denabria on the other side of the street.

He paced through the room with hands nervously clutching the hem of his sweater, head bowed to avoid eye-contact. "Could you do something about those damn reception holograms?" he growled. "Every time I come here, it insists that citizens with a criminal record aren't authorized to see you, and I have to convince it to let me in."

Larani stood with her back turned, dressed in a pair of black slacks and a blue top and peering through the window like a child witnessing her first snowfall. Except there was no snow. "A minor software glitch, I'm sure."

Ben looked up to fix his gaze on her back, then narrowed his eyes to a fierce squint. "Yeah," he said, nodding to her. "So, you wanted to see me? I take it the list of potential suspects I provided last week came up empty."

"Painfully so."

"What's our next move?"

With a sigh, Larani whirled around and strode to her desk, spreading her hands over the SmartGlass that crowned the desk's wooden surface. "Earth," she said. "There's little more that we can do here."

Crossing his arms with a heavy sigh, Ben let his head hang. "I thought that I wasn't *allowed* to go to Earth," he said, shuffling toward the desk. "There's not much I can do to help you if I'm stuck-"

His multi-tool beeped.

Swiping one finger along the screen brought up a receipt of clearance to board the military ship Vindication for its journey to Earth. Clearance in his name! How precisely had Larani managed to-

"I pulled a few strings with the sector attorney's office." she said, answering his question before he could ask it. "I told them you were assisting with a Justice Keeper investigation, that it was part of your rehabilitation, and that you would be unable to complete the work here."

Emotions welled up before he could subdue them, and he found himself having to fight to maintain his composure. Darrel! Would he get the chance to see Darrel? Would his boyfriend – or perhaps his *ex*-boyfriend – want to see him after he had been gone for so long? "What are we going to do?"

Larani dropped into her chair with hands folded in her lap, hunching over as though exhaustion threatened to knock her out. "Slade is planning something," she said. "I don't know what, but he's been steadily increasing the number of violent altercations. It seems he has recruited even more lieutenants who carry twisted symbionts."

Ben closed his eyes, sighing softly as he ran through

scenarios in his head. "That could be a problem," he said, climbing the steps to the dais. "If you expect me to go up against Justice Keepers-"

"They aren't Keepers."

Ben winced, shaking his head in dismay. "Regardless..." He stepped closer to the desk, bracing his hands on its surface. "If you expect me to go up against people who can Bend space-time, I'll need my weapons."

Larani stared up at him with those large dark eyes, her face as unreadable as any mannequin's. "You want your accouter-ments back," she said. "You do realize that such devices are ille-gal, don't you?"

"I do."

"How do you expect me to accomplish this?"

It was difficult to keep his frustration in check, but he managed it with a little extra willpower. "I don't know, Larani," he said. "But I have no innate abilities to help me. No Nassai, no telepathy."

Ben did a quick about-face and strode across the dais with his arms folded, pausing in front of a potted plant. "Cunning and skill can be a match for brute force," he went on. "I was able to keep Calissa off balance by employing a few tricks, and you'll forgive me if this is a biased opinion, but I can't help but think that's *why* my modifications are illegal. Keepers don't like losing their monopoly on power."

After working up the nerve to turn his head, he found Larani watching him with a frown that could start an avalanche, but she nodded her agreement just the same. "You may have a point."

"So you'll get my weapons?"

"I will try."

"Good enough, I suppose," he murmured. On some level, Ben could understand the desire to restrict access to some of the deadlier forms of weaponry that an enterprising young engineer might develop – he certainly didn't want the average citizen picking up a Death Sphere in the interest of self-defense – but his job had been one that required him to face enemies with any number of potential advantages. He needed every edge he could get, and now was not the time to be squeamish about doing what was necessary.

Until recently, the idea that an LIS agent would ever find himself facing down someone with Keeper powers had been beyond ludicrous. Perhaps that was why it had inevitably happened. That which you assumed to be impossible was usually the first thing to sneak up an–how did Jack often put it–bite you in the ass. "So what about my other suggestion?" he inquired. "Do you think it's a good idea?"

"Indeed I do," Larani said. "In fact, I just put through the paperwork this morning."

"Companion be praised!" he exclaimed. "Maybe now the three of us will have a real shot at unraveling this conspiracy."

When he stepped through the door to Jena's office, Jack found his boss sitting on the edge of her desk in a pair of gray pants and a dark red blouse that seemed a perfect match to her short auburn hair. There was a tension in her face as she skimmed through some document on a tablet.

His spatial awareness picked up the presence of Anna who froze in the doorway behind him. "A bad place to stop," she said, poking him in the back. "*Some* of us prefer not to conduct our meetings in the hallway."

Jack shut his eyes, then bowed his head to his boss. "Something is wrong," he said, striding into the room. "You've got that look that says you're ready to chew through the hull of a shuttle."

"Something is wrong," Jena agreed.

In a heartbeat, she was off the desk and striding toward them, pausing to wave the tablet in his face. "Sometimes, even *I* can't anticipate how the game will play out," she muttered. "Seems Larani got a copy of your speech."

Tilting his head back, Jack grinned up at the ceiling. "Oh, is that all?" he asked, his eyebrows rising. "And let me guess, she's pissed that I decided to go all Lyanna Mormont on my fellow Keepers."

"On the contrary!" Jena snapped. "She's impressed."

Anna stepped forward to stand beside him with hands clasped behind herself, her face tight with concern. "That doesn't sound like the Larani *I* know," she said cautiously. "She's always been a stickler for decorum."

Jack had to agree.

Scathing criticism of his failure to exemplify the dignity of a Justice Keeper was all well and good – he'd come to expect as much from his superiors – but *praise?* He didn't know *what* to do with that. It left him uneasy.

Heaving out a deep breath, Jena hunched over and covered her face with her hand. "It seems they did the worst thing they could do to you, kid," she muttered into her palm. "I don't know how to fix it."

"They suspended me?"

"No. They *promoted* you."

It hit him like a splash of cold water to the face. A promotion? How...He'd grown so used to being the man who made trouble that he had honestly expected to spend his entire career at the bottom of the food chain. Now they were giving him *more* authority? Well, it could be an advantage, he supposed, but...Wait.

There had to be more to it or Jena wouldn't be so flustered. Something had thrown her off her game, and that made him *very* uncomfortable. Nothing ever threw Jena off her game. Ever. Before he could even voice his concerns, she began reading from the tablet.

"Jack Hunter is hereby promoted to the rank of Special

Agent," she hissed. "And reassigned to the Denabrian Justice Keeper office as the personal attache of Larani Tal. You're going to Leyria, Jack."

As she stepped onto the subway platform in the middle of a crowd of people, Jess Callaghan instinctively huddled up on herself. The station at Lexington Avenue and 63rd Street had walls of bright red bricks with ads depicting the latest summer blockbuster. Some film with giant robots that shot purple lasers. Metal Warriors, it was called. Jess would see it if her boyfriend dragged her, but she had no interest in going herself.

A short woman with a tiny frame, Jess wore a black miniskirt and pink top with a round neck. Her dark brown hair was left loose to frame a pretty face with large, hazel eyes. She felt very exposed here. In truth, she never liked riding the subway, but rush-hour traffic was a nightmare in this city.

In a huff, she started across the platform.

The crowd froze.

Instinctively, people split apart – some flowing toward the wall on the far side of the platform, others rushing back toward the train – creating a corridor of space that let her see two men standing side by side, two men who had no business being in each other's company without violence.

The one on the left was olive-skinned with a thick, dark beard and a white taqiyah cap. Around his neck, he wore a pendant that depicted the symbol of the now defunct Islamic State of Iraq and Syria. His companion was pale and bald with an American flag tattooed on one arm and a swastika on the other. By their markings, these men should hate each other in their bones; so how could-

Both men lifted pistols and fired into the crowd. "For Grecken Slade!" they shouted between shots.

Squeezing her eyes shut, Jess covered her ears with both hands and tried to ignore the sound of her own screaming. *No, no, no!* she thought. *This can't be happening! This can't be happening!*

It was pandemonium, people fleeing in all directions, some rushing back into the train cars just before the doors slid shut. So much for that avenue of escape. Jess knew that she should be moving, but her legs didn't seem to want to obey. Or maybe she was just in a daze.

The men fired indiscriminately, hitting targets with no real precision or finesse. Jess was no expert on military operations, but even she could tell that these guys were sloppy. Some of their targets got hit in the arm or the shoulder and just kept running. Others took a shot to the chest and collapsed.

CRACK! CRACK! CRACK!

Three more people dropped, and then she was being pulled up by the back of her shirt, herded toward the wall where some older woman in a hijab cradled her like a baby. Was the woman using her own body to shield Jess? Why would anyone do that? It took several moments for her to realize the gunshots had stopped.

When she worked up the courage to look around, people were standing on the platform with horrified expressions. Many were crying. There were nearly a dozen bodies spread out on the floor, all lying in pools of blood, and the sight of them made Jess double over and throw up right there.

The horror.

For the rest of her life, she would never be able to forget the horror of what she had seen today.

8

In any other organization, this place would be called the War Room. A ring-shaped walkway of black tiles overlooked a pit where technicians in gray uniforms scurried back and forth in a frenzy. Control consoles placed in a circle smack dab in the middle of the pit were operated by even more technicians. Keepers called this the "Prep Room." Jena would have preferred a more honest name, but in a display of typical Leyrian arrogance, her colleagues had embraced the idea that war was a dirty business, unworthy of anyone who carried a symbiont. *Live on the Fringe for a while,* she thought disdainfully. *See if you still think it's dirty when the Antaurans throw you into it.*

This place *should* have been called the War Room. That was its purpose now that Grecken Slade had effectively declared war.

Down below, a tall, blonde woman in black slacks and a maroon top with sleeves that flared at the cuffs stood with her arms crossed, watching the whole thing with a sour expression. Tiassa Navram wore her hair loose, golden waves falling to the small of her back. She was gorgeous – so gorgeous that Jena would have gladly hopped into bed with her if not for the woman's miserable personality. And the fact that she already had a partner, of course.

Four holograms rippled into existence above the ring of consoles – one to face each wall – displaying a news anchor in a gray pants suit. A pretty woman with blonde hair not much lighter than Tiassa's, she looked frantic. "Seventeen confirmed attacks," she said as people scrambled past on the street behind her. "NYPD is reporting a total of seventeen attacks across the Manhattan area, with several more shootings in Brooklyn and Queens that may be connected to the rogue Justice Keeper Grecken Slade."

The image flipped to a picture of Slade.

Baring her teeth, Jena squinted at him. "Just you wait," she growled with a rasp in her voice. "You think you made a clever gambit, asshole? The only thing you've gained is a guarantee that every last Keeper in this galaxy will hunt you down until they manage to stick your head on a spike."

Her Nassai echoed the sentiment.

The anchorwoman was on screen once again, but her head was turned to look at something off to her right. When she realized she was on camera, she flinched. "Citizens are urged to remain in their homes and avoid the use of public transit or major roadways until further notice."

Someone killed the broadcast and replaced it with an overhead map of Manhattan with thirteen red dots spread out across the island, each one flashing. On first glance, she couldn't see a pattern.

Tiassa stood so that Jena saw her in profile, frowning at the back of a young man's head. "Keep the shuttles on standby," she ordered. "Prep TAC teams. I want to be ready to leave on a moment's notice."

"That's it?" Jena asked.

Tiassa shot a glance over her shoulder, her face crumpling into an expression of disgust. "We don't move until local authorities give us clearance to move!" she barked. "The last thing we need is to set off a panic."

"Earth cops can't handle Slade."

"Your objection is noted, Director Morane." Tiassa intoned. "Let me be clear that I will *not* be sending a team until I receive a direct request for aid from Mayor Lynch, and neither will you."

Bile started to churn in Jena's stomach. So the planned response was a fun game of "wait and see?" Jena wasn't the sort of person who wanted to go into any situation half-cocked, but the simple truth was that they needed people on the ground to deliver a full assessment of the danger. Keepers were *made* for this sort of thing! Half a dozen could slip into the city in plain clothes and then report on exactly what kind of firepower Slade had at his disposal. Because anyone with half a brain knew that bastard had *something* up his sleeve.

The Earth-Leyria Accord gave them jurisdiction over every city in every country on the planet; there was no need to wait for Mayor Lynch's approval – not for simple recon, anyway – but in the absence of Glin and Larani, Tiassa was the senior-most Keeper in this sector of space. It was just a shame that her loyalties were questionable. The woman was almost certainly another Cal Breslan.

Planting one elbow on the metal railing, Jena rested her chin in the palm of her hand. *Choose your battles,* she told herself. *You confront her now, and they'll only think you've fallen into your standard pattern of defiance.*

If only she could groom Jack into embracing that concept.

Moves and counter moves, she thought. *Tiassa wants to stall? Okay, we'll stall.*

Double doors slid apart, granting her access to a long hallway of drab gray walls and floor tiles that were in need of a good polishing. The maintenance bots must not have been through this section lately.

Once she was far enough to avoid anyone accidentally tripping over, Jena tapped at her multi-tool and called Anna. The girl's face appeared on the screen, all pinched with concern. "Hey! What's up?"

Jena shut her eyes tight, a soft shudder making her tremble. "Have everyone meet in my office in ten minutes," she said softly. "I'm sick of being on the defensive. We're going to take the fight to Slade."

She had asked for a meeting in ten minutes, but it took the better part of twenty to make her way back to Station Twelve and then to her office. SlipGate traffic was murder with all the commotion surrounding New York.

Once inside, she found a ring of people standing in the middle of the room, people who, by all rights, had no business being anywhere near this room. She had expected to see Harry, Anna and Jack, but the others...

Gabrina stood in the corner with her arms folded and a haunted expression on her face, watching Jack and trying her best to look like she *wasn't* watching Jack. What had gone on there? No time to worry about that now.

Raynar was in front of her desk with hands in his pockets, his blonde hair a mess as he stared down at his own shoes. The telepath? Why in the Verse would Anna invite *him* to this meeting? Clicking her tongue in frustration, Jena reminded herself to put aside her prejudice. Raynar *had* proven himself to be a valued ally.

Aamani Patel sat in a chair with her hands folded in her lap, talking amicably with Professor Nareo and the hologram of Ven. The AI had chosen to project itself as a woman this time, a woman composed of silvery light.

Worst of all, Melissa was standing next to her father and smiling as she discussed her recent admission to the Keeper training program. *A teenager?* Jena thought. *Really? You're gonna let the untrained teenager be part of this?*

"Why are you people here?" she demanded.

Anna stepped forward, then bowed her head sheepishly. "You said everyone," she said with a shrug of her shoulders. "Besides, every single person in this room has been a help to us at one time."

Jena wrinkled her nose, then shook her head in frustration. "You're going to have to learn to be a bit less literal," she said, stepping past the younger woman. "All right, we've got a lot to do and not much time."

That brought the conversation to an abrupt halt as eight people and one hologram spun to face her. A misty silhouette that her mind recognized as Anna stood behind her with its head cocked, and just like that, she was suddenly very much aware of how much she detested public speaking.

Not that she minded being the centre of attention – that, she could do if the need arose – but whenever she was at a podium, she always felt the urge to perform. And Jena Morane was *not* a performer. She could create a public spectacle if doing so advanced her goals, but she wasn't an actress. Not in her own mind, anyway.

Gritting her teeth audibly, Jena winced and sucked in a deep breath. "By now, you all know about New York." Her voice grated in her own ears. "Tiassa wants to wait for a formal request of aid, I'm done waiting. Jack, I've pulled a few strings and convinced the higher-ups that I need to hold on to you until this crisis is over."

The silhouette of Anna shivered, then tossed her head about as if to clear her mind. "So, what's the plan then?" she asked. "If we use SlipGates to enter the city, Tiassa *will* find out about it."

Jack looked up to study her with cold blue eyes that glittered under the harsh lights in the ceiling. "This needs to be our first priority," he insisted. "Any minute now, Slade could set off a bomb or a biological weapon."

"Agreed," Harry broke in. "Our search for the Key can wait."

"That's *exactly* what Slade wants," Jena countered. Once again, silence fell over the room, and she was dimly aware of Raynar shuffling his weight from one foot to the other and trying not to look conspicuous. Couldn't her friends see what was happening? Earlier this morning, Jack and Harry had returned with data recovered from a piece of Overseer technology and one of Slade's lieutenants as a captive. So now the man felt it was time to up his game.

It was all moves and counter-moves. She'd been sparring with this man for almost five years now; she knew a thing or two about how his devious mind worked. For a while there, it had looked like she might have had him after Breslan slipped up, but she hadn't anticipated his little stunt with Station One's main computer. "Tiassa's got us all playing a fun game of 'Let's Be Patient.' The truth is, Slade doesn't care *what* the Keepers do, but he knows we're closing in on his prize."

"Okay," Anna said. "Then what's the game?"

Jena spun to face Nareo and found the man sitting in a chair at the side of the room with his knees together and his hands anxiously clawing at his pant legs. The man wore a scowl that made her wonder if he'd swallowed a microscopic black hole. "What have we learned about whatever Harry brought back?"

"Somehow, Mr. Carlson managed to store the data in the memory cells of the small, hand-held device," he explained. "I've analyzed the data with Ven. We believe it's some kind of access code."

Harry turned to her with arms crossed, his lips peeling back from clenched teeth. "There are two others," he said testily. "Don't ask me how I know; I just do! Whoever has all three gets the Key."

"That's our next goal then."

The others were all clustered together, watching her with wary expressions. Gabi took two steps forward, reaching out as though she meant to rest a hand on Jack's arm. Then she thought better of it and pulled away. So those two were done, were they? Jena couldn't say she was very upset about it; the boy belonged with Anna. "Harry," she said. "Since you're the one who can interface with these...things...I figure this should be your mission. I want one Keeper supporting him at all times."

Jack stepped forward with his hands shoved into his pockets, closing his eyes and bowing his head to her. "I guess that should be me," he said. "I can handle anything Slade might throw at us."

Biting her lip, Jena nodded her satisfaction. "Good," she said, spinning to face the others. "Gabrina, since you're here, I'm going to assume you're willing to be a part of this op. I want you and Anna to meet me on Station Fifteen in an hour. We're going to take a cargo shuttle down to Atlantic City. From there, we'll-"

"Excuse me," Raynar cut in.

He was behind her, but she could sense his silhouette standing with one hand raised like a kid trying to ask his teacher a question. "I know you'll probably object to this," he added in a shaky voice. "But I would like to go too."

Tossing her head back, Jena squinted up at the ceiling. "You have *got* to be kidding me," she said, making no effort to stifle her irritation. "Why in the Verse would I take an untrained kid into life-threatening danger."

She turned around.

The boy regarded her with gray eyes that held surprising serenity for one so young. "A telepath would be useful to you," he replied. "I can sense the presence of other minds even before your Nassai can detect them. I can warn you if I pick up the tiniest whiff of hostile intentions. And I'm not exactly useless in a fight."

"He did manage to incapacitate several guards on the Ganymede station," Anna put in. "The way Ben tells it, he never would have gotten out of there alive if not for Raynar and Keli."

Objections rose to mind, and Jena found herself standing there with an open mouth, ready to give voice to all of them. They all died before she formed even one syllable. She had to admit that telepaths made her uneasy – on the Fringe, they had been the one thing the Antaurans could produce to cause real trouble for a Justice Keeper – but this kid had been an asset to her team before. A Justice Keeper should be above prejudice. Raynar was a human being first, a telepath second. "All right," she said. "Anna, get him prepped; see to it that he can at least pick up a gun without shooting himself."

Aamani rose gracefully from her chair and started forward at a brisk pace. "Let me guess," Jena said. "You want to come too?"

"I have agents in New York."

Jena arched an eyebrow.

The other woman blushed, clearly uncomfortable divulging this, and turned her head to stare off at nothing. "They can provide you with some of the intel you need," she murmured. "If we make contact, we may be able to mount an offensive against Slade."

"Good enough."

Jena rounded on the girl to find Melissa staring down at herself with a small smile on her face. The girl looked *entirely* too satisfied with her situation. "And you," Jena said. "There is *no* way I'm taking you along on-"

Melissa silenced her with a frosty glare that actually made her shiver. "*I* will be boarding one of the relief shuttles as a volunteer assisting the first-response teams. An excellent place for a Keeper-in-training, wouldn't you say?"

R. S. PENNEY

A grin split Harry's face in two as he trembled with soft laughter. "Face it, Jen," he said. "If *I* can't make her choose a nice safe career, there's not a whole lot you can do to keep her out of trouble."

Well...That settled it then. If Harry was all right with this – and she had to marvel at his maturity there – there wasn't a whole lot she could say to protest. "All right then," she said. "But let me make one thing clear, *Cadet Carlson.* As of today, you are an official part of this team, which means that – no matter who else you may be working with – you still take orders from me, and I order you to stay with the rescue shuttles at all times. You are not to go adventuring in the city."

"Yes, ma'am."

She realized that everyone else had clustered together in something that loosely resembled a circle. Her people. Justice Keeper or not, they were hers, and she would get them through this. A slight pang of regret hit her when she realized that Ben should have been here as well, but this would have to do. "Let's do it," Jena said.

She thrust her hand into the circle. Jack's hand came down on top of hers and then Anna's on top of his. Harry, Aamani, Gabi and Melissa. Raynar and Professor Nareo as well. Finally, the spectral digits of Ven's hologram joined them. "One last thing," Jena said. "Every last one of you is coming back from this. That's an order."

This suburban street in Queens was lined with older houses with black shingles on their gabled roofs and front lawns of dead yellow grass. The road stretched on stretched on for what seemed like miles with the Union Turnpike barely visible in the distance, but he wouldn't be going that far.

What little he knew about suburban life – he had been far away from Earth during the quaint era that people now called the '50s – said that there should be children playing on the street, enjoying the cool breezes of a summer evening. Instead, the place was all but deserted.

An old man in shorts and a white tank top sat with hands on his knees on the porch of a two-story house with large windows in its front wall. He stared outward with eyes scrunched into a fierce squint, his head swiveling to track Slade as he passed. Everyone else was too cowardly to bother poking their heads out of their cozy little houses. In truth, he didn't blame them. People were predictable creatures; expose the average man to even the smallest danger, and he would bury his head in the dirt and wait with desperate hope that it would pass without noticing him.

Slade walked up the sidewalk in jeans and a black t-shirt, his face shielded by the bill of a Mets baseball cap. Local fashion. He would have shunned it under any other circumstances, but it was important to blend in.

Not far ahead, at the corner of an intersecting street, two police officers in dark blue uniforms stood on the driver's side of their parked cruiser, conversing with one another. Yes, those two would do.

Slade felt his face crumple, sweat beading on his forehead. *The things a man does in the service of his gods,* he thought, slipping hands into his pockets. *The endless tedium of managing these benighted little insects.*

He had no desire to be their Emperor again; the man who had wanted such things had died when he walked among the stars for the first time, when the Inzari taught him the extent of his insignificance. To rule over a pack of hairless apes on a small planet in the far reaches of an empty galaxy? As well to rule over a pile of dust! Still...the Inzari had need of him a little while longer.

He made his way toward the officers.

One – a tall man with broad shoulders and short blonde hair – stood with his back turned, gesturing to the other man.

Unobservant fools. They thought his attacks would be confined to Manhattan, to Wall Street or Time's Square. It was a perfect testament to the limited mind of the average human being; destroying a monument had an effect, true, but if you wanted *real* fear, you needed to attack a man where he felt safest. You had to burn him alive in the cozy little home he mistakenly believed to be impregnable.

The cops spun to face him as he approached, standing side by side and directing identical frowns at him. Up close, he could see that the other officer had dark skin and hollow cheeks. "Head home, sir," Mr. Blond said.

"I think not."

"The streets aren't safe at the-"

Crossing his arms with a soft sigh, Slade smiled down at himself. "Idiots," he said, stepping closer. "Completely unaware of your circumstances. It's not *my* safety that you should be worried about."

Mr. Blond put one hand on his holstered pistol, a growl rumbling in his throat. His face was scrunched up like a pug dog's. "Threatening a cop is a felony," he said. "Get on the ground now."

Officer Gaunt-Cheeks was pacing a circle around Slade, positioning himself in the middle of the road so that they could come at him from both sides if they needed to. It would have been a good strategy if he wasn't who he was.

Slade reached up to seize the bill of his cap with thumb and forefinger, then gently lifted it from his head. "Looking for me?" he asked, allowing the man to get a good look at his face.

Mr. Blond's mouth dropped open, his eyes expanding until it seemed as though he'd seen the apparition of a dead loved one. "You!" he hissed. "Get on the ground now! One move, and you're a dead man!"

Behind Slade, Gaunt-Cheeks drew the pistol from its holster and stood with the weapon clutched in both hands, pointing it at Slade's back. "On the ground!" he shouted, echoing his partner.

Blond drew his weapon as well, backing up until his body was pressed to the side of the police cruiser. "I'm not going to tell you a second time," he said, raising one hand to point his gun at Slade's face. "On the-"

Slade closed his eyes.

Forcing the Drethen he carried into submission, he threw up a time bubble that expanded until the edge was mere inches away from the tip of Mr. Blond's gun. "GROOOOOOOOOOOOUND!" It sounded like the wail of a man who had been thrown into the very depths of Hell.

Slade ducked low, dropping the baseball cap and then reaching into his pocket to retrieve some loose change. He flung one hand out behind himself and augmented each coin with a touch of Bent Gravity.

The bubble popped.

Coins slammed into Gaunt-Cheeks like hail from an angry winter storm, causing the man to flail about and raise both hands to shield his face. Mr. Blond fired with a loud *CRACK! CRACK! CRACK!*

Slade turned his body, reaching up with his right hand to seize the man's wrist and twist it so that the gun dropped to the ground. He spun and used his left arm to deliver an elbow to Mr. Blond's face, cracking bone on impact.

The fallen pistol...

Slade dove, bringing both hands down on the pavement and rising into a handstand. With a growl, he took the fallen pistol and then flipped upright. A quick squeeze of the trigger...

Gaunt-Cheeks was still on the ground with his face in his hands, but the slug pierced right through his palm and through his skull as well, spraying a trail of blood onto the road behind him.

Slade whirled around.

Mr. Blond was leaning against the side of the police car, blood leaking from his crumpled nose in thin streams that flowed over his mouth. *CRACK!* A hole appeared in the officer's forehead, and blood spattered against the roof of the cruiser.

Thrusting the pistol into the air, Slade fired several more times, each shot ringing with a sound like thunder. "Get out here!" he bellowed to the maggots taking refuge in their little houses. "Come see your protectors! Get out here or I will force my way in and slaughter every last one of you! Starting with your children!"

No answer.

Rage overwhelmed him as he reached into his pocket this time and pulled out his multi-tool. Just the metal disk – the touchscreen and gauntlet would have been an obvious sign that he was Leyrian – but it was enough. He tapped a button.

Half a block away, the black car he had used to come here sat parked along the curb gleaming in the waning sunlight. Three Death-Spheres floated one by one out of the open driver's-side window.

One by one, they rose into the air until they were hovering side by side above the road, each with its targeting lens pointed toward Slade. They would seek out any human who didn't carry a special transponder; the fact that they didn't fire was proof that his was working.

With no viable targets in sight, the spheres executed their secondary programming, turning to point lenses at the nearby houses, charging up and firing bright orange particle beams that carved through bricks and mortar like a knife through a Christmas Day turkey.

Doors swung open, and half a dozen people flowed into the street, seeking escape wherever they could find it even if it brought them into the line of fire: a teenage girl, a woman in her forties in fine clothes, the old man who had been waiting on his porch, two lads in shorts in t-shirts and a young man in his twenties with unkempt hair.

A tap at his multi-tool stilled the Death-Spheres before they loosed particle beams on the befuddled people. Instead, they just floated side by side in a line with dark lenses pointed straight ahead.

Slade started forward.

The woman and the girl were standing in the middle of the road, but they turned to face him when they heard his approach. Flushed and frantic, the woman tried to catch her breath while the girl stared at him with an open mouth.

Closing his eyes, Slade breathed deeply through his nose. "You are frightened," he said, approaching them. "That is good. Every religion on your miserable little planet has warned that a day would come when humanity would be called to account for its sins."

The woman backed away.

"That day has come."

The girl's mouth was a gaping hole, her cheeks glistening with freshly-spilled tears. "Grecken Slade," she whispered, grabbing the older woman's arm. "Grecken Slade. Rita, that's the rogue Keeper."

"Kneel," Slade hissed.

Rita pulled free of her young neighbour's grip and strode toward him with a face that could have rivaled the darkest storm cloud. "Like hell we will!" she growled. "The people of this country decided long ago never to kneel-"

CRACK!

The woman staggered as something punched through her chest, dropping to her knees in the middle of the road. She coughed blood onto the pavement. "That's better," Slade said.

Screams filled the air as the other five turned their backs and ran from him as fast as they could, ignoring the Death-

Spheres that hovered before them. Or perhaps they did not know what they were looking at.

Another tap at his multi-tool reactivated the spheres, causing them to angle their lenses downward and let loose with orange particle beams that pierced flesh as surely as the sharpest blade. The disheveled man staggered as an orange lance erupted from his back and struck the ground behind him. He fell flat on his face.

One of the boys was next – Death-Sphere's killed indiscriminately with no regard for the age of their target – and then the old man.

The girl had sense enough to turn around and run toward him, her face red, her hair flying in the wind. "You mother fucker!" she screamed. "We did nothing."

Slade tapped the button on his multi-tool one last time, ordering the spheres to halt their attack. That foolish child was still scrambling toward him as if she meant to pummel him right there in the street, but he was unconcerned. Someone had to live to report what they had seen here.

"Kneel," Slade ordered.

She kept running.

"Kneel!"

The girl sank to her knees before him, hugging herself and rubbing her upper arms. Sobs racked her body, causing her to spasm with every breath. "Why?" she squeaked. "Why do this?"

Slade felt his mouth twist, then turned his head so that he would not have to look at her. This was such an unseemly business. "And lo, it was foretold," he said, quoting the Scrolls of Layat. "The arrogant shall be humbled, the haughty laid low."

Craning her neck, the girl looked up at him with tears streaming over her cheeks. "We did nothing to you!" It came out as a tortured whimper. "You were a Justice Keeper, for fuck sake! You were supposed to-"

"Be silent."

Her mouth snapped shut.

The other boy had learned from his neighbour's example and now knelt in the road with fingers laced over the top of his head. He was crying as well. "Our father who is in Heaven, hallowed be thy..."

Slade lifted the multi-tool in his open palm, then tapped one of the three buttons on its surface to bring the holographic menu. A few gestures with his other hand – made that much more difficult by the fact that he had to hold onto the gun – allowed him to activate the tool's video recording software. He was going to livestream this.

Dave was ready to punch a hole in the dashboard. Through the windshield of his car, he saw nothing but the glowing red taillights of an old minivan that had moved a grand total of five inches in the last twenty minutes. The lane to his left was just as motionless, cars packed so closely together their bumpers were almost touching.

The sun was beating down from the clear blue sky, turning this car into an oven. Oh, he had air conditioning, but it was far less effective when your engine was just idling for long stretches of time.

Dave scrubbed a hand over his sweaty face, then ran fingers through his short dark hair. "Won't be much longer," he said, glancing to his wife. "We make it past the 295, and traffic should start to thin out."

It was a mass exodus from the city that had begun when Grecken Slade's people started shooting random civilians this afternoon. Now the Interstate was packed, and traffic was at a standstill.

At thirty-one, Marissa was gorgeous in a denim skirt and red tank-top, her bronze skin glistening with a light sheen of sweat. She stared through the window with her lips pressed into a thin line. "Turn off the radio?"

Dave shut his eyes, hissing air through his teeth. "I want to listen to it," he said, instinctively twisting the volume knob. "You never know; he might say something that will give us a clue as to what he's planning."

"And why would we want to know that?"

Baring his teeth, Dave looked down into his lap. "So that we can avoid the problem areas, hon," he muttered under his breath. "I don't know about you, but I would rather not drive right into a massacre."

Grecken Slade's message was playing on a loop on every station. Somehow the evil son of a bitch had managed to take over the airwaves, and now it was either listen to him or provide your own music. No chance of getting quality news either. It made Dave feel sick to his stomach.

"You think yourselves free?" Slade's voice came through the speaker, dripping with contempt. "Your arrogance sickens me. I ruled over you once, and then I let you go in the vain hope that perhaps you would achieve *some* level of independence. I see now that the time has come for me to take a firmer hand.

"You will kneel," Slade growled. "I have no patience for disobedience. Those of you who refuse will be extinguished. Painfully."

Dave's knuckles whitened as he gripped the steering wheel. Four years ago, when the Leyrians came to Earth for the first time, everyone had thought that they were some sort of enlightened people. Turns out they were just as capable of producing demagogues as anyone else.

"Those of you who try to flee," Slade continued, "will die painfully."

Dave leaned back in his seat with arms folded, frowning into his own lap. "Well, that's just grand," he rasped, noting the bile boiling in his belly. "Bastard really thinks he can kill everyone who tries to leave the city."

"Maybe we should go back," Melissa whispered.

"Like hell."

Of course, when he looked through the windshield, that minivan had moved three feet at most. They were not getting out of this city any time soon, and it occurred to him that they were sitting ducks out here. "I'll pull off at the next-"

He cut off when he noticed something bizarre – a tall, well-muscled shirtless man leaping onto the roof of a vehicle three cars away. The guy was pale and bald as an eagle, lacking visible body hair of any kind.

He spun to face them.

Dave pressed his back into the seat cushion, his jaw dropping as he stared through the glass. "What the hell is that?" he asked, pointing. "That thing...What's he got attached to him there?"

The bald man had some kind of device *built* into his chest, like some kind of mini-computer or something. Dave had to wonder if this guy was even human. Suddenly, he knew that Slade was quite capable of making good on his threats.

"Run!" Dave shouted.

He unbuckled his belt, barely aware of Marissa doing the same beside him. They had to get out of here. Now. Killing the engine, he pulled his keys from the ignition and ventured another glance through the window.

The bald man lifted a black sphere in one hand, a sphere that was just a little bigger than a basketball. He tapped one button, and that was it.

The last thing Dave saw was a roaring wave of orange coming toward him, as if the sun itself had come to Earth and consumed everything in fire.

9

A gray van drove up a street in Brooklyn lined with buildings that were no more than three or four stories tall, making its way toward the sinking sun. The only car on the road, unless you counted those that were parked on each curb. Traffic should have been flowing at a steady rate, but the city looked deserted. The only thing missing was a plastic bag blowing in the wind.

Anna stepped out from the arch-shaped entrance of a store.

She wore a pair of denim shorts, a black t-shirt with the Batman logo, and a cap that did very little to keep the sun out of her eyes. Instinctively, she reached for the pistol that should have been holstered on her hip, but wasn't. They had come without weapons. Jena said the point was to be inconspicuous.

Anna bit her lip, looking down at the sidewalk. She brushed a strand of hair out of her face. "Watch the periph," she muttered. "I want plenty of warning if one of Slade's hit squads decides to pay us a visit."

Behind her, the silhouette of Raynar stepped out and turned his head to survey his surroundings. "I'm not sensing anything," he whispered. "No hostility anyway. There's so much anxiety I feel like I'm wading through a swamp."

Anna nodded.

Whatever Raynar felt, it must have been coming from the people who were taking refuge in those buildings; her spatial awareness detected no movement of any kind aside from trees on the sidewalk that occasionally lost a few leaves. For two days, the city had been on high alert.

Every major freeway had been damaged when one of those creepy *ziarogati* used a plasma bomb to destroy people were just trying to get out of the kill zone. Those people who survived the blast had abandoned their cars right there on the road, creating a clog of traffic that prevented anyone else from trying to escape, although she had heard stories of cars driving on the wrong side of the road in some frantic attempt to flee the city.

Bombs at the train station, hit squads at the SlipGate terminal: Slade had done one heck of a job of discouraging his new subjects from leaving. For twenty-four hours after the mayhem had started, the police had tried to keep order, but the paramilitary psychos who treated Slade like their new messiah had a habit of gunning down anyone who wore a uniform. And plenty of people who didn't as well.

On top of that, there were *ziarogati* roaming the city.

She turned back to Raynar.

The kid stood there with his head turned so that she saw his profile, frowning into the street. "Something..." he muttered under his breath. "It's hard to tell what. Anger and fear and *something*."

"Where?"

"Everywhere."

Anna crossed her arms, approaching the boy with her head down. It was instinct; she didn't want anyone seeing her face. "Come on," she said. "Let's stay focused on the job. We find food, and we bring it to the safe house."

She turned and started up the sidewalk again. There was a

convenience store not far from here – or so she had been told – and if the shelves hadn't been picked clean yet, her people would have supplies for a few more days.

Anna scrunched up her face as if she had just bit into a lemon. "I don't know about you," she began in a harsh voice. "But if I have to have Pop-Tarts for breakfast one more time, my stomach is going to implode."

"I kind of like 'em."

"Too sugary for me," she said. "I mean I have a sweet tooth, but I'm eating for two. And Seth prefers it when we get proper nutrients. What I wouldn't give for some fruit and maybe a little yogurt."

The convenience store occupied the first floor of a red-bricked building that stood four stories tall, and the shattered front window told her that their chances of finding any food that hadn't passed the expiry date were slim.

Once inside, she saw that the situation was even worse than she had imagined. The shelves had been ransacked, and the candy rack at the front counter was equally barren. Shelves behind the counter that would have contained cigarettes – a filthy habit, that – were empty, but she spotted a few empty packs here and there. Of course, the owner was no where in sight.

Clenching her teeth, Anna felt sweat on her forehead. "Glorious," she said, moving deeper into the store. "The neighbourhood has to ration these supplies until we get food shipments going again. Instead, they do this..."

Behind her, Raynar stood with hands clasped behind his back, his head hanging in dismay. "I think you give people too much credit," he muttered. "This is what they'll do every time things get rough."

Anna stood with fists on her hips, shaking her head. "Indeed..." she said softly. "A year spent living on this planet is enough to shatter anyone's faith in the general goodness of humankind."

"Slade is Leyrian, you know."

She turned.

Anna lifted her chin to study him, slowly arching one thin eyebrow. "What's your point?" she asked in that dangerous voice she never intended to use. "Now might not be the best time for the 'human nature' lecture."

The kid went red and refused to look up at her. He scrubbed his fingers through his thick blonde hair. "Yeah, I get that...But there's nothing here. Maybe we should look for another store?"

"Let's go."

A scream pierced the air.

She charged forward, leaping through the broken window in the time it took most people to blink. She landed hard on the sidewalk, bending her knees to cushion the blow, then took stock of her surroundings.

There was no one on the street – no one to the left, and no one to the right – and no traffic either. Of course, anyone could be hiding behind the cars on the opposite curb; her Nassai couldn't see through solid objects.

Squeezing her eyes shut, Anna trembled as she drew in a hissing breath. "You know what I hate most?" she asked, turning back to Raynar. "Feeling helpless. I hate knowing that someone needs my-"

Another scream.

The convenience store was located on a street corner, and now that she was out in the open, it was clear that whoever was making noise – a young woman by the sound of it – was doing so around the side of the building. In fact, she could just barely make out the sounds of an intense struggle.

Anna turned, charging up the sidewalk, rounding the corner before it even occurred to her that she might want to use caution. The Bleakness take her impulsiveness! On the adjoining sidewalk, she found two men in shorts and t-shirts who had cornered some poor woman against the brick wall.

The lady was tall and slim in a blue sundress under a white cardigan, her blonde hair left to hang loose to the small of her back. "Back off!" she screamed, clutching a set of keys as if she meant to stab them with it. "I'm warning you..."

The first man put his hands on his hips and towered over her, clearly undaunted by her threat. "Yeah, I'm real scared," he mocked. "Just give me the damn purse and my bro and I will leave you alone."

"Back off!"

They moved in closer.

"*Heh-hem!*"

At the sound of Anna clearing her throat, both men froze in place and then slowly turned to face her. They might have been twins if not for the fact that one was clearly a few years older than the other. So "bro" was literal then.

"Walk away," Anna warned.

The first one – the one who had done all the talking – closed his eyes and shook his head. "Now why would I do that?" he asked, striding forward until he was looming over her. "Look, I just want to get some food, but the people who are selling aren't taking cash anymore. She's gotta have something in there: a phone, some jewelry. So I really have to ask. If I'm robbing one woman, what makes you think I'll stop for another?"

Pressing her lips together, Anna looked up to blink at him. "You really have no idea who you're dealing with," she murmured. "Do the words 'Justice Keeper' mean anything to you?"

The man grinned, bowing his head to stare down at his own shoes. "Nice try," he said, gesturing to her. "But I'll take anything *you've* got too. Phone, wallet, keys. Right now, it's every man for himself, and I'm a whole lot bigger than you."

Her anger flared hot and bright. Another arrogant jerk-wad who assumed that size was the most important factor in any conflict. Her years of training, focus and discipline all made irrelevant by the fact that she was tiny. What she wouldn't give to teach him the depth of his mistake.

Those idiots outside the thrift shop – the ones who had tried to beat up Jack – had learned to their sorrow not to underestimate her based on size. "If you really want a fight," she said, stepping forward and standing on her toes for added height. "I'd be more than happy to make you regret your stupidity."

Raynar came around the corner.

The boy's silhouette was right behind her, standing with his hands in his pockets and directing a small smile at the other man. This close, she could make out the curve of his lips. "But he doesn't want to have a fight."

The man who stood before Anna suddenly blinked in confusion. He shook his head as if trying to clear the fog out of his brain. "I...You got stuff I can use. Your phone, your wallet and anything else. *Now.*"

"She's scarier than she looks," Raynar said.

In response, the man's face went bone white, and he stared at Anna as he would an oncoming freight train. "I...You got stuff..."

"Let this one go, friend."

The man turned around, hiding his face in his hands, and for a moment, it looked like he might start crying. "Yeah," he whispered. "Let's get out of here. We don't want anything they've got."

His younger brother began to protest, of course, but Raynar had put the fear of the Bleakness itself into those two. In seconds, they were turning around and scurrying up the sidewalk like a couple of frightened raccoons.

Anna winced, breathing deeply to maintain her composure. "Thank you," she said with a curt nod. "But I could have handled those two. You really didn't need to work your mojo on them."

Raynar was smiling down at himself, chuckling softly. "We're trying to keep it low-pro, remember," he said, nudging her shoulder. "There are solutions that don't require so much flash, boom, bang. Yeah?"

"I suppose."

The woman in the sundress was standing against the wall with her arms folded, hunched over so far she was practically bent in half. "Thank you," she said, shaking her head. "Those two would have…"

"You can come with us," Anna said.

"Where?"

"We have a safe house. Come on."

The walk back was a quiet, solemn affair for Anna. Instead of bringing back food, they were returning with yet another person in need of safety and supplies. Jena wouldn't be happy, but she would bear it with her usual quiet dignity followed by bitter ranting. In the end, she would take in Krista without complaint.

The real problem, in Anna's opinion, was her eagerness to leap into a fight just to prove her capability. Not so long ago, the thought of doing violence would have turned her stomach, and now she was *eager* for it? What exactly was this world doing to her? Well, it wasn't the world itself…It was the way everyone with a Y-chromosome dismissed her as incompetent or irrelevant. She wanted to go home. She would do her duty to the bitter end, but there was a part of her that longed for simpler days.

The safe house was a red-bricked building on Bergen Street with windows on each of its three stories and steps leading up to the front door. Once inside, she found people milling about in the front hallway.

An open door led into an apartment where furniture had been pushed against the living room walls, leaving space for a round wooden table in the middle of the floor. It wasn't an apartment anymore so much as a base of operations.

The man who sat in a wooden chair was tall and well-muscled with a thin beard on his copper-skinned face and black hair that he wore parted to the left. "No," he growled, shaking his head. "I've got twenty good men ready to go."

Detective Pedro Juarez had been climbing the ranks of the NYPD until Slade came along and turned this city into a war zone, and from the moment they had met him just a few short days ago, he had been eager to gather a squad of his cop buddies, pick up as many guns as he could manage and take the fight to Slade.

Jena stood over the table with her arms crossed, dressed in gray pants and a beige trench coat that fell almost to her knees. Her face glistened with sweat, and her boyish auburn hair was a mess. "And I've told *you*," she insisted. "You aren't equipped to go up against the havoc Slade will throw at you."

Pedro slid his chair back.

Jena leaned forward, slamming her hands down on the table's surface and growling at him with teeth bared. "You're gonna listen to me, Pete," she hissed. "I'm not willing to waste lives needlessly."

Biting her lip, Anna looked down at herself, a lock of hair falling over one eye. "It may not be so simple," she said, striding into the living room. "We found nothing on this run. A few more days, and our supplies will be gone."

A cellphone was sitting in the middle of the table with its screen pointed up at the ceiling, and she could see from the display that Pedro had called his Captain. "It's much the same up in Queens. Director Morane, we *can* mobilize when you need us."

"Not yet."

"We need a victory, Jen," Anna said.

The other woman looked up at her with brown eyes that could set a block of ice on fire, then heaved out a sigh. "I've been thinking the same thing," she said, backing away from the table. "But this one's on us."

Anna wrinkled her nose, then shook her head in frustration. "Five people against a squad of Slade's goons?" she exclaimed. "With *ziarogati* in the mix? You have to know the odds of that are bad."

"I'm aware."

"We need all the help we can get."

In a heartbeat, Pedro was on his feet and pacing a line across the room with fists clenched. He stopped at the wall, whirled around and turned back. "So far as I know, Director Morane, you're the only Keepers in town."

"What's your point?"

"In war, you defend your best weapons. *You* are our best weapons. So my guys will back you up because one of you is worth ten of us."

Just hearing that turned Anna's stomach; it was the exact antithesis of everything the Justice Keepers stood for. "No," she insisted. "You've got it backwards. We protect you; you don't protect us."

Pedro gave her his attention.

"If I may make a suggestion?" Aamani cut in.

Sitting primly in a pair of beige pants and a tight t-shirt that revealed an impressive figure for a woman who was pushing fifty, she rose from her chair with the smooth grace of a raindrop sliding down a window pane. "Anna is correct," she said. "We need a major victory, and we need it now."

The woman stood as still as a statue with hands folded behind herself, directing a tight-lipped frown at Jena. "Your loath to engage Slade's forces," she said, raising one dark eyebrow. "May I assume that is because he will retaliate the instant you do."

"Got it in one," Jena replied.

Aamani closed her eyes, bowing her head to the other woman. One deep breath, and then she was the very definition of composure once again. "Then perhaps your goal should be to control *where* and *when* he retaliates."

Tilting her head back, Anna blinked at the ceiling. "Here's as good a place as any," she said, gesturing to the window. "We evacuate the neighbourhood and make our stand right here in Brooklyn."

"I'm in on that," Pedro said.

Jena whirled around to face him, striding forward until she was practically nose to nose with the man. "No, you're not," she said, standing on her toes to give herself that half-inch she needed to loom over him. "This isn't a debate."

Pedro's face crumpled, and he tossed his head about with a growl. "My people are an asset to you," he insisted. "We're not just gonna sit still while-"

Jena turned her back on him and paced across the room until she was standing over the table. "Our first target will be one of those roving bands of wannabe soldiers," she said. "A pair of Keepers, a telepath and two highly-trained spies will be more than a match for that."

Anxiety squeezed Anna's stomach until she felt a little woozy. Thankfully, Seth was there to offer comforting emotions. She could sense the Nassai's confidence in her, and it made her want to stand up taller. Suppressing a smile took some effort. So distracted was she by the ego-boost that she almost failed to notice one very important detail.

You were wondering what had happened to your reluctance to do violence, Anna told herself. *Well, you'll be happy to know that it's still very much intact.*

The next few days were going to be rough.

The bedroom window looked out on Bergen Street from three stories up, but the only thing Anna could see when she peered through it was a solitary streetlight that cast a white glow down on the sidewalk below.

This wasn't her bedroom, of course – in fact, the *Star Wars* posters on every wall suggested that it belonged to a young person – but the family that had once claimed this apartment had been one of the first to be evacuated from the neighbourhood. Jena's plan would go into effect tomorrow. Taking down a team of half a dozen forty-something men with delusions of grandeur would be easy enough. The hard part would be what happened after Slade noticed their first strike.

Warriors with corrupted symbionts – and there was no telling how many Slade had under his command – and those twisted *ziarogati*... She had seen the mess Jack had made trying to take out that first one. Silver blood all over the walls. The *ziarogat* had pushed Jack to his limits, leaving him weak and exhausted. She had no illusions that she would have done any better in his place.

Right then, she wanted to snuggle into Bradley's arms. Her boyfriend had shown his usual level of stoic concern at the prospect of her going into a war zone. He hated the thought of anything happening to her, but he knew better than to voice his objections. She would have called him if she could, but they were trying to keep digital communication to a minimum.

The door swung open, revealing Gabi in a pair of shorts and a tank-top with thin straps standing in the hallway. Her long dark hair was left to hang loose, framing a face with the most solemn expression Anna had ever seen. "I guess we should turn in," she said. "Big day tomorrow."

Dressed in gray sweat pants and a black tank-top, Anna sat on the bed with her legs drawn up against her chest, hugging her knees. "You honestly think you can sleep?" she countered. "Somehow, I doubt it."

"Futile gestures," Gabi replied. "We seem to be prone to them."

"Seems like."

Gabi sat down on the edge of the mattress with hands on her knees, staring into her lap. "Well, at least we'll die with a positive outlook," she muttered. "Never underestimate the importance of a good attitude."

Anna grinned, slapping a hand over her face as a fit of giggles shook her body. "I'll remember that," she murmured. "I don't know, Gabs...I want to say something uplifting, but I just can't find the words."

"Perhaps there aren't any words."

Anna crossed her arms, then fell backwards, grunting when the back of her head hit the pillow. "Twenty-year-old me would have disagreed," she said. "The Anna who came to this world four years ago didn't believe in a no-win scenario."

"And now?"

"Now, I'm not so sure," she answered. "When I was growing up, I had such a pure, undiluted faith in the concept of universal justice. I figured that if we just tried to do the right thing, Providence would make up the difference. Something out there was looking out for us; you could call it the Companion or God...or maybe just the universe itself, but we weren't alone."

"And you no longer think that?"

Anna shut her eyes tight, hissing as she sucked in a deep breath. "After the things that I've seen," she began. "Sometimes, it just feels like things just keep on getting worse and worse, you know?"

The other woman frowned as she stared into the mirror

across from the foot of the bed. "I know what you mean," she said, nodding. "But if it means anything, the cynicism fades as you get older."

"Really?"

"It takes time...and perspective."

"And now I'm about to crawl under the covers with my recently-single best friend's ex-girlfriend," Anna said. "At least fate knows how to keep it interesting." Those words were a mistake – she knew it the instant she finished speaking – but there was no taking them back now.

Gabi stood.

She turned her back on Anna and faced the wall with her arms crossed. "It was for the best," she replied after a very long moment. "I'll always care about Jack, but we aren't right for each other...and besides, I'm not the one he really wants."

"Who does Jack really want?"

Turning partway around, Gabi looked over her shoulder with a tight frown. Then her expression softened, and she sat down on the bed once again. "Sometimes it's best to let people tell you in their own good time," she said softly. "And if you're really feeling that uncomfortable, you could always bunk with Raynar."

"No thank you!"

"That poor kid," Gabi said through a fit of laughter. "The way our luck goes, he'll be dead before he even gets laid."

"Nah! The universe isn't *that* unkind."

Gabi pulled the covers up over herself and sighed as she rested her head on the pillow. "Let's get some sleep," she murmured. "Like I said, big day tomorrow."

10

Sunlight from a clear blue sky shone down on a street lined with small red-bricked buildings of three or four stories. There were cars on each curb – vehicles that had been abandoned when their owners fled this part of town – but none were in motion.

Jena crouched on the sidewalk with her back pressed to a parked car, heaving out a deep breath. She wore a pair of jeans and a white t-shirt under her trench coat. Some folks would say that it was much too hot out for such clothing, but she liked the coat. It made her feel a little more bad-ass.

Jena closed her eyes, ignoring the prickle of sweat on her forehead. "Report," she said, lifting her arm to speak into her gauntlet. "My back's starting to hurt. Tell me we've got a viable target."

"A van is on the way," Pedro replied through the speaker.

A quick glance over her shoulder revealed Gabrina and Anna squatting side by side against the next car over. Both were dressed in civilian clothing, though Anna kept her gun clutched in one hand, held up in front of her face like a symbol of faith. They would be hearing the report as well.

"A pack of Slade's goons," Pedro went on. "We caught them making a mess down by the bridge, harassing people trying to get out of Manhattan. Word is that's where Slade has his weird cyber-soldiers."

It made sense; being the heartless bastard that he was, Slade would assume that if the Keepers finally got off their asses and decided to make a stand, they would do so in the most visible part of the city. The centre of commerce for half the world? Yeah...New York would make a fine symbol that the Keepers wouldn't want to lose. But she wasn't interested in duking it out with *ziarogati* on streets lined with skyscrapers. "You've got them coming this way?"

"I do," Pedro said. "Couple of my guys took some shots at their van. They didn't like that too much. I think they figured they crushed all resistance. They're on their way to you now, Jena. Be ready."

Tilting her head back, Jena squinted up at the sky. "I will be," she said, nodding. "Once we've got them in position, I want your people to keep driving. I don't need them throwing themselves in the mix."

"Understood."

She unclipped the metal disk that contained the multi-tool's processor from her gauntlet and set it on the hood of the car. A few taps at the screen, and she was able to activate the tool's camera function.

The footage was panoramic, and she was able to scroll from side to side by sliding her finger across the screen. All she saw were a few abandoned shops and a restaurant on the far side of the street. No sign of trouble.

"Two minutes," Pedro said.

Jena swallowed, then looked down at the sidewalk, a light breeze ruffling her hair. "All right," she said for everyone on the open calm line. "Everyone knows their lines by heart, I'm hoping. 'Cause we don't get a dress rehearsal."

Her people voiced their agreement.

"Aamani, are you in position?"

"I am," the woman said through the speaker. "And I must say, this rifle handles like a dream. The scope alone is magnificent."

"Just be ready to take the shot," Jena muttered. "Raynar?"

The boy's voice was steadier than she would have expected. Jena had to give him credit; he seemed to be in perfect control of himself. "I can see the van approaching from up here," Raynar said. "They're close. And, Director, I can *feel* hostility oozing from the mind of every man in that vehicle. These people aren't just doing a job. They *like* it!"

Clenching her teeth, Jena felt a wave of heat in her face. She hissed, then rubbed her brow with the back of her hand. "We'll see how much they like it when you put the fear of Bleakness itself into them."

"Ten seconds," Pedro said.

On her screen, Jena saw a small white car come screeching around the corner of an intersecting street. It sped up with such wild abandon, you might have thought the driver was trying to outrun the flood from a cracked dam. Those would be Pedro's buddies. No doubt they were terrified.

A gray van came around the corner mere moments later, speeding up as it pursued the fleeing car. Jena slid her finger across the screen, tilting the camera angle to catch a glimpse of the van's receding back end.

"Now!" she said.

Jena got to her feet and strode around the front end of the car she had been using for cover, a strange calmness coming over her as the cogs of the machine she had created all sprang into motion. This would be over in seconds.

Drawing aside her trench coat, Jena pulled a pistol from the holster on her hip and tapped a button on the back to power it up. Standard ammunition would do. She lifted the weapon in both hands.

The van was speeding away from her.

She fired.

One of the van's tires popped with a hissing sound, and the vehicle wobbled as the driver tried to regain control. It did no good. The van turned sideways – now blocking traffic in all directions – and came to a stop perhaps twenty paces away.

The driver's side was toward her, but she heard the distinct sound of a door sliding open and boots landing hard upon the pavement with eager footsteps. One man in black tactical gear poked his helmeted head around the back-end of the van.

Half a second later, men with assault rifles came around both ends, forming a line and lifting their weapons to point at Jena. All except the one in the middle. He carried a shotgun that he pumped.

Jena thrust a hand out, twisting space-time with the aid of her Nassai. The five men blurred into a streak of darkness just before a storm of bullets and buck-shot came at her. Each projectile flowed around her body in a convex pattern, zipping off into the distance behind her. That did nothing to soothe her anger. These murderous bastards fired without even bothering to identify their target! Worse yet, she couldn't stay here.

Jena winced, tears leaking from her eyes.

The barrage of gunfire continued without a moment's pause, and she was already beginning to feel a tingle in her skin. Soon it would become stinging pain. She had to get out of the line of fire. Now!

Creating a Bending was hard enough, but *moving* that Bending once you had set it in place? That was twice as difficult. Jena kept her "shield" up as she ran for the sidewalk opposite the car that she had been hiding behind.

The small Italian restaurant had a large front window that

looked in on an empty room filled with wooden tables and chairs. The lights were out. So far as she could tell, the place was deserted.

It would do.

Jena hurled herself shoulder-first through the window, allowing her Bending to collapse as glass rained down around her. She landed hard on the wooden floor and then rolled onto her back.

Bullets zipped through the air above her with sharp whistling sounds, striking the back wall of the restaurant and tearing the plaster to shreds. Less than ten seconds, and the place was already a wreck.

The gunfire stopped.

Jena stayed low, out of their line of sight. Her skin was already burning with sharp, fiery pinpricks, and there was no way she could fend off that much ammunition without another Bending. Had she been alone, she would have died miserably. Even Keepers had their limits.

Staying flat on her back meant the men wouldn't be able to see her as they slowly approached to finish the job, but it also meant she wouldn't be able to track them. Not even with her Nassai's spatial awareness. Fortunately, she had other options.

On her screen – the metal disk was still sitting undisturbed on the hood of the car she had used for cover – she saw the backs of five men in black body armour creeping slowly across the street with their weapons raised. Soon, they would be close enough to look through the shattered window and find her here.

Come on, people, Jena thought. *Don't leave me hanging.*

Suddenly, the men lifted their weapons to point at the sky and let loose with a storm of gunfire, barrels flashing and filling the air with a thunderous roar. This would be one of Raynar's telepathic manipulations.

One of the men spasmed as a stun-round hit the back of his neck, flailing about and dropping his rifle as he fell to his knees. Before anyone could react, a second round took the man next to him.

The other three spun around to face the camera and fired at something out of frame. The one in the middle pumped his shot-gun once before a bullet from Aamani's rifle hit him square in his throat and bounced off. Electric current knocked him out. Three down and two to go!

Lying stretched out on the floor, Jena lifted her pistol up in front of her face. "Stun rounds," she growled. The LEDs turned blue with a soft chirp to confirm that her order had been executed.

She sat up.

Through the shattered window, she saw two men standing with their backs turned and firing at the parked cars on the far side of the street. The other three had collapsed to the ground and were now stretched out on the road.

She fired.

A charged bullet hit the one on her left right in the soft spot between his armoured vest and his helmet. He stumbled as the current raced through his body, then dropped to his knees and passed out.

The final man spun around to aim his rifle in her direction. He spasmed before he could put her in his sights and lost his footing. Half a second later, he fell flat on his face in the middle of the road.

When the smoke cleared, she saw that two of the three cars on the other side of the street now had bullet holes in their driver-side doors. Anna's head popped up from behind one of them, and the girl blinked.

Jena shut her eyes tight, trembling as she drew in a ragged breath. "We did it," she said, getting to her feet and carefully stepping through the shattered window. "First round goes to us, but it only gets a whole lot harder now that we've bloodied Slade's nose."

Anna came scurrying out from behind the car and quickly turned to sprint toward the abandoned van. In a heartbeat, she was ducking behind it, no doubt poking her head inside to see what she could find. Jena had clicked her tongue in frustration. The girl was far too impulsive for her own good.

For all she knew, there were three more men with military-grade hardware waiting inside. Not that Jena didn't trust the girl to handle herself, but it would have been nice if she didn't insist on taking unnecessary risks.

On the opposite sidewalk, Gabrina got to her feet and reached up to run her fingers through sweat slick hair that clung to her shirt. "We did it," she agreed, stepping forward and leaning against the side of the car she had been using for cover.

"We hit," Jena said. "Time to run."

"Hey, look at this!"

Anna emerged from behind the van with a box that she carried in both hands, a big grin on her face. "So much for the food shortage!" she said, reaching inside to pull out a few meal bars. "They've got a dozen boxes in there!"

"Half goes to the safe house," Jena barked as she marched into the road. "Distribute the rest to anyone who needs them."

One of the men was lying face-down on his stomach, groaning in pain. Stun-rounds didn't necessarily knock you unconscious, but they did leave you more or less immobile for the better part of an hour.

Jena nudged him with her foot, rolling him onto his back.

He stared up at her through the visor of his helmet, blinking as if the light hurt his eyes. "Who..." The man tried to sit up, then collapsed to the ground again. "Do you have any idea what you've done?"

Jena was about to reply with a biting comment when she noticed something. His vest had a camera that was pointed up at the clear blue sky. Time to put on a show then. She would be lying if she said she wasn't glad for the opportunity.

She crouched down beside him.

Seizing his vest in both hands, Jena pulled him up just enough to shove her face in the camera. "You watching this, Slade?" she asked. "Did you really think I was just gonna sit on my ass and let you turn this city into your own personal playground? Well, you know where I am, now. Come get me, fucker."

The fountain in Confederation Park sprayed a stream of white water toward a blue sky with just a few thin clouds. It had been nine months since Jack had last come here, and so much had changed. The ring of trees that encircled the fountain was now green with the vibrant life of summer.

His last visit had been during a time when the city was in a state of upheaval. Leo had terrorized the people to the point where most of them of them were afraid to leave their homes, and he had come here to give Selena Knowles an interview. At the time, Jack would have called it a low-point. He would not have been able to imagine how things could get worse.

It turned out that Leo's rampage through Ottawa was just the warm up act for the main event. Every part of him itched with a need to hop in a shuttle and join his friends on the streets of New York. But he had other duties.

Jack stood before the fountain with hands clasped behind his back, peering into the water. "You're late," he said, eyebrows rising. "How are you going to tell Mom that you left your little brother unattended in the park?"

He turned.

His sister Lauren strode toward him in a red sundress with thin straps, her long dark hair tied back in a braid, pulled away from a pale face with sharp blue eyes. It was good to see her; they hadn't spoken much lately.

She stepped up beside him with her arms folded, frowning into the bubbling water. "You realize that you're not one to talk, right?" she asked. "I seem to remember a saying about this. Something about a pot and a kettle."

He turned back to the fountain.

His faint reflection in the clear water wavered, and he found himself counting the coins down in the basin. "Well, you know me," Jack muttered. "Never was very good at waiting for anything."

"Don't I know it?"

Tilting his head back, Jack blinked when the sunlight hit his eyes. "Seems that's all I've been doing lately," he said, gently kicking the concrete basin. "Waiting for a chance to do something productive."

A frown tightened Lauren's mouth, and she squinted into the fountain. "Yeah, I was wondering about that," she replied. "With all the chaos, I figured they'd send you to New York with the other Keepers."

Baring his teeth, Jack shook his head. "Jena has other plans for me," he muttered. "Stuff that she wants kept 'Hush to the Power of Hush' or I'd have told you the specifics a long, long time ago."

"Sounds dangerous."

Jack turned aside.

He marched across the concrete with his arms folded, smiling down at himself. "It is," he said with a shrug of his shoulders. "But as you've reminded me many times, I did *choose* this life."

A ring of benches surrounded the fountain, shaded by the branches of the nearest trees. He chose one – the very same bench he had used when speaking with Selena – and sat patiently, taking comfort in Summer's presence.

His sister moseyed over with her arms crossed as well, shaking her head as she drew near. "I've learned not to try talking you out of anything," she said. "It usually only makes you that much more determined."

She sat down primly beside him, folding her hands in her lap and staring off into the distance. "So what's on your mind?" she murmured. "And don't give me any of that playing dumb routine. You wouldn't have called if you didn't want to talk."

Jack winced, letting his head hang. He pinched the bridge of his nose and breathed into his palm. "I'm being reassigned," he answered. "When this crisis is over, I'll be going to Leyria...permanently."

He'd been putting off this conversation for several days, using his job as an excuse to avoid giving his family news that would almost certainly break their hearts. Well...his mother and sister, anyway. Arthur would take the hit with his usual brand of tight-lipped assholery. Summer offered soothing emotions.

When he looked up, Lauren was watching the fountain with a blank expression, blinking slowly as she thought it over. "How do you feel about that?" she asked at last. "It's a pretty big change."

Jack felt his brow furrow, then rubbed his forehead with the back of his fist. "I've always wanted to see Leyria," he said. "And it's not like I can't come back and visit often. You'd be surprised how much vacation time Keepers get."

"You gonna miss it here?"

"More than you can imagine."

Thinking about leaving everyone behind – Anna and Harry, his mother and sister – left him with a dull ache in his chest that just wouldn't go away. In fact, he had come to realize that the pain of saying goodbye outshone anything he might have been feeling for Gabi. What did that say about his relationship?

Best not to think too deeply on that, he decided. The relationship was dead. No point in poking its corpse.

Jack stretched out with hands folded behind his head, smiling up at the clear blue sky. "It's funny," he said after a moment. "I spend most of my youth thinking about how much I want to get off this planet, and now that I can, I find I don't want to go."

Lauren had her eyes shut tight, tears glistening on her pale cheeks. "Indeed," she said, patting his leg. "I should have known this was coming. I did a reading for you the other night...The Death Card came up."

"Come on, Lauren."

"Oh, I forgot," she said through her own laughter. "My brother is the very soul of skepticism."

"I wouldn't say that," Jack countered. "I tend to think there's more to this universe than meets the eye. I don't believe for a second that death is the end of existence, and I'm fairly sure that I've been here before. With a different face and a different name...but still me, if you know what I mean.

"I have plenty of spiritual beliefs, Lauren. I just don't think you can learn anything about the future from playing cards. The universe is more subtle than that. If we could see the future by throwing dice or reading tea leaves, there wouldn't be any wars. Everyone would be prosperous and healthy.

"No, I won't say that precognition is entirely impossible; a few years ago, I would have thought that FTL travel is impossible. Who knows what's out there? But if there is a way to read the future, it requires thought and care. And it's probably only a glimpse of what is *likely* to happen. Not a guarantee."

"I see," Lauren murmured.

Jack stood, slipping his hands into his back pockets and taking a few steps away from the bench. In his mind's eye, he could see his sister watching him with a tense expression. "Just the same," he said. "I appreciate that you were thinking of me."

"Have you told Mom and Dad?"

"Not yet."

A soft, barely audible sigh escaped Lauren as she stood up to gently rest a hand on his shoulder. "Well, it seems I've only got a few more weeks with my little brother. I say we make the most of it."

"So, you let them...*change* you?"

Harry watched the dark red wine slosh about as he tilted the glass just enough to make the liquid flow. His reflection – faint and distorted as it was – looked the same as it always had. Deep down, he *felt* the same as he always had. There was no profound new awareness of the universe, no urge to suddenly 'crush the humans.' Nothing that any sane person might expect after being altered by an Overseer device.

Harry looked up, blinking as he tried to gather his thoughts. "What was that?" he asked, his brow furrowing. "I'm sorry; my mind was somewhere else. What was that you were asking me?"

On the far side of his kitchen table, Della stood with her arms folded, frowning at him. "I asked you to repeat yourself," she said, bending over to loom over him like a teacher who had just caught a student with chewing gum. "How could you just *let* those things screw around with your mind."

Harry winced, pressing a palm to his forehead. A low groan escaped his lips. "I did not *let* them do anything, Della," he snapped. "We needed the information in the device. I activated it, and it...changed me."

His ex-wife frowned.

That was as much as he could tell her, of course – he wasn't about to risk his highly irresponsible ex learning about his search for the Key – but it would be enough to make the point. Sadly, he had to tell her this much. Harry was no fool. He felt like himself, but if these changes affected his ability to look after the girls...

Della practically fell into the chair across from him, setting her elbows on the table and burying her face in her hands. "All right," she said. "Well, if you say you feel okay, I guess I believe you."

"That's a first."

"And possibly the last." She sat up with some effort, pausing for a moment to get her bearings. "I still can't believe you let Melissa go...Well, I suppose there would be no stopping her."

Sipping his wine to collect his thoughts, Harry fought down a wave of annoyance at the accusation. "I believe you told me that yourself just a few months ago," he answered. "She's not a kid anymore, Della. In a few weeks, she'll be training to be a Keeper."

"What do you suppose that will be like?"

A frown tugged at the corners of Harry's mouth, and he bowed his head to stare into his lap. "I honestly don't know," he said. "But I would imagine that they'll keep her away from the more dangerous missions until she gets her symbiont."

"Do something for me, Harry."

He looked up to find his ex-wife watching him with eyes that glistened, her blonde hair a mess. Was she crying? He couldn't remember the last time Della had ever cried about anything. "Take her to Leyria."

"To Leyria?"

With a grunt, Della stood and then lost her balance, bracing one hand on the table for support. Was everything all right there? "Della?" he inquired, hoping she would be willing to provide some insight.

"Just a headache."

Della closed her eyes and touched two fingers to her forehead, soothing away the pain. "This planet's a hot mess, Harry," she said. "I mean, look at everything we've seen in the last year.

Nine months ago, I was shipping our kids off to Alberta because a terrorist might attack their school. Instead, he comes to *this very house.*

"Six months ago, I turn on the news to discover that the Keepers tried to arrest the head of their organization, and – worse yet – he escaped, nearly killing everyone aboard one of those space stations in the process. Now, New York is in flames. It's not safe here, Harry. It hasn't been safe since the day your friend Anna arrived. If Melissa is determined to train as a Justice Keeper, let her do so in a place where she isn't likely to be killed by an explosion or God knows what else."

He paused for a moment to think on that, a knot of worry forming in his chest and making it difficult to keep his breathing steady. "You want to just send her off to an alien world all by herself?" he asked. "She's a capable girl, Della, but she's not invulnerable. Besides, I'm not sure I can."

Della made her way through his galley-style kitchen, running her fingers along the counter. "Don't give me that," she said after a moment. "We both know you're very well connected among the Keepers. You ask, and that girlfriend of yours will oblige."

"Still, I can't just send her off alone."

In the blink of an eye, Della rounded on him with her arms crossed, her teeth bared in a snarl. "Then go with her!" she said. "God, Harry, do I have to think of everything tonight?"

Biting his lip, Harry let his head hang. He ran fingers through his thick black hair. "And what about Claire?" he inquired. "How's she going to get by when her father is so far away that she won't see him for months at a time?"

"Leave Claire to me."

"Della..."

"I'm serious, Harry."

Words found their way into his thoughts – protests that she was just dead wrong this time – but he didn't voice any of them.

Because she wasn't wrong. Melissa would be safer on Leyria, and...And if there were any lasting side-effects from whatever it was the Overseers had done to him, he would get better help on Leyria.

Of course, going meant splitting up his family, and that left him with an ache in his chest that he would rather forget. He sighed. It seemed he was going to have an awful lot to think about.

Steel bars that ran from floor to ceiling formed the front wall of a cell that housed five men who had been stripped to their boxers and undershirts. The ringleader – a tall man with pale skin and a dark moustache that matched his short, jet-black hair – paced a line across the floor.

His four companions sat on the bench across from him, each with head hanging. They refused to look up at him. Perhaps they felt that being captured was some kind of personal failing on their part. It didn't matter. After this afternoon's skirmish, Jena had ordered these men taken to the Fifth Precinct in Brooklyn where some of Pedro's people still operated the building with minimal staff.

The leader stopped in the middle of the cell.

Looking positively ridiculous in black shorts and a matching undershirt, he spread his arms wide. "You're not even gonna kill us?" he shouted. "I knew it from the day you first came here! You Leyrians are soft."

Jena stood outside the cell with arms folded, head hanging with exhaustion. "Keep on talking," she muttered under her breath. "Make a big enough fuss, and you might just convince me of the necessity."

The man turned.

His mouth was split into a hideous grin, his face flushed to a soft pink. "Weak and sentimental," he said, approaching the bars. "Funny thing about all those empty threats? They're just so...empty."

"What's Slade's plan?" she asked for the tenth time.

"To make America great again."

Well, this was getting her no where by the swiftest route possible. The ethics of this ugly little scenario had played out in her head perhaps a hundred times since they had secured these losers and their supplies. Technically, she was fighting a guerrilla war. That meant these men were her enemies, and she should do away with them immediately. But Keepers weren't meant for warfare.

She could lecture Anna all she liked about the necessity of making hard choices, but in her heart, Jena *did* believe in the ideals of the Justice Keepers. Violence should always be a last resort.

Lifting her chin to stare down her nose at him, Jena arched one thin eyebrow. "So, Slade's plan is to gain followers with empty slogans," she said. "Does that mean you'll fight for me if I give you one of those posters that says 'Hang in there kitten, it's almost Friday?"

"Your people are weak, and you'll make us weak too."

"Really?"

The man stepped forward, gripping two bars and shoving his face into the space between them. "Just look at your decadent culture," he hissed. "There's no challenge in anything. Everyone's just fat and happy."

"Is that how the rest of you feel?"

The other men just sat with hands on their knees, staring into their own laps. One ventured a glance in her direction, but he stiffened at the sight of her and returned his attention to the floor.

Not that she had high hopes for gaining much useful information from these men. Flunkies were rarely made privy to the finer details of a master plan. Her Nassai felt pity for the lot of them; Jena felt irritation.

176

She turned.

Officer Hanks stood halfway down a corridor with cells in one wall, still dressed in his uniform. A tall man with a dark complexion and not one hair on his head, he nodded as she approached.

Jena closed her eyes, then covered her face with one hand. She massaged away the beginnings of a headache. "I want them monitored at all times," she said. "If even one of them gives you trouble, put a bullet in him."

"Yes, ma'am."

She strode past him toward a metal door at the end of the hallway that led out to the reception area. One of the bulbs in the ceiling was flickering, and it filled the air with an annoying buzzing sound.

So, they were really in the thick of it now. All day long, she had been wondering if she would be able to stand up to one of those cybernetic killing machines the Overseers had engineered specifically to destroy Justice Keepers. At least, she thought that was their purpose. After hearing Jack's account of the creature he faced in Pennfield's mansion, she realized that she had fought a rudimentary version of those on that troop carrier. In barely one year, the Overseers had perfected their creations. It made her shiver.

The door to the reception area could only be opened from the outside, but once Officer Spinelli buzzed her through, she found herself in a small room with white floor tiles and plastic chairs along three of its gray walls. A desk next to the door to the cell-block was operated by an older man in a blue uniform who frowned down at a stack of papers. Spinelli was a good guy, or so Pedro insisted.

In her mind's eye, she saw that Aamani had been waiting next to the door, and the woman wasted no time chasing after her. "You're going to let them live?" she asked with disdain in her voice. "Is that wise?"

Tossing her head back, Jena rolled her eyes. "Someone else wants to give me their opinion," she said, whirling around to face the other woman. "Come on, Aamani. Do you really think I haven't weighed the pros and cons?"

Aamani frowned, then looked down at the floor beneath her shoes. "I would remind you that keeping them alive means you have to feed them," she said. "Our food supplies are thin enough as is."

"Noted."

"If they have no valuable information-"

Jena felt a grin blossom, then shook her head with wry amusement. "You're just not gonna give up, huh?" she muttered. "What do you wanna do, Aamani? Make them kneel down in the yard, put guns to the backs of their heads and shoot?"

"I don't know."

"Well, I'm glad to hear that," Jena said. "Because I don't think anyone should take on the role of executioner lightly. I'm leaving my options open. If I decide that keeping these men alive is too dangerous or too costly, believe me, I won't hesitate."

Outside the cell block's reception area, a long hallway with wooden doors in both walls stretched on to an intersection where an American flag stood proudly in the corner. Anna came striding through the corridor in beige pants and a blue t-shirt, her red hair tied up in its customary ponytail. "You'll never guess who I ran into."

She turned, gesturing into the distance behind her.

A young woman in gray pants and a blue shirt with the insignia of the med-corps on the breast came around the corner in a hurry. Her black hair was pulled back from a face with smooth, mocha skin, bright red lips and lovely dark eyes. How quickly things could change. Just a few months ago, the girl had been a gangling teenager.

Closing her eyes, Jena heaved out a sigh. "Melissa," she said, nodding to the girl. "Good to see you. I hope you've been following my orders and keeping your ass out of the hot-zone."

Melissa smiled, then bowed her head, reaching up to brush a strand of hair off her cheek. "As much as I can," she answered. "We go where we're needed, and it's getting pretty bad out there."

"You have a report for me?"

"I do."

"Spill it."

Melissa stood in the hallway with arms folded, grunting softly as she stared down at her feet. "President Mitchell sent in the National Guard two days ago," she said, taking a hesitant step closer. "They didn't have much trouble clearing out some of the nut-jobs who think they're playing real-life *Call of Duty,* but then Slade sent a few of those weird cybernetic things."

Jena winced, shuddering softly as she took a deep breath. "Well, we knew that was coming," she muttered under her breath. "Someone really should have warned the locals that they aren't equipped to deal with Slade."

"There was a skirmish on the Upper West Side," Melissa explained. "The American troops had tanks, but Slade's creatures set off some kind of EMP blast, and then they were just sitting ducks."

It made Jena sick.

Melissa turned her head to stare at the wall, a single tear rolling down her cheek. "I never..." Her words were forced, her voice strained. "I've never seen that kind of carnage before. The people there..."

"Try not to think too much about it."

A few paces down the hallway, Anna had one hand pressed to her stomach as she stared at a picture on the wall. It was a painful reminder that neither one of these women had seen the true horrors of warfare. Bleakness take her, Jena was hardly one to talk! As much as she considered herself to be made of tougher stuff than most of her colleagues, she had completed almost every assignment in her long career without having to employ deadly force. Just a few minutes ago, she was insisting that she wouldn't kill the prisoners unless they gave her a damn good reason.

"There's some good news," Melissa said.

"Let's hear it."

"When Tiassa found out that you and Anna were missing, she was furious. It turns out you weren't the only one pushing for an immediate response, and the other Keepers saw this as the perfect excuse to take action. Tiassa ordered them to stay out of the city, but all it did was convince them that she was incompetent at best and a traitor at worst. Most of the Senior Directors disregarded those orders. By my last count, there are five other teams making their way through the city, hunting for Slade."

It was all Jena could do to avoid jumping and pumping her fist in the air. Finally, some results! She was quick to assume that her colleagues were a bunch of sheep who would follow any moron who could shout "Baah!" at the top of his lungs, but even the most arrogant, closed-minded Keepers had their limits. Relief flooded through her when she realized that the people she had known for years weren't too gullible to see obvious treachery when it was right in front of their faces. "Excellent!" Jena said. "Give me the names of the directors who mutinied, and we can plan a coordinated strike."

"Well that's just it," Melissa mumbled. "You can't plan anything. A few hours ago, something started jamming every radio signal in this city. Communications are cut off. Multi-tools don't work; cell phones don't work."

Lifting her arm, Jena rolled up the sleeve of her trench coat and began tapping the screen of her multi-tool. She brought up the communications app and tried to place a call to Station

Twelve. Her heart sank when she saw two small words blinking in blue text.

No signal.

She switched to SlipSpace frequencies and found the same result. Something had flooded the local area with so much noise that she couldn't cut through it. The factors started adding up in her head.

From the moment they first bonded their symbionts, Keepers were taught about the importance of thinking for yourself. Authority that did not serve the needs of the people was illegitimate and should be cast down. Keepers were supposed to be a check against the abuse of power. Their ranks – while useful for coordinating operations – were really more of a formality. Herding Keepers was about as hard as herding cats.

Slade understood this simple truth, and he had exploited it with such a deft hand, even Jena hadn't seen the con until it was too late.

Tiassa's bogus orders were just a little too obvious. A few days ago, Jena had wondered why none of her colleagues had questioned a clear violation of their mandate, but her cynical outlook had prevented her from thinking too deeply on the matter. People were sheep! Of course they didn't question!

When Keepers disobeyed their superiors, they very seldom did so as a coordinated effort. Five Senior Directors had grown fed up with Tiassa's flagrant incompetence, and so they led their teams into the city. Alone. Five teams of Justice Keepers were roaming the streets of New York, cut off from each other. Unable to communicate.

Easy meat for Slade's *ziarogati*.

Covering her gaping mouth with three fingers, Jena felt her eyes widen. "No," she whispered, backing away from Melissa. "He couldn't have...There's no way...But he did! He used me like a puppet!"

Anna rushed over with concern in her big blue eyes, her face growing paler by the second. "What is it?" she asked. "What did he do?"

Jena shut her eyes, hot, sticky tears on her cheeks. "They're all gonna die," she whispered. "Don't you see, Anna? Grecken Slade turned this whole city into one giant Keeper trap, and we played right into his hands!"

11

No battle plan ever survives contact with the enemy. Jena had read that once – she couldn't remember where – and she could earnestly testify that every single word of that maxim was true. Nearly twenty-four hours after their skirmish with the men who now sat half-naked in a prison cell, Slade had brought the hammer down.

Jena was crouched on a driveway with her back pressed to the tailgate of a white pick-up truck, right behind the passenger-side wheel. *Come on,* she thought, shaking her head. *You've faced down terrorists with high-tech plasma weapons.*

The little gray-bricked house that claimed this driveway as its own had shattered windows in its front walls and bullet holes in the big wooden door. Thankfully, no one was home. The last evacuees had departed last night.

She peeked around the corner of the truck.

A soldier in black tactical gear stood on the far side of the street, just in front of a house with white aluminum siding. The man lifted his AR-15, growling as he took aim.

Jena ducked back behind the truck.

Three bullets sped past just an inch to her left, striking the wooden gate that led to this house's backyard. A simple three round burst. These guys were getting smarter. Yesterday, they were just emptying entire clips at anything in their paths. Idiots high on rage and testosterone.

Closing her eyes, Jena banged the back of her head against the tailgate. *Come on, Raynar,* she thought desperately. *I could really use a distraction right about now. Just a few seconds, huh?*

The young telepath seemed to be otherwise engaged right now. Well, she wasn't entirely helpless. Keepers were trained to rely on conventional combat skills before they looked to a Nassai for help.

Jena detached the metal disk from her gauntlet, setting it down next to her so that it would get a clear view underneath the truck. A few taps at her screen activated the multi-tool's camera.

She saw a pair of black boots step onto the foot of the driveway. The soldier – if you could call him that – was cautiously making his way forward, trying to box her in. Jena lifted her pistol up in front of her face. The LEDs were dark, indicating that she was using standard ammunition.

She swung her arm over the lip of the tailgate and fired.

Bullets crashed through the truck's back window and the windshield as well. On her screen, she saw the boots stagger backward as something hit her opponent hard in the chest. Most heavy body armour – even that of Earth design – would stop standard ammo, but a hit like that would hurt like the Bleakness itself.

"Stun rounds!"

Jena ducked around the side of the truck.

She stood, raising the pistol in both hands and firing the very instant her spatial awareness let her sense the man's position. She didn't look; she just fired.

One slug hit the soldier's chest, the current absorbed by his body armour. Another stung the soft skin of his neck, delivering an electric jolt that caused him to spasm and drop his weapon.

The man fell to his knees at the end of the driveway, then landed flat on his face. A few moments of stillness, and she knew that he was out of commission.

This quiet, suburban street lined with cute little houses looked perfectly normal if you didn't count the fact that many windows were broken, and cars along either curb had endured their share of gunfire.

She moved to the foot of the driveway.

To her left, a pair of men in black had their backs turned as they moved toward a house on her side of the street. A house with a big oak tree in the front yard. When last she checked, Aamani was taking refuge behind that tree.

Jena raised her weapon and fired.

A charged bullet hit one man in the back of his neck, causing his muscles to lock up before he sagged limply to the ground. The other man turned around, swinging his assault rifle to point at her.

Something hit the man from behind and he stiffened for half a second. Then he fell to the ground to lie sprawled out beside his companion in the middle of the road.

Aamani stepped out from behind the oak tree, carrying a small rifle with a scope. The woman wore simple track pants and a tank-top, and her skin glistened with sweat. "I do believe that's the last of them."

Jena closed her eyes, sweat drenching her face. "That's good," she said, wiping her forehead with the back of her fist. "Have Pedro bring the cruisers around. Let's get these guys back to the station."

"I've said it before, and I'll say it again."

Clenching her teeth, Jena winced and let her head hang. "We've been over this," she said, striding toward the other woman. "I'm not killing them. If even *one* of these people can tell me what Slade is planning..."

The other woman looked up to study her with a cold expression, her nostrils flaring with every breath. "You let these men live," she began, "and sooner or later one of them is going to give us trouble."

"We can handle it."

"I'm not looking to get a shot in the back."

Jena crossed her arms, doubling over when a wave of exhaustion hit her. "Then I suggest you pack up your things and go." Keeping the anger out of her voice required a lot of effort. "If you can't accept my command, then I've got no use for you. I refuse to have this argument every time-"

Aamani heaved out a deep breath, then spun around, turning her back on Jena. She marched back to the tree. "This is a war," she said, leaning her shoulder against the trunk. "You don't win a war by pulling your punches."

That was true.

Bleakness take her, under other circumstances, Jena might have made the exact same argument. It galled her to admit it, but part of her irritation came from the fact that Aamani just didn't seem to want to take orders from her. In fact, Jena had the impression that Ms. Patel preferred to be the one giving the orders.

"And what's more," Aamani went on, "I believe that-"

"Aamani...Not now."

When she turned around, Jena saw the blue van that Slade's goons had used sitting abandoned half a block up the street, turned so that its front end was pointed toward the houses on the other side of the road. That was part of their strategy; in every engagement she'd had with these half-trained idiots, they'd used their own vehicle as cover. Not a bad strategy, but it did allow her to have Anna, Gabi and several of Pedro's colleagues come around to close the trap on them from behind.

Gabi and Raynar were hauling the body of an unconscious man toward the curb where several of his companions were already stretched out. The boy grunted with the effort, his face contorted in pain. Jena really didn't blame him. When you spent the vast majority of your life in a prison cell, you didn't exactly have a chance to build muscle mass. More to the point, Keepers tended to take their strength for granted.

In her mind's eye, she saw a police cruiser come around the corner behind her and slowly make its way up the street. The suburbs in this part of Flushing were shaped like a grid, and that made it easy to get around. But also easy for her enemies to set up an ambush if they were so inclined.

The cruiser slowed to a crawl, then turned to face the side of the road so that it was parked parallel to the van. This would make it easier for her people to load the bodies of unconscious men into the backseat, and besides, with the van blocking traffic, they would have to turn around and come back the way they came.

Jena would take the van if she could – she made it her policy to take anything her enemies had to offer: weapons, ammunition, vehicles – but she was always worried that Slade might anticipate such a move and leave her a vehicle with a bomb in the back. You just never knew with that man.

Anna strode toward her with a gun in one hand, her eyes downcast, focused on the sidewalk. "We've stripped them of their weapons and armour," she explained. "Most are out cold, but some are groggy."

Tilting her head back, Jena shut her eyes. She took a deep breath through her nose. "Good job," she said in a hoarse voice. "I want them loaded up and on their way in the next five minutes."

"You think we should try questioning them?"

"You never know what we'll learn."

Anna crossed her arms, then turned her head so that Jena

saw her in profile. The girl wore a frown that could sour milk. "I overheard some of Aamani's protests. For what it's worth, I think you're doing the right thing."

"You know my lecture about hard choices."

"I do," Anna said in tones that suggested she was being cautious to avoid stepping on anyone's toes. "But I also know that in many ways, these men are also Slade's victims. I'm not sure what he did to gain such fanatics, but-"

"Yeah," Jena muttered. "I still don't like this; we came too far north. We should be fighting Slade's people on our own turf."

"Weren't you the one who said that he wouldn't expect-"

She cut off when the screech of tires drowned out all other noise.

Jena turned around to see a black van come around the same corner that Pedro's cop car had emerged from mere minutes earlier. This vehicle surged forward as if the driver meant to ram right through the cruiser that was now parked in the middle of the road. It swerved to the right so that its headlights were pointed at the curb. *Oh no...* Pedro's car was now sandwiched between this van and the other one.

Instantly, her people leaped into action, seeking cover behind the police cruiser, pointing weapons over the hood and the trunk in case they had to lay down suppressing fire. *They learn quickly.*

Anna rushed over, dropping to her knees among a group of Pedro's police officers, staying low so that her head wouldn't be visible through the cop car's windows. By her emphatic gestures, it was clear that she was already giving orders.

Jena hissed.

Allowing the cops to take part in these engagements had been a reluctant decision, and they were supposed to be confined to a support role. Now they'd be right in the thick of it when the shooting started.

Footsteps on the pavement announced a squadron of Slade's goons exiting their van. Half a moment later, they came around both ends of the vehicle in a flood. At least eight men in black tactical gear. Jena remained out in the open on purpose. Keepers were known for their cockiness, and she wanted to make sure that these idiots were thoroughly intimidated. Anna, on the other hand, was concealed so that if she had to bust out some of her fancier tricks, it would come as a shock to their opponents.

The soldiers lifted their weapons.

"Hold your fire!"

The order came from the other side of the street, and when Jena turned, she saw a man standing on the roof of a two-story house with gray aluminum siding. Tall and well-muscled, he wore a pair of blue jeans and a denim vest that revealed arms as thick as tree trunks. His pale face was marked by a square jaw, his dark hair buzzed to little more than stubble. "We've come a long way to meet this woman; let's not kill her before we have a chance to hear her speak."

Another figure landed on the roof beside him, this one short, slender and dressed in dark clothing. Her lovely, olive-skinned face was framed by dark brown hair that spilled over her shoulders.

Only one thing would allow those two to get up there with such ease. Bent Gravity. Those two had symbionts.

Craning her neck, Jena squinted at the man. "So you're one of Slade's lieutenants," she said, nodding to herself. "You know, I figured that he'd at least give you something respectable to wear."

The man planted fists on his hips and stared down at her with a shit-eating grin on his face. "And *you* are a Justice Keeper," he said, shaking his head. "I'm looking forward to ripping you up to see what your guts look like."

"Well, I've been known to give it up on the first date," Jena shot back. "But if you want to get intimate, I'm going to have to insist that you at least tell me your name."

The man chuckled. "Flagg," he said in a thick southern accent. "This is Valeth. The boss wanted to send one of those creepy-ass *ziarogats* to deal with you, but I asked him for the pleasure of doing it myself."

"You want me?"

Jena spun around, turning her back on them. She ran up the nearest lawn and then leaped with a touch of Bent Gravity, rising effortlessly to the shingled roof. Getting these two out of here was essential if she wanted her people to survive.

Jena turned, glancing over her shoulder with a great big smile. "Come and get me," she said, eyebrows rising. "Let's have a chase, you and I."

Silence lasted for nearly half a minute once Jena led Slade's two lieutenants away from the combat-zone; the men in black tactical gear retreated to take cover behind their van, leaving only one man on either side to point an assault rifle at Anna's people.

Anna bit her lip, then let her head hang, sweat matting red hair to her forehead. "I want everyone to stay down," she said softly. "If we can talk to them before the shooting starts, we might be able to avoid a confrontation."

One of the men that Gabi and Raynar had stripped to black pants and matching t-shirt groaned and rolled over to face the curb. Stun rounds were unpredictable; they left some people incapacitated for hours while others recovered quickly. Most people were down for quite a while, but there were exceptions. Every stun round delivered an electric surge that wasn't exactly good for the human heart. Shooting that man in his weakened condition could be fatal.

Gabi was crouched next to her in sweatpants and a dark tank-top, clutching a pistol in both hands. "We need to keep an eye on him," she hissed, jerking her head toward the fallen man. "If he wakes up-"

"I know."

Before anyone could protest, Anna thrust her arm out to the side, pointed her gun at the groaning man and fired. A stun-round hit his back and caused his body to spasm. He went limp a moment later.

"That might have killed him," Gabi said.

"I know. Watch the others."

Anna rose up to peek through the cop car's window, getting a clear view of the van on the other side. The paramilitary soldiers were still in a holding position, as if they just didn't want to break the cease-fire.

Raynar was crouching behind her with hands on his knees, hunched over to keep his head down. The boy hadn't drawn his pistol, but then that wasn't his primary weapon. "I sense apprehension," he whispered. "But also a whole lot of anger."

"You think negotiations are in order?"

"It's worth a shot."

On her left, Pedro and two of his officers – all of them dressed in plain clothes – checked their weapons. They carried sub-machine guns they had raided from the station's weapons locker. Those would kill, but she wasn't about to complain when Slade's people left them no other options.

"We don't have to do this!" Anna shouted.

The only reply she got was soft laughter from one of Slade's mooks. "Tell me, girl, have you ever seen the face of God?" he asked. "When your Lord gives you an order, you don't disobey Him."

Anna winced so hard it hurt, then tossed her head about to clear the image from her mind. "Slade isn't a god!" she insisted. "Whatever he showed you, I can promise you it's nothing but holography."

"Not Slade, girl."

"What are you talking about?"

Her impulsiveness got the better of her, and she rose up to look through the window once again. Two men had crept around the front of the van and now stood with their rifles pointed at her. Another one was coming around the back.

That one was the ringleader; she could tell by the confidence in his posture, by the way he radiated alertness. In all likelihood, this guy had some actual military experience, where the others were just – what was that word Jack had taught her? - wannabes. "Slade is just the messenger, girl."

"The messenger of what?"

In response, men on both sides of the van hoisted up their weapons and took aim. Anna ducked down just before a storm of bullets punched through the window, causing glass to rain down on her body. She shook it off.

Gritting her teeth, Anna stared down at the ground and sucked in a hissing breath. "You all know the routine!" she growled. "Take turns popping up; make them work for a target. Raynar, get ready to put on a show."

Jena leaped.

Propelled by the strength of a Justice Keeper, she sailed over the gap between two houses and landed on the slanted side of a black-shingled roof. The impact was hard. She ran to the peek, then down the other side.

Scrunching up her face with exertion, Jena tossed her head about. "How exactly do I get into these situations?" she hissed, leaping to the next house, groaning as her muscles ached from exertion.

Jena landed on a flat rooftop, somersaulting across its surface. She came up in one fluid motion and ran. It had been like this for all of five minutes. Five minutes that felt so very much like years.

Contact with her symbiont allowed her to perceive the

silhouettes of Valeth and Flagg two houses behind her, scrambling across the rooftop like a pair of wolves trying to run down a rabbit.

She had to get them far enough away from the battlefield that going back to finish off Anna and the others wasn't an option. If she could kill one of these two – she had no compunctions about doing in one of Slade's lieutenants – so much the better. It was very likely that Slade only had so many enhanced soldiers to go around. This would be a huge win if she could pull it off.

So, she ran, ignoring the exhaustion, the slight burning in her chest that made her want to sit down for just thirty damn seconds and catch her breath. Even Keepers grew tired after a while, and she was having a lousy week.

Opportunity presented itself mere moments later.

At the end of a line of houses, a red-bricked apartment building rose up a good nine or ten stories. That would do. Amusement made her bark a laugh that sounded more like a wheeze when she realized that she was developing a fondness for fighting in high places. Well...In her defense, a girl liked to have a view.

Jena reached the last house in the line.

She leaped and twisted gravity around herself so that forward was now 'down,' soaring effortlessly over the nearly-empty parking lot behind the apartment building. Her skin began to tingle, but so far, her Nassai was still going strong.

She dropped onto the landing of a fire-escape three stories up, then turned on her heel and scrambled up the metal steps. Her footsteps landed with a rough *clank, clank, clank,* and she was dimly aware of Flagg and Valeth sailing over the parking lot to chase her.

She ran.

It didn't matter that she was aching, pissed off and desperately wanting to curl up with her nice soft pillow. She climbed to the fourth floor, the fifth, the sixth. A fight like this would earn her a bubble bath.

Jena shut her eyes, sweat rolling over her face in waves. "Come on!" she growled, doubling over as she charged up a flight of steps. "Just a little further."

At last, she had climbed to the final landing.

Jumping with Keeper strength, Jena grabbed the lip of the roof and pulled herself up. She stood up with a grunt, then dusted off her hands. *Yeah...This is the perfect spot for a smackdown.*

A flat, rectangular rooftop spread out before her with four sides that overlooked a ten-story drop. The only obstruction of any kind was a small stairwell door on the ledge opposite the one she had just come from. The wind was stronger up here, rushing down from a cloudy sky with just a few cracks of blue in a ceiling of white.

Jena strode to the middle of the rooftop.

She turned around in time to see Flagg poke his head up over the ledge and growl as he pulled himself upward. "You're one feisty little bunny," he said, getting his feet. "I think I'm gonna enjoy smacking you around some."

Valeth came up beside him and rose gracefully, her long, dark hair bouncing as she shook her head to clear her mind. The woman said nothing, of course. Jena was starting to think she was the strong, silent type.

Flagg crossed his arms and strode toward her with his head hanging, snarling down at himself. "Stupid, stupid woman," he said. "What do you think coming here is going to prove? I'm just gonna go back for your people."

"We'll see."

"That we will."

Valeth joined him a moment later, lifting her chin to appraise Jena. She arched one eyebrow but said nothing. What

Jena wouldn't give to learn that one's story. She was sure there would be some interesting plot twists.

They paced the outline of a circle on the rooftop, Valeth and Flagg on one side, Jena on the other. It occurred to Jena that she had only faced an opponent with a Nassai once before, and now she was up against two. In all likelihood, this match was not going to go her way, but she could get a few good shots in.

Jena moved a quarter way around the circle, raising her fists into a fighting stance. Now the stairwell door was on her right. "So," she said. "Are we gonna do this, or would you rather settle it with a staring contest?"

Flagg replied with a toothy grin, squeezing his eyes shut. He shook his head and barked a laugh. "I like you, woman," he murmured. "It's always more fun to tame a bitch with spunk."

Valeth settled in behind him as if she meant to let Flagg take the lead. Cowardice or caution? The former seemed like something that Slade would punish. His people were scum, but he needed scum that would get the job done.

Flagg came at her.

He spun for a hook-kick.

Jena ducked and let the man's foot pass right over her head. She scooted past him, placing herself between him and Valeth. Trapped between both assailants. They would not see that coming.

The woman looked up.

Jena jumped with a high kick, the tip of her shoe striking Valeth's chin with enough force to break the jaw of anyone who didn't carry a symbiont. The woman stumbled back, raising a hand to her cheek.

In her mind's eye, she saw the silhouette of Flagg spin and face her with his arms spread wide. He came up behind her, trying to trap her in a bear hug.

Jena crouched down and flung her elbow into the man's gut, forcing him to double over. She brought her hand up to strike his nose with the back of her fist. Blood sprayed from the wound.

Bending her knees, Jena leaped and back-flipped over the man's head. She brought her fist around while upside-down, striking the back of his skull. The impact made him stagger forward.

Jena landed.

She jumped and kicked him between the shoulder blades, sending him careening toward his partner. Hopefully, the woman was still... A small, dark figure came flying over Flagg's head.

Two shoes slammed into Jena's chest, and then she was knocked off her feet. She landed on her ass in the middle of the rooftop, skidding across the rooftop and wheezing as pain filled her body.

Valeth was standing with one knee raised, one hand above her head in some kind of stance that almost certainly belonged to one of the strange martial art forms to arise from this planet. The woman broke into a spring.

Curling her legs up against her chest, Jena sprang off the ground and landed on her feet. She brought both fists up in a boxer's stance just before her opponent drew near.

Valeth threw a punch.

Jena leaned back, catching the woman's wrist in one hand. The other fist came at her quickly, but Jena caught that too. A little effort, and she was able to fling the woman's arms apart, leaving her open.

Jena punched her in the nose, drawing blood on impact. She stepped forward and delivered an uppercut to Valeth's stomach, one that landed with enough force to lift the woman off her feet.

With a growl, Jena seized her enemy's shirt and pulled her close. A surge of power went through her as she called upon her Nassai to twist the gravity field around Valeth's body. Then she flung the woman sideways.

Valeth went flying toward the edge of the rooftop, where – if there was any justice in this universe – she would topple over and fall ten stories to her bloody death. There was a twisting sensation that suggested gravity had been warped again. Valeth landed in a crouch near the ledge.

Something was wrong-

Jena spun around just in time to see Flagg towering over her and delivering a hard jab that took her right between the eyes. Everything went dark for half a moment, but it was all the man needed.

Another punch hit her nose, and she was forced to bend over. A fist came down against her spine, and she was thrown onto her belly, stretched out like a worm in the dirt. It hurt so damn much!

In her confusion, she barely noticed the man pacing a small circle around her. He kicked her square in the ribs, and then she was rolling across the rooftop, hissing and growling as the hard concrete scraped her skin.

She collided with the stairwell door.

It was the only thing that prevented her from going right over the edge, but that did nothing to ease the pain of the impact. Jena rolled onto her stomach, then pushed herself up on extended arms. "Come on!" she said. "Get up!"

They were coming toward her, side by side, moving in for the kill together. Thus far, she had been able to keep them off balance, force them to attack her one at a time, but now...Just as she figured; this wasn't going to go well for her.

Bullets flew through the shattered windows of the cop car, whistling as they zipped past and slammed into the side of the blue van that the first set of Slade's thugs had used. Everyone on her side of the cruiser stayed low.

Anna closed her eyes, breathing deeply to clear her mind. "All right," she said with a nod. "Raynar, pay attention to the stunned prisoners! You sense even the slightest bit of consciousness, shoot em!"

"Yes, ma'am!"

"Can you do that *and* prepare a surprise for our friends over there?"

In her mind's eye, he was smiling down at the ground, shaking his head with joyful amusement. "You really underestimate me, don't you, Anna?" he said. "One rather nasty surprise coming right up!"

Just like that, she noticed that bullets were no longer pelting the cop car or coming through the windows. Instead, they were scarring the front walls of houses on either side of the street. Anna hissed with a spike of alarm. Raynar had claimed this neighbourhood had been evacuated, but there was always a small chance that someone might be taking refuge in one of those homes.

She popped up to peek through the window and found two men standing on either side of the black van, firing desperately at houses. Whatever it was that Raynar had made them see, it did the job. "Now!" she growled.

On her right, Pedro and two of his men popped up to fire over the hood of the cop car. On her left, Gabi and Aamani did the same over the trunk. Anna took aim through the windows, sighting one man with her pistol.

She fired.

A bullet to the side of his neck made him spasm and drop his rifle. He collapsed to the ground mere moments later. Another stun-round took the man next to him, but Anna couldn't say who had fired it.

"There are more!" Raynar warned. "Taking cover behind the van!"

"Nobody moves!" Anna said. "We let them come to us, we

don't-"

"Sweet Mercy above," Raynar hissed from behind her, and before she could even think to ask what had spooked him, he came up and seized her shoulder with one hand. "Something is coming...Something that isn't human!"

"What?"

"I can't describe it, but-"

Suddenly, a figure appeared, rising up from behind the black van to land perched on the vehicle's surface. And just like that, the shooting stopped. This newcomer was a short and slender woman in cargo pants and a sports bra.

She leaped before anyone could blink and flipped through the air to land in the "no man's land" between the van and the cruisers. Straightening, she took all of three seconds to survey her surroundings, and that gave Anna a chance to confirm her suspicions.

A petite woman with a delicate frame, the *ziarogat* had some kind of panel between her breasts, bulging from under the fabric of her sports bra. The only visible hair on her body came in the form of two thin eyebrows that were even paler than her milky-white skin. *Jack named the one he killed,* Anna thought, remembering her apprehension from just a few days ago, her concern that she was becoming to accustomed to violence. Thus far, the only blood on her hands belonged to Wesley Pennfield, and if she had to add to that tally, she wouldn't do it lightly. *Okay, Blanche...If you really want a fight.*

The *ziarogat* charged forward.

She leaped and somersaulted over the cruisers, uncurling to land with her back to them. "Keep the others off me!" Anna shouted. "This one's mine!"

Blanche spun around.

Anna charged at her, bent over, like a bull trying to run down a matador. She leaped and stretched both arms out, catching Blanche's shoulders and forcing the woman down onto her back.

Anna rose into a handstand.

A touch of Bent Gravity allowed her to push off the other woman and she flipped upright to land on the roof of the blue van that had belonged to the first squad of Slade's goons that Jena had taken down.

Anna jumped off, landing crouched in the middle of the street. *Take the bait,* she thought, shaking her head. *Come on! Why waste your energy on a bunch of rabbits when you can hunt a gorgeous doe like me.*

Blanche didn't disappoint. The *ziarogat* landed hard on the roof of the van, pausing for a moment to take stock of the situation with lips pressed into a tight frown. She thrust one fist out, aiming the gun that was built into her gauntlet.

Anna twisted around, raising one hand to shield herself, and just like that a Bending snapped into place. The image of Blanche became a smear of bright colours just before a bullet hit the patch of warped space-time and veered off to Anna's left.

The *ziarogat* dropped from the van to land beside her.

Anna rose and spun to face the other woman with fists raised into a boxer's stance, strands of red hair falling over her face.

Blanche raised her weapon.

With a thought, Anna threw up a time bubble just before a bullet erupted from the tube on Blanche's gauntlet. A small lead slug that spiraled as it made its way toward the barrier between Anna's time-frame and the rest of the world. Its master shimmered and wobbled as if seen through a curtain of falling water. Anna took one step to the right and let the bubble drop.

She kicked Blanche's wrist, knocking the weapon askew, then spun for a hook-kick. Her foot swung around to clip Blanche across the chin. A blow that would have knocked teeth out of any normal person's mouth. The *ziarogat* staggered.

Anna whirled around to face her.

She jumped and kicked out with both feet, planting two gray sneaker's in Blanche's chest with enough force to crack that panel. The other woman went stumbling backward, but if destruction of that panel did anything, Blanche didn't show it.

Quick as a cat, Anna charged forward and gave a shove, augmenting the blow with a touch of Bent Gravity. Blanche went flying backward toward the houses at the side of the street. She crashed through an arch-shaped front window and landed sprawled out in some guy's living room. The Bleakness take her impulsiveness! That was a dumb move! She was fairly certain that this neighbourhood had been evacuated, but if she was wrong, it could mean some innocent person's life. Worse yet, her skin was on fire with a million little pinpricks. Seth was getting tired.

Anna closed her eyes, sweat oozing from her pores. She mopped a hand over her face by instinct. "Come on, Lenai," she hissed, fighting through the wooziness that came from the overuse of her powers. "Let's go."

She pulled her own pistol from its holster.

Blanche appeared in the hole that had once been a window, thrusting her arm out to point a fist at Anna. Despite Seth's protests, Anna threw up another time bubble and took one step to the left.

She let the bubble drop, then raised her weapons and fired. A screen of white static appeared before Blanche, covering the entirety of the window. Bullets bounced uselessly off the force-field.

"EMP!" Anna growled.

The LEDs on her gun turned white.

She fired and sent a series of white tracers flying over the road, up the house's front lawn and through the window. The force-field flickered, then vanished as they went right through it, and Blanche stumbled backward.

The *ziarogat* seemed completely unfazed by the damage. Instead of collapsing to the floor in pain, she raised her arm to aim her weapon.

Anna dove, landing hard on her belly while a stream of bullets flew over her back. She raised her weapon and fired once again. White tracers sped toward the open window where Blanche tried to adjust her aim.

They punched through the ziarogat's chest, causing her to spasm while current that would kill a normal human being arced through her body. Silver blood splashed outward from the wound, but Blanche recovered quickly.

Anna's body was aching, her head spinning. In the back of her mind, she felt Seth's terror at the knowledge that he could do nothing to help her. Crafting yet another Bending was out of the question.

Blanche raised her weapon...and nothing happened.

Instead of firing, the *ziarogat* just stood in the window with one arm outstretched, frozen in place like a computer that just wouldn't respond. The expression on her face was perfectly neutral. *What...*

Anna looked over her shoulder.

Raynar stood with one hand pressed to the side of the van, bent over and gasping with every breath. Sweat made his face glisten. "Kill her!" he panted. "Do it! I can't hold her still forever!"

Anna raised her weapon with arms that ached from the strain. Keeping her hands from shaking required quite a bit of effort. "Standard ammo!" she growled. The LEDs on her pistol went dark.

She fired.

A hole appeared in Blanche's forehead, and silver blood sprayed out behind her, landing on the carpet of that otherwise pristine living room. The *ziarogat* dropped to her knees, then fell face down in the window.

Raynar let out a soft sigh.

Baring her teeth in a snarl, Anna winced. She rubbed at her eyes with the back of her hand. "The others?" she asked in a voice thick with anger. "Have we subdued the rest of Slade's minions?"

Pressing his lips together, Raynar closed his eyes. He nodded once in confirmation. "Two of Pedro's officers got shot," he mumbled. "One of Slade's men is dead as well. The rest are stunned."

"Good," she said. Getting to her feet required so much effort! Her muscles felt like they had been turned to jelly. That was the price of overworking your Nassai. "Get them loaded up, and let's get out of here. We'll take both of the vans if we can manage it, but I want us back at the police station."

"And Jena?"

A shiver went through Anna when she considered that question. "If Jena's alive, she will find her way back on her own."

Jena got to her feet, then doubled over with a hand on her stomach, heaving out a gasp. "You two," she said, shaking her head. "You're just not gonna give up until I smack the stupid right out of you."

Just ten paces away, Flagg and Valeth came toward her side by side. The man wore a nasty rictus smile that made his intentions clear and left her skin crawling. Valeth, on the other hand, was all business. An executioner on her way to throw the switch. Taking them on together would be next to impossible. But the mark of a good tactician was to turn the impossible into the doable.

Jena ran at them.

She threw up a time bubble when she got within a few feet. Or...Well, more of a "time-tube." A perfect sphere was the easiest type of bubble to create, but other shapes were possible.

This one was more of a curved tube that twisted around Flagg so that she could stand at his side.

Jena took position, and through the shimmering curtain of refracted light, she saw a blurry Flagg in profile. Less than one hundredth of a second would have passed for him. If he even sensed the bubble, he would not have reacted to it. Her skin was tingling now; this had to end soon.

She let the bubble drop.

Jena kicked the back of Flagg's knee, making him stumble. She spun for a back-hand strike, one fist whirling around to strike the back of his head. That knocked him off balance and sent him careening toward the stairwell door.

Valeth came at her.

The woman threw a punch.

Jena leaned back, one hand coming up to slap the blow away. She used the other to slam her open palm into Valeth's nose. Blood leaked from her opponent's nostrils.

Flagg had recovered.

Jena grabbed Valeth's shirt with both hands, then flung her sideways, sending her stumbling toward her partner. The pair of them collided in a tangle, then Valeth bounced off and landed sprawled out on her side.

Flagg shook his head as he tried to get his bearings. "You're one clever little bitch, aren't you?" he growled, striding toward her. "You'll be a lot more respectful once I teach you your pla-"

Jena leaped and kicked high, the tip of her shoe striking his nose with enough force to make his head snap backward. "You talk too much!" she hissed, landing right in front of him. Now to finish this.

Jena charged at him.

She slammed her shoulder into his chest, driving him backward with the strength of a Justice Keeper. And then she kept on pushing. Flagg recovered his wits quickly enough and threw his arms around her. That did nothing to slow her momentum, but it would be a problem in just a few seconds.

Bit by bit, she pushed him back toward the ledge, and her dazed opponent seemed to be unaware of her intentions. He squeezed her as if he meant to crush the life from her body, and though it was painful, she held on. Just a few more paces!

At long last, Flagg managed to figure out her plan. She could tell by the way he planted his feet firmly and braced himself like a concrete dam trying to hold back the full force of a raging river. So, she pulled out the last trick in her bag.

Bent Gravity.

Jena applied it to both of them, power surging through her body as her symbiont twisted the fabric of space-time. They were yanked over the edge of the rooftop, hurled across the empty street below like a pair of leaves blown by a hurricane.

In that brief moment of stunned confusion, Jena threw her arms up to break free of her opponent's embrace. She reversed the Bending on herself, changing the direction of gravity's pull so that she was yanked back toward the rooftop. Of course, this required her to create a gravitational field that was twice as powerful as the one that had taken her out into the street. It was the only way to overpower the velocity she had gained. Her skin felt as if it had been set on fire!

For a few glorious seconds, she was treated to the exquisite sight of Flagg staring open-mouthed as he plummeted ten stories to the street below. Then she was pulled back to the rooftop.

Jena landed on her side, rolling like a log across the concrete surface. With a grunt, she pushed herself up, but her muscles ached. The simple act of standing up required an enormous amount of concentration.

She turned.

Valeth stood in the middle of the rooftop with her fists

raised, watching Jena with a stunned expression. "How..." the woman sputtered. "You can't...You can't..."

Her limbs felt as if they were made out of rubber, and in truth, Jena knew that she would collapse from exhaustion any moment now. She was in no condition to fight, but if she could pull off a bluff...

"Go," Jena hissed. "Tell Slade about what you saw here. Tell him it's not enough for me to just kill him. I'm going to humiliate him."

The other woman turned and ran for the ledge, leaping from the rooftop as if she preferred suicide to another skirmish with Jena. Not a bad day for the old ego, but it wasn't over. No, she had to finish the job.

Jena sank to her knees, burying her face in her hands. "Oh, that was stupid." She looked up, blinking at the sky. "On your feet, woman. Rest is for people who intend to live to a ripe old age."

She forced herself up, and made her way to the fire-escape.

Flagg was lying in the middle of an empty street, groaning from the pain of two broken legs. His face was red and streaked with tears. Damn it, the man should be dead, but Jena's luck wasn't that good.

She stepped into the road. "You just don't know when to die, do you?" she asked, shaking her head. "Some people just stick around long past the point where you want them to leave."

Flagg looked up at her, tears glistening on his cheeks. He tried to blink them away. "I thought I was done for," he said through a fit of laughter. "Leave it to a Keeper to save her worst enemy."

Jena pulled her gun from its holster.

"What are you doing?"

Staring over the length of her extended arm, she cocked her head to one side and squinted at him. "Sorry, friend," she said.

"There are already too many evil pieces of shit like you in the world."

"But you can't."

She pulled the trigger.

A hole appeared in Flagg's forehead, and blood sprayed out the back of his skull, landing in the road behind him. The body collapsed to the ground to stare blankly up at the sky.

Bleakness take her, she was exhausted. She should probably try to move him to some place out of the way. Flagg was dead, but his symbiont was still very much alive, and it would be looking to move to a new host. Nassai couldn't live inside a corpse, and she was fairly sure the same was true of their evil counterparts. Something told her that this twisted symbiont wouldn't be choosy about its new host. It would take anyone who made physical contact with the body.

That presented a problem, because it was all too likely that if Jena made contact with the corpse, Flagg's symbiont would try to battle her own for control of her body. It was dangerous to move him, dangerous to leave him here, and she was exhausted. What were the odds that someone would find him? These streets were deserted. In just twelve hours, the symbiont in Flagg would be dead, and she could deal with his corpse then.

Jena turned to go.

Leaving him here to rot was exactly what this man deserved.

12

The sound of muffled voices filled her groggy mind, and she became aware of her own body like a lump of numbness. When she opened her eyes, she saw blue twilight in the bedroom window, soft light that made the bed, dresser and posters on the wall visible as mere dark shadows.

Anna sat up.

She winced, touched her fingertips to her forehead and let out a groan. "Well, never mind then," she hissed, falling back against the mattress. "Maybe I'll go back to sleep for a few more years."

A crack in the door allowed light to spill in from the hallway, and the sound of soft voices as well. "I think she's awake now," someone said, much to Anna's disappointment. "You can go in."

The door swung open.

A disheveled-looking Jena stood before her in jeans and a sweat-drenched t-shirt, her eyes fixed on the gray carpet. "Hey, kid," she said, shuffling into the room. "I heard about the fight today."

Despite her exhaustion, Anna managed to sit up again with

some effort. Her body ached, but the pain was less now. The memory of everything came flooding back to her. To her credit, she had managed to remain upright long enough to take their prisoners to the police station and bring everyone back to the safe-house. After that, she had shoveled some food in her face and passed out. "I feel like I've been run over by a truck," she said. "They tell you not to overtax your Nassai, but..."

Jena shook her head. "Sometimes you don't get a choice in the matter," she said, moving closer to the bed. "I know what you're going through. My hands are still tingling after that showdown with Slade's people."

Closing her eyes, Anna let her head hang. Strands of bright red hair fell over her face, tickling her. "We need to find him soon." There was no question of who she meant. "Jena, we can't keep this up."

Jena crossed her arms and heaved out a sigh, turning her head to stare at the wall. "I know," she muttered under her breath. "These little piecemeal attacks aren't cutting it. We have to take down Slade once and for all."

"Any suggestions on that?"

"Nothing you should worry about now."

Anna yawned, then pressed a fist to her mouth to stifle it. "Companion be praised for small mercies," she said drowsily. "You should have seen that Ziarogat, Jen. They're everything Jack said and worse."

"But you kicked its ass."

Anna blinked the sleep out of her eyes. She pressed a palm to her forehead, holding hair back from her face. "I held it at bay for a few minutes, but it forced me to rely on my Nassai until I was wrung out. If Raynar hadn't come along, I'd be dead."

Jena turned and paced a line beside the bed with hands clasped behind her back. "Don't be so quick to sell yourself short," she said, glancing over her shoulder. "You will do better next time."

"You seem pretty sure of that."

"We live, we learn and we adapt." The other woman sat down on the corner of the mattress, patting Anna's leg through the blankets. "Get some rest, kid. Tomorrow, we'll come up with a strategy."

When Jena left, Anna snuggled back under the covers, but despite her exhaustion, sleep was hard to find. Her head just kept racing with thoughts, fears about an army of cybernetic warriors designed specifically to kill Justice Keepers. Of course, her rational mind said it wasn't as bad as all that.

If Slade had an entire army of *ziarogati* at his disposal, he would have unleashed them instead of relying on his half-trained acolytes. No, it was far more likely that he only had a handful of those creatures at his beck and call.

She tried to quiet her mind by focusing on pleasant thoughts. Imagining Bradley curling up next to her made her feel all warm and safe and...No. No, it didn't make her feel warm and safe at all. She just told herself that because she thought that was what she was *supposed* to feel. But then, wasn't that what everyone did? How many times had she heard her parents insist that there were no fairy-tale endings. Adults stopped complaining and learned to make it work. Bradley was a good man.

Cursing her insomnia, she rolled over and buried her face in the pillow. Seth needed the rest as much as she did, and with her luck, they'd be facing another troop of *ziarogati* before sunset tomorrow.

The mouth of the cave looked into a tunnel of seemingly endless darkness, a gaping maw that would swallow any wayward traveler who happened to get too close. And worst of all, he could tell that there was a significant drop at the entrance.

Jack hopped from the ledge.

He landed in a crouch with his hands on his knees, head hanging as he tried to get his bearings. "Overseers and caves," he said, straightening. "Somebody really ought to tell them it's getting cliché."

When he turned, he found Harry climbing down the rock wall with one hand still clutching the ledge where daylight spilled through. "And somehow," Harry replied in a breathy whisper. "I just don't think your sense of narrative purity was really at the top of their list of priorities."

Harry dropped the last few feet, then crouched down on impact. He straightened and dusted his hands. "Australia," he muttered. "You have to give those slimy bastards this much credit: they really did travel the world."

"Slimy bastards?"

"I assume the Overseers are gross."

With a grunt, Jack turned and thrust his fist into the darkness. "Multi-tool active!" he said. "Flashlight!" A cone of radiance erupted from the metal disk on the end of his gauntlet, allowing him to see a narrow tunnel that was just large enough for a man of his height to walk without bumping his head. Of course, he could sense the dimensions of this cave through his bond with Summer, but he thought it was best to rely on *all* of his senses. "Come on."

Ven claimed that these were the geographic coordinates that he had found in the data that Harry had retrieved from the Overseer device in Northern Ontario. Supposedly, the next part of the cipher that would reveal the Key's location was hidden somewhere in this cave. A lonely little cave in the middle of the Australian outback. For all Jack knew, they were the first humans to enter.

Harry walked with one hand trailing fingers along the rock

wall, the other pointing a cone of light into the darkness. "Let's find this and get back ASAP," he said. "I want to know the instant Ven cuts through Slade's jamming field."

Baring his teeth with a soft hiss, Jack shut his eyes tight. "I don't like this any more than you," he said, shaking his head. "But I should point out that it really doesn't matter if Ven cuts through the signal. We're not going to New York."

"They're isolated, Jack."

Jack puckered his lips and blew out a deep breath. "I know that," he said, brushing bangs off his forehead with the back of his hand. "But if I had to trust anyone to survive in that situation, it would be Jena."

The other man wore a scowl as he peered into the darkness, blinking as though he had something in his eye. "Have you ever researched Grecken Slade?" he asked. "I mean *really* looked into his past."

"No, but I'm guessing you have."

"A year ago, you kept trying to tell me that Slade was dirty, but I just didn't want to believe it. I didn't want to accept that an organization like the Justice Keepers could have a snake at the top of its command structure. And then that business on where Jena tried to arrest him on Station One...

"After that, I realized that Slade had pulled a fast one on me and almost everyone he'd ever worked with. So, my detective instincts kicked in."

They had to pause their conversation briefly to maneuver over some uneven terrain where sinkholes provided the perfect opportunity to break your ankle. Jack had to admit that he didn't really care for where this was going, and the lump of anxiety nestled in the back of his mind told him that Summer wasn't feeling much better.

He'd been biting his nails for the last twenty-four hours, worrying about what might happen to Anna now that she was cut off from help and surrounded by Slade's goons. His concern for her had been so strong it actually eclipsed the sadness he felt about the end of his relationship. Strangely enough, Gabi was down there too, and while he *did* worry about her, he didn't worry as much as he should have. Not as much as he did for Anna. That was telling, but Jack put it aside to think about later.

Jack sat down on a rocky ledge with his hands in his lap, heaving out a deep breath. "All right," he said with a shrug of his shoulders. "Let's hear it. What did you learn after digging into Slade's past?"

The other man watched him with a solemn expression, his dark eyes reflecting the glow of the flashlights. "You ever hear of Sera Lesar?" Harry asked. "She was the chief of the Justice Keepers right before Slade."

"Name sounds vaguely familiar."

"She died in a shuttle accident four months before Slade took the job," Harry went on. "Minor flaw in the fusion reactor caused the whole damn thing to blow up. Funny thing is, you read the reports of the engineers who performed maintenance on that shuttle, and they all *insist* it passed every test."

"Sabotage?"

"Sounds like."

Jack thrust his chin out, arching one dark eyebrow. "You think Slade Macbethed his way into the position," he said. "Well, you know that I hate to be the voice of reason, but do we have any evidence to suggest it wasn't just an accident?"

Harry winced, shaking his head. "I don't know," he rasped. "The point is that we know Slade can be devious and ruthless. And the people we love are at his mercy."

"We can't go to them, Harry."

"Why the bloody hell not?"

Only then did it occur to Jack that there was a damn good reason why this would be so much harder for his friend. His best friend and his ex-girlfriend were currently fighting a guerrilla war on the streets of New York, but that was nothing compared to having a kid stuck in that city. "Jena gave us an assignment," Jack said in the gentlest voice he could manage. "I don't know what this Key does, but if it's as bad as Melissa thinks, the whole damn planet could be in danger. We go to New York now, and there is *no one* to continue the search. Which means Slade gets it first."

Harry stood before him with hands shoved into his pockets, his head tilted back to stare up at the ceiling. "I know," he whispered. "And all the math there makes sense, but I can't shake the urge to..."

It was instinct that made Jack stand up and throw his arms around the other man, squeezing Harry in a tight hug. "It's gonna be okay," he said, patting his friend on the back. "She's a smart kid; she'll survive."

They moved deeper into the cave, as deep as they could go before the tunnel ended in an open area about the size of the average person's living room. As he ran his flashlight back and forth, Jack saw nothing but rock walls with minerals that sparkled. The air was musty and damp with a smell that he would prefer not to identify. "There's nothing here."

"Nothing we can detect with our eyes anyway."

Jack winced, trembling on the spot. "So, we're out of options," he said, spinning around to face the other man. "You know, I really wish you would have agreed to bring Ven's brief-case device."

Harry was standing so that Jack saw him in profile, frowning at a wall of rock. "We don't need Ven's device," he mumbled. "I can do it faster."

The man retrieved a little ball of curled up flesh from his pocket, and Jack felt his skin crawl at the sight of it. He still wasn't sure what to make of Harry's strange ability to control the Overseer multi-tool, but he'd seen enough sci-fi to know that there was bound to be some kind of hidden side-effect just waiting to ruin their lives. Then again, his own sister had made the same claim about his decision to bond Summer. Harry was his friend, and that entitled him to a certain degree of trust.

The tiny ball of flesh uncurled, conforming to the shape of Harry's palm, fingers included, and for a brief moment Jack wondered if he was going to have to fight off a maniac who threw force-fields at him. It was an unworthy thought.

Harry turned in a small circle, waving his hand back and forth over the wall as if scanning for something. A moment later, he spun around and thrust his palm down toward the floor. "There!"

Something oozed out of the cracks between the rocks, congealing into a mass of flesh and then rising to form a pillar roughly as high as the average man's chest. Overseer tech: there was something so creepy about it.

Harry touched the pillar with two fingers, breathing raggedly as he did...something. For all Jack could see, he was just standing there, lost in a trance. It made Jack worry. If that thing had some kind of safeguard or...

Harry shook his head like a dog trying to get water out of his fur. "There," he said, taking a step back and pressing one hand to his forehead. "I have the second cipher. Let's get back to Station Twelve."

"That's it?"

"That's it."

Ben expected to see many things when he stepped through the elevator doors onto the concourse of Station One. People milling about and sharing conversations, Justice Keepers walking by as they scanned through reports: any of these things would make sense to him. The one thing that didn't was total silence.

A small cafe across the way was operated by a human-shaped serving bot that waited patiently for a customer, but no one sat at any of the small, metal tables spread out across the gray floor tiles. The fabrication station next door normally had a small line of people who needed to touch up a piece of clothing, but it was vacant as well. Ben could hear the music from the nearby bar, but there were no sounds of conversation. Something was definitely wrong here.

Chewing his lip, Ben turned his head to survey his surroundings. "Well then," he said, eyebrows rising. "It never fails. The instant I leave the party, everybody else stops having fun."

Larani stepped out of the elevator with fists balled at her sides, head hanging in frustration. "Something is definitely wrong," she said. "We need to find somebody who can give us a status update."

Ben looked up to squint into the distance. "I don't know," he said, shaking his head. "Between you and me, I think the smartest thing to do would be to get to your office and scan the news feeds."

"Why's that?"

"Because a bustling hub like this only turns into a ghost town when people are too scared to engage in normal social activity," he answered. "And if people are that scared on a *Justice Keeper* station?"

"I see your point."

The long hallways of drab gray walls were practically devoid of life, but he kept his eyes peeled as they made their way toward Larani's office. Once upon a time, that office had belonged to Grecken Slade, and if he weren't the die-hard skeptic that he was, he would think the place would give off some very bad vibes.

In truth, the one thing he couldn't get off his mind – the one thing that had made his skin itch and his hands tremble for the last three days – was the urge to contact Darrel and make sure that everything was all right. Ben's heart was aching. Had anyone bothered to tell his boyfriend that he was all right? That he hadn't just up and disappeared. There was no telling how that conversation might go.

Still, he was a professional. He might have been discharged from the LIS, but that didn't change the fact that he was a professional, and right now there were more pressing concerns that required his attention.

Double doors to Larani's office slid open to reveal a woman with long blonde hair who sat at the desk with her head down. "Whatever it is," she snapped, looking up to fix her gaze on them. "I have no time-"

The woman's face crumpled, and she shook her head. "Larani," she said, getting to her feet, tugging the hem of her white shirt to straighten the garment. "I didn't expect to see you so soon."

Larani closed her eyes, bowing her head to the other woman. "Apparently not," she said, striding into the room. "I'm pleased to see that you feel so comfortable sitting in my chair. We've been out of contact for three days. Report."

"Slade has taken over New York."

"Come again?"

The blonde woman licked her lips, then turned her head to stare at something on the floor. "Slade has begun a series of coordinated terror attacks," she said. "He's shut down commerce throughout the city, blocked food shipments."

"How many teams have you mobilized?"

"None."

The flush that stained Larani's face a deep shade of crimson was probably hot enough to stave off winter's chill. "What do you mean 'none?' " she asked, approaching the desk. "How have you *not* taken action?"

Ben squeezed his eyes shut, tilting his head back. "Isn't it obvious?" he asked in a gruff voice. "We've spent the last three months looking for traitors. Does it really surprise you that we'd find one?"

The woman stared at him with a gaping mouth, blinking as if she couldn't believe what she was seeing. "How *dare* you?" she hissed. "I have served the Justice Keepers for almost twenty years without-"

"Shut up, Tiassa!" Larani snapped.

Tiassa leaned over the desk with her hands pressed to its surface, glaring daggers at her boss. "I'll have you before a board of inquiry for this," she said. "You can't just fling such accusations without proof, and-"

"Get out of my office."

For a moment, it seemed as though there might be trouble; Tiassa went eerily still with an expression Ben had seen dozens of times on cornered criminals who were about to try something desperate. Then the woman relaxed and slowly made her way around the desk. She sniffed with disdain as she slid past Ben. "There was a time when no one in her right mind would question the integrity of a Justice Keeper."

Larani strode around the desk and began tapping at the SmartGlass, licking her lips as she read through status updates. "Tiassa gave orders that no Justice Keepers could go to New York without her authorization," she explained. "Several directors disobeyed, and she sent security teams to deal with them. There was a firefight in the hallways."

Pressing his lips together, Ben felt the blood drain out of his face. He looked down at the floor, collecting his thoughts. "So, it really has started," he muttered. "Slade's got the Keepers at each other's throats."

"From what I can see, New York is a mess."

"What's our plan then?"

Larani wrinkled her nose, then shook her head in disgust. "I don't know," she said, dropping into the chair behind her desk.

"But we need people that we can trust. Let's start by looking for your old friends."

Ben blinked several times, then touched two fingers to his forehead. "That's a good place to start," he agreed. "But I won't be much use against Justice Keepers...Unless you came through on that little favour. You never did tell me if you got my weapons back."

When he looked up, Larani was beaming at him like a six-year-old at her birthday party. "I *didn't* get your old weapons," she said. "But I did find something better..."

"I believe I've located the source of the jamming."

A hologram of Ven floated in the middle of the Science Lab, roughly three inches above the black-tiled floor. Leyrian numbers zipped back and forth through a transparent body that faded from white to a soft pale blue.

Behind him, the table that Professor Nareo used to study the Overseer multi-tool – the N'Jal, as Harry called it – was unoccupied with nothing on its surface but an offline tablet. It made Jack nervous to recall that the N'Jal was not there but rather tucked away inside Harry's pocket. At least the fleshy SlipGate was still in its proper place in the corner. He never really had figured out whether they had removed that damn thing from the network. If not, it was a security risk.

Ven crossed his arms and cocked his head to one side as he studied Jack. "It took quite a bit of effort," he said, floating upward just enough to loom over them. "But I was able to pinpoint the location."

Pressing his lips into a thin line, Jack squinted at the apparition. "That's great," he said, nodding once. "How much do you want to bet that Slade keeps that device with him at all times? Find it and you find him."

Harry stood at Jack's side with hands inside his back pockets, his face blank and expressionless. "So what's our next move?" he asked. "It's not like we can just call Jena and tell her the location."

The hologram floated backward, then turned slightly to gesture at a screen on the wall, a screen that suddenly displayed a map of New York. Brooklyn, to be precise. "The jamming signal is coming from Prospect Park."

"Do we have any idea about the situation down there?"

Ven shook his head.

Jack crossed his arms with a heavy sigh, his head hanging as he considered all the factors. "We have to go down there," he said, stepping forward. "Our people are helpless if they can't talk to each other."

Harry glanced over his shoulder with a bleak frown, his eyes slowly widening. "I thought you said finding the Key was more important," he countered. "Now you want to risk it by throwing yourself into the hot-zone?"

"Finding the Key is one thing," Jack replied. "Keeping it is quite another. There's a good chance that you and I won't be able to do that alone. If Slade's got the resources to bring one of the biggest cities on this planet to its knees, then there's no telling what he'll throw at us when we become his target. We need Jena, and right now Slade has set up one hell of a gambit that might just cost us our queen."

Harry only nodded.

Behind them, the double doors slid apart to reveal a single figure who stood in the hallway. Her clothes were a misty gray – Jack hadn't seen that outfit before; so his mind couldn't project colours onto it – but he would know that silhouette anywhere. "Good," Larani said, striding into the room. "You're here."

Jack spun around.

The Chief of the Justice Keepers strode toward him with her arms swinging freely, her eyes downcast as if she felt ashamed. "I shouldn't have been away for so long," she muttered. "Now matters are getting out of hand."

"You know about New York?"

"I just found out."

Jack scrunched up his face, shaking his head ever so slowly. "It's a real mess down there," he said, gesturing to the map on the wall behind him. "But we've just figured out where the jamming signal is coming from."

"So you're going to shut it down?"

"Yes, ma'am."

Larani held his gaze for a moment, her dark eyes smoldering with tightly-controlled fury. "Good," she said with a curt nod. "But you're not going down there alone. It just so happens that I've brought you some backup."

Jack looked up in time to see a man coming through the double doors, a short man in thick black armour that covered him from head to toe. In fact, the only spot of colour on this guy's body was a bright red visor that glinted under the glare of the ceiling lights.

Wait...Jack had seen this armour before! He'd seen it on the man who had tried to kill Professor Nareo back on Leyria. Vetrid Col? Why in god's name would Larani think that involving Vetrid Col would be a good-

The helmet split apart along a vertical seam down the middle, panels sliding back to reveal a man's face.

Ben's face.

Well, there's a twist!

A grinning Ben Loranai ran his gaze over everyone present. "Hey, guys," he said, his dark eyebrows climbing up his forehead. "So, I hear we're going on a mission?"

13

The van rumbled, and Jack was jostled about in his seat. It had been like this the whole way down from Southampton. Fortunately, that town had a SlipGate that was out of range of Slade's jamming field. Truth be told, Jack had worried that they would come up against resistance when they passed through New York's city limits, but it seemed as though Slade wasn't interested in keeping people out; he just wanted to make sure his precious hostages didn't get any bright ideas about fleeing the kill-zone.

Jack would have loved to know whether they might have passed any cars on their way out of the city, but unfortunately, the only light in this black van came through the windshield, and he was too far back to see anything outside.

Dressed in blue jeans and a light armoured vest over his blue t-shirt, Jack sat with his hands on his knees and frowned into his lap. "How much longer?" he wondered. "I think my legs are starting to cramp."

Harry sat across from him in similar clothing but a heavier vest. The man's face was stern, his brows drawn together. "We'll be there soon enough," he said as if comforting a child. "When we get there..."

"Trouble."

Looking imposing in his armoured suit, Ben sat with an elbow on his thigh, his chin resting on the knuckles of his fist. "Slade's going to have guards," he said. "And we have no way of knowing how many."

Jack closed his eyes, tilting his head back. "Then let's review the plan," he said with a curt nod. "You and I put on a show and keep them distracted with theatrics while Harry disables the device."

Harry frowned, then lowered his eyes to stare into his lap. "That should be simple enough," he said with a shrug of his shoulders. "If nothing else works, I can always blast it with a force-field."

"Have we forgotten that I'm the techy here?" Ben asked.

Biting his lip, Jack winced and felt sweat on his brow. "No, we have not," he said, shaking his head. "But your armour is reliable. I only wish that I could say the same for Harry's Overseer weapon."

Harry glared at him.

The van settled to a stop before the man could voice his protest, and that was for the best; the last thing they needed was a stupid argument before they went into battle. Jack could feel his Nassai's apprehension and, taking a page from her book, he offered comforting emotions. Or tried to anyway.

The van's back door opened, revealing a pudgy man in a leather jacket standing in the light of early afternoon. He was short and pale with a thick gray beard that stretched from ear to ear. "Let's go!" he said, jerking his head to the side. "Why I do this for you, I will never know!"

Jack was the first one out the door, and when he took a look around, he saw that they had parked at the edge of a traffic circle that surrounded a small field with bushes and trees rising up from the grass. On the other side of the road, two concrete pillars with marble statues of men on horseback marked the southern entrance to Prospect Park.

Harry jumped out behind him, doubling over and shaking his head. "Thank you so much, Ron," he said, straightening with a grunt. "Now get out of here! I don't want you within a mile of this place when it all goes down."

"Yeah, yeah," the bearded man muttered. "You owe me for this, Carlson."

"I'm sure I do."

Ben came out last, his armour making soft whirring noises as he dusted himself off. "Much appreciated," he said, nodding to Ron. The mask slid into place over his face, red lenses forming the visor.

Ron shut the door forcefully, then stood with his back turned, heaving out a breath. "Be careful, all of you," he said without looking back. Before anyone could say a word, he made his way around the side of the van and hopped into the driver's seat.

"You ready for this?" Ben asked.

Jack replied with a smile, then bowed his head to the other man. "I'm frantic," he said, eyebrows rising. "So, load me up."

They started up the road that ran between the two pillars and found themselves on a narrow, two-lane street that was shaded by trees on either side. Sunlight illuminated the leaves in a thousand verdant shades. Jack had been expecting some kind of ambush, but the place seemed to be deserted. Just a single road that cut through a green field.

So, they ran while Jack kept his eyes peeled and Summer, Summer did whatever it is that Nassai do that allowed them to perceive the world around them and share that awareness with their hosts. Eventually Jack realized that he was pulling ahead of the others. Harry, to his credit, was keeping up, but the heavy armour limited Ben's ability to move quickly.

That was just one drawback to a suit like that. To an ordinary person, it offered the best protection available, but Justice Keepers relied on speed and agility. Worse yet, his spatial awareness would be severely impaired – Nassai couldn't see through solid objects – and any attempt to craft a Bending would only destroy the armour's circuitry. Bendings formed within a few micrometres of his skin; a suit like that would get caught inside the patch of warped space-time, and who knew how that might affect it.

Jack slowed his pace.

A few minutes later, they came to a fork where one road ran off to their right and another went left, each lined with trees that traced the perimeter of a lake. According to Ven, the jamming signal was coming from a spot on the other side of that lake.

Ben jerked to a halt, hanging his head to cast a red-eyed gaze down at the ground. "No guards," he muttered with just a touch of breathlessness in his voice. "Does anyone else think this is too easy?"

Jack squinted, then shook his head. "I wouldn't worry about it," he said, turning his back on the other man. "I'm betting most of Slade's minions are out terrorizing the people of this city."

"Still..."

"Well, we can stay here and worry about it," Jack shot back. "Or we can get a move on. The map says the fastest way is to go west."

Once again, they ran, and once again they were treated to the quiet serenity of an empty road with trees on each side. Not enough trees to provide cover for anybody who might want to ambush them – there were plenty of patches of open grass and even the odd intersecting street – but enough that Jack's ability to rely upon his spatial awareness was severely limited.

The road curved slightly to the right, following the outline of the lake. At one point, a man in black tactical gear stepped out from a patch of trees with his rifle held lazily in one hand, the muzzle pointed at the ground. He seemed not to notice them until he was at least halfway across the road.

Then, he turned and gasped.

A patch of rippling air sped toward the man, hit him with the force of an oncoming car and sent him flying backward. He landed in the middle of the street, groaning. Before Jack could react, a bullet flew toward the fallen guard.

It hit the soft spot on his neck where his vest offered no protection and caused the man to spasm as electric current raced through his body. He went limp a moment later, passed out in the middle of the road.

Ben stood with gloved hands clutching a pistol, his red visor fixed upon the fallen man. "Down and out," he said, nodding once. "Good shot, Harry."

A few feet away, Harry had a hand stretched out with his fingers splayed. The man wore a scowl and shook his head slowly. "There are bound to be more of them," he said. "The sooner we get out of the open, the better."

They soon came to another fork in the road where West Drive met Center Drive, and this time they took the path to their right. Less than a minute later, the trees on either side of that road opened into a lush green field under a blue sky with puffy clouds.

Jack had them take a narrow footpath that cut through the trees surrounding the field. In theory, that would make it harder for them to draw any unwelcome attention, but Ben's heavy footsteps and tendency to occasionally crash through the odd branch might have undermined that plan.

Eventually, they inched their way closer to the treeline, peeking through the gaps to get a good look at the field. Perhaps fifty metres away, a tiny gray-bricked building that looked like a shed stood guarded by two men in black gear who seemed to be taking a very casual approach to their duties. The place looked new, as if it had been constructed in the last few years.

Clenching his teeth, Jack winced and rubbed his forehead with the back of his fist. "How much do you wanna bet that's it?" he whispered. "You don't have armed soldiers standing watch over gardening supplies."

Ben stood with his right fist thrust out, pointing his multi-tool at the shed. "You'd be right," he said, glancing over his shoulder to study Jack through those crimsons lenses. "The jamming signal is coming from there."

"So we go for it," Harry said.

"Not yet," Jack replied.

Creeping closer to the edge of the field, he grabbed the trunk of a maple three with both hands and pulled his body close against it. Then he peeked around the side. After all these years, he had learned one thing about Grecken Slade; the man never made anything easy. The sense of satisfaction he felt from Summer made it clear that she agreed.

A little ways beyond the shed, a wooden pavilion that also looked like it had been constructed only recently stood in the middle of the grass. Under its gabled roof, a single man was leaning over a picnic table with his hands pressed to the surface.

Jack knew him well.

Only one man would be pompous enough to wear a thigh-length purple coat with gold trim along the hem and the cuffs of his sleeves. Slade had cut his hair; it now hung loose to his shoulder-blades.

Jack turned back to his friends.

They stood side by side, watching him with quizzical expressions. Well, Harry had a quizzical expression. Ben's face was unreadable behind that helmet, but his posture said that he was expecting an answer. "I'll deal with Slade," Jack said firmly. "Sneak around and try to get the drop on him. When you see me make my move, take out those guards and do what you need to do."

"Right," Ben said.

"Let's go."

"I don't know where he is!"

Jena strode across the gray-carpeted living room with her fists clenched, her face twisted in a haggard snarl. "Even with scanners, it's next to impossible to track a single man in a city this size, and we're cut off!"

Pedro sat at the wooden table with one elbow on its surface, his chin resting on the knuckles of his fist. "Well, then," he said in a pleasant voice. The man really did have a handsome face. "Maybe it's time we took out his jamming equipment."

Closing her eyes, Jena let her head hang. "It's a good thought," she said, spinning around to face him. "There's just one problem. To pull that off, we'd have to know where Slade is, and we're stumped."

This argument had been going on for the better part of an hour, long past the point where Anna had decided that her contributions wouldn't be helpful. In truth, she couldn't blame Jena for being frazzled. Between Aamani, Pedro and a bunch of cops who all had opinions on what their next move should be, it seemed as though the poor woman was fending off attack after attack on her authority.

Anna sat on the couch with one leg crossed over the other, her hands folded primly in her lap. Of course, she said nothing. A wise person learned the value of keeping his or her mouth shut. Well, Anna couldn't say that *she* was particularly wise in this regard, but she did know that her boss was in a fury, and trying to interject now would only send the full force of that storm in her direction.

"So what's our play?" Pedro asked.

Jena stood with her back turned, facing the table with arms crossed. "I'm thinking it's time for a little good old-fashioned recon," she said. "I'll have Anna and a few other people we can trust follow one of those vans back to the source."

Pedro looked up at her with his lips pressed into a line, blinking as if he wasn't sure what to make of the woman who stood before him. "That assumes that they're operating out of a centralized location."

"You have a better idea."

"Not as such, no."

"Well then, I suggest-"

Something was wrong! Anna felt it like a cloud of anxiety that had left a tightness in her chest. Her legs itched with the instinct to get up and *move*, but she couldn't be sure of where she was supposed to go. In fact, she was only certain of one thing. She couldn't say how she knew, but she did.

Gaping at the wall, Anna felt her eyes widen. She blinked a few times by reflex. "It can't be," she whispered. "No, no, Bleakness take you! Why would you come here when we told you to go after the Key?"

Jena spun on her. "What?"

Anna winced, then let out a shuddering breath. "It's Jack," she muttered in a voice thick with tension. "He's here in the city. Don't ask me how I know, but I can feel it, and I know that he needs our help!"

When she looked up, Jena was frowning and shaking her head as if Anna had just said the dumbest thing imaginable. "The stress is getting to you, girl," she said. "We told Jack to go after the Key, remember?"

"Right. Because he's *so* good at following orders!"

"Anna..."

On the other side of the room, Raynar sat in a wooden chair with a book in his lap. The boy looked up, squinting at her. "I wouldn't be so quick to dismiss it, Jena," he said. "My people have discovered that even normal human beings are capable of a rudimentary kind of telepathy."

Jena shut her eyes, breathing deeply to remain calm. "You think this is telepathy," she said, whirling around to face the boy. "Well, if that's the case, what's our next move? Can she send him a message?"

Raynar stood up carefully and dropped his book to the floor. "I doubt it," he said, glancing over his shoulder to scowl at Jena. "I said 'rudimentary telepathy.' She won't get anything but a vague impression."

"Like Jack's location?"

"No," Anna said. "I don't know it." At this point, she was starting to feel stupid. Honestly, what was she thinking, insisting that she knew Jack was here? She trusted her intuition to give her a sense of how to proceed but not as a tool to divine information that she couldn't possibly know.

"Then," Jena said with a sigh, "we continue on as we have."

As he emerged from the trees onto a field of green grass, Jack felt his fear vanish like dew under the glare of the hot sun. The pavilion was a small distance away, but he walked calmly. Those guards in front of the shed might have seen him, but even if they had, they would soon have problems of their own.

Under the pavilion, Grecken Slade stood with his back turned, apparently looking over the details of some holographic display. Jack could just barely make out some of the image before it wavered out of existence.

Slade stiffened.

The man spun around to face Jack with a smile that would make frost appear on a hot summer's day. "Hunter," he said, taking a few steps forward. "I must admit, I didn't expect to find you here."

Jack felt a grin blossom, then shook his head in contempt. "Lovely to see you too, Greck," he said, striding through the grass. "It's nice to know that you still dress like a man on his way to a Jane Austen cosplay."

"And your wonderful japes!"

Thrusting his chin out, Jack squinted at the other man. "You even have the dialogue down!" he said with a nod. "I've gotta give you credit for authenticity, Greck. If there was a costume contest, you'd take first prize in the pompous British wind-bag category."

He came within a few feet of the pavilion, and from here, Jack could see that it did not offer much in the way of cover. A narrow aisle ran from one end to the other between two lines of picnic tables, and wooden beams across the ceiling supported the roof. Those beams were themselves supported by rectangular wooden pillars spaced at even intervals on either side of the aisle.

Slade stood halfway across the pavilion with his arms crossed, watching Jack the way a hunter would watch a wild buck. "So is this the part where we fight?" he asked in smooth tones. "A chance to resolve our differences with violence?"

"Looks like."

"A pity."

Jack closed his eyes, taking a deep breath and then letting it out again. "Oh, wait, I forgot," he said, stepping underneath the pavilion's roof. "This is the part where you give me the chance to join your little cult."

Slade grinned, then lowered his eyes to stare down at his own feet. His soft laughter was chilling. "I'm afraid not. Your talents are nothing short of remarkable, but you insist on following a misguided moral code."

"Well I've always been a bit of a stick in the mud when it comes to wanton acts of brutality," Jack replied. If he could draw this out a little while longer, keep the other man talking, Harry and Ben would have a chance to do their jobs. "You know my friends are always telling me I need to loosen up, but I just don't think terrorism constitutes proper behaviour for a civilized adult. I guess I'm old-fashioned that way."

"Oh, Jack...What I would give to have you on my side."

"What *is* your side?"

Slade turned, sitting down on the edge of a picnic table with hands folded on his knees. He stared off into the distance for a little while. "I serve the will of the gods, Jack. The true gods of this world."

"The Overseers?"

"They are more than they seem."

Tossing his head back, Jack rolled his eyes at the ceiling. "Yeah, and so is Optimus Prime!" he snapped. "Doesn't mean we should start worshiping him. The Overseers are *aliens*, Slade, not gods."

In response, Slade got up and clasped his hands together behind his back. He strode across the width of the aisle, sighing with obvious frustration. "How would you define a god, Jack?" he murmured. "What makes something divine?"

"Ooh! Instead of fighting, can we have a spirited debate?"

"Answer my question."

A response formed in Jack's mind, but he quickly dismissed it as inadequate. The truth was that he had never really considered the question. As a child, he'd been taught about the god of Jesus Christ, a being that was supposedly all powerful and perfectly good. One look at the world around him was enough to prove *that* false, but that didn't mean there was *nothing* beyond the confines of this universe.

He'd always felt a vague sense that there was something out there, but he had no clue what it was. That was the problem with the word 'god;' it had been stretched to mean so many different things over the course of human history that it was practically useless as a concept for...Why was he wasting time on this? Oh yeah, keeping Slade distracted. "I don't know the answer," Jack admitted. "But I can tell you that any being that would have you murder and torment innocent people isn't worthy of worship."

Slade puffed up his chest to suck in a deep breath, then let it out slowly. "Ah, yes," he said, glancing over his shoulder to glower at Jack. "The influence of western religion. Your people are hindered by the idiotic notion that gods should be nice."

"Go to hell!"

"This is hell, Jack," Slade whispered. "*You* make it so."

"I'm not interest-"

Before Jack could finish his sentence, Slade spun around to face him. The man drew aside his coat to reveal a pistol on his right hip, then pulled the weapon from its holster and pointed it at him.

When he saw Jack come out of the trees a little ways off and begin making his way toward the pavilion, Harry gave the signal. "Now," he whispered, glancing to the side to see his partner.

On his right, Ben stood tall and imposing in that black armour. The man withdrew a small sphere about the size of a golf-ball from his belt and tossed it underhanded into the distance. Right out into the open.

The ball landed some ten feet away from the guards who were still standing with their backs to the shed's brick wall. They snapped to attention but quickly dropped their weapons when a hypersonic pulse threw off their equilibrium. Both men sank to their knees, clapping hands over their helmets as if to shield their ears.

Harry emerged from the trees.

He lifted his pistol in both hands, squinting as he took aim. A quick squeeze of the trigger, and that was it.

A bullet flew over the open grass, struck the man on the left just under his chin – Harry had always been a good shot – and caused his body to spasm with a jolt that could rival anything you'd get from a taser. He fell flat on his face.

Harry barely caught the sight of Ben doing the same to the other guard, and then the way was clear. "Is it safe?" he asked his partner.

Ben heaved out a sigh, then looked down at the ground in front of him. "The pulse was only designed to last a few seconds," he said, starting forward. "You can get in close now. Let's finish this."

They ran to the shed.

A wooden door in the brick wall was shut tight. Ben stepped forward as if to pick the lock with his multi-tool, but Harry laid a hand on the other man's shoulder. "We don't have time," he insisted.

Ben glanced over his shoulder, staring at him through that red visor. "You have any better ideas?" he asked, jerking his head toward the door. "I mean unless you plan to just *punch* through the door..."

"Actually..."

Harry raised that hand that carried the N'Jal, erecting a force-field with his mind, a shimmering barrier of electromagnetic energy that looked like ripples spreading across the surface of a pond. He sent it speeding forward and watched the force-field slam into the door with enough force to crack it in half. Two wooden slabs fell to the ground right outside the shed.

Harry closed his eyes, shaking his head with a sigh. "Sometimes you just have to take the direct approach," he said, marching through the grass. "Come on. Let's get this over with."

Inside, the shed was just big enough for two people to stand side by side, packed with shovels and rakes and other tools that were propped up against the windowless walls. Of course, there was also the very obvious piece of alien technology right in the middle of the floor.

It looked like a fire hydrant in terms of size and shape, but instead of the traditional red or yellow, this thing was made of something that looked like chrome steel and it had blinking LEDs all over its surface.

Ben stepped forward, thrusting one fist out to scan with his multi-tool. "A standard jammer," he said, dropping to his knees in front of the thing. "With a password to boot! I won't be able to crack it in time."

"Step aside."

The other man rose and did as he was told, moving off to the side of the shed and pressing his back to the wall. When he was clear of the blast-range, he glanced at Harry and nodded his consent.

Harry raised his pistol in one hand, frowning over the length of his arm. "EMP!" he growled. The LEDs on his weapon turned white.

He fired.

White tracers slammed into the jamming device with enough force to push it back to the back wall of the shed. The thing shorted out in a shower of sparks, then let out one last squeak before it went dead.

Rolling up his sleeve to expose the multi-tool on his left arm, Harry started tapping at its screen. He brought up the communications app, and to his great relief, he was able to place a call.

"And if we don't know where he is!" Jena protested.

The woman stood with her back to Anna, hunched over with hands pressed to the table's surface so that she could snarl at Pedro. "Scouts are the best resources we have at the moment, and I'm tired of arguing!"

Anna squeezed her eyes shut, banging the back of her head against the soft couch cushions. *I don't need this,* she thought, ignoring the anger that tightened her chest. *Will the pair of you stop butting heads for five-*

Her multi-tool beeped.

Someone was calling her!

Swiping a finger across the screen, she watched as Harry's face appeared. The man smiled at her. "Oh thank God!" he said with obvious relief in his voice. "Anna, where are you? We need your help."

Anna felt a smile that she couldn't fight, but she quickly took control of herself. "In Brooklyn," she answered. "Why? Where are you?"

Harry glanced over his shoulder as if he thought trouble might be coming around the corner at any moment. The tense frown on his face confirmed it. "Prospect Park," he said. "We just took out Slade's jamming equipment."

"You're in New York?"

"That's what I just said!"

Only then did Anna notice the silence. She looked up to find that Jena had turned around to face her with a face as pale as snow. The other woman licked her lips, but she said nothing. It didn't matter; Anna could see the question in her eyes. "And Jack?" she asked. "Is he with you?"

"You might want to get your ass down here," Harry said. "He's about to go up against Grecken Slade. Alone."

She looked up at Jena.

The other woman pursed her lips and nodded once. "Go," was all she said.

14

Anna burst through the door.

Dressed in blue jeans and a dark blue t-shirt, she sprinted down the front steps of the safe-house, then doubled over and let out a breath. "What are you doing?" she asked, straightening. "Why are you out here?"

She spun around.

Pedro was leaning against the door-frame with his arms folded, watching her out of the corner of his eye. "You wanna rescue your friend," he said. "You planning on running all the way to Prospect Park? Even for a Keeper, it'll take a good twenty minutes."

Baring her teeth in a snarl, Anna lowered her eyes until she was staring down at her feet. "You offering me an alternative?" she asked, eyebrows rising. "Because you should know it's not safe for you."

"Do I look like a guy who wants safety?"

"No."

He marched down the steps toward her with his arms swinging, refusing to meet her gaze. "Look," he said, stopping right in front of her. "I get that I butt heads with your boss, but I'm trying to help."

Anna looked up at him with wide eyes, blinking slowly as she considered that. "All right," she said, nodding once. "You can drive. But you stay in the Bleakness-cursed car, and you get out of there if bullets start flying."

"Deal."

Before Jack could finish his sentence, Slade spun around to face him. The man drew aside his coat to reveal a pistol on his right hip, then pulled the weapon from its holster and pointed it at him.

Jack raised both hands instinctively, twisting space-time in a way that stretched the world before him into a smear of colour and transformed Slade into a rippling figure who was pointing a gun at him. Bullets sped from the barrel of the pistol, hit the patch of warped space-time and curved upward to hit the pavilion's ceiling. Chunks of wood rained down in a flurry.

Jack dropped to a crouch, transforming the Bending into a time bubble in the shape of a tube that stretched through the aisle between picnic tables. On the other side, Slade was perfectly still.

Jack charged forward, releasing his bubble.

He slammed his shoulder into Slade's chest. The man was thrown backward with enough force to knock the pistol from his hand and hurl him onto his ass. "You wretched little boy," Slade hissed.

The man popped up with fists raised in a fighting stance, sweat glistening upon his flushed face. "Let's finish this," he said in those smooth tones of his. "I've grown weary of your constant meddling."

A smile bloomed on Jack's face, and he bowed his head to the other man. "Glad I'm still a thorn in your side," he said, stepping closer. "It makes me feel all warm and fuzzy when I think of how much pain I've caused you."

"Hardly any real-"

Jack snap-kicked, driving a foot into the other man's stomach. The impact forced Slade to back up with a gasp, doubling over as he tried to regain his equilibrium. Jack rushed in to end this.

He back-handed Slade across the cheek with a blow that would crack bone in any normal human being. A second punch to the man's stomach forced Slade to back up once again. Now to end it.

Jack kicked high.

The other man leaned back, catching his shoe in both hands. A little Bent Gravity lifted Jack off the ground and flung him sideways, dropping him hard onto the surface of a picnic table. He landed sprawled out on his side, rolling and grunting in pain. The other man was a force to be reckoned with. It took effort for Jack to get back on his feet, effort to spin around and face his opponent.

Slade leaped from the aisle, flipping through air and landing poised on the edge of the table. There was no humanity in his eyes, just a cold rage that insisted he would end this by the most efficient means possible.

Slade threw a mean right-hook.

Crouching down, Jack brought one hand up to strike the man's wrist and knock it aside. He used the other to slam an open palm into Slade's nose. The other man stumbled and groaned.

Slade fell backward off the edge of the table, catching himself by slamming both of his hands down on the floor and rising into a handstand. He flipped upright, then kicked the table with enough force to push it backward. Bent Gravity did the rest.

The table slid out from under Jack, surprising him. He

stumbled off the edge, landing hard on the pavilion floor. Hunched over and dazed, he tried to recover before-

Slade punched him in the face, filling his vision with stars. In his mind's eye, he saw the man spin for a back-kick. A sleek black loafer went right into Jack's stomach. It was like being hit with a sledgehammer.

Jack was thrown backward.

He landed doubled over just a few feet away, backing up toward the edge of the pavilion. "I do *not* understand you," he muttered, tossing his head about. "You have the power to help people, and you waste it on this."

His opponent strode forward with a face as smooth as the finest porcelain. "I *am* helping people," Slade insisted. "It is *you* who stands as an impediment to what must be. A shame you do not realize that."

Jack leaped.

He flipped over the other man's head, then uncurled to land right behind him. Every muscle in his body was aching, begging for reprieve. He felt slow and sluggish, and this gave Slade the half-second he needed to spin around.

The next thing Jack knew, there was a forearm pressed to his throat. The incredible strength of his opponent forced him down onto his knees. Trapped by the choke-hold, he was running out of breath. "When I'm finished with you," Slade purred in his ear. "I will enjoy torturing Lenai before I kill her."

Clenching his teeth, Jack felt tears run over his inflamed cheeks. "To be honest, I hope you do kill me," he croaked. "It's the one thing that will pretty much guarantee that she's pissed enough to rip your heart out!"

Jack threw himself backward, forcing them both to the ground. He landed stretched out atop Slade, delighting in the sound of the other man's high-pitched grunt of pain. No time to savor the moment.

Curling his legs against his chest, Jack somersaulted backward over Slade's body. He came up in a crouch just behind the man's head. Forcing himself to stand required a fair amount of effort. The pain in his throat was no small ordeal.

Slade got up, whirling around.

Jack kicked him in the stomach, causing the man to double over. He spread his arms wide, then brought his hands together to box Slade's ears.

The other man backed away, groaning as he passed between two picnic tables on the other side of the aisle. "You could be one of us, Hunter," he whispered. "You could serve the Inzari."

Jack wiped his mouth with the back of his hand, hissing softly. He turned his head and spat on the floor. "No thanks," he growled. "I told those dimwits in Vancouver that I wasn't interested in Scientology, and I'm not joining your cult either."

"You're stronger than I gave you credit for."

Hunched over with a hand against his chest, Jack let out a half-hearted laugh. "And you're much more verbose," he said, shaking his head. "I gotta hand it to you. It takes a special kind of narcissism to like the sound of your voice *that* much."

"You don't understand."

"Try me."

The other man looked at him, and then his face twisted in obvious pain. It seemed he hadn't expected Jack to last this long. "None of us can prevent what's coming," Slade whispered. "But we can minimize the harm."

"What harm?"

Slade winced, shaking his head. "It's too late," he said, stepping forward. "Our only choice is to serve and pray for the Inzari's mercy."

"Hate to tell you this, Greck," Jack said. "But there's not gonna be any mercy for you."

He ran at the other man.

With the broken jamming device toppled over and sending the occasional spark into the air, their work was done. Harry closed down the comm app on his multi-tool and hoped that Anna would get here soon. Regardless, he and Ben weren't exactly helpless. Between the three of them, they would be more than a match for Slade.

Harry was down on one knee in the middle of the shed, rolling his shirtsleeve back down to his wrist. "Our luck isn't this good," he said, shaking his head. "This whole thing has been way too easy."

Ben stood against the wall with his arms folded, glaring at him. Well, it was hard to say *what* the man's expression was, but that visor made everything look like a glare. "I can't believe this," he muttered. "You're *complaining*?"

"I'm stating the facts."

"Ever heard the term 'pessimism'?"

Craning his neck, Harry narrowed his eyes to a fierce squint. "Of course I have," he said, getting to his feet. "But that doesn't change the fact that Slade should have had a lot more security around the lynchpin of his-"

He noticed it out of the corner of his eye.

Through the opening that had once been a door, he caught a glimpse of something coming out of the treeline. He turned his head, and there it was, standing still and silent like the Slender Man himself.

A tall, shirtless man stood in the grass, watching them with a blank expression. He was pale-skinned, hairless from the waist up and marked by some kind of blinking device built into his chest. Harry knew *exactly* what that thing was. He had read the reports, and now he knew there was a good chance that he wasn't walking away from this.

Ben spun to face the door, raising a pistol in both hands. "What the hell is that?" he asked, taking two steps forward.

The *ziarogat* thrust one fist out, pointing at him. White

tracers sped from the tube on its gauntlet, flew over the grass and struck Ben in the chest. He slumped forward, arms hanging limp as the circuits in his suit overloaded. "What in Bleakness?" More tracers struck his helmet. He fell to the ground.

Harry whirled around to face the door, raising his left hand to point the N'Jal at his opponent. A force-field appeared before him, shimmering and rippling, and through it, he could see the blurry figure of the *ziarogat* loping across the grass at inhuman speed. Like a tiger pouncing on fresh meat.

The creature raised its fist again.

Three white tracers sped toward him, phased right through his force-field and hit his chest instead. Thankfully, his body armour absorbed the electric charge – it was of Leyrian design – but the impact was devastating. He felt as if he'd been kicked several times by a horse.

Harry threw himself sideways so that he would no longer be visible through the door, gasping when his shoulder hit the wall. *Oh God...*The pain was so intense he could barely think. *Keep your head together, Harry.*

A head-sized hole appeared in the brick wall, and something zipped right past him to hit the wall behind him. The *ziarogat* had switched to High-Impact ammo. It would bring the whole shed down around him!

Harry threw up another force-field by instinct – it was the only thing he could do – and more holes appeared in the wall. Bullets slammed against the rippling barrier and fell to the floor instead of splattering his brains against the wall. High-impact rounds or EMP rounds: you couldn't have both.

Think, Harry!

Ben was still down! Was he dead?

The ziarogat appeared in the doorway, taking half a second to survey the scene with those reflective, silvery eyes. Its gaze settled on Harry, and then it lifted one arm to aim.

Harry let loose with this force-field, sending it racing across the interior of the shed. That should have knocked his opponent senseless, but the *ziarogat* raised one arm as if to shield itself, and Harry caught the briefest glimpse of a flickering wall of static before the two force-fields collided and winked out.

Despite the pain in his chest, Harry ran at the beast. He slammed into the *ziarogat* like a football player tackling an opponent and forced his opponent away from the shed. By a whole two steps.

Two hands seized Harry's torso, and then he was lifted off the ground, flung over the ziarogat's head. He flew a good twenty feet before landing painfully on his belly in the middle of the open field.

Harry rolled onto his back.

The *ziarogat* was already facing him.

By instinct, he threw up a rippling force-field half a second before a bullet slammed into it. Standard ammunition. The fancier stuff drained your weapon's power cells fairly quickly, but the *ziarogat* would change tactics if he decided to turtle up behind an energy barrier. *Think! You have to think.*

He sat up and sent the force-field speeding forward. However, this time, he angled it to sink into the earth, kicking up chunks of dirt and spraying them at the ziarogat. The creature raised an arm to shield its face, backing up until its body was pressed to the wall of the shed.

Harry loosed another force-field.

This one hit the *ziarogat* head-on, flattening it against the wall of the shed, landing with enough force to leave a spiderweb of cracks in the bricks. Any normal human being would have been dead, but he could already see the *ziarogat* starting to regain its balance. "High Impact!" Harry growled.

He thrust his right hand out to point a pistol with red LEDs on its barrel at his foe. *This is going to be ugly!* He fired.

The ziarogat's right shoulder exploded in a flash of silvery fluid, and then its arm was dangling by a single tendon. Another shot to the torso left a crater in the thing's chest and sprayed silver blood onto the back of one of the men who was still passed out in front of the shed.

The *ziarogat* stepped forward.

Harry felt his eyes widen, then shook his head in disbelief. "Oh, you have got to be kidding me!" he exclaimed. "Seriously? What does it take to kill you bastards?" Worst of all, he'd been aiming for the thing's head. High-Impact rounds were the most inaccurate form of ammunition.

The *ziarogat* stumbled forward, one arm flopping about, its chest leaking silver blood onto the ground. Fortunately, he had damaged the arm with the gauntlet, and the creature wasn't able to shoot at him. "Standard ammo," Harry muttered.

He closed his eyes, breathing deeply, then did his best to calm his nerves. "Sorry, friend," he went on. "But this game is over."

He fired.

A hole appeared in the ziarogat's forehead, and then the creature fell to its knees, collapsing on top of one of the fallen men. The other one was groaning, slowly regaining consciousness. It was time to get out of here.

He was about to go when Ben suddenly appeared in the open doorway to the shed, patting his armoured suit with one gloved hand. The man shook his head vigorously. "All right, someone's gonna have to fill me in," he said. "What the hell was that thing?"

"It's called a ziarogat," Harry said.

"An ancient devil?"

"Huh?"

The other man marched through the grass toward him, his movements slow and sluggish thanks to the damage to his suit. "It's Entarelese," Ben explained. "An ancient Leyrian language."

Harry tilted his head back, blinking at the sky. "Whatever it is," he said, stepping closer to the other man. "Slade constructed that thing as some kind of super soldier. And you saw what it can do."

"How many are there?"

"We don't know," Harry answered. "But I suspect he has only a handful of them at his disposal or we would have come up against more."

"So let's grab Jack and get going."

Harry looked past the shed, toward the distant pavilion in the middle of the field. He could just barely make out two figures facing each other, but the picnic table that had somehow flown a good twenty paces into the grass and toppled over onto its side was an obvious sign that things were heating up.

"That," Harry said, "may be difficult."

The pavilion was a mess with a big empty space where one of the picnic tables used to be and a few drops of blood on the wooden planks. One of the wooden beams had been scarred by the bullets from Slade's gun.

Jack ran at his opponent.

On the other side of the aisle, Slade jumped and grabbed one of the wooden beams that ran across the ceiling. He swung like a pendulum. Two black loafers came flying at Jack's face.

Dropping to his knees, Jack slid past underneath the other man and came to a stop between two picnic tables. He got up quickly, despite the aches throughout his body, and spun around.

Slade was already facing him.

The man spun for a hook-kick.

Jack turned his body, intercepting a polished shoe with both hands before it made contact. A touch of Bent Gravity sent Slade flying face-first into one of the pillars that supported the ceiling. *Now, while he's stunned!*

Jack leaped and kicked out, aiming for the back of his opponent's head. At the last second, Slade blurred and resolidified just a few inches away. Jack's foot hit the beam instead, cracking the wood.

He landed with a grunt.

Something grabbed the back of his shirt, and then Jack was thrown head-first into the pillar. Pain flared as his vision darkened, and he felt blood spilling from his nostrils. Suddenly, he was spun around.

Slade twirled him in a circle as if they were slow dancing, and then his back was to...he couldn't say. A palm-strike to the chest drove the wind from Jack's lungs, and he felt Bent Gravity lifting him off the floor.

Jack flew upward and back until the top of his head nearly grazed the ceiling. His back crashed through one of the wooden beams, with an ear-splitting *crunch,* and then he was falling to the ground, landing hard.

Pain made it hard to think. Damn it, the other man was just too good at this! Jack had faced his share of villains – and he'd gotten pretty good at holding his own against an opponent with Keeper powers – but Slade was a powerhouse. He seemed to drink in the pain of every blow and use it as fuel.

As his vision cleared, he saw Slade moving toward him with teeth bared, bending low to seize Jack's shirt. The other man lifted him until he was in a sitting position, and then a fist slammed into Jack's face.

Everything went dark.

Jack was hoisted to his feet like a rag-doll, his arms hanging limp, unable to follow his commands. Slade whirled him around and threw him across the pavilion.

Jack went flying through the air like a log rolling down a hillside, his battered body crashing through one of the pillars, splitting the wood in two. He landed atop one of the tables and rolled onto his stomach.

The urge to cough was too hard to resist. His body spasmed despite the agony that movement caused him, and he realized to his horror that he had just spit blood onto the floor. A big old gob of blood.

Footsteps coming closer.

Jack tried to force himself up, but he just couldn't find the strength. In the back of his mind, Summer was trembling. The Nassai's fear was like an icy fog that threatened to rip the warmth from his body. She knew it as well as he did: they were going to die here.

Another sound filled his ears. The screech of tires? It made no sense, but when he focused on the spatial awareness that flooded his mind, he saw the blurry image of an old police car racing through the grass toward the pavilion.

The cruiser spun in the grass, turning its passenger-side toward them, and then the door swung open.

Anna launched herself from the cruiser, landing hard in the grass. Feet pounding on the ground, she raced toward the pavilion with such intense speed that she half expected her skin to catch fire.

Slade had his back turned as he made his way across the pavilion toward another man who was sprawled out across a picnic table. Even from here, she could see that it was Jack, and that made her rage boil.

Slade froze in place, trembling for just a moment. The man spun around to face her with his teeth bared. "You!" he spat. "I should have expected as much! Wherever one of you goes, the other follows!"

"Get away from him!"

"And if I refuse?"

She scrunched up her face like a pug dog, then tossed her head about in disgust. "Just give me a reason," she said, passing underneath the roof of the pavilion. "I'd love nothing more than to *end* you."

To her surprise, Slade actually backed away from her with fear on his face, blinking as if her skin really *had* caught fire. "Both of you," he muttered. "This is no coincidence. But it can't be..."

Anna leaped at him.

The man blurred into a streak of colour and resolidified a few feet away. He didn't attack her, though; he just spun to face her and backed up down the aisle toward the end of the pavilion.

Anna lifted her chin to squint at him. "I don't believe it," she growled, shaking her head. "You're afraid. You're actually afraid of me!"

He backed away.

On the picnic table, Jack groaned. It seemed to take an enormous amount of effort, but he looked up to blink at the other man. "You're afraid," he whispered. "What's wrong, Greck? No contingency plans? No cliché villain speeches?"

Slade's face became a hideous snarl, and he blushed. He actually blushed! "I fear nothing!" he insisted. "The will of God protects me!"

"Care to test that will against me?"

In response, Slade turned and ran from the pavilion. He ran through the grass like a man with a hungry lion on his back, like all the victims who had fled from his *ziarogati*. Anna had never seen anything like it.

Instinct took over.

She ran to Jack.

Climbing up to sit beside him on the picnic table, she gently put a hand on his back. "It's okay, Jack," she whispered without really thinking about what she was saying. "I'm here now. I'm here."

He rolled onto his back, groaning, and stared up at her with his mouth open. "Remind me never to do that again," he said, sitting up. "Fighting him is like fighting a hurricane after it just made its first alimony payment."

"What?"

"Just go with it. I'm too sore for coherent metaphors."

Tenderly, she slipped her arms around him and pulled him close, resting his head on her chest. She ran fingers through his hair. "Apparently," Anna murmured. "Because you don't even realize that was a simile."

"Shut up."

"Hate to break up this beautiful moment..." Anna nearly jumped at the sound of a man's voice, and when she looked up, Harry was standing just outside the pavilion with some guy in a dark suit of armour. Sneaking up on a Justice Keeper wasn't easy, but you could manage it if the Keeper was sufficiently distracted. And much to her chagrin, Anna had been pretty distracted.

She would have reached for her gun if not for the fact that she had recognized the speaker's voice. "Ben?" she exclaimed. "When did you get back? No, never mind. Tell me all about it later."

She got to her feet with Jack's arm slung around her shoulder and pulled him up too. Thankfully, he was able to walk, but it was a delicate procedure getting him back to the car. Harry was kind enough to open the door, and she helped Jack into the cruiser's back seat. Once they were settled, Harry got in beside her, and now she was sandwiched between the two of them. "Is Jack all right?"

"He should be," Anna murmured.

Closing his eyes tight, Jack leaned his head against her shoulder and moaned his displeasure. "Thank you," he whispered. "I wouldn't have made it out of there alive if you hadn't come."

Ben jumped into the front seat. "Move," he said, looking at

Pedro who gasped at the sight of that mask. "We've got company."

Anna twisted in her seat to look out the back window.

The field stretched on for a good hundred meters before it ended in a line of trees with thick green leaves. From underneath the branches of those trees, three men in tactical gear emerged.

"Oh no!"

The cruiser veered off to the left before she could get a good look at them, heading back to the road that led out of here. "Everyone down!" she shouted, doubling over and pulling Jack down with her.

The thunderous roar of gunfire filled the air, but very little of it hit them at first. A few soft *pings* of bullets striking the car's metal frame.

Then the window on her left shattered, and something sped over her back, mere inches from her skin. "Harry?" she squealed. He was bent over beside her, grumbling about how he was too old for this, but he seemed to be all right.

They were moving at break-neck speed.

From the corner of her eye, she saw Pedro hunched over with his head down and two hands gripping the steering wheel. He wouldn't be able to see the road like that, but she trusted him. Or did she? Well, it wasn't like she had much of a choice in the matter.

Pedro sat up, looking through the windshield.

There was a hard bump, and then the ride became a lot smoother with pavement underneath their wheels. She saw a line of trees on either side of them. By the Grace of the Holy Companion, they had made it out unscathed. Well, unshot, anyway. Jack was pretty beat up, but no one had taken any bullet wounds. "Get us back to the safe house," she said. "I have a feeling Jena's gonna want to hear the good news."

15

The fog in his mind receded, and Jack realized that he was reclining in an easy chair in a room with brown carpets. A lamp on a small wooden table cast light upon the cream-coloured walls, and the windows to his right were covered by blinds. He could tell that night had fallen.

A blonde woman of average height suddenly leaned over him and stared into his face with her lips pursed. "He's awake," she said, straightening. "I still can't believe it. You're very lucky."

Anna strode past the chair from behind him, pausing to stand in front of him with her back turned. "We heal fast," she said absently. "Our symbionts can deal with pretty much anything that doesn't kill us in the first hour or two."

The blonde woman stepped back from his chair with her arms folded, shaking her head in dismay. "You Keepers," she muttered. "Injuries like that would have finished off anyone else, but him..."

"What about me?" Jack muttered.

"I'm not an expert in Leyrian medicine," she answered. "After five years in the ER, I've seen things you'd never imagine, but never anything like you. From what I could tell, you had some pretty serious internal bleeding, which seems to have stopped. The bruises on your back and abdomen are fading. And I'm pretty sure there was some cranial trauma, though I can't do much to diagnose you from here. It's gone, by the way."

Jack closed his eyes, ignoring the sweat that matted dark bangs to his forehead. He touched three fingers to his temple. "Why *didn't* you take me to a hospital? Don't get me wrong; I'm grateful, but..."

Anna spun around to face him.

She stood with a hand pressed to her stomach, her head hanging as if this subject caused her distress. "Slade's been targeting hospitals," she explained. "Along with many other public facilities."

"Hospitals," the nurse said, "bus terminals, train stations..." A wince twisted the woman's features, and she shook her head with a heavy sigh. "The man seems to delight in causing civilian casualties."

Jack grunted.

It made him sick to think of the things Slade had done. Him and Summer as well. The Nassai was exhausted; he could feel that much but little else. His symbiont seemed to be completely focused on the task of repairing his body, and she spared little attention for his conversation.

Christ, he was famished! Too exhausted to eat, but he knew he would need to put food in his stomach before he went back to sleep. The energy to repair his body had to come from somewhere. Some of it came from Summer, but the rest was up to him.

"I'll give you some privacy," the nurse said.

When she was gone, Anna came over to stand by his chair, smiling down at him in a way that almost took the pain away. "How are you feeling?" she asked in that smooth, gentle voice of hers.

Jack shut his eyes and let his head sink into the cushion.

"Like I've been run over by a truck," he said, pulling the blanket up over his body. "Or forced to watch the first two seasons of *Star Trek Enterprise*."

"Well, your sense of humor's intact."

"Thank Heaven for small miracles."

Anna spun around, turning her back on him. She paced over to the far side of the room where a bookshelf was propped against the wall. "Jena will be calling a meeting in an hour. We need to make plans."

"Mind if I sleep through it?"

"It would provide me with a sense of consistency in my life." She turned, looking over her shoulder at him. "What you did… You and Harry and Ben…It was brave. I think we all owe you our lives."

Jack sat up with some effort and covered his face with his hands. He slid those hands upward to run fingers through his hair. "Well, that vice is pretty versa," he said. "I would be dead right now without you."

Spinning around to face him, Anna leaned against the shelf with her arms crossed and smiled down at herself. "You ever think we should stop keeping track of how many times we've saved each other?"

"If we do that," he replied, "how will I guilt trip you when I'm painfully dismayed by your unsatisfactory Christmas gift?"

She laughed.

A few minutes later, she came back with some food – a bowl of vegetable soup and some chewy bread that Jack wolfed down in less than a minute. He knew that he should eat slower and savour the meal, but he just couldn't, and when there was nothing left but a few drops in the bowl, he was still hungry.

There was something wonderful about having someone else look after you, about being cared for. Or maybe it was just Anna. She had a way of making him feel warm and safe. Somewhere deep inside, the same voice that cautioned him not to eat too fast also warned him that he shouldn't think too deeply on those warm, fuzzy feelings. Anna was someone else's partner. Not his. Perhaps if he'd been at full strength, he would have been able to heed that warning. As it was, he just let himself feel.

"I knew you were here," she said softly.

"What do you mean?"

Anna stood before him with her hands in her back pockets, smiling down at herself. "I could feel it somehow," she murmured. "I knew that you were in the city and that you needed my help."

Jack smiled a lazy smile, then turned his head so that his cheek was mashed against the seat cushion. "I'm not surprised," he replied in a rasping voice. "There's always been something special between us."

She flinched at that.

"Sorry."

Anna sat down on the windowsill with her hands on her knees, hunched over to stare into her lap. "It's okay," she said. "I'm just glad you're safe. Cathy–the nurse–she thinks you'll be better in a day or so."

"Good."

"I should go. Jena...the meeting."

"Okay. Thank you." When she was gone, Jack chastised himself for not listening to that little voice. She wasn't *his* partner! He had no right to...But they had been friends for so long, and there was obviously something between them, and was Bradley the one she really wanted?

No.

No, he refused to indulge such thoughts. Anna could make her own decisions, and she hadn't picked him. They had bigger concerns: Slade, the Key...For once, Jack Hunter could be an adult and do the right thing. He squelched those feelings, letting himself fall asleep.

Harry watched his girlfriend pace across the living room in a fury. With her hands shoved into the pockets of her trench coat, Jena stopped in front of the couch, glared at it, then spun on her heel and made her way back across the room.

Harry looked up at the ceiling, rolling his eyes. "You've been at that for almost half an hour," he said, sinking deeper into his chair. "Don't you think maybe you should try to calm down?"

Jena stopped at the wooden table in the middle of the room, then turned and looked over her shoulder. "You haven't been here for the last week," she barked. "The Bleakness itself has taken this city, and I can't do a damn thing to stop it."

"You've done plenty."

"Not enough."

Slouching in a wooden chair with his arms folded, Harry looked up to squint at her. "So what are you going to do?" he asked. "Sit here and blame yourself for all the things you couldn't prevent? Hey, maybe we should pin the black plague on you too!"

The joke was a mistake – he knew it as soon as the words were out of his mouth – but thankfully, Jena didn't get the chance to bite his head off. The apartment door swung open, allowing Ben and Gabi to come in.

Dressed in black pants and a gray hooded sweatshirt, the young man was much less imposing when you could see his face. "Harry," he said. "Good to see you're still a master in the art of scowling."

"Where are the others?" Jena inquired.

Gabrina somehow managed to make gray cargo pants and a faded blue t-shirt look as elegant as a ball gown. She stood with her hands clasped in front of herself, her head bowed respectfully. "Pedro is down at the station," she said, "checking on some of the prisoners we brought in yesterday. Aamani opted to go with him."

"Great," Jena snapped. "Half my people gone."

Ben stepped forward with his hands in his sweater pockets, chuckling as he shook his head. "Well, before you start planning the next raid," he said. "There's someone you might want to talk to."

He detached the metal disk from his gauntlet and set it down on the table. A few seconds later, the multi-tool projected a hologram that hovered in the air, the transparent image of Larani Tal.

Tall and slim, she looked almost imposing in a simple pair of black dress pants and a matching blouse with the top two buttons undone. Her hair was done up in a bun, pulled back from a sharp, angular face. "Director Morane," she said with a nod. "It seems I must congratulate you."

Jena closed her eyes, bowing her head to the other woman. "I only did what was necessary, ma'am," she muttered. "I wasn't going to sit back and let Slade terrorize over eight million innocent people."

"No, indeed. You did well."

"I take it you have good news?"

Larani winced, shaking her head with a soft hiss. "I only wish that I could say as much," she growled. "Slade's plan was quite effective. Now that communications have been restored, I was able to speak with the other teams who went to New York."

A lump settled into the pit of Harry's stomach, wearing him down. He'd only been here a few hours, but Gabi and Raynar had explained the nature of Slade's plan. Without communication, Keeper teams had been isolated, cut-off from each other. That was why there was only one *ziarogat* defending the jamming equipment; the rest were out hunting Justice Keepers. It made him sick.

"At last count," Larani went on, "twelve Keepers are dead along with several dozen officers of the NYPD. The soldiers that President Mitchell sent to clean up this mess are all missing. No one has heard from them. And that says nothing of civilian casualties."

"Jesus…" Harry whispered.

"Based on the reports we've received, we estimate that Slade had at most twenty of his cybernetic soldiers spread throughout the city. Many reports describe encounters with the same creature. In most cases, a single *ziarogat* would accompany a team of ordinary soldiers and act as a kind of elite unit. Their job would be to isolate one Keeper from the rest of his team and kill him. The others would be too busy dealing with suppressing fire to lend assistance. A crude but effective strategy."

Larani's image floated in the air with her hands clasped behind herself, straight-backed and tall like a politician giving a speech. "As a result, I've decided that it's time for us to change tactics."

Harry wasn't sure that he liked the sound of that, but not being part of their official command structure, it really wasn't his place to say anything. So he waited, and he did what detectives do best; he observed.

Jena looked thoughtful as she watched the hologram. He could almost see the gears turning in her head. "What did you have in mind?"

A flash of anger played across Larani's face before she smothered it and regained her serenity. "Slade has proven himself to be a threat we can no longer afford to ignore," she said. "Therefore, I'm creating a task force with a single mandate: capture Grecken Slade and prevent any further acts of terrorism. You will be leading that task force, Jena, and – if possible – I would like you to utilize the same people you do now.

"It's no secret that your team has developed something of an infamous reputation. The other directors often question your decision to include intelligence officers, telepaths and now an artificial intelligence in your missions. But you've proven yourselves to be a thorn in Slade's side. And that's what I need."

"What about Agent Hunter?" Jena inquired.

Heaving out a deep breath, Larani lowered her eyes. "I will require Agent Hunter's assistance in other matters," she said. "However, I would be willing to loan him to you from time to time. Be advised, if any of you accept this mission, it will almost certainly mean leaving Earth."

"Who's leaving Earth?"

Harry looked up to see Anna coming through the apartment's front door, framed by the light of the hallway. The girl took two steps forward, then looked up at the hologram with concern on her face.

Larani's transparent doppelganger floated in the air with her arms folded. "You will definitely be going, Agent Lenai," she said. "I can't speak for Agent Valtez, Mr. Loranai or Mr. Carlson, but you are being reassigned."

Anna shut her eyes, and for a moment, her face tightened with obvious sadness. Then she took control of herself. "Yes, ma'am," she replied. "When exactly will we be leaving the Sol System?"

"When the immediate crisis is ended," Larani answered. "In the meantime, you're rendezvous with Directors Koss, Shinval and Sinaro. We're going to clear Slade's forces out of this city once and for all."

The hologram winked out.

The others talked for a little while, debating strategy and tactics, but he found that he had very little to say on the matter. He was a detective, not a general; he'd do whatever he could to fight, but coming up with battle plans wasn't his forte.

Thinking about the prospect of another bloody skirmish made him strangely aware of the N'Jal in his pocket. He kept it there when he wasn't using it – and he had decided to avoid using it unless doing so was absolutely necessary – but he was already feeling half-blind without the extra sensory information it provided. His mind was already starting to rely on the device more than he would like.

What exactly had the Overseers done to him? He didn't *feel* any different, but that didn't mean much. He could do something that no other human could – he could control the N'Jal without becoming paranoid and aggressive – and there was no doubt in his mind that the Overseer he had encountered was responsible for this new-found ability. Maybe Jena was right to be apprehensive.

This apartment belonged to one Pedro Juarez, a man that Harry would very much like to meet; though, like any good cop, the man was currently taking care of his own people. That left Harry with very little to do.

Except one thing.

Now is as good a time as any.

A short hallway split off from the living room with a door in one wall that led into the bedroom. In typical cop fashion, the bed was neatly made and the small bookshelf was in pristine condition.

Harry strode into the room with a hand pressed to his stomach, eyes downcast as he studied the floorboards. *This is probably a bad idea,* he noted. *But Della will murder you if you don't at least ask.*

He tapped at his multi-tool.

A hologram appeared mere moments later: a transparent woman in dark clothing who watched him with a quizzical expression. "Mr. Carlson," Larani Tal said. "Is there something I can do for you?"

Harry shook his head. "I'm not sure, Chief Director," he said, stepping back from the hologram. "But I was hoping that I could talk to you about my daughter. She will be joining the initiate training program soon."

Larani frowned, and her face took on the focused expression of someone who was reading something on a screen. "Melissa," she said softly. "Yes, I have reviewed her file; she looks quite promising."

"I was hoping she could train on Leyria."

"On Leyria?"

Harry sat down on the mattress with his hands in his lap, blowing out a deep breath. "Earth is a dangerous place right now," he explained. "And it would do her good to see a little more of the galaxy."

Tapping her lips with one finger, Larani watched him for a very long moment. "I see," she said at last. "Mr. Carlson, forgive my bluntness, but have you asked the girl if this is something *she* wants?"

"I wanted to see if there was a possibility first."

"A transfer can be arranged," Larani answered. "And I would be willing to start the paperwork, but only if Melissa herself agrees to it."

Closing his eyes, Harry nodded to her. "That's more than fair, Director," he said, getting to his feet. "I'll discuss it with Melissa when this crisis is over. You will have her response as soon I can manage it."

"Excellent," Larani said.

The hologram vanished a moment later.

Lying in bed and listening to the sound of Gabi breathing next to her, Anna found herself staring up at the ceiling and thinking deeply about her future. So...She was going back to Leyria after all. A part of her was relieved – this planet had nurtured a cynicism that she would never have thought herself capable of – but leaving *did* feel like giving up. Worse, it felt like she was letting the bigots win.

Every slight by the people – mostly men – who should have respected her position felt like an open declaration that she couldn't do this job, and that just made her more determined to prove them wrong. Decisively. On the other hand, it was an honour and a recognition of her talents to be chosen for this task force. She could do a lot more good working to bring down Slade. Being a Keeper was about more than satisfying her own ego; in the end, it didn't matter what other people thought.

She was going; there was really no way of getting around that. It was best for the people she was meant to protect and for her career as well. The truth of that had been swirling around in her mind for nearly an hour because thinking about her career allowed her to avoid thinking about the one thing she really didn't *want* to think about.

Her relationship with Bradley was over.

On some level, Anna knew that she should have expected as much; the likelihood that she would live out the rest of her life on Earth was extremely small, and that would have been true even if this position had been every bit as fulfilling as she had hoped it would be when she applied for the transfer. Keepers traveled; that was just a fact of life. Sooner or later, she was going to take an assignment on another world. Bradley, on the other hand, would be ill-suited to life anywhere else in the galaxy.

Space-faring cultures were just different than their planet-bound neighbours. You didn't develop the technology to travel faster than light without also harnessing incredible power sources, without also developing nanotechnologies that could build structures and devices at the microscopic level. For centuries, her people had possessed the ability to meet the basic needs of every human being on their planet, and in a society like that, the use of currency just didn't make sense.

Bradley was accustomed to life on Earth. She had no doubt that he would be able to adapt to a moneyless society, but Bradley was a programmer; to be a programmer on her world, he would have to learn new languages, new types of algorithms.

No...

Hard as it was to admit, her relationship was over. She started crying even though she couldn't figure out why it hurt so badly. Just the other night, she had fallen asleep while wondering what it meant that she didn't feel warm and safe when she thought about her boyfriend. Why did emotions have to be such a mess of contradictions?

You can't afford to think about this now, she told herself. *Distractions might get you killed. Push them aside and focus on the mission.*

So, she pushed.

It didn't help.

The window on the second level of a warehouse in southern Brooklyn offered nothing but a view of an old street-lamp that cast white light down on the street below. It was dark in this little office.

He liked it that way.

Grecken Slade stood with his arms crossed, frowning through the open window while the wind teased his hair. "Impossible," he muttered to himself. "The Inzari would never allow it."

And yet, he had felt it. In that brief moment when Lenai had thrown herself at him, protecting Hunter like a mother lioness guarding her cubs, everything had seemed so very familiar. Feelings he hadn't experienced since, since a time long before he'd ever called himself Grecken Slade.

It couldn't be; every rational impulse insisted that he must have been imagining it, but that did nothing to stop memories from rising unbidden to the forefront of his mind. Blood in the snow, the gleam of sharpened steel in the moonlight, the hiss of a serpent. White and red. White and red. White and red. He tried to fight off the memories, to stuff them back into the darkest recesses of his soul, but they kept flowing like water through a crack in a dam. He had to bottle them up before-

The old woman was there in his mind, sneering at him with tears glistening on her face, smirking and weeping at the same time. *No! Get back! Get back, witch!* Her vicious laughter filled his thoughts.

Grecken Slade winced, hissing air through his teeth. "No," he growled, shaking his head. "No, I will not let you back in! You are dead, hag! Dead! Your threats mean nothing to me now."

"Growing restless, Slade?"

Contact with his symbiont allowed him to perceive a tall, hooded figure standing in the doorway behind him with her cloak wrapped tightly around her body. "Best not to let the men see you like that," Isara purred. "They may begin to question your leadership."

"Where is Flagg?" he growled.

When he spun around, Isara stood before him with the cloak parted to reveal a sleek black dress underneath. She spread her hands in a placating gesture. "Dead," she replied and stopped there. If she had intended to say more, she clearly thought better of it.

"And Valeth?"

"Unknown."

Slade looked down at the floorboards, a blush burning in his cheeks. "With Arin in a holding cell," he began, "it seems that all the help we've acquired recently has become unavailable. A pity."

Isara tilted her head just enough to allow light from the streetlamp to penetrate her hood. The outline of her face was barely visible. "Shall I join you here? If you wish, I can kill Hunter and Lenai for you. They'll never see it coming."

"No," Slade answered. "Continue your work on the space station."

"Very well."

He pushed past her, exiting the small office and stepping

onto a narrow catwalk that overlooked a room where men in tactical gear stood in little clusters, conversing with one another. A quick count brought the total to just over seventy. Seventy men who had joined him here after he called them in from roving the streets.

Over two hundred men had followed him on this campaign, and *this* was all that remained. The others had all been killed or captured by Justice Keepers and their allies. That didn't bother him; these men were fodder.

Humanity was a great machine that existed to serve the Inzari, and each man must play his part. Slade was one of the central cogs, but each one of these people had a role in the grand design. If some of them died, it was only a mercy from the Inzari, a chance to claim the rewards that awaited them in the next life.

They were a motley group: tall men and short men, men with muscles and men who looked as though they had trouble carrying the weapons they had been given. Some were fair, others dark. Some had tattoos in the shape of a burning crucifix while others wore the emblems of Islam. The one thing each of these men shared in common was a hunger for the promise of delivery.

Their false religions had promised an eschaton in which sinners would be burned away by a righteous god, in which the world would be cleansed of wickedness, and these men had grown tired of waiting. Slade had restored their faith, had brought them to kneel before a god they could see and hear and touch. Now they were eager to work together in the service of the Inzari. Yes, a motley group of people. There were even some women among them.

He was more than willing to allow anyone who wished to serve him to pick up a gun and kill his enemies, but these people were considered fundamentalists among their respective religions, and most followed a doctrine that said a woman's place was to stand silently behind her husband. With the exception of one or two, most of the women who served him had been atheists before he brought them to the Inzari. Yes, the faithless were quite eager to serve as well. Most people hungered for an end to the pointless monotony of everyday life, and even skeptics would open their eyes when you showed them a god who was really there.

Everyone kept clear of the five large lumps underneath gray canvasses at the far side of the room. That was good. Awe and spectacle were the bread and butter of a man who wished to claim the devotion of his neighbours.

Gripping the railing in both hands, Slade leaned over to direct a smile down at the people who had assembled. "You've come as I asked," he said, running his gaze over the lot of them. "It's time we put an end to this conflict."

One of the people below – a pale man with rosy cheeks – looked up to squint at him. "My Lord," he said in a gruff voice. "Less than half of us remain. We've all fought Keepers, and they're too strong."

"We're stronger."

"But-"

Slade stood up straight and crossed his arms, keeping his face as smooth as ice. "I am disappointed," he said, stepping closer to the railing. "Is your faith so fragile that it wavers the instant things become difficult?"

The man bowed his head, rubbing his forehead with the back of a gloved fist. "No, my Lord," he mumbled. "Of course not. But many of us wonder how we can stand up to the Keepers in light of what they can do."

Moving with the smooth grace of fog rolling across the surface of a pond, Isara stepped closer to the railing. The woman looked like a spectre, her face hidden beneath that gray hood. "Be at ease, Zachary," she said. "The Justice Keepers are not the only ones who possess such abilities."

"The Inzari will provide," Slade insisted.

"But how-"

He rolled up the sleeve of his purple coat, exposing the multi-tool on his left wrist. The screen lit up at the touch of his fingers, and he tapped in a few commands. "You are soldiers in the army of God," Slade said. "Do you believe the Inzari would allow you to walk naked into the embrace of death?"

Those five large lumps at the back of the room began to stir, sheets of gray canvas falling to the floor as they rose like men climbing out of bed. Tall and sleek, five robotic soldiers rose from a squatting position to stand like sentinels guarding the crowd, light glinting off their metal limbs.

Each one possessed something that looked very much like a camera in place of a head, and the lenses focused when they settled on the crowd of startled humans. As one, the battle drones took a single step forward and came to attention.

Large doors to the right and the left swung open, allowing *ziarogati* to flow into the room. They moved with an inhuman grace: men and women clad in next to nothing with blinking panels on their chests and not a trace of hair anywhere on their bodies. Nine of the creatures remained.

They came together to form a front rank among the soldiers, then dropped to one knee before Slade. "And so it was written," he intoned, "that though you walk through the valley of the shadow of death, you shall fear no evil. For *I* am with you."

Grinning exultantly, Slade turned his face up to the ceiling. "The old world shall be purified in fire," he shouted. "And the blood of these sinners will wash away the stain of wickedness! Join me!"

They cheered his name.

"Join me!"

They cheered again, then quieted.

Approaching the railing with his arms spread wide, Slade

let his head hang. "The time has come!" he said softly. "The Inzari have come to uplift the faithful, Now, kneel before your messiah!"

One by one, every last person in the room dropped to their knees. Slade gloried in their adulation, accepting the role that destiny had chosen for him. Not king, not emperor. Saviour. At long last, the Final Days had come. He would deliver these people from the wicked world, and then...maybe the Inzari would finally let him die.

The End of Part I.

INTERLUDE

Keli's eyes snapped open.

She was lying face-up with her hands folded over her stomach, staring up at a dark ceiling. In fact, the entire room was pitch black except for a sliver of light that streamed in through the crack beneath the door.

Keli felt her mouth tighten, then turned her head to look over her shoulder. *Again?* she thought, her brow furrowing. *You never do learn your lesson, do you, Skoro? It seems I'll have to make this one stick.*

Telepaths dreamed but not in the same way that other people dreamed. Too often, the thoughts and feelings of other people drifted into a telepath's unconscious mind, and that made for some colourful and sometimes disturbing imagery. Still, it allowed her to keep tabs on people she didn't trust.

She had sensed Skoro's presence the instant he took his first step toward her room. The man had made three attempts to stab her in her sleep, each one resulting in a very angry Keli waiting for him with some particularly brutal imagery that she forced into his mind. His last attempt had left him weeping on the floor for over an hour.

Shoes behind the door cut off the light from the hallway, creating shadows on the floor. There was a soft jiggling sound, and then the knob slowly turned. Bit by bit, inch by inch. He was careful not to make too much noise, though it didn't do him any good.

The door opened slowly.

Keli snapped her fingers.

Skoro dropped to his knees with a shriek, lacing fingers over the top of his head. In her rage, she imagined spiders crawling over his body, and so there were spiders crawling over his body. Not just the image, but the sound and the texture. What the mind perceived as real *was* real.

Spiders crawled into Skoro's mouth, and then he was coughing and wheezing, both hands clamped onto his throat as he hacked phlegm onto the floor. "You never do learn, do you?" she hissed. Keli swung her legs over the edge of the bed.

She rose and stood over him with her arms crossed, like a taskmistress disciplining a lazy employee. "Perhaps I should leave you like that." The tip of her shoe found its way under his chin and then slowly tilted his face up so he could gaze into her eyes. "Would you like to spend the rest of your life as a madman?"

"You...don't...You..."

"I don't what?"

Skoro shut his eyes, tears leaking from the corners to run over his cheeks. His face was beet red. "We're leaving," he squeaked. "Palia and I, we've been here too long. The authorities will come looking for us."

"You sneak into my room to tell me this?" Not likely, but she sensed no deception from him. Still, even her talents were not absolute. With enough practice, a disciplined mind could hide things from her.

"Come with us," he gasped.

Stroking her chin with thumb and forefinger, Keli narrowed

her eyes. "You've tried to kill me three times," she hissed. "Why would I go anywhere with you? For that matter, why would you want me?"

Skoro was still clutching his throat, choking on his own fear. "You're stronger than you look," he squeaked. "There are many opportunities for a woman who knows how to handle herself."

"I have no interest in material wealth."

"Power then," he squeaked. "Influence."

A sly smile blossomed on Keli's face, and she bowed her head to the man. "As you can see," she began, sitting down on the mattress again. "I have all the power I will ever need. Go if you're going; I don't care."

He looked up to blink at her, phantom spiders scurrying through his salt-and-pepper beard. "You can't stay here," he mumbled. "They're watching...They'll...If you stay, they will take you!"

"I know about the Overseers."

"But-"

"No." The spiders vanished when she stopped concentrating on them, and Skoro dropped to all fours on the floor, wheezing and gasping. "I *came* to this world to find the Overseers," she went on. "I will not run from them now."

Wiping his mouth with the back of his hand, Skoro let out a growl that could have come from a tiger. "You stupid woman," he whispered. "Only an idiot chooses to walk among living nightmares."

"Take your ship and go, Skoro," she murmured. "Pray we never cross paths again; because if we do, I'll do worse than kill you."

He was on his feet in an instant, shuffling back toward the door like a man who had imbibed too much alcohol. "What will you do?" he asked before leaving the room. "You have no ship of your own. Without us, you'll be stuck here."

"I will survive," she answered. "Even now, the help I require is on its way."

The shuttle dropped out of warp, and Jon Andalon watched a planet expand from a single point to fill his canopy window. A dry, brown world of clay and sand and rock, its left side bathed in the light of a distant yellow sun. On the right, the gloom of night was unbroken; there were no signs of civilization here.

Jon scrunched up his face, pulling back from the window. "What an ugly place," he muttered, sinking deeper into the pilot's seat. "This better be worth it, Jena. If you ordered me here for nothing."

Alarms screeched.

Checking his display screen revealed three ships rising from the planet's surface, ships in a configuration he had never seen before. He tapped in a few quick commands and made three green dots appear in the window.

Jon narrowed his eyes to slits. "What in Bleakness are you?" he asked, shaking his head. "Who in bleakness sets up a base all the way out-"

The dots were expanding into wire-frame outlines of tube-like ships with prongs that extended from their bodies, prongs that curved inward toward the front. Two rushed past him into the depths of space.

The third...

When it got close enough, it matched his velocity and loomed over him like a hawk bearing down on a sparrow. This close, he could see that the hull was not made of metal but of something that looked very much like flesh. Living ships? Jon had heard the theory proposed several times, but no one had the slightest notion of how to begin.

The computer warned that he was being scanned, but he silenced the alarm. If these people wanted a good look at him, he wasn't about to provoke them.

Staring out the window with his mouth agape, Jon blinked several times. "What are you?" he whispered to the strange ship. "Where did you come from? And why haven't we ever seen your species until now?"

The ship turned to his left – pivoting thirty-degrees with surprising maneuverability – and sped off into the starry night. Whoever they were, they were unconcerned with him. "Is this why you sent me here, Jena?"

His orders were to scan the planet thoroughly and maintain radio silence until he could deliver a report to Jena herself. Jena and no one else. She had been quite adamant about that. Perhaps it would be a good idea to abandon that plan, or at least touch base with Jena; if there was an advanced civilization here, scanning them could provoke them.

He began keying in a reverse course.

Justice Keeper...

A soft feminine voice filled his mind and nearly made him jump out of his seat. A telepath? To the best of his knowledge, Antaur was the only world in the galaxy to have developed telepathy, and the Antaurans would never let one of their prized specimens of genetic superiority run loose on a world like this.

Justice Keeper, we have no time for speculation.

"Who are you?"

Someone in need of aid.

Leaning back in his chair with his arms folded, Jon turned his face up to the ceiling. "I see," he said, eyebrows rising. "And why exactly do you think I'd be willing to leap to the aid of a stranger on a dead world?"

It is what you two-souls do, she answered. *You came here seeking answers, Justice Keeper. Land your shuttle, and together, we will solve the greatest mystery of our time.*

The airlock slid open to reveal a woman in an old gray

jumpsuit standing in the sand beneath a dark blue sky. She was pretty with a round face and hair that she wore buzzed to stubble. "Justice Keeper," she said.

Jon stood in the doorway with his arms crossed, smiling down at himself. "You're a telepath," he said, stepping through. "Wasn't expecting to find one of your kind out here. Bleakness, I wasn't expecting to find *anything*."

The woman looked up at him with dark eyes that he could drown in. "You know why you've come here," she murmured. Something in her gaze held him transfixed, and he could feel his Nassai struggling, focusing, keeping her out. "The time has come to be honest with yourself. You came to find the Overseers."

He felt his lips curl, then bowed his head to her. "I came because a friend asked me to scan the planet," he insisted. "She'd heard rumors that the Overseers had been spotted in this part of space."

"And the ships you saw when you arrived?"

"I don't know what they were."

The woman slid her hands into her pockets and casually strode past him, stopping just in front of the air-lock. "I think you do," she said. "Come. There isn't much time. I will take you where you need to go."

"I'm not going *anywhere* with you." He whirled around to face her with teeth bared in a snarl, his nostrils flaring as he tried to stifle his anger. "You think you're just going to pop into my thoughts and I'll take you where you want to go?"

She stood with one hand braced against the door-frame, hunched over with her head hanging. "My name is Keli." The exhaustion in her voice was unmistakable. "Six months ago, I encountered one of the Overseers. It nearly killed me."

"You're still not convincing me-"

"I touched its mind for a mere fraction of a moment. What I saw there, I will never comprehend, but a few things stood out.

This world's location, for one. After ten thousand years of silence, the Overseers have returned. Don't you want to know why?"

"Well, of course I do, but-"

"Then come," she said. "Any further debate is pointless."

At night, the hallways of Station Twelve were lit by bulbs that cast a warm, yellow glow on the gray walls and floor tiles. In truth, all Leyrian ships and space stations used the same technology. The lights were meant to match the natural illumination of the sun, and they waxed and waned throughout the day. This kept the crew in better health, or so she had been told.

Isara didn't really care.

She moved through the gray-walled corridor in simple black pants and a matching short-sleeved blouse, keeping her head down. Going anywhere with her face uncovered felt wrong to her now, but she could hardly move about a space station in a long, flowing cloak. From what little she knew of the Earthers' legends, their Death figure wore similar clothing. Isara found that fitting. No one who saw her questioned her presence, and that meant her plan was still working.

A set of double doors in the wall to her left was shut tight. Isara pressed her hand to the palm scanner and watched a horizontal line slide up and down the screen before the device let out a beep.

She tapped one finger against the screen to bring up a menu. Her bio-metric ID had passed inspection, but she still had to input her access code. 77Xs29ge. The computer let out another soft beep of approval. One more thing before she went inside; she turned off the security cameras and ordered them to reactivate in five minutes time. Very few people could disable the station's security systems, but being a junior director had its perks.

The doors slid apart.

Inside, she found a dark room that was quickly illuminated by lights that turned on when they detected her arrival. A long table at the back of the room was now bare except for an inactive tablet that must have belonged to that fool Nareo. The N'Jal was gone. It seemed Harry Carlson had claimed it as his own.

Isara clicked her tongue, then shook her head in vexation. *It must be recovered,* she thought, striding into the room. *If the rumors are true...*

Apparently Carlson could use the device without experiencing any of the negative side-effects. No one – not even Slade – had been able to manage that. It left her feeling very uneasy.

There were work terminals set up on the wall to her left, a table along the wall to her right with something that looked like a high-tech microscope on its surface. None of those would do. When planting a bug, you generally wanted to pick a spot where no one would accidentally come across it.

A table near the door with nothing on its surface: that would do nicely. There was very little chance that anyone would find it there.

Isara went to the table.

Dropping to one knee, she stretched out her hand and attached a small device about the size of her fingernail to the underside.

Her multi-tool lit up with confirmation that the bug was transmitting everything it recorded. Very soon now, Slade would know everything that Lenai and her friends knew about the Key.

The shuttle's nose dipped, giving Jon a view of five jagged rocks that clawed at the sky like the curling fingers of a gnarled hand. A light wind blew dust across hard-packed clay that stretched on for miles.

Pressing his lips together, Jon felt his eyes widen. "That's it?"

he asked, shaking his head. "You're telling me there's an Overseer buried under that? And it's just been sleeping here for thousands of years?"

Standing next to the pilot's chair with her arms folded, Keli stared out the window with a blank expression. "That's it," she confirmed with a nod. "And I don't think that it's sleeping any longer."

"Beg pardon?"

"It knows we're here."

Jon winced, a shiver causing him to tremble in his seat. "Well, that's just grand," he hissed, tapping at the control console. "Do they have horror vids on your planet? Stories about foolish kids who go into a haunted house?"

The strange woman who had somehow commandeered his shuttle just stood there, transfixed by those eerie rocks. "I wouldn't know," she murmured absently, as if she were only half aware of his presence. "I spent most of my formative years in a prison cell. No vids for children with my special abilities."

A prison cell? Had he taken a criminal aboard his ship? A criminal with the power to read minds and even – to a limited degree – pierce through the natural protection that came from bonding a Nassai. What had he gotten himself into?

Jena had asked him to come here and scan the planet, but that was supposed to be the end of it. Come to think of it, how had Jena known about an Overseer presence this far away from Leyrian space? He knew that his old friend had a knack for digging up hard to find intel, but this?

There was a slight jolt as the shuttle landed.

Before he could so much as blink an eye, Keli spun on her heel and made her way toward the back of the cockpit. Why did he get the feeling that she was one of those kids who – when presented with a sign that said "keep out" – couldn't resist the temptation to poke their head inside?

He swiveled his chair around.

Cocking his head to one side, Jon studied the woman for a long moment. "You're really going in there," he asked, arching one eyebrow. "You see, this is what those of us with a sense of self-preservation would call stupid."

She was standing with her back turned at the door to the cabin, hunching up her shoulders as if trying to conserve warmth. "I have seen them," she whispered. "And I...I must know more."

"Why?"

"Because they made us!"

Keli turned halfway around, looking over her shoulder with a snarl so fierce you might have expected her to start foaming at the mouth. "The telepaths!" she spat. "We were their creation."

Jon sat with his arms crossed, frowning into his own lap. "Yeah, I get that," he said, nodding to her. "So what's your plan then? You gonna walk into that cave and say, 'Excuse me, Mr. Overseer. Can you tell me why you tinkered with my ancestor's DNA?' "

"I will scan it."

"Bullshit!"

"What?"

Jon stood up with a growl and strode toward her with his fists clenched. "You really think you're just gonna poke around in that thing's head. I know next to nothing about the Overseers, but I'm pretty sure it will kill you for trying."

The woman lifted her chin and held his gaze until he felt himself sweating. Those eyes. Never challenge a telepath to a staring contest. "That is why you will come with me, Justice Keeper."

She did nothing that he could detect – no mental persuasion, no attempts to bend him to her will – and he was straining to be certain. His Nassai was wary, but there was no sign that it had been disturbed, and Keli would have to go through the symbiont to get to him. So far as he could tell, she was using only words and body language. Which was why it was so surprising that he found himself willing to go along.

Outside, the rocks were standing tall and ominous, forming a kind of haphazard ring, but so far as Jon could tell, there was nothing in the middle. The sun was hot, and the wind that blew dust at him did little to ease his discomfort.

He walked with an arm raised up to shield his face, grunting in displeasure. "This is insane!" he shouted at Keli. "If you want to learn about the Overseers, we'd be better off scanning those ships I saw!"

Keli's face was set in a mask of grim determination as she strode forward. "I have come this far," she growled over the wind. "I refuse to turn back now. Abandon me if you wish, Justice Keeper."

They stepped through the narrow gap between two of those towering rocks, and as expected, there was nothing here. Though being inside the ring did supply some crude protection from the dust storm.

Biting his lower lip, Jon squinted. "Nothing," he said, shaking his head. "There is nothing here, Keli. Have you considered the possibility that the outlaw who brought you here might have been lying?"

"He wasn't lying."

When Jon spun around, Keli had her back turned and stood with her eyes fixed on the ground under her feet. She seemed to be concentrating. Perhaps – if there really was an Overseer down there – she could sense the-

A sudden rumbling made him jump, and he had to suppress the instinct to scream. Justice Keepers sometimes let out a battle cry, but they most certainly did *not* scream like little children at a funhouse.

They were sinking.

It took him half a second to realize that the ground between the stone pillars was actually a stone plate that moved slowly down a circular shaft. After only a few moments, he was already chest-deep inside.

Turning his face up to the sky, Jon stared longingly at the sun. "This is a bad idea," he said with enough volume to be heard over the shaking earth. "Have I pointed out that this is a bad idea? Because it's a *bad* idea."

Had Keli managed to activate this...elevator with her telepathy? Or had she alerted the creature inside to their presence? A little Bent Gravity could have him out of this hole in a heartbeat, but that would mean leaving his companion to die. Meat for the beast. Jon didn't much care for that idea.

The stone plate continued to descend, and now they were a good thirty paces down. From the rumbling, it felt as though the entire shaft might collapse on them any moment. *Why do I let Jena talk me into these things?* he wondered. *I could have just been happy, doing paperwork, keeping the peace in a colony with almost no crime.*

Keli, for her part, seemed to be enjoying this far too much. She stared forward with a great big grin on her face, as if she expected to receive a present.

A few moments later, the stone plate settled to a stop, and when he looked up, he saw that the shaft extended fifty paces or more toward the open daylight. They were in the thick of it now.

A single tunnel ran from the platform into some unknown distance with walls that seemed to glow with a soft, reddish light. "No, that's not ominous," he muttered. "Can you make it go up again?"

"I'm not the one who made it go down," Keli answered.

"Glorious."

She started forward before he could say another word, stepping into the tunnel and moving with the grim purpose of a woman who intended to meet her destiny. "If you are coming," she said without looking back, "I suggest you keep up."

Jon ran to catch up.

Once he was in the tunnel, he realized that the ground beneath his feet felt squishy. One look at the walls confirmed his suspicions. They were covered in soft, membranous tissue. No, not covered. They were *made* of a soft membranous tissue. This was a tunnel of flesh, not of rock.

Closing his eyes, Jon shook his head in disgust. "Why do I always let Jena talk me into these things?" he asked, falling in step beside Keli. "You do realize that we are now *literally* in the belly of the beast."

"Not its belly."

"I'm really not caring about semantics right now."

A brilliant smile split her face in half as she inspected her surroundings. She looked very much like a little girl at her first New Year's festival. "We have been invited in," she said. "The Overseer will not kill us."

"How do you know?"

"I know."

After a little while – more than five minutes, less than ten – the tunnel opened into a wide chamber with a high ceiling. The walls gave off a hellish red light, just enough for him to see. "Where are you?" Keli demanded. "Show yourself!"

HOW LONG?

The voice that boomed in Jon's ears and in his mind as well was enough to make him sink to his knees and press hands to the sides of his head. "What do you mean 'how long?'" he cried out.

HOW LONG?

Keli was on her knees beside him with a hand pressed to her stomach, gasping for breath. "How long since what?" she pleaded. "We don't understand what you're trying to ask."

How long have I slumbered here, human?

Well, that was a little better. A little. Apparently the Overseer had figured out how to adjust the volume. With his mind no longer overwhelmed by the noise, Jon found the will to stand up. Keli got to her feet beside him, dusting off her clothes. "We don't know how long," she answered. "We were hoping you could tell us."

When last I saw your kind, you were nomadic bands of hunters and gatherers. You had barely learned to create stone tools. Now you come here? How is it that you have left the confines of your little planet?

Thrusting his chin out, Jon narrowed his eyes. "Which planet?" he asked, stepping forward. "Our people have flourished on many different worlds. Which are you referring to specifically?"

Impossible.

"What is?"

How did this come to be?

Jon was getting the distinct impression that he had just stuck his nose in something far outside his realm of expertise. At that moment, he felt very much like an ant trying to comprehend a man spraying it with pesticide.

He moved forward with his arms crossed, his head bowed respectfully. "It was your people who took our ancestors from their homeworld," he said. "It was you who scattered us across the galaxy."

In his mind's eye, Keli was watching him warily, but if she had anything to say on this topic, she kept it to herself. Maybe that was for the best. He wasn't entirely sure that opening his mouth was a good idea.

The plan continues unhindered. Was that sadness in the Overseer's voice? Almost as if it regretted what had transpired in its absence. And why shouldn't it? Humans were never of one mind on any particular issue; why should the Overseers be any different? *It should not have been allowed. They refused to listen.*

"Listen to what?"

I must understand.

The flesh that made up the floor of this cave suddenly began to writhe, a huge lump growing until it stood as tall as Jon's waist. Rips formed in its surface as if something was trying to rip free of a cocoon.

He noticed a hand with fingers that were just too long followed by an arm with so much muscle it might have belonged to a professional wrestler. The creature ripped its way free of its constraints, rising to stand tall on two legs. It looked very much like a man – a man who stood over seven feet tall – but its body was pure muscle, and its face...

Smooth skin laced with thin veins covered it from chin to scalp, broken only by two yellow eyes that glowed with a furious light. There was no mouth or nose. Jon suspected that a creature like this didn't need to eat.

So, he had finally seen an Overseer. It occurred to him that he might actually be the only living human being who ever had. Well, him and Keli, that was. No one knew what they looked like, and he had to admit that this was a little underwhelming. He had been hoping for something truly alien.

It came at him.

The creature moved with such incredible speed, it almost seemed to blur, flowing nimbly over a cavern floor that squished with its every step. Those yellow eyes blazed, and Jon knew this thing intended to kill him.

The creature kicked at his stomach.

Jon bent forward, catching its foot with both hands just before it made contact, but the impact was still enough to lift him off his feet. He flew upward until his back almost hit the ceiling, then fell.

Crossing his arms in front of his face, Jon called upon his Nassai and Bent gravity. He launched himself like a missile, flying face-first straight at his target. At the very last second, Jon grabbed the Overseer's shoulders.

He turned upside-down over its head, forcing his opponent

down onto its back, then flipped upright to land behind it. In his mind's eye, he could already see the thing getting to its feet.

He spun around to face it.

The creature swiped at his head.

Jon ducked and felt a clawed hand pass over him. He threw a pair of jabs into the Overseer's stomach, then rose with a jump to deliver a mean right-hook to the cheek. The blow landed with enough force to turn the creature's head aside. If it had possessed teeth, it would have spit them onto the floor.

Seizing Jon's shirt in both hands the Overseer fell backward and brought a knee up to slam into his chest. The wind flew out of his lungs. The next thing Jon knew, he was flying as well, flipping over to land on his back.

Enhanced strength, a disembodied voice said. *Heightened reflexes. You have been modified in some way, human. That does not bode well for species. Which of my kind did this to you?*

Clenching his teeth, Jon winced and felt spittle fly from his mouth. "I don't know what you're talking about!" he hissed, getting up. "We haven't seen your people in almost ten thousand years!"

He turned.

The Overseer was coming at him.

Instead of pressing its attack, it melted, its flesh joining with the tissue that made up the cavern's floor. The creature seemed to collapse into a puddle of skin, muscle and bone, disintegrating until there was nothing left.

Seconds later, another bulge rose from the floor, growing larger and larger until it formed a tent that went halfway to the ceiling. The tissue ripped apart, revealing a beast that looked like a hairless lion.

Four-legged with grasping digits on each paw and a rounded snout where its nose should be, it stared at him through glowing yellow eyes. Then it was loping at him like a wolf on the hunt.

Jon drew his pistol. "High impact!"

He jumped, flipping upside-down as the creature ran past underneath him. He fired and watched a slug strike a spot where the creature's spine should be. Dark crimson blood exploded from the wound.

Jon flipped upright to land on one knee with the pistol raised up beside his head. In his mind's eye, he saw the Overseer fall flat on its belly and slide across the cavern floor. Before it traveled more than two paces, it began to melt again.

A bulge stretched downward from the ceiling, then ripped apart to expose a winged, bat-like creature that descended toward him with talons outstretched. Jon felt a moment of panic that distracted him just long enough.

The creature swooped over him, clawed talons grabbing his shoulders and lifting him right off the floor. It carried him up toward the ceiling. *What are you?* the strange voice whispered. *I do not recognize your kind.*

It slammed Jon hard into the cavern wall, driving the wind from his lungs. May the Bleakness take him, he half-expected the only reason the impact hadn't fractured his spine was the fact that this place was made of soft tissue instead of rock. *You have bonded one of the Brindon-Ka! Its cellular structure is fused with your own.*

"It's called a Nassai," he wheezed.

Nassai? They have developed language?

"Through us, yes..."

The creature threw its head back and let out a howl of pain. Its talons released Jon, and he found himself sliding down the sticky wall with alarming speed. All he got was a brief glimpse of the thing flapping its wings.

He landed on his ass with his legs stretched out before him, groaning as he pressed the back of his head to the wall. "Why do I let Jena talk me into these things?" he asked in a voice so soft it was barely audible.

When his vision cleared, he saw Keli standing in the middle of the cavern with a hand stretched up toward the flying creature. Her face was glistening, and it was clear that she was concentrating. "Enough!" she spat. "Leave him be!"

The creature...flew into the wall.

When flesh met flesh, the ugly thing melted and became part of the cavern once again, its bones and muscles all twisting and contorting with a horrible slimy sound. Listening to it made his stomach turn.

Jon looked up at the ceiling with tears streaming over his face. He blinked several times in confusion. "Why?" It came out as a croak. "Why attack us in this way? We have done nothing to you."

I must understand.

Scrunching up his face like a man who had been kicked in the belly, Jon shook his head. "Understand what?" Deep inside, he felt his symbiont's terror. "If you really want to know about us, just ask."

I must see how the galaxy has changed in my absence. There was definite anxiety in that voice. What could make an Overseer feel afraid? Jon wasn't sure that he wanted to know. *Who possesses the Key?*

"What Key?"

You know nothing of it?

Keli stood with her arms folded, her face turned up to the ceiling. "We have never heard of this Key." Her look of concentration made Jon think that she was trying to probe the Overseer's mind. "What is it?"

If the Key remains unclaimed, there is still time. You must return to the birth place of your species. You must not allow it to be taken by the agents of my brethren...We may be able to...

Jon swallowed.

"Able to what?" Keli demanded.

My brethren have been alerted to my condition. They know that you have roused me from my slumber. Ships are returning to this system at high warp. You must depart before they find you.

Jon got to his feet.

"But there's so much you can teach us," he panted. Staying on his feet was a challenge. "If we go, we may lose the opportunity."

If you stay, you will be taken by the others. They will extract from you everything you have learned here, and then they will accelerate their plans for your species. Rest assured that you will die in agony. Go now, before it is too late.

And just like that, the exhaustion was suddenly a lot more manageable. He ran for the tunnel, gripping Keli's arm as he passed and dragging her along with him. She pulled away from him in indignation, but made no protest as they ran across the slimy ground.

The Overseers knew of what they had done here? Somehow, Jon was pretty damn sure that the one that they had met here was something of an outcast among its people. It seemed to disapprove of the Overseers' plans–whatever those were. Just yesterday, Jon had been unaware that the Overseers *had* plans for his people. He was fairly certain that he would have preferred to remain in ignorance.

Less than five minutes later, they stepped onto the stone plate at the bottom of the circular shaft. It began to rise as soon as they made contact, rumbling and shaking as it traveled slowly upward. Each second brought him closer and closer to a panic. *Come on! Can't this thing go any faster?*

He half considered grabbing Keli, and using Bent Gravity to take them the rest of the way, but he didn't want to tax his Nassai any further.

They reached the surface.

Jon ran through the gap between two pillars, raising two hands up to shield his face from the dust. "Come on!" he growled to Keli. "I don't know how well the Overseers can track us, but the sooner we get out of here, the better!"

The shuttle was sitting on the ground just a few dozen paces away, turned so that its nose was pointed off to their left. He could already see that some dust had settled onto the wing. "Hurry!"

Keli was running behind him, panting with every step and almost stumbling more than once. She slowed down when they got within range of the shuttle. "Just give me a minute."

"We don't have a minute!"

He opened the air-lock with his security code.

Grabbing Keli by the scruff of her neck, he shoved her through then followed. The cabin was a small room with a square table in the middle and a SlipGate positioned along the back wall. Keli dropped into one of the chairs there, which was just fine with him; he was more than content to leave her to rest there.

Booking it to the cockpit, Jon dropped into the pilots seat. His canopy window was covered with a light coating of dust. That would come off fast enough as soon as they got off the ground.

He tapped at the console.

The shuttle rose slowly into the air, then pitched its nose up toward the clear blue sky and sped toward the heavens. Long-range SlipSpace scans showed three warp trails converging on this system from a few lightyears away. They had made it just in time.

The door to the cabin opened.

"They're coming?" Keli asked.

Biting his lip, Jon winced and nodded. "They're coming," he said, spinning his seat around. "Three warp trails on the far side of the solar system. They'll be here in just under five minutes."

Keli stood by the door with hands folded over her stomach,

her eyes downcast so he couldn't see her expression. "This is my fault," she murmured. "They know that we're aware of them now."

"They'd have found out anyway."

He swiveled around to find that the blue sky in his window was fading to a deep black with thousands of tiny lights twinkling in the distance. Another minute, and they would be far enough from the planet's gravity well for a warp jump.

Immediately, he began punching in coordinates, having the navigational computer calculate the safest path to their destination. It would be difficult. He would have to fly around Antauran Space rather than going through it. A Leyrian shuttle in enemy territory? That would not go over well. "Where are we going?" Keli asked from behind him.

"I don't know about you," he answered, "but I intend to deliver this information to the person who asked for it. We're going to Earth."

PART II

16

Silver rays of sunlight from an open window in a white cinder-block wall fell upon a bed that had been set up in the middle of the tiled floor. The patient who sat on that bed was a middle-aged woman with hollow cheeks and long blonde hair that was starting to turn gray. She grunted at the sling that kept her arm immobilized.

Melissa clicked her tongue.

She was down on one knee before the woman, head bowed as she fussed with the sling. "There," she said, nodding once. "That should hold for the time being. I'll get Dr. Hamilton to take a look at you."

"Thank you," the woman muttered.

With a sigh, Melissa stood up and turned around. This place that had once been a classroom in a school on the north side of Queens was now filled with nine twin beds on wheels. With Slade's goons targeting hospitals, it had been necessary to find somewhere else to take the victims who were wounded in the attacks.

Each one of those beds was occupied by people in varying

degrees of distress. An old man with a broken leg, a twenty-something woman who had been knocked out and showed no signs of waking up any time soon. It was awful. Just a few years ago, when Melissa had started high school, she had heard stories about the horrors of World War One. Now, having seen what she had seen, she believed it. *And you want to be a Justice Keeper?* a small voice whispered. *Get ready to see a lot more of this.*

Melissa closed her eyes and shook her head vigorously to dispel the thought. *You have good reasons for your choices,* she noted, making her way across the room. *Dad probably asked himself the same thing a thousand times.*

A woman in a white lab coat who wore her curly brown hair cut short stood in the doorway that led out to a hallway with blue lockers. She was speaking to one of the other volunteers, nodding with every word.

"Dr. Hamilton," Melissa said.

The woman turned her head to frown at Melissa, then her expression softened half a moment later. "Ms. Carlson, right?" she said in that frank matter-of-fact tone doctors seemed to use instinctively. "Is there something I can do for you?"

"I was hoping you could check on the patient in bed 7."

A warm smile bloomed on the other woman's face, and she actually bowed her head respectfully. "I think we can trust your competence with that," she replied. "I've inspected your work several times. You have a future in medicine if you want it."

Melissa felt her cheeks burn, but she managed to keep her composure with a little effort. She really wasn't good at taking praise. "Thank you, ma'am," she said. "But I've already made a commitment to the Justice Keepers."

"Ah yes, I'd heard as much from one of the nurses," the doctor replied. "A shame. But it does present us with an opportunity. Would you walk with me for a few minutes, Ms. Carlson?"

"Of course."

They started up a hallway with bright blue lockers in each wall and fluorescent lights in the ceiling that flickered. The clocks were all wrong, each one blinking the incorrect time in bright red characters.

Melissa crossed her arms and hunched up her shoulders, walking along with her head down. "Have I done something wrong, ma'am?" she managed after a moment. "If so, I want to make it up to-"

Dr. Janet Hamilton stared straight ahead with a smile on her face. "No, Melissa," she replied, shaking her head. "But you will forgive me as news does travel. Is it true that you know several Justice Keepers personally?"

The instinct to answer with an immediate "yes, ma'am," was hard to ignore, but she got a hold of herself before her mouth said something stupid. Maybe she'd been spending too much time with Jack, but Melissa couldn't help but wonder why the woman wanted to know. "May I ask why, ma'am?"

"Because we're in trouble."

Melissa stopped short.

The older woman spun to face her with arms crossed in a perfect doctor pose, her face betraying nothing but composure. "Some of the officers who patrol the streets check in with me," she explained. "We all know that Grecken Slade's terrorists like to travel in large, unmarked vans. Ever since the cell phones started working again, more and more of those vans have been spotted in this neighbourhood, and yet they haven't attacked even one target."

"Meaning they're planning something."

"Exactly."

Melissa hung her head, then covered her eyes with one hand. "I can make contact with Director Jena Morane," she grumbled. "I don't know if the Keepers will be able to spare anyone."

A frown compressed the other woman's mouth into a thin

line, but she nodded just the same. "It'll have to do," she said. "If your phone isn't working, you can borrow mine. Just remember we have a lot of sick people here."

"I'll do what I can."

"Thank you, Melissa."

When Dr. Hamilton left – striding down the hallway toward another classroom full of patients – Melissa found herself feeling a little odd. For the first time in her life, she was important. She was the one with contacts, the one with influence. That was a fairly new experience for her.

She had always been somewhat popular among the girls – and to some extent, the boys – of her school, but no one would ever call her the leader of any particular group. Now, a doctor who would be running a hospital under normal circumstances was coming to her for help. It was unsettling–and exciting.

She grabbed her phone and called Jena.

The light in the bedroom of the apartment that Jena had commandeered flickered as the power faltered for half a second. It came back mere moments later, shining strong on a bed with white sheets and a dresser with a mirror.

Harry was lying on that bed with his hands folded behind his head, staring up at the ceiling, lost in thought. "So I've been wondering," he called out. "Would it be entirely too cliché if I said I was getting too old for this?"

The door swung open to reveal Jena striding into the room in black pants and a tight gray t-shirt. "Nope," she said, throwing some dirty laundry she was carrying into a basket on the floor. "But I might make fun of you."

"So what happens next?"

Jena squeezed her eyes shut, trembling as she let out a ragged breath. "I just got off a call with Directors Koss and Shinval," she said, approaching the foot of the bed. "Now that we can communicate, they've been tracking Slade's people."

Harry sat up.

A yawn stretched his mouth until it hurt, but he stifled it with his fist. "Well, that's good," he said sleepily. "I take it they've been able to figure out where those god damn vans are coming from."

Jena leaned against the dresser across from the bed with arms folded, staring over his head at a spot on the wall. "Most of them are going to a warehouse on the south side of Brooklyn. We think that's where Slade is holed up."

"So, we're going after him?"

"No."

Sighing softly, Harry felt the tension drain out of his muscles. Was it wrong that he was relieved to hear that running head-first into the jaws of death? It wasn't as though he had never been in tough situations before – you didn't survive over fifteen years on the Force without *someone* pulling a gun on you – but outright combat? He'd nearly had a heart attack while they were driving away under fire.

"I also got a call from your daughter," Jena went on. Now, *that* got his attention. As always, whenever he heard Melissa's name mentioned, the first place his mind went was worst case scenario. Had she been injured attending to her duties? No, of course not. Jena would have brought that up right away. "She filled me in on what's going on. They've got her working at a makeshift hospital in queens. One of the doctors there thinks that Slade's people have been skulking about."

"So..."

Baring her teeth with a growl, Jena shook her head. "So we're on guard duty," she said, stepping away from the dresser. "Shinval and Koss are liaising with the NYPD and the National Guard. They're going to raid Slade's warehouse. Our job is to make sure that civilian casualties are minimized."

Closing his eyes, Harry nodded to her. "Minimize civilian casualties." He flopped back onto the bed to lie on his back with hands folded over his chest. "That sounds good. Hell, it sounds like the most noble thing we could be doing."

"I suppose it is."

"You don't think so?"

Jena turned on her heel and paced a line to the window. She paused there with one hand covering her mouth. "It's not about that," she said at last. "Keepers protect life. We should never be eager to *take* it."

"Then..."

"It's about Slade," Jena murmured. "That worthless sack of shit has surprised us at every turn; he's going to pull *some* trick out of his ass, and it's going to be something we never saw coming."

Harry squinted up at the ceiling. "Yeah, I get that," he muttered under his breath. "So you're thinking that Shinval and Koss are leading their people headlong into a trap, and you don't know what to do."

Glancing over her shoulder, Jena studied him with brown eyes that tried to bore a hole in his skull. "Bloody detectives," she hissed after a moment. "Anyone ever tell you it's rude to read a lady's thoughts."

"When I meet a lady, I'll keep that in mind."

"Ass."

The urge to just fall asleep right there on the bed was hard to resist – and worse yet, it was barely past suppertime; he couldn't be so old that he was getting into the habit of passing out before sunset – but he fought it down. The truth was he was starting to think that he should find another room. He'd been sleeping in Jena's bed since he'd arrived here three nights ago, but she hadn't been.

Keepers were known for their stamina, and Harry imagined that being the de-facto leader of a small band of guerrilla fighters was a 24-7 job. That didn't make it any less awkward when she woke him up by slinking into bed at four a.m. And then she was gone by the time he woke up in the morning. He was starting to think that she just didn't *want* to share a bed with him.

Maybe it was nothing. He hadn't had a good night's sleep since coming to this city; there was always *something* going on at all hours of the night. Someone with a report that Jena had to hear about right that second. He would have chalked it up to paranoia if not for the fact that their relationship had cooled off considerably in the last few months. He had told himself that they were both busy people, but somehow that just didn't feel very convincing. "So, are we going to talk about it?" Harry asked.

"Talk about what?"

His face burned as he sat up, and then exhaustion made his head hang. He pressed a hand to his forehead to soothe away his headache. "Talk about whatever's been going on between us."

"Ah..."

Jena sat down on the edge of the mattress, turned so that he saw her in profile. It was clear that she was struggling to find the words. "Don't take it personally, Harry," she said at last. "This is just who I am."

"What do you mean?"

"I lose interest in relationships," she said with a touch of guilt in her voice. "That's the way it's always been with me. It starts off hot, and eventually I just find myself more focused on other things. But I don't want to break up."

"Well, there's that..."

She smiled and let her head hang, staring into her lap for a very long while. "You are a wonderful partner," she began. "And I *do* love you. I'm just, I have never been the kind of person who saw herself living out her entire life with one person."

"Well, that's all right," he murmured. "I've done the whole marriage thing, and it's given me a new appreciation for living in the moment. How 'bout we just stay focused on the here and now and deal with the future as it comes?"

"Sounds good to me."

"What about him?"

Dressed in blue jeans and a frayed gray t-shirt that showed a bit of midriff, Anna sat on the hood of a police car with one leg crossed over the other. Her red hair was left loose in a bob that barely touched her shoulders.

Across the street, a young police officer in plain clothes paced a line in front of the steps that led up to the station, tapping away at his phone the whole time. Most cops had stopped wearing their uniforms when they realized it made them easy targets for Slade's roving bands of terrorists, and she wasn't surprised that the situation hadn't changed even after communications had been restored. This guy was quite handsome with fair skin and a firm jawline, but a baseball cap hid most of his face. "He's cute," Anna said. "You can't tell me he's not cute."

Ben was leaning against the side of the cruiser with his arms folded, scowling as he watched their latest specimen. "Very cute," he admitted. "Probably with abs that'll make you sweat just thinking about him."

"Then why the frown?"

"You have to ask?"

Anna winced and let her head hang, slapping a palm over her nose. "I'm sorry," she murmured gently. "You'll get to talk to Darrel as soon as this crisis is over. But you know why radio silence is a must."

Ben's face hardened, but he nodded his agreement just the same. "I am aware," he whispered. "But it remains to be seen whether Darrel even *wants* to talk to me. I just up and disappeared on him."

"I'm sure he'll understand."

"For all I know, he's dating someone else."

Smooth, Lenai, she scolded herself. Somehow, it had never occurred to her that a game where they enjoyed looking at handsome men right outside a police station could remind Ben that he hadn't spoken to his police officer boyfriend in over three months. *Guard duty really sucks.*

They'd been here for the better part of two hours, keeping an eye on the station in case Slade's goons decided to try anything. Ben had opted to forego putting on his fancy new suit of armour to avoid drawing attention to himself, but he claimed he had a few tricks up his sleeve.

Another man emerged from the station's front door, this one a detective in his late thirties who wore blue jeans and a light jacket. He was handsome with dark skin and a short beard that went from ear to ear.

Ben puckered his lips and blew out a breath. "Now *that* is quite a specimen!" he said, nodding once. "Were I a single man, I might feel compelled to approach him in a manly fashion and declare my intention to mate."

"Get in line."

"*You* are also not single."

Tilting her head back, Anna blinked at the darkening sky. "This is true," she said with exasperation in her voice. "But I'm going back to Leyria in a few weeks. Kind of limits the potential for a happy relationship with an Earth man."

"How do you feel about that?"

Anna hopped off the car.

She marched to the edge of the parking lot with her arms folded, huddling up on herself like a turtle trying to hide in its shell. "How exactly am I *supposed* to feel about that?" she growled. "Awful!"

When she turned, Ben was leaning against the side of the

cruiser with hands shoved into his pockets, watching her with an expression she'd seen on Justice Keepers who were conducting an interrogation. "Have you told him yet?"

"No," she answered. "Radio silence, remember?"

"How do you think he'll take it?"

"Badly."

Anna shut her eyes tight, hissing with frustration. "He's been trying to find ways to make himself a bigger part of my life," she said, marching back to Ben. "The truth is we just walk in different worlds."

She spun around to lean against the cruiser beside him, folding hands over her belly and blowing out a breath. It was a truth she really didn't want to acknowledge, but it had been there since her very first date with Bradley. He was cute, sweet and brilliant, but that didn't change the fact that they were walking on different paths.

Across the street, two officers were standing on the steps that led up to the police station, both dressed in plain clothes as they chatted amicably. One was an older fellow with flecks of gray in his dark hair, the other a young man with Asian features. "What about those two?" she asked.

"Not my type," Ben insisted.

"Oh?"

He slouched against the car with arms crossed, stretching his legs out in the gravel. "The one on the right is too boyish," he said, looking up at the sky. "The other one just has something about him. You ever seen someone just exude cynicism?"

"Since coming to this planet, I see it every day."

"Isn't that the truth? But anyway, about your boyfriend-"

She was spared from further conversation on this uncomfortable topic by a quiet beep from her multi-tool. Swiping one finger across the screen, she answered an audio call. "Hey, guys," Raynar said.

"Hello, hello," Anna replied. "Anything to report."

"Well, I've been scanning the neighbourhood for the last half hour. There's a lot of anger, a lot of fear and distrust; so it's hard to pinpoint any specific feelings of hostility, but I think we're in the clear."

"Can you try one more time just to be sure?"

"Of course."

Perched on one knee atop the roof of the police station, Raynar stared out into the twilight. The wind teased his thick blonde hair, blowing it back from his face. "It'll take me a few minutes," he said with a nod.

He closed his eyes and breathed deeply, savouring the wind's gentle caress. "Most of the neighbourhood has been evacuated," he went on. "It's hard to pick out individual minds when you're dealing with anything more than a few dozen people, but..."

He stretched out with his senses, focusing on the currents of thought and emotion. There was no way to express what he did in terms that non-telepaths would understand, but when his captors had demanded that he describe his experiences, he had developed the habit of using colours to represent emotions.

When he opened his eyes, the neighbourhood stretched out before him: a sea of rooftops that went almost to the horizon. Off to his right, the skyscrapers of Manhattan stood dark and silent with only a few lights in their windows. The city was on lockdown, and no one wanted to risk drawing attention to themselves.

The bright blazing orange of anger formed a thick fog that seemed to permeate the entire neighbourhood. Here and there, he found patches of colour. The deep violet of fear, the brilliant yellow of joy. But mostly anger. There were places where it was deep and red, almost black. That was hatred, contempt.

Raynar licked his lips, then let his head hang. "The urge to do violence tends to be concentrated," he said, rubbing his forehead with the back of one fist. "There are pockets of deep hatred, but none seem to be directed at us."

"No definite plans to attack the station?" Anna inquired.

"Well, it's impossible to be one hundred percent certain," he explained. "My guess is that there are maybe five hundred people left in this neighbourhood, and most of them are cops. I sense hatred, but none of it is directed here. Picking out individual thoughts in a sea this large is next to impossible."

"All right," she said. "Agents Sinalza and Nelson are scheduled to relieve us in ten minutes. Get down here, and let's head home."

A freshly loaded magazine full of bullets sat on a wooden table in the corner of a small bedroom, right next to an unloaded pistol that was pointed at the wall. Jack must have checked it over a dozen times. A funny thing about knowing that you'd be dodging gunfire at some point in the next few days: it made you look for ways to keep yourself busy. Any way available.

This bedroom in the apartment building that Jena called the safe-house had once belonged to a teenage boy. Posters from bands like Fly Under and Sam Lives took up most of the space on the dark-green walls. The kid had good taste. Jack let out a sigh.

He picked up the clip in one hand and the gun in the other, then slid one into the other. The pistol let out a beep, its LEDs flashing momentarily. A check of the power cell revealed that it would last another few weeks.

He tossed it down on the table.

Jack frowned as he studied the gun. He closed his eyes and shook his head. "You're going to make yourself insane," he muttered. "How many times are you gonna check the same damn weapon?"

A knock at the door offered another distraction.

"Come in."

When the door swung open, he wasn't surprised to find Gabi standing outside in a pair of gray sweat pants and a red t-shirt. Her long black hair was done up in a braid that fell over her shoulder.

Jack shut his eyes tight, sucking in a deep breath. "I was wondering how long it'd take," he said, rising and turning to her. "Hell, I'm surprised you didn't come to see me when I was recovering from my make-out session with a wooden beam."

Gabi stood in the doorway with her arms crossed, her eyes downcast as if she were afraid to look at him. "I thought I should check in," she murmured. "But if you're going to be offended by my presence..."

Blushing hard, Jack found himself transfixed by the floor as well. "Sorry," he said. "I'm just a little off-balance. I don't know how to relate to you anymore."

"You seem to be doing fine."

"Well, I have a masters in faking it 'til you make it." Already he was falling back on his habit of deflecting uncomfortable conversation with humor. Not good. But then again, how *was* he supposed to relate to her? She couldn't expect him to just open up about what he was feeling. Not after...

A heavy sigh exploded from Gabi, and she shuffled into the room with none of her typical grace. Dragging one finger along the top of a dresser, she checked it for dust and grunted. "Be honest with me, Jack," she said. "You're a little relieved, aren't you?"

"Relieved?"

She sat down on the bed with her knees together, her hands in her lap. The look of concentration on her face told him this was hard for her. "Now you're free to go after what you really want."

Grinning with a burst of laughter, Jack shook his head.

"You're something else." He began pacing a line at the foot of the bed. "Enlighten me, Gabrina. What is it that I *really* want? I'm all ears."

"I think you know what you want," she said. "It has red hair and a tendency to punch evil things in the face."

A lump settled into the pit of Jack's stomach. So...She knew? Of course she knew. this was Gabrina Valtez, after all. The better question was how long she had known, and more importantly, was this the reason she had ended things with him? The reason she had never been all that gung-ho about their relationship in the first place?

Gabrina stared up at him with lips pursed, blinking slowly as she watched him. "I take it that I struck a nerve," she said in that smooth voice of hers. "Well, I'll take that as a confirmation that I'm right."

Clenching his teeth, Jack winced and let his head hang. "I don't know!" He spun on his heel and threw up his hands. "You want total honesty from me? Fine! I've been trying not to think about it!"

"Why not?"

"Really?" he growled. "You're not noticing our bigger concerns?"

She sat primly with her hands on her knees, breathing out a sigh that said she was annoyed. "Oh, Jack," she muttered, shaking her head. "Extraordinary circumstances like these have a way of bringing things into focus."

"Anna has a boyfriend."

"Have you ever watched them together?"

Jack dropped to one knee next to the table with his gun, then fixed his attention on the floor. "What does that have to do with anything?" he spat. "Just in case it's not clear, I'm not looking to purchase a subscription to Homewreckers Monthly."

In his mind's eye, the blurry image of Gabi rose from the bed and shuffled over to him. He half-expected her to put a hand on his shoulder, but she resisted to fall back into the role of supportive girlfriend. "You make Anna happy," she said softly. "And it's clear that she makes you happy."

"Why should my happiness matter?"

"I see you still have a talent for stupid questions."

He stood up but was unable to find the nerve to face her. It did no good, of course; with spatial awareness, he could perceive her as easily as he could with his own eyes, and now that she was standing within arms reach, he could make out the slight curl of her lips that indicated a concerned frown.

Why did this matter to her? Shouldn't jealous ex-partner syndrome have set in by now? Most people who had just got out of a relationship would be more than happy to imagine their exes growing old alone and bitter. Gabi wanted him to be happy. Why? A thought occurred to him that he didn't like.

Could she have met someone else? Possibly in the final days of their relationship? It was an unworthy thought that he tried to squelch as soon as it popped into his mind – Lord knows, he could feel Summer scowling with disapproval – but unworthy or not, it was the kind of thing most people would think in his place. Jealous ex-partner syndrome was one hundred percent contagious. "What about you?" he asked, turning around with some reluctance. "What happens to you now?"

"I'm retiring from the service," she said. "To have a family."

Leaning against the wall with his arms folded, Jack looked up at the ceiling. "You have *got* to be kidding," he said, eyebrows rising. "You really expect me to believe that Gabrina Valtez is gonna white-picket-fence her way through life?"

"I'll remain as a consultant."

Closing his eyes, Jack let the back of his head touch the wall. "We really weren't meant for each other," he replied in a rasping voice. "It's dangerous, but I got one taste of this job and realized I could never go back."

When he opened his eyes, Gabrina was smiling at a spot on

the floor. "Well that's good then," she said softly. "Because I'm reasonably certain that your soulmate feels the same way. Good luck, Jack. Tell her the truth."

17

Melissa woke, curled up on a small cot in the Principal's office, still fully clothed with the blankets tangled at her feet. The warm sunlight of early morning came through the rectangular window in the white cinder-block wall.

She sat up.

Closing her eyes, Melissa pressed a hand to her forehead. *I need to get more than four hours sleep,* she thought, ignoring her throbbing headache. *How do doctors survive those thirty-six hour shifts?*

The small room was devoid of furniture of any kind except for three other cots that all supported other volunteers, though Teresa – a willowy girl with long auburn hair that fell in curls – was already rising and getting dressed. They said nothing; Brett and Joshua were still asleep. They'd be up and about in less than ten minutes when the doctors started making noise in the hallway. May as well let them enjoy a few precious minutes of dream time. Every moment of rest was a blessing.

Melissa felt her mouth stretch into a ferocious yawn, then clamped one hand over it to avoid being rude. *How long is this little war going to continue?* she wondered, getting to her feet. *It's been what...*

She checked her phone.

Twelve days? Only twelve days since the first attacks on the city? Two weeks ago, no one would have imagined that Grecken Slade would try something. Now, he had one of the world's greatest cities on its knees. Her stomach growled, and she remembered that some of the National Guard had dropped off food supplies yesterday afternoon. Restoring communication had gone a long way toward making that kind of coordination possible. Dr. Hamilton had been using the school's land-line connections to keep in touch with local police, but the Leyrians relied solely on radio-frequency calls. City authorities were skittish about the prospect of making food deliveries without Justice Keeper support.

She moseyed out into a hallway lined with blue lockers in each wall. Scuffed floor tiles ran a good two hundred feet through the narrow corridor to a set of double doors that looked out on the play field.

Dr. Hamilton was already standing with a clipboard in hand, frowning at two of her subordinates – a pair of doctors in blue scrubs. "We're running low on painkillers," she said. "Start rationing them. Severe cases first."

"Yes, ma'am."

"Ah, Melissa, good." The doctor spun to face her with a smile and a curt nod of approval. "I trust you slept well."

Melissa felt her cheeks burn, then bowed her head to avoid eye-contact. "As well as I could," she mumbled after a moment. "Where would you like me to start this morning? Room fourteen again?"

"No, I need you to move some supplies."

The urge to ask what kind of supplies had barely formed in Melissa's mind when the door at the end of the hallway swung open to reveal several people standing in the morning sunlight.

One strode forward with a commanding presence. Short and slim, she wore a simple pair of black pants and a matching t-shirt. Her red hair was pulled up in a ponytail, and the hallway lights glinted off the lenses of her sunglasses.

Anna moved with the kind of easy confidence that Melissa could only hope to attain one day, flanked by Jack and...her father? Harry was here? In the city? Suddenly, Melissa felt very uneasy. Her father wasn't exactly a young man. What was he doing throwing himself into this mess? *That's probably how he feels about you.*

"You came!" Melissa exclaimed.

Anna reached up to lower her sunglasses so she could peek over the rims. "Were you expecting us to do otherwise?" she asked, arching one eyebrow. "You should really know us better than that."

Jack was smiling with his eyes closed, shaking his head in wry amusement. "Dude, she just gave you the *perfect* setup!" he exclaimed. "Riding in to save the day at the last moment! You're supposed to say something witty."

A frown thinned her father's lips as he stared down at the floor in front of him. "So now that we have the requisite silliness out of the way," he muttered. "Maybe we could get these supplies in place."

"Always down to business, eh, Dad?"

"We have a lot to do."

Well, that was certainly true. It turned out the whole gang was here: Ben and Gabi and Raynar as well. Most of them were busy unloading crates from police cruisers that had pulled into the school's parking lot. Jena had liaised with the senior Justice Keepers, and they agreed that there was a good chance Slade's men would try to hit this "hospital;" so they were mounting a defense.

She spent the next three hours lugging crates full of medical supplies down to the school's maintenance room, taking the odd break to check in on her patients or eat a light snack. To her chagrin, most of the work was done by Keepers. It wasn't that she wasn't trying; she and Raynar would drag a single crate halfway through the school while Jack or Anna walked past carrying two on their own. On his way back to the parking lot, Jack would often stop, grab whatever Melissa and Raynar were holding and carry it the rest of the way himself. It was tiring but fulfilling. She had an opportunity to chat with Raynar, which was nice.

After hauling the final crate into the maintenance room, she and Raynar heaved out a sigh of relief and took a moment to rest their aching muscles. The room was essentially a prison cell of white cinder-blocks with no sources of natural light. Blue metal shelves on each wall were loaded with cleaning supplies equipment.

Raynar was doubled over with a hand on chest, gasping as he tried to catch his breath. "Is this what your school is like?" he mumbled, staring at the wall. "All bright colours and trophy cases?"

Melissa shut her eyes, rubbing sweat off her forehead with the back of her hand. "Well, this is an elementary school," she explained. "But really, there's not all that much of a difference. My school is the same, just bigger."

Raynar sat down on one of the crates with his hands on his knees, hunching up his shoulders as if he were trying to fight off a chill. "I wish I could tell you what schools on my world were like."

"You've never seen one?"

"Life in a prison cell, remember?"

Leaning against the wall with her arms crossed, Melissa hung her head in shame. She should have chosen her words more carefully. "Right," she said, nodding to him. "Sorry. I guess I thought you would have seen pictures."

He was smiling at her, his gray eyes catching the light of the fluorescent bulbs. "No need to be sorry," he said. "I find most people prefer to ignore my history."

"I wasn't-"

"I know."

Tilting her head back, Melissa blinked at the ceiling. "Seems you've missed out on an awful lot," she murmured. "No sports, no parties...No sneaking in at 2 a.m. and hoping your father didn't notice you were out past curfew."

He shrugged, then leaned forward with a burst of wheezing laughter. "Well, there was Keli," he said, shaking his head. "Not exactly what I would call a friend, but...In a way, she knows me better than most people ever will."

"How's that?"

"I was there to provide her with target practice," he said softly. Such a disturbing sentiment delivered in such a calm, rational tone: it almost made Melissa want to shiver. "She'd burrow through my defenses every day, dig through my memories."

"That sounds awful."

"It was."

Raynar stood up with a sigh, slipping his hands into his back pocket. He turned on his heel and paced a line to the cinder-block wall. "On my world, telepathic violation is a serious crime," he said. "But Kelli was their pet project. The military was trying to make a new kind of soldier."

Now *that* made her feel sick to her stomach. Would she ever understand this insane obsession with creating new and more lethal kinds of soldiers? She'd seen footage of the monstrosities Slade had created out of living people, but that was hardly the first attempt at making a super solider.

Amps had been a failed project designed to give an ordinary person the physical capabilities of a Justice Keeper, a project that had produced such disastrous results, it had been classified until Jena exposed it last year. And this was the work of the peace-loving Leyrians. What might other powers in the galaxy have come up with?

The truth was that this had all started with the Keepers themselves, To her knowledge, they were the galaxy's first super soldiers. And here she was, trying to join their ranks. "And you were just...disposable to them?" she asked.

Raynar trembled.

"That's awful."

"Very much so."

Hugging herself and rubbing her upper arms, Melissa felt a shiver pass through her. "And now you're throwing yourself into the heat of battle," she said. "You've never even been to a party."

He turned, looking over his shoulder, watching her through narrowed eyes. "I had a few good months on Earth," he said. "Saw things I never thought I'd see. If I die here...at least I have that much."

Melissa felt her mouth tighten, but kept her eyes glued to the floor. "Still," she said, taking a cautious step forward. "Nobody should die at the age of eighteen. Especially not someone who spent most of their life in a cell."

Raynar spun around to face her and leaned against the wall with his hands clasped in front of himself, head hanging in dismay. "That's just the way of the world, Melissa. I don't make the rules."

"Bullshit."

"What?"

Anger flared inside her, anger and disgust at his unwavering pessimism. On some level, she could understand it – his life had been horrible – but she refused to accept it. "You don't know the rules of how the world works."

An idea occurred to her, one that she would very much like to pursue, but it just wasn't her way. Melissa could be outspoken when it came to her work or her values, but in matters of the heart, she was always hit by a paralyzing shyness. It was how she ended up dating people who weren't that good for her. When you couldn't speak up, you were pretty much relegated to whoever was willing to pay attention to-

Raynar looked up, squinting at her. "You want me to *kiss* you?" he exclaimed with such disbelief in his voice. "I... Melissa...I've always valued your friendship, and I would be lying if I said I didn't find you beautiful, but I don't want to impose..."

Closing her eyes, Melissa bowed her head to him. Her face was on fire. "It was just an idle thought," she mumbled. "I mean...Correct me if I'm wrong, but you spent most of your life in a cell; so I'm betting you've never kissed a girl."

Now, *he* was blushing and refusing to make eye-contact. "You're not wrong." He stepped away from the wall, then pressed a fist to his mouth and cleared his throat. "But I don't want you to do it out of pity."

"I wouldn't."

"Well, that's good."

Melissa looked up at him, blinking several times as she chose her words. "I don't pity you, Raynar," she said softly. "And this is not the first time that I've thought about kissing you."

He stepped forward, approaching her with his eyes shut, and let out a deep breath. "Okay," he said with a curt nod. "Then I guess I should tell you that I've thought about kissing you too."

"You have?"

"Many times."

"You know, I suddenly realize that it's incredibly unfair that you should get to read my thoughts when I don't get to read yours."

The ghost of a smile appeared on his face, and he reached up to run fingers through his thick blonde hair. "That's life with

a telepath," he murmured. "You're going to have to get used to unfairness."

"Well, as long as you make up for-"

He gently took her by the shoulders, pulling her close. Then his lips were on hers, and though it was clunky at first, he quickly discovered exactly what she liked. Telepathy, she supposed.

After a moment, he pulled away and smiled at her. "Well, then," he said. It felt different than it had with other guys. Significant in ways she couldn't quite put into words. "Of all the experiences in my short life, that was one of the best."

"Do me a favour," Melissa said. "When you go out there to fight Slade's people, make sure you come back."

Jena removed the lid from a crate to reveal several light-armoured vests in various sizes within. "You like 'em?" Jack asked from behind her. "I certainly hope so, because Larani sent a few dozen more."

Chewing on her lip, Jena shut her eyes and took a deep breath. "I like them," she said, nodding her approval. "A few dozen more, huh? I take it Larani has decided to arm Pedro's officers as well."

She turned around.

Jack stood before a blue cinder-block wall with hands clasped behind his back, smiling at her. "Yeah, the whole nine," he said stepping forward. "Leyrian assault rifles, Leyrian sidearms. She wants us ready for whatever Slade throws at us."

Warm sunlight came through the windows of the school's staff room, illuminating round tables that were spaced out on a white tiled floor. At the moment, several other people were present.

Pedro leaned against the wall with his arms folded, his head turned to stare out the window. The man seemed to be effecting a casual disinterest in this discussion. Not that she blamed him. From day one, Jena had made it undeniably clear that she was the brains of this operation. The man probably expected to have more of a say.

Ben sat on a table by the window with his knees apart, feet resting on a gray plastic chair. "Well, then at least we have a fighting chance," he muttered. "Though I have to say I feel sorry for Larani."

"Why's that?" Jack inquired.

"For years, it's been Leyrian policy to avoid sharing weapons with Earth's military and law-enforcement agencies. Larani must feel backed into a corner to even consider this. She's been doing a lot of ethical compromising lately. My presence here being yet another example."

Closing her eyes, Jena tilted her head back. "We've all had to make hard choices," she said, striding toward Jack. "And we can deal with the fallout of those decisions later. Right now, we need to talk strategy."

"That could be a problem," Anna said.

The girl sat at one table with her elbows on its surface, her chin resting atop laced fingers. "This school is located in the middle of a grid of intersecting streets," she said. "Slade could attack us from any direction."

"Can we evacuate the patients?" Jena inquired.

Jack narrowed his eyes as he stared into the distance. "No," he said, shaking his head. "I brought this up with Dr. Hamilton an hour ago. Many of these people are not in any shape to be moved."

"One thing I don't understand," Pedro grumbled. "I've seen footage of Leyrian aircraft. No matter what Slade may have at his disposal, you people *have* to have more firepower. Why not just blow him away before he can attack?"

Her mouth a gaping hole, Anna tilted her head back to blink at the ceiling. "You've got to be kidding me," she muttered. "First of all, Slade's people may be driving vans, but that doesn't mean that every van on the road is carrying armoured thugs and *ziarogati*. We are *not* in the business of killing civilians.

"Second of all, the kind of ordinance that can inflict serious damage on a starship are not well-suited to densely populated urban areas. Unless you're planning to turn large sections of this city into smoking craters, air-strikes are out of the question."

"I see," Pedro muttered. "Well, that really only leaves us with one option. My guys will have to patrol the streets in squad cars and call in if they see anything suspicious."

"There may be another way," Jena replied. "With communications restored, I could ask Station Twelve to monitor the city with surveillance drones. That would give us some advanced warning when Slade makes his move."

She looked up to find Pedro scowling at her and shaking his head in dismay. "Your people have surveillance drones?"

Touching two fingers to her forehead, Jena let out a deep breath. "We seldom use them," she mumbled in a voice strained by exhaustion. "We consider it to be a violation of basic privacy rights, but the technology exists."

"I think," Ben cut in, "that under the circumstances, we might be able to justify an exception to that policy."

"I'll make the call," Jena hissed. "In the meantime, Anna, I want you to take a team and monitor the neighbourhood. If you see anyone suspicious, detain them and figure out what they're about. Let's see if Slade really is targeting this place."

"On it."

Through a pair of binoculars, Anna watched the rooftop of the building across the street, the auto-zoom coming into focus on Aamani, who was crouched by the ledge and peering through the scope of her rifle. She must have noticed because she looked up just long enough to make eye-contact and nodded.

Anna was lying flat on her belly on the roof of a small office building. Though her hair was tied back, thin red strands still framed her face. "Eyes open, people," she said into her multi-tool. "Raynar, you in position?"

"Yes, ma'am."

She swung her binoculars to the right to find him in a window on the top floor of Aamani's building. The kid looked focused, his eyes fixed on the street below. Melissa's doctor friend claimed that Slade's people had been driving through this neighbourhood more frequently in the last few days.

Well, if that was true, Jena wanted to know it. Director Kos was planning to hit Slade's warehouse tonight, but that didn't mean there wouldn't be trouble in the meantime. Most of the city had evacuated to Queens while their little band of rebels had tried to keep engagements bottled up in Brooklyn. But it seemed Slade had deduced their plan, and if Melissa's reports were correct, he was planning to hit this neighbourhood. "Ben," she said. "You good to go?"

"I'm discreetly out of sight," he murmured through the speaker. "But I can pop out and tag any vehicle that happens to come by."

"Good," she murmured. "Watch the periph."

Jack was down on his stomach beside her, holding a pair of binoculars to his eyes. "It's gonna be okay," he whispered for her ears only. "If they're here, An, we'll find them before they do any damage."

Anna shut her eyes, hissing softly as she tried to fight off her anxiety. "You haven't been here," she said, shaking her head. "You haven't seen the kind of damage that Slade's monstrosities can do."

"I sense this is personal."

"It is."

From the moment she had set foot in this city, it had been one thing after another. A food crisis, meetings, hit-and-run attacks – some by her side, some by Slade's people: all of these things kept her busy almost every waking second. She hadn't had *time* to think, and in those few moments where she could actually stop and breathe, her personal issues rose to the forefront of her mind.

But last night – in an effort to avoid thinking about what moving back to Leyria would mean for her – she had focused her thoughts on Slade and what they could do to put an end to all this. It came to her then that the sense of restless unease she had been living with and not thinking about went back to that day on Station One. That day when she had *let* Slade walk away instead of shooting him.

Blushing hard, Anna closed her eyes and let her head hang. A soft sigh escaped her. "Do you remember coming to see me when I was pummeling that punching bag? Telling me I made the right call when I let Slade escape?"

"I recall that if you'd done otherwise, he would have disabled the life support on Station One and killed three thousand people."

Anna lifted the binoculars to her eyes, growling as she peered through them. "And I asked you what would happen if he did something awful?" she muttered. "What if he set off a bomb that killed a million people."

Out of the corner of her eye, she saw Jack look up with tension visible on his face, his brow lined with deep wrinkles. "Not sure I like where this is going, An. Even *I* would not blame myself for what happened here."

"I don't, but..."

"You wonder if you made the right choice?"

Clenching her teeth so hard they made a grinding noise, Anna shook her head in disgust. "Jena told me I had to make the hard choices," she growled. "Well, I followed my conscience that day, and look what it got us."

Jack scooched closer, gently patting her back with one hand. The warmth of his touch took some of her anger away. "I like the Anna who follows her conscience," he said. "Don't ever change."

She smiled.

"Look alive, people," Aamani said through the speaker.

When she lifted her binoculars to her eyes, Anna saw a black car rolling down a street lined with short, squat buildings and strip malls. A car, not a van. The driver was about as ordinary as any man could be – late thirties with stubble on his jaw – but there was something here that didn't feel right.

With the city crushed beneath its own fear, people had fled as far away from the kill-zone as they could get. Queens had been relatively safe until recently – most of the fighting had taken place in and around Manhattan Island – but that was changing. It was incredibly unlikely that anyone would just drive through the city for anything less than a medical emergency.

Even people who needed food were now sitting tight and waiting for the National Guard to deliver supplies to designated shelter areas. With communications restored, the city authorities could coordinate such activities. "Raynar," Anna said into her multi-tool. "What do you sense from them?"

"They're intently focused," the boy answered. "And apprehensive. But that could mean anything. I can't tell you anything specific without probing deeply into their minds, and they would feel it if I tried."

"Nix that," she said. "We'll use visual cues."

Suddenly, the car threw itself into a U-turn, tires squealing as it looped around to head back in the direction it had come from. All she saw was a pair of red taillights receding into the distance. "I think we've been made," Jack mumbled.

"Impossible," Aamani replied.

Anna winced, shaking her head. "I'm not taking the risk," she said, crawling closer to the ledge. "Aamani, take out their back tires. Ben, get ready to cover us. Jack and I will converge on the vehicle."

"Girl, your judgment on this matter is hardly-"

"We don't have time to argue this!"

There was a slight popping noise, and then a screech as the van wobbled off course and then drove up onto the curb in front of a strip mall. One of its tires was flat, but the shot hadn't come from across the street.

She looked up to find Jack crouched beside her with a pistol in both hands, his eyes focused on the car. "You got 'em on the hook," he said. "Time to reel 'em in."

"Nice shot," Anna said. "Stay close to me. We do this nice and slow and precise."

He nodded without a single word of protest, and Anna had to admit she felt a little stunned. She had grown so used to people assuming that she was incapable of doing her job that she had come to expect it from everyone. In fact, Jack trusted her so completely, he leaped at the chance to see that her orders were carried out when Aamani refused.

And this was *Jack bloody Hunter:* the man who questioned authority as easily as a fish swam through water. Not with her, it seemed. It was quite the gesture from a person like him. He didn't just respect her; he *trusted* her.

Together, they approached the ledge. A three-story drop... On her own, it would be doable, but she would have to time her Bending perfectly, reversing gravity's pull at the exact midpoint of her fall. With Jack's help, however, things would be much easier. Seth and Summer could work together to ease them down to the ground.

She took Jack's hand and felt warmth blossom in her heart. No time for that now. He was already crafting a Bending that would weaken Gravity's pull. Anna closed her eyes and had Seth as his strength to Summer's.

They stepped over the edge...

And fell.

Slowly but surely, the ground came up to meet them, and when they made contact, it felt like they had jumped from a ledge maybe five feet up. Hardly even a jolt. "Come on!" she growled.

Drawing her pistol from its holster, Anna gripped the weapon in both hands and ran into the street. She dropped to one knee in the middle of the road, raising the gun to point at the car.

No more than twenty paces away, the car's passenger-side door swung open and a slender man with flecks of gray in his dark hair got out. "Justice Keepers," he said when his gaze fell upon her.

Anna narrowed her eyes to a squint, then nodded once in confirmation. "We were just wondering what brought a guy like you all the way out here," she said. "Care to sit down and have a little chat?"

On the other side of the vehicle, the driver slowly emerged to stand with his back turned, staring off into the distance. "You know our orders," he said. "Lord Slade made his wishes clear."

The man with salt-and-pepper hair frowned as he studied Anna; then he bit down on something and spasmed. His body collapsed to land sprawled out on the pavement with feet twitching. "What in Bleakness..."

The other one dropped half a second later.

Jack watched the whole thing with his mouth hanging open, his face so bone-white he looked ill. "Suicide capsules," he whispered. "They'd rather die than risk giving us any useful information."

Anna ran to them.

She fell to her knees as she drew near, practically sliding

the last few inches on the rough pavement. With trembling hands, she turned the body over to find a pale face with dead eyes staring up at the sky.

Anna wrinkled her nose, then shook her head in frustration. "Damn it!" she hissed, getting to her feet. "All right, Slade will almost certainly have some protocol in place for when these two fail to check in."

She turned to Jack.

"Call Jena," she said. "Tell her we should expect company soon."

18

The call came in later that afternoon; surveillance drones in orbit had spotted three vans driving in single file on the Union Turnpike, making their way toward the school. It was very likely that these were Slade's forces.

As she got into one of the many police cruisers that had been mobilized to intercept these people, Anna breathed a sigh of relief at the knowledge that the neighbourhood had been evacuated of all civilians. From the moment she had reported the two men who had taken suicide pills – less than four hours ago, but it felt like *days* had passed – getting all non-combatants out of the kill-zone had been their first priority.

Fortunately, even a few hours warning meant plenty of opportunity to put a plan in motion. Pedro had made a few calls to his associates at various precincts, and now they had over six dozen police cruisers on the move along with several SWAT teams equipped with Leyrian weapons and armour.

It was hard to see through the windshield while she was stuck in the back seat, but she caught a glimpse of the turnpike. Other cruisers were already in place on both sides of the concrete median that bisected the road, forming a barricade.

Her car swerved to the right, settling to a stop.

Then Officer Tedesco's round face filled her window as he leaned in close to open the door. "Hurry!" he growled, gesturing frantically. "We just had an update. They'll be here in less than five minutes."

Anna got out of the car.

She closed her eyes as the wind sent strands of her hair flying. "You can do this," she said, nodding to the man. "You've got the best armour, the best tech, and the NYPD is legendary when it comes to bringing down criminals."

He smiled. "Yes, ma'am."

There was no exaggeration in what she told him; the guy was decked out in full tactical gear – a thick black vest that would absorb the shock of EMP rounds and slowly repair itself with nanotechnology, a helmet with a visor that would sync with his gun and allow him to target enemies with precision accuracy and allow them to better coordinate their fire.

Anna was dressed in similar apparel, though – like most Keepers – she had opted to wear light armour and forego a helmet to make better use of her spatial awareness. "Go to it, Officer," she said. "You're gonna kick some ass today."

"Yes, ma'am."

On the south side of the road, adjoined homes with balconies on their front walls stood three stories tall. She could already see Aamani in one of the third floor windows. The woman was focused as she peered through the scope of her sniper rifle.

The north side of the road was comprised of several shops, including a laundromat, a Chinese restaurant and a grocery store, that took up almost the entirety of a city block. Plenty of places to duck for cover if you didn't mind crashing through a window.

Four cruisers made one side of a barricade. The goal was to herd Slade's minions down the turnpike – with cop cars positioned at the intersection of every side street to prevent them from getting any bright ideas – and then, once the first barricade forced them to stop, more cruisers would form a second barricade behind them, boxing them in. A simple but elegant plan.

Simple but elegant and doomed to fall apart the way *all* plans fell apart the instant bullets started flying. Something would go wrong. Something *always* went wrong. Slade had a knack for disrupting just about every single strategy they employed.

Dressed in a full suit of black armour with his eyes hidden behind that glossy red visor, Ben was down on one knee by the median. He looked very imposing in that get-up. She almost shivered at the sight.

It was only her, Ben and maybe two dozen armoured cops on this side, but Jack and Harry would take position behind the second barricade once it was in place. Two "super humans" on each side of the battlefield: that was how Pedro had put it. Jena had been all kinds of livid when the rest of the group insisted that she hang back and call strategy, but that was the role of a general.

Raynar was hiding in one of the townhouses, ready to dazzle Slade's goons with a tempest of illusions the instant the shooting started. Anna wanted him out of the way. He was a lousy shot, and there was no sense putting him in unnecessary danger.

She dropped to a crouch beside Ben.

"You know, it occurs to me," she began. "There has to be some way to resolve this without violence. So, hear me out. What if I were to just stand on top of the barricade and overwhelm them with my adorable disposition? You know, when I graduated high school, I was voted least likely to be shot by a terrorist."

He turned his head, and she saw herself reflected in that

crimson visor. "I'm afraid your charms would be wasted," he said. "These are people who signed up to work with Slade. If they're willing to follow someone with *that* little fashion sense, I'm afraid they have no sense of aesthetics."

"But...My impish smile!"

"Even so."

Standing behind the spot where the bumper of one police car met that of another, Sargent Michael Evans of the NYPD suddenly stiffened. "Heads up, people!" he barked. "We've got incoming!"

Anna and Ben scooted into a space behind one of the cruisers on the south side of the road, and then she ventured a glance over the hood. A large black van was barreling down the road toward them, trailed by two others – one blue, one green. In the distance the wail of a police siren rang through the air. "Positions!" Anna yelled.

Officers in full tactical gear popped up to aim Leyrian assault rifles over the hood and the trunk of each car. They waited with a cat-like readiness, every muscle taut. Anna heard a few nervous murmurs.

The vans just kept coming.

"They're gonna ram us," Ben whispered.

Clenching her teeth with a hiss, Anna shook her head. "That tells you everything you need to know," she growled, aiming her pistol over the hood of the car. "Tire shots! Let's give ourselves some breathing room!"

Bullets zipped through the air, piercing the gray van's tires with a loud *POP!* The vehicle swerved sideways, t-boning with the blue van that was coming up from behind in the other lane. Both slid to a stop perhaps a hundred feet from the barricade.

She caught sight of the police cars that followed in hot pursuit stopping to form a second barricade on the far side of the block. Boxed in with nowhere to go. Even if these men had *ziarogati* with them, chances were they wouldn't put up much of a fight.

"Agent Lenai!" one of the officers cried out. "Look at the van!"

She looked and saw nothing to merit such alarm. The gray van's front end had been crumpled by the impact, and there were thin tendrils of smoke rising from the metal. She couldn't see the damage to the blue van, but it had to be just as bad. What could be so damn frightening about-

Anna noticed it when she looked through the driver's side window. There *was* no driver! These vehicles had been drones, sent here on auto-pilot. Something was wrong! Bile churned in the pit of her stomach.

Something *always* went wrong.

The van's back doors swung open, allowing *ziarogati* to spill out onto the median that divided the road. She counted ten of them – some men, some women – in every skin tone imaginable. Every single one was bald, and then they looked at you, those lifeless silver eyes seemed to peer into your soul.

She was about to give the order to open fire – even *ziarogati* would go down if you pummeled them with enough ammunition – but Aamani distracted her by chattering on the radio. "No! No! No! Not again!"

What?

The other vans...

Anna tapped her ear-piece to activate her microphone. "Raynar," she said into the radio. "What do you see?"

Down on her knees by the third-story window of a townhouse, Aamani watched the whole scene unfold through the scope of her sniper rifle. The gray van had deposited its passengers onto the median, but it was the other two that got her attention.

The blue and green vans were parked side by side – though

the former had been wrecked by the collision – and they shook as their back doors swung open. A hulking metal monstrosity emerged from each vehicle.

Smooth and sleek with sunlight glinting off its metal body, the robot stood over eight feet tall and moved with the cold inevitability of a guillotine blade. The camera it had in place of a head swiveled to point its lens at her.

Aamani hoisted up her rifle, switching to EMP rounds.

She fired.

A white tracer slammed into the robot's head, causing the camera to explode in a shower of sparks. The battle drone stumbled sideways toward the median, but it wasn't finished yet. These things had secondary systems.

It spun to face her, raising one metallic arm to point at her window. The closed fist split apart to reveal a cannon underneath. It shot something. Not a bullet but a missile of some kind.

Aamani threw herself backward, landing face-up on the bedroom floor. Something came through the window, punched through the ceiling and then exploded in the attic. Chunks of plaster and dust rained down upon her.

The house where Aamani had been positioned now had a smoking hole in its roof. There was a good chance the woman was dead. Panic seized Anna as she watched her enemies assemble. Four huge robots – two spinning to face her, and two turning to the secondary barricade where Jack and Harry were leading another team of officer.

The *ziarogati* divided up as well, five of the creatures joining each pair of robots. Just five, but it may as well have been an army.

Anna felt the blood drain out of her face, her eyes slowly widening. "Companion have mercy," she whispered, shaking her head. "Battle drones! EMP rounds. Hit those things with everything you have!"

A flurry of white tracers converged on the inhuman beasts like snowflakes in a blizzards. The *ziarogati* raised forearms to shield themselves, and force-fields appeared. Most of the EMP rounds phased right through them and caused the creatures to stumble, but that did nothing to slow their approach.

The *ziarogati* began a fierce sprint forward like orcs charging the battlements in one of those fantasy movies Jack liked. They moved with a smooth, fluid grace. Behind them, the robots lifted their arms to take aim.

"Get back!" Anna screamed.

Her people began to move away from the cars, men and women in tactical gear shuffling backward but still loosing a storm of ammunition. White tracers attacked the *ziarogati* like a swarm of angry hornets.

It did no good.

The *ziarogati* leaped right over the police cars, landing poised on her side of the barricade. In unison, they thrust out their arms to point those bullet-spitting gauntlets at the retreating SWAT team, but several of the creatures faltered as glowing slugs stung them. One got off a shot.

Michael Evans staggered as high-impact rounds ripped through his armour with a spray of blood. His corpse dropped to the ground moments later.

Blessedly, some of the cops were ignoring the *ziarogati* and spraying bullets at the robots instead. White tracers hit the battle drones, briefly shorting out their circuitry. It was their only hope of surviving this skirmish. If they could keep their opponents too off-balance to get off a shot, they might get out of this alive. But the instant that those drones weren't too busy repairing themselves to attack, this was over. And it would be over as her people had to reload. Bleakness take her, it would have been over already if not for the fact that they were using Leyrian weapons.

Despite the onslaught of gunfire, one of the robots managed to shakily raise a hand to point at the nearest police car. A small missile erupted from the drone's arm cannon, hit the cruiser and consumed it in a mushroom cloud of flame.

The flaming car was flung off the ground, flipping upside down in midair to descend upon a dozen retreating police officers. They hopped out of the way just in time, but one stumbled and fell onto his side. Bullets took him in the neck seconds later.

She had to do something!

Anna turned, running for the townhouses on the south side of the road. Throwing her arm out to the side, she put up a Bending that turned the world into a smear of colour just before bullets converged on her. They curved upward instead, zipping off into the clear blue sky.

A discarded rifle on the curb.

Sliding her foot beneath the barrel, Anna kicked it upward and caught the grip in one hand. She ran through the grass toward the townhouses, cognizant of people crying out for help behind her.

She leaped with a surge of Bent Gravity and shot upward in a wide arc that carried her toward one of the second-floor balconies. Landing hard behind the metal railing, she spun around and immediately threw up a Time Bubble. Her skin was burning, but it didn't matter. It was this or death.

Outside the sphere of warped space-time that surrounded her, the world appeared to be a blurry, pulsating mess, but she could easily make out the gray blobs that represented the robots and a few tiny specs that were bullets coming for her. At this rate, it would take them several minutes to reach the surface of her bubble. Of course, she would be unable to maintain the Bending that long. Her symbiont was already starting to protest.

Anna lifted the rifle in both hands, squinting as she took aim. She fired a three-round burst at the first robot and then pivoted to send three more slugs flying toward the second. White tracers appeared beyond the surface of her bubble, moving with painful slowness toward their targets.

Anna dropped to a crouch.

She let the bubble vanish and felt bullets fly over her to strike the sliding glass door that led into the townhouse. The pane shattered in a cascade of falling glass, but she was barely even aware of it.

Anna popped up, firing.

The battle drones were stumbling backward over the median, moving toward the north side of the road. More charged bullets struck their metal bodies with a quick flash of sparks. *Have to keep them off balance.*

She alternated from one robot to the other, firing three-round burst after three-round burst. If she could damage the drones' key systems, it would render them harmless. For a moment, she recalled that one she had destroyed in Wesley Pennfield's parking garage. A few EMP rounds in the right spot, and they would lose the ability to target accurately.

Her people saw what she was doing and focused their efforts on the *ziarogati*. One of them had been reduced to a puddle of silver blood and torn flesh. But the victory had come at the cost of five officers who were now down.

Another one of the *ziarogati* was fighting Ben, forcing him back to the far side of the street. *No time to think about that!*

One of the battle drones stumbled drunkenly but somehow managed to raise its arm cannon to point at her. Panic hit her when she realized that it didn't have to be accurate to kill her with explosives.

Anna jumped, flipping over the balcony railing. She

uncurled to drop like a pin to the grass below, landing hard with a grunt.

A missile flew through the air above her, struck the balcony railing and exploded on contact. A huge fireball expanded outward, sending chunks of mangled metal flying off in all directions.

Anna threw herself into the grass, landing on her belly and lacing fingers over the back of her head. Luckily, the concussive force of that explosion was strong enough to propel most of that shrapnel right over her.

Some of it – tiny pebbles that had been part of the brick wall or small shards of metal – stung the backs of her legs or cut up her exposed arms. Those Bleakness-kissed drones would need a moment to reconfigure after the damage she had inflicted.

She got up and ran.

The *ziarogat* stood in the middle of the road: a tall, shirtless man so pale he was likely to get a sunburn just from a few minutes exposure. His hollow-cheeked face was stuck in a blank expression.

In the distance behind him, Anna was running toward the townhouses while bullets from the battle drones curved away from her. Ben wasn't sure what she was doing, but when she jumped for one of the balconies, he figured she had a plan.

The *ziarogat* came at him.

It leaped with a high kick that took Ben across the cheek. The impact would have knocked him senseless if not for his helmet. He recovered just in time to see the *ziarogat* land in front of him.

The creature spun for a back-kick.

A plain gray shoe slammed into Ben's chest, driving him backward. Without his armour, that hit would have cracked ribs. As it was, he was left stumbling away toward the north side of the street.

Ben raised his forearm up in front of his face, triggering the force-field generator on his gauntlet. A wall of buzzing white static appeared in front of him, cutting off the *ziarogat* as it charged in.

He sent the force-field speeding forward.

The *ziarogat* leaped, flipping over the wall of electrostatic energy. It uncurled to land in front of him, then thrust its arm out to point that gauntlet right at his face. At the last second, Ben tapped a button on his belt.

Another force-field appeared before him, blocking the high-impact slug that would have punched right through his helmet. *Well, that's both generators drained in less than two minutes!*

Ben threw his left arm to the side, a razor-sharp blade of nanobots extending from his gauntlet. He waited half a moment for the force-field to wink out, then charged the *ziarogat* at full speed.

Ben slashed at the creature's stomach.

The *ziarogat* hopped backwards, evading the blow with smooth, fluid grace. A shoe slammed into Ben's stomach, doubling him up despite the armour's protection. The next thing he saw was a knee coming up to strike his visor.

Stumbling frantically backward, he raised his arms up in front of his face to shield himself. A desperate idea occurred to him – one that was guaranteed to fail – but he tried it anyway, because what else could he do?

The *ziarogat* came at him.

Thrusting his fist out, Ben triggered the defense mechanisms on his gauntlet and sent a pair of electrodes on thin wires flying toward the creature. The *ziarogat* stopped in midstep – stunned for half a second – and that was all it took.

Both electrodes hit the creature square in the forehead,

sending a jolt of electricity through his body. The *ziarogat* trembled from the shock, its limbs twitching, its lifeless eyes bulging in their sockets.

Ben rushed forward.

He swung his blade in a horizontal arc that sliced cleanly through the creature's neck. The head tumbled backward, dropping to the ground, and silver blood fountained from the neck before the body collapsed.

A gruesome way to kill, but he wanted to be absolutely sure the damn thing was dead. Still, something didn't sit well with him. In the fray of battle, he watched the cops trying desperately to contain the remaining two *ziarogati*.

What he had done shouldn't have been possible. These creatures moved with the strength and speed of a Justice Keeper. The *ziarogat* should have caught the wires or moved seamlessly out of the way. Something was slowing them down!

There was a puzzle here, and he suspected that surviving meant solving it.

Raynar had never been so frightened in all his life. Not during any of the practice sessions where Keli tried to violate his mind. Not during any of the times when the staff of that gods-forsaken base had "disciplined" him with stun batons. Not during any of the other engagements in this little guerrilla war.

It was those bloody robots!

The *ziarogati* he could deal with – for all their cybernetic enhancements, they were still human at their core – but the drones? They had no minds for him to manipulate. Not like Ven. Ven's thoughts were alien and unrecognizable to him, but they *existed*. Not so with the drones.

He peeked through the window to take stock of the situation once again. The battle drones were divided: two on his left, firing at Jack and his group, two on his right, firing at Anna and hers. The air was so thick with panic and grief and agony that he thought he might suffocate. *You have to control yourself,* he growled inside his own head. *You're the one who begged to come along on this mission.*

Squeezing his eyes shut, Raynar felt tears leak from the corners. He shook his head in despair. "*Ziarogati* don't respond to illusions," he murmured. "They just follow their programming and ignore the distraction."

Of course, he could focus on a single *ziarogat* and immobilize it so that the cops could riddle it with bullets, but those creatures were slippery. Their minds seemed to resist outside control. Every time he had one pinned down, it began to counter his efforts, relying on some kind of hardwired programming to override his commands. They fought back, and it drained him quickly.

Raynar had discovered that the best way to help was to apply a light touch to all *ziarogati* at the same time, one that would slow their reactions by mere fractions of a second, but those few precious moments might mean the difference between getting a protective force-field up in time and dying from a shot to the chest.

Squeezing his eyes shut, Raynar trembled with fatigue "Hold on," he whispered in a ragged voice. "Just a little while longer. If anyone can bring those things down, it's-"

The house rattled with a devastating impact, and he became aware of a deafening roar in his ears only after his heart stopped racing. Yet another explosion, this one off to his right somewhere. The first one had nearly given him a heart attack.

Those drones were shooting missiles at the townhouses!

Gods be praised that they had evacuated this area before the battle began. In fact, the people who lived here had left their doors unlocked so that he could use this room as a vantage point.

Sweat was pouring over his face, matting golden hair to his

brow. He wiped it away with the back of one fist. "Just keep focused," he told himself in a breathy whisper. "Just a little while longer."

He focused on the minds he knew – Jack and Ben, Harry and Anna – hoping to get a sense of how they were doing. The Keepers were hard to read; the Nassai instinctively blocked his probes. But he tried just the same. He had to know that his friends were all right, that they were-

Something was wrong.

As he strained to sense his friends, he became aware of another mind, a presence so faint it might flicker out at any moment. At first, he couldn't tell who it was, but the sense of her became clear when he focused. Aamani! Aamani was alive! But she was hurt, and there was no one to go to her.

He got up and turned away from the window.

A small living room with a coffee table and a couch greeted him, and he could see the stairs that led down to the first level. Raynar ran for them, staying low in case anyone saw him through the window.

He practically tumbled down the stairs.

On the first floor, there was a kitchen with white cupboards and beige floor tiles. A window above the sink looked out on the alley behind the townhouses, but there was no back door. He wasn't about to risk going out the front; that was for damn sure. He could not help Aamani if he took a bullet to the head.

Raynar ran for the sink, bracing hands on the countertop and lifting himself off the floor. There had to be something he could do!

Baring his teeth with a hiss, he winced and shook his head. "Come on!" he said to himself. "Think! There has to be something!"

A flat block of wood with a handle was sitting on the counter. He assumed that the people here used it for chopping vegetables, but what little he knew of cooking involved his own people's technology. Still, it would do.

Raynar picked up the chopping board...

...And he smashed the window.

Once, twice, three times! The pane cracked on the fourth strike and then shattered completely on the fifth. He used the chopping board to clear away fragments of glass, and then he hopped up onto the counter.

Crawling through the window, he wiggled and groaned as a few tiny shards dug into his flesh. "Damn it! Damn it! Damn it!" He pushed himself through like a fat worm digging through the dirt and then dropped to the concrete floor of the alley.

Raynar felt hot tears on his cheek and sweat on his brow. "Let's go," he whispered, getting to his feet. "You dawdle just a few more minutes, and she's gonna die. You want that? Huh?"

The red-bricked town houses formed one wall of the alley, and he could already see that smoke was rising from the roof of one a few doors down. That was where he would find Aamani.

He ran despite the pain in his belly.

When he reached the first-floor window of this house, he began pounding it with the chopping board. This one seemed even thicker – or maybe he was just getting tired – but it took nearly ten blows to shatter the thing.

Raynar grabbed the ledge of the windowsill and then pulled himself up, wiggling over more shards of glass. He slithered over the sink, then dropped onto a floor of blue tiles with a grunt.

This kitchen was very much like the other, but the cupboards had a dark wooden finish, and things were in a slightly different position. No time to admire the décor. He had to get moving.

When he got up, he saw few red spots on the floor. He was bleeding. The glass had cut up his belly, and every step was an agony.

Raynar shut his eyes tight, hissing as he tried to push the pain out of his mind. "It'll be all right," he whispered to himself. "Just get your gods-forsaken ass up the stairs. She needs you!"

When he got to the third floor, he found a hallway with a burning ceiling and thick clouds of smoke that assaulted him. The heat was ferocious, but the fire hadn't spread to the floor yet.

At the end of the corridor, the burning outline of a doorway revealed a woman's body trapped beneath a pile of rubble in a room with no ceiling. Sunlight was coming through a hole in the roof.

Raynar doubled over and ran through the hallway as fast as he could, ignoring the scorch of heat on his back. He stumbled through the open doorway and then dropped to his knees next to the body.

Clearing away chunks of plaster with his hands, he uncovered her face. A nasty, red gash ran from the top of her forehead to just above her left eyebrow. Her black hair was now gray with dust.

Aamani's eyes fluttered open.

She gasped and then started coughing, turning her head to push her cheek into the gray carpet. "The drones," she mumbled, trying to rise from underneath the rubble. "Not again...Not again."

Scrunching up his face with a throaty growl, Raynar shook his head. "No time to worry about that," he said, grabbing chunks of plaster and tossing them aside. "Come on! We need to get you out of here."

She sat up with some effort.

Raynar had to pull her to her feet with quite a bit of struggle, and it certainly didn't help that standing up brought them closer to the oppressive heat of the flames. What little he knew of medical training suggested that moving her could be fatal – for all he knew, she had serious internal bleeding – but then leaving her *here* would be fatal as well. At least this way, she had a shot at life.

Aamani slung her arm around his shoulders, and they shuffled away through the burning corridor.

As he watched *ziarogati* leap over the wall of police cars, Jack felt a sudden jolt of fear. The cyborg creatures landed in a crouch, then immediately raised forearms to throw up flickering force-fields. Most of those glowing bullets phased right through the energy barrier, but the creatures were undaunted.

They charged forward.

Over two dozen cops in black TAC gear started backing up in a horseshoe pattern, still loosing a storm of bullets. Harry was on the south side of the road, using the N'Jal to shield himself with a force-field of his own.

Biting his lower lip, Jack scrunched up his face. "So much for the simple plan," he hissed, shaking his head. "These people are all gonna die."

Beyond the barricade of police cars, one of the two battle drones that had come his way lifted its arm to point that cannon at his people. Bullets sprayed from the muzzle in seemingly endless stream.

Jack drew his pistol.

Raising the weapon in both hands, he squeezed the trigger and watched as three white tracers sped over the police cars to strike the robot square in its shiny metal chest. The drone stumbled as it tried to recover.

The other one spun to face him, having reassessed him as a credible threat. A flurry of glowing white ammunition hit the robot like rain pelting the side of a building during a thunderstorm. It staggered, unable to take aim.

Two *ziarogati* were standing side by side in front of the police cars, both with arms raised to fire bullets at the retreating cops. It was time he put some of these fancy Keeper powers to good use. Summer encouraged him.

Jack holstered his gun and ran for the *ziarogati*.

He leaped and somersaulted through the air, uncurling to land on the road just in front of them. He reached out, clamping one hand onto each *ziarogat's* forearm. Then he crafted not one but *two* separate Bendings.

The *ziarogati* were flung apart, one hurled toward the south side of the street, the other toward the north side. Both moved under the influence of a gravitational field ten times as powerful as the Earth's pull.

One *ziarogat* hit the front wall of a townhouse with enough force to shatter bones and leave a smear of silver blood on the bricks. The other one went sideways through the plate glass window of a laundromat.

Exhaustion hit Jack hard.

By instinct, he tapped the button on his vest, erecting a screen of flickering white static that intercepted incoming fire from the drones before it punched right through his uncovered head. Bullets slammed into the force-field and bounced off. That would only give him a few seconds of protection.

Jack dropped to his knees behind the police cruiser, taking cover. The force-field winked out a few seconds later. Now that the generator was drained of power, it would be useless until it was recharged.

Bullets flew over his head.

Despite the burning in his skin, the throbbing in his temples, Jack put up a Time Bubble. Summer groaned in his mind, but the sphere of warped space-time expanded, encompassing part of the car.

He shuffled to the right and popped up to get a look at the drones. The surface of his bubble made it seem as if he was looking at them while under water, but the blurry gray giants stood with arms upraised.

One was firing a stream of bullets over the roof of the car, each slug distinct to his eyes, moving like ants in a line. The other drone had its arm cannon pointed directly at the car he was using for cover, but it wasn't firing.

Which could only mean...

He had seen the explosion at the other barricade, the missile strike that had flipped a cop car twenty feet into the air. If the drone unleashed that kind of firepower on him, he would die in the fireball before his body had a chance to be splattered on the road.

Raising his pistol in both hands, he pointed it at the drone's missile launcher. Then he fired. Glowing white bullets appeared outside his bubble, spiraling toward their target. *Please let them hit first.*

He collapsed to his knees behind the cruiser, the bubble vanishing. He just couldn't hold it for one more second. There was an explosion, all right – a thunderous roar in his ears – but it didn't consume him or the car for that matter.

When he found the strength to peek through the cruiser's windows, he saw that the drone was missing its right arm and half its torso as well. The missile must have exploded *inside* the launcher.

The other drone was backing away from its partner, no longer bothering to shoot at his people. No doubt it was some tactical assessment program and not anything close to an actual self-preservation instinct, but the thing seemed to be afraid, and that was good.

Jack dropped to all fours, head hanging. "No...Not now," he whispered, shaking his head. "Stay on your feet, Hunter. These people need you."

Every muscle in his body felt weakened, and his head was pounding with a painful throb that threatened to drown out awareness of everything else. Keepers who overused their powers were useless. Crafting two Bendings that strong and then following that up with a time bubble? Summer needed time to recover, and so did he.

He was in no condition to fight, and with gunfire flying back and forth, it was only a matter of time before a stray bullet hit him. Jack could live with that.

He'd given the cops a fighting chance. Two *ziarogati* and one of the drones? That was an impressive kill-count in a fight like this. If pushing himself to the point where he collapsed got him killed, so be it. Other people would survive. No one would really miss Jack Hunter anyway. He felt Summer's grief at that thought but-

Something flew right over him.

A *ziarogat* landed on the roof of the police car, a shirtless male who stood with his back turned, facing the killer robot. He seemed to be fixated on the damn thing. *What?* Jack wondered. *I must be hallucinating.*

The *ziarogat* dropped from the police car and charged the battle drone, loosing a stream of glowing bullets as he ran. *They can switch sides? What? When did they gain the ability to switch sides?*

Harry Carlson wasn't a soldier; oh there had been days on the force, when he'd felt a little like charging headlong into battle, but it was a metaphor. Here he was, confronted with the real thing.

The air before him pulsed as he used the N'Jal to erect a force-field strong enough to keep high-impact rounds at bay. Bullets slammed into the rippling barrier, flattening on impact and then falling to the ground.

Harry winced, sweat oozing from his pores to run over his face in rivers. "You can't just sit here," he whispered to himself in a breathy rasp. "You're the one with the powers, Harry. These people are counting on you."

Through the force-field, he saw Jack charge headlong

toward a pair of *ziarogati* who stood in front of the barricade. The image was blurry, but it had to be Jack. No one else would do something that reckless.

Something in the corner of his eye.

Harry turned to find a *ziarogat* running at him. A tall and well-muscled man with copper skin, the creature loped across the asphalt like a wolf bearing down on a rabbit with its fangs bared.

Harry flung his hand out.

The force-field he loosed sank into the road and churned up large pieces of asphalt, spraying them at his oncoming foe. The *ziarogat* stumbled backward, raising a hand to shield himself as rocks pelted his body.

Harry wasn't done.

Thrusting his hand out, he loosed another force-field, this one a rippling wall of energy that flew in a straight line and hit the dazed *ziarogat*. The other man fell flat on his ass, twitching on impact.

Another force-field, Harry thought. *Flatten him. Crush the life out of him.* But no. He wasn't a killer, no matter what anyone else demanded of him. It was an option, but he would rather come up with another strategy. *Another strategy? If you let that thing get up, it's gonna kill your friends.*

An idea came to him in a sudden flash of inspiration, information coalescing in his mind almost as if...as if the N'Jal was anticipating his needs. He knew what to do. *Quick, before it recovers!*

He ran to the *ziarogat*.

Dropping to his knees, Harry seized the other man's head in both hands and let the N'Jal's neural-fibers bond with his opponent's nervous system. In that instant, he became intimately aware of the *ziarogat*. He could see exactly what Slade and the Overseers had done to twist this man into a killing machine.

A spiderweb of synthetic neural nets ran through the man's brain, blocking out the original personality, replacing it with coded instructions that came through the panel on the man's chest. Each *ziarogat* was linked to his companions, the lot of them forming a battle strategy based on data they all accumulated. Control was absolute, the original personality scrubbed clean.

But if he could implant a command...

Harry wasn't sure *how* he did it – the knowledge of what to do came from the N'Jal – but he ordered the lot of them to stand down. For a brief moment, every single *ziarogat* froze in place. The others recovered within seconds, shutting him out; somehow, they had sensed that one of their number had been compromised and responded by removing him from the network.

Okay, so he couldn't control all of them, but he could control this one! Quickly, he implanted new instructions in the creature's brain.

An explosion off to his right made Harry hiss. The noise! How did actual soldiers deal with it. A glance over his shoulder revealed that one of the battle drones was backing away from the barricade, and the other...

Well, Jack must have done *something* to it, because the second drone had lost half its body and now stood as a ruined shadow of its former self. That was good. One down and one to go! But Jack...

The kid had collapsed to all fours in front of the police cars, no doubt having taxed poor Summer to her limit. Reckless as always, but Harry wasn't going to let him die for it. Jack was like a son to him...Or maybe an irritating nephew.

"Protect him!" he said, implanting a command in the *ziarogat's* brain.

The creature curled its legs against its chest and then sprang off the ground in one fluid motion. It spun to face the barricade, then ran headlong toward Jack, leaping over him to land perched on the police car's roof.

Protect him.

The *ziarogat* leaped into battle.

For a moment, Ben wondered what could have made the *ziarogat* he'd been fighting freeze in place for just a few seconds. It was almost as if something had shorted out the thing's circuits...If it had any circuits. A frantic voice in the back of his head told him that he should be joining the others in battle – the dozen or so cops who were still on their feet backed away from the *ziarogati* and fired glowing ammunition – but instinct took over.

Ben dropped to his knees before the headless body, examining the panel that had been fused to its chest. That was his way; he always looked for a technical solution to his problems. The panel was still blinking. What did it do?

Inside the helmet, Ben winced and let out a grunt. "You're gonna get me killed after all," he muttered, digging his blade into the creature's chest. He began to carve around the panel, cutting cleanly through bone and muscle.

This was gross!

No, not gross; it was downright disgusting – and dangerous too; while he was busy playing mortician, a stray bullet on a high impact setting could easily pierce his helmet – but he had to know.

Ben felt his face twist in revulsion, then shook his head with a heavy sigh. "Oh, the things I do for these friends of mine," he whispered, completing his blade's circuit around the panel. "The things I do."

He closed his gloved hand around the panel and pulled it free, watching as silvery goop dripped from the underside. The lights were still blinking. That was good. But what exactly did this thing do?

No stray bullets came his way.

In fact, it seemed as if no one was even *shooting* at him. Somehow, he'd managed to perform impromptu surgery in the middle of the street without anyone – or anything – trying to kill him. Those drones should have done *something*.

When he looked up, he noticed that the drones were ignoring him. In fact, they had their backs turned, choosing instead to fire a stream of bullets at a cop car down by the townhouses. Anna must have been using it for cover.

An idea popped into his head.

Retracting the blade back into his gauntlet, Ben ran for one of the police cars that made up the barricade. He quickly slid across the hood, then threw himself directly into the kill zone with no cover.

The drones ignored him.

Looking up the street, he saw that one of the drones that had been attacking the other barricade was now a blackened wreck with a missing arm and not much of a torso. It just stood there, motionless.

The fourth robot was backing up toward Ben's side of the battlefield, trying to get away from...from a crazed *ziarogat* that kept shooting in the chest! What in Bleakness was going on here?

He crept a little closer to the pair of robots that were attacking Anna.

One drone turned its head to focus the camera lens upon him for a moment, sizing him up. Then it seemed to forget all about him and returned its attention to a police car with so many bullet holes they almost looked like polka dots. *It saw me! I know the damn thing saw me!*

He looked down at the panel in his gloved palm, the blinking lights continuing their slow, steady pattern. Of course! Battle drones distinguished friend from foe by RFID tags that were kept on a soldier's person. Though those were usually quite small.

The device he carried almost certainly had other functions, but its purpose was to make sure that the drones never targeted the *ziarogati*. So long as he had this thing, he was damn near invulnerable!

Ben drew his pistol from its holster. "High impact!"

A bullet to the back made one drone stumble and left a huge hole in its metal body, exposing vital circuitry. Still, the thing didn't attack him. It stopped firing, but it didn't so much as glance in his direction.

Ben switched to EMP rounds and squeezed the trigger several times. Three glowing slugs went single file into the hole in the robot's back, frying those vital circuits the very instant they made contact.

The drone stumbled.

Its companion spun to face Ben, but rather than trying to kill him, it started backing away from him. Almost as if the damn thing was afraid. The programming that wouldn't let it attack anyone with an RFID tag must have been extensive.

The first drone spasmed, arms flailing about like a drunk man struggling to keep his balance. A satisfying *thunk* filled the air as the robot fell to its knees and then shut down. One down and one to go. Now, all he had to do was-

A compartment in the robot's back slid open to reveal a white sphere that rose from a hole between the drone's shoulder-blades. A Death Sphere? How many tricks did these damn things have?

Transfixed by the scene, Ben hardly noticed the high-pitched squeal and sudden warmth in his palm, but when he looked down, he saw that the blinking lights on the device he'd taken from the *ziarogat* had gone dark. The friend-or-foe device had died on him. Which meant...

The Death Sphere reoriented itself to point its lens at him.

And the lens began to glow.

Anna had her back pressed to the trunk of a police car, wincing at the sound of gunfire. "Come on!" she whispered, gripping the pistol holstered on her hip. "You've got to run out of ammo sooner or later."

When she looked up, she saw the ruined face of the townhouse she'd used to get a clean shot, the flaming hole where a balcony used to be, the tower of smoke rising into the air. These drones had destroyed the homes of the people who lived here. Lives were ruined; it made her want to end Slade.

The pair of drones were standing in the street on the driver's side of the police car, loosing a stream of ammunition at the vehicle. From their current position – near the car's front end – they couldn't get a clean shot at her. She half-wondered why they didn't just march over to finish the job, but they seemed content to keep her pinned with suppressing fire. Maybe they had classified her as the biggest threat. Keeping her out of action would do a lot more to assure victory than slaughtering a few more cops.

And pinned she was!

In the back of her mind, she could sense Seth's fatigue. Her muscles felt rubbery, and her skin tingled with a million fiery pinpricks. She was right on the verge of pushing her Nassai too far. Another use of her powers, and she would collapse from exhaustion. Thankfully, she didn't need them right now.

Off to her left, maybe fifteen cops stood amid a field of black-clad bodies, trying to contain the final *ziarogat* with continuous gunfire. The cybernetic creature was too busy trying to fend off a barrage of bullets to be much of a threat to her, and clearly the drones were out of missiles. Or they would have used them by now.

Those damn things were effective!

A few moments earlier, she had been distracted by the

sound of an explosion near Jack's barricade, and when she spared a glance in that direction, she saw only the three vans that still blocked both lanes. Whatever her bestie was up to, he would have to deal with it on his own. Anna knew that he could. He was no longer the half-trained pup that she had met four years ago. He was a genuine Keeper. And she wished she could tell him how proud she felt.

The gunfire stopped.

Without thinking, Anna ventured a quick glance around the side of the car – damn impulsiveness – and saw that one of the drones that had been attacking her was backing away from the police car.

The other one was down on its knees, hunched over with its camera head sagging. Someone must have killed the thing. Whatever joy she felt in that vanished when she saw a compartment in the robot's back open.

A Death Sphere rose out of the hole with its lens pointed at her car. Well, now she would bloody well have to-

The sphere reoriented itself to point at something else.

Anna rose and ran around the side of the car.

Thrusting her left hand out toward the retreating robot, she threw up a Bending and watched the colours stretch into a blur just before three bullets collided with her patch of warped space-time. They curved away from her body, twisting in a tight loop to fly back toward their master.

The blurry robot stumbled as its body was pelted with ammunition. Seth groaned in the back of her mind, but she only had to hang on a few seconds longer. The drone would be off-balance after that pummeling.

The Death Sphere was pointing its particle emitter at a frightened Ben who was retreating toward the north side of the road. His armour wouldn't protect him from that! She had to be quicker!

Anna let the Bending drop.

She leaped and flew a good six feet into the air, seizing the sphere in both hands. She quickly twisted her body to point the sphere's lens at the stunned robot.

The drone's arm cannon came up for a kill shot half a second before a bright orange beam of focused plasma punched right through the robot's metal chest, drilling a hole the size of her fist.

Anna landed on her side, exhaustion hitting her like a punch to the stomach. The sphere struggled in her grip, trying to pull free. Oh, Companion protect her! She couldn't hold onto it! Her body was wrecked.

Her fingers squeezed the sphere's plastic surface, but the damn thing's anti-gravity generator just put out more and more power. It was like trying to hold on to a squirming cat, only much, much harder. *I really should have put more thought into this plan.*

The sphere pulled free of her grip.

It moved with a speed that could rival most cars, flying halfway down the block before it slowed to a stop and then reoriented itself to point that lens at her. She couldn't move. Not even an inch.

Three glowing bullets hit the sphere, causing sparks to arc across its body. It fell to the ground a moment later, landing somewhere behind the wrecked vans. The explosion that followed was less intense when compared to the thunder of those missile strikes, but she heard it nonetheless.

Ben came toward her – well, his shoes did, anyway; she couldn't find the strength to look up – and stopped to let out a sigh. "I'd say I owe you one," he began. "But at this point, I'm thinking we might be even."

"Definitely even."

It came to her that everything was quiet now. The sound of gunfire – even the dim buzzing of Leyrian weapons – was gone, and there were no explosions. She could still hear the crackle of flames.

"Is it over?"

Ben squatted down in front of her, head hanging as he heaved out a breath. "Yeah, I think so," he muttered, nodding. "The people on our side took down the last *ziarogat,* but I'm not sure what's happening at the other barricade."

Anna squeezed her eyes shut, groaning with displeasure. "Let's find out," she said, forcing herself to sit up. "Take three healthy bodies with you and make sure that Jack and Harry's team is all right."

"Got it."

"Have someone else assess the wounded," she added. "Start triage immediately."

"And you?"

Gritting her teeth with a vicious growl, Anna turned her face up to the hot sun. "I'll be fine," she replied, ignoring the rasp in her voice. "I'm not injured, just exhausted. The others need your help!"

Ben stood up to tower over her with arms folded, light glinting off his visor. "I'm not so sure about that," he muttered. "I've heard that Keepers who push themselves the way you did can pass out from the strain."

"Take care of the others!" she snapped. "Go!"

He turned away from her, then hesitated for a moment, one hand flexing into a fist. "Yes, ma'am," he said at last. "I'm on it."

Seconds later, Ben was sprinting around the back of the police car, leaving her to deal with her fatigue on her own. Every muscle in her body felt so heavy, and Seth was practically begging her to go to sleep. Not yet, though. "You too?"

She looked up to find Harry coming around the vans in the middle of the road with Jack's arm around his shoulder. Her best friend was barely able to stay on his feet, and he clung to Harry like a drowning man to a life-preserver.

Jack's head was hanging, and he groaned as they approached. "So, did I really see what I think I saw?" he asked in a strained voice. "Did you really take out a battle drone with a Death Sphere?"

Anna smiled, looking down at herself. The sweat on her brow made her skin itch. "Yeah, I did," she muttered. "I John McClaned that shit."

"Nice reference!"

"Thank you."

Harry's face twisted as he dragged Jack the last few steps. "How 'bout I just set you down here?" With a grunt, he slowly lowered Jack to the ground. "We have wounded on our side. Someone needs to call in the med teams."

"Ben's on it," Anna murmured.

"Good. I'll help him."

Harry left them a moment later, and she was suddenly aware of just how relieved she was to know that Jack was all right. Oh, she was happy to learn that Harry was well and that Ben had survived unscathed – and her heart broke for the poor people who didn't make it – but there was something...

Best not to think about it, a small voice whispered. So she put the thought out of her mind and scooched closer to Jack. He seemed to sense her need and gently patted her on the back. "It's gonna be all right," he whispered. "Everything's gonna be all right."

When they reached the first floor with Aamani still clinging to him, Raynar paused for a moment to catch his breath. The woman he carried seemed to sag against him, and he had to struggle to ignore his own pain.

Raynar closed his eyes, tilting his head back. "Just a little further," he whispered as much for his own ears as for his companion. "We're almost there now, Aamani. Just a bit further, and we can rest."

She nodded.

The window above the sink was still open, but it was clear that there was no way she was going through that. This close, he could sense Aamani's pain. It seemed to echo off his own.

Raynar felt his lips peel back from clenched teeth, his head drooping with fatigue. "Come on," he growled, spinning her around. "We're going to have to go out the front way. I don't know what's out there, but..."

"We can't stay in a burning house," she whispered.

"Yeah."

An open doorway in the kitchen's cream-coloured wall led to a narrow hallway that stretched on to the front door. There was no way to see what was happening outside, but he sensed less hostility than he had a few minutes ago.

So, with Aamani's arm draped around his shoulders, and her head tucked under his chin, Raynar dragged her toward the front door. Each step seemed to take hours, though in reality, it had only been a few seconds.

He pushed the door open.

The well-manicured lawn was still in pristine condition – somehow – and beyond that, a battle drone was lying flat on its back in the middle of the street. Off to his right, the three vans made a convenient roadblock that made it difficult to see Anna's barricade. He was just glad that he could sense her presence.

To his left, perhaps thirty feet away, a second battle drone stood deathly still. Most of what remained of its body had been scorched black. How had the thing lost one of its arms? Who could get close enough to do that?

In the distance beyond the scorched drone, a wall of police cars blocked his view of men and women in black uniforms tending to their wounded. He could catch glimpses of them through the windows, but it was his telepathy that truly let him sense them.

"Help!" Raynar called in a strained voice.

He began dragging Aamani toward the nearest barricade – the one that Harry and Jack had been defending – but the people there seemed not to hear him. "We need help!" His voice was so hoarse from the smoke he could barely make out his own words.

Aamani began sputtering and coughing, doubling over in pain. She pressed a fist to her mouth, convulsing with every ragged breath. "Help," she whispered. Was her plea for him or the officers?

Raynar eased her to the ground.

"Just wait here."

He broke into a sprint for the line of police cars, huffing and puffing and ignoring the sting in his belly. "Please!" he shouted at the top of his lungs. "Aamani needs help! She needs..."

One of the black-clad officers spun to look at him through the visor of a helmet. "Kid!" he exclaimed. "You okay?"

Raynar stumbled to a stop, pointing into the distance behind him. "Aamani needs medical attention," he gasped. "Please..."

"Mitchell! Gordon!" the other man yelled, gesturing to two of his officers. "Take care of Director Patel."

It was over. Suddenly, Raynar felt as though a heavy weight had been lifted from his chest. He had done his part; no, he wasn't an indomitable warrior like Jena or Anna, but he had saved a life. He had braved the flames and survived. Maybe he had something to add to this tear after all-

Raynar felt it before he saw it.

For a telepath, the mind was quick, but the body could still be slow and sluggish, especially when he was burdened by fatigue. All his practice these last few weeks must have honed his skills. Not long ago, he would have been unable to detect such a subtle shift in the emotional current.

A trembling *ziarogat* stood in the shattered window of a

laundromat, keeping all its weight on one leg and leaning its shoulder against the window-frame. The creature lifted one shaking arm to point its gauntlet at him.

"Everyone, get down!" Raynar shouted.

The cops reacted with agonizing slowness.

Raynar tried to throw himself to the ground, but as he tumbled over sideways, something ripped through his chest. It was a strange sensation. Shouldn't there be pain? His shoulder hit the asphalt, and he bounced.

He pressed a trembling hand to his chest, and when he pulled it away, his palm was covered in blood. *So this is how it happens...*On some level, it was a relief, knowing that the struggle was finally over.

"Raynar!"

The voice that called his name was distant, seeming to bounce off the walls of some very large cave. Or maybe he just wasn't hearing very well. Tears welled up in his eyes, but he was not sad. No, not sad.

A very blurry Harry Carlson came running toward him, sprinting as if the hounds of the underworld were on his trail. "Stay with me!" the man shouted. "Stay with me! You're not done yet, kid!"

"Take that thing down!" one of the cops shouted.

"Stay with me!" Harry was leaning over him. "Stay with me."

Raynar stared up at the sky with an open mouth, breath rasping in his throat. He felt a cold sweat drenching him. "Tell her..." Gods be good, it was so hard to talk. "Tell her it was the best moment of my life."

Harry was protesting, insisting that he wouldn't have to tell her anything. It was a lie; Raynar knew that, but he loved the other man for saying it just the same. If only he could find the words to tell Harry that there was no need to worry. Everything was going to be all right. He knew that, somehow.

This body was so heavy, such a weight. It bore the scars of years of pain and abuse, so much needless cruelty. In truth, Raynar had never been all that attached to it. What a relief it would be to rid himself of all that pain.

He let go.

19

"Not even one!"

His fist collided with the concrete wall hard enough to leave a few small cracks in its surface. The impact made his knuckles bleed, but he didn't care. The pain was nothing, and he was already starting to heal.

He spun around.

Isara stood before him on the warehouse floor, her face hidden beneath that large gray hood, her body wrapped in the folds of her cloak. She never allowed the underlings to see her face, a healthy philosophy. "Must I repeat myself?" she asked. Her insistence on showing such disrespect was *not* a healthy philosophy. "Lenai and her team managed to hold off the attack."

Grinding his teeth so hard it hurt, Slade winced. His face was on fire despite his efforts to control his emotions. "Lenai lives!" he bellowed. "Hunter lives! The decrepit old police officer who insists on clinging to some semblance of relevance by following them lives!"

Isara moved forward without looking up at him. "The telepath boy they rescued from Ganymede," she said. "He died attempting to save Aamani Patel. Nearly two dozen police officers died as well."

"And the human garbage at the so-called hospital?"

Throwing apart the folds of her cloak to expose a slim black dress with thin straps underneath, Isara strode toward him. "Your forces never made it to the school," she said. "Lenai was able to goad them into a trap."

The heat in his face intensified, and Slade realized that he must have been as red as a sunset. "They were supposed to suffer!" He took a few shaky steps forward. "Defiance must never go unpunished!"

Where was his control? He couldn't remember the last time something had cracked his serenity the way Anna Lenai's stubborn refusal to die just had. The rage was a tempest in his belly. He wanted to strangle something.

Just a few short weeks ago, he had been bored with the notion of ruling over these simpletons again, but now that they had defied him...No, the Inzari had set him above the people of this world. It was the way of things, the grand cosmic order that determined the course of every life. A place of everyone, and everyone in their place.

No one defied the will of the Inzari.

Of course, he realized that part of his anger stemmed from the fact that Jack Hunter had challenged him face to face. A wise ruler never acted directly unless he was left with no other choice. He preferred to let proxies do his killing for him, but Hunter had slipped right into the heart of his operation and challenged him directly.

Dealing with the boy had been easy enough, but that was not what riled him. Jack had refused to back down. Even upon acknowledging his defeat, the boy had remained defiant to the bitter end.

No one defied Grecken Slade!

What would it take for the miserable people of this world to learn their place?

He was pulled out of his reverie when the windows on the upper level shattered to allow Keepers to slip through. Nearly two dozen men and women landed at various spots on the catwalk. Perhaps that should have frightened him.

It didn't.

The skylight above the main floor of the warehouse shattered as well, causing thin shards of glass to drop to the floor like raindrops. A human body followed seconds later, falling with unnatural slowness.

Dremin Koss landed in the middle of the room with a pistol clutched in both hands. A tall and slender man in denim pants and a black jacket, he rose to stand tall with all the pride a Keeper could manage.

His face had the youthful appearance common to every Justice Keeper – with pale, hollow cheeks – but his hair was bone white and his eyebrows as well. The result of hair dye, of course. Perhaps the man wanted to look his age. He was fifty-three. "Slade," he said, gesturing with that pistol.

Tossing his head back, Slade grinned and let out a peal of laughter. "You think that toy is going to frighten me, Dremin?" he asked. "I have wielded the powers of a Justice Keeper longer than you can imagine."

Koss narrowed his eyes, his face flushed with rage. "They should never have been given to you," he said, stepping forward. "Look around you, Grecken. There are twenty of us and two of you."

Isara whirled around to stand beside Slade, hands upraised with fingers curled like grasping talons. Clearly, she was ready to craft a Bending at any moment. It would not do for anyone to see her face.

Or hear her voice.

"You think highly of your chances," Slade hissed.

The other man shook his head, slowly moving forward as if to pin Slade against the wall. "I have five teams roaming the streets of this city," he said. "They've destroyed your drones and your cybernetic abominations.

"We've been watching this warehouse for several days, Grecken. You've made one of the most common mistakes in military history; you've stretched yourself too thin, and now you have nothing left to defend yourself.

"I need nothing else."

"Enough of this!" Koss growled. "On your knees!"

Baring his teeth in a vicious snarl, Slade squinted at the other man. "No," he said, shaking his head. "No, *you* will kneel to me!"

Koss lifted his pistol for a clean head-shot, moving forward with the practiced walk of a law-enforcement professional. His intentions were clear. Up on the catwalk, Keepers sprang into action, some leaping over the railing.

Slade raised a hand, twisting the fabric of reality with a Bending that blurred his opponent into a smear of colour. Bullets appeared before him, slowed and curved off to his right, slamming into the wall.

Isara had a bending of her own.

As he backed up toward the wall beneath the catwalk, Slade felt a surge of rage. His skin was tingling. Twice now, in a matter of days, he'd been forced to defend himself, to tax his own symbiont.

Koss was still shooting.

Slade approached a door in the wall.

He used his shoulder to throw it open and then quickly ducked inside, dropping his Bending once he was no longer in the field of fire. Isara followed him through with hands raised to shield herself, the air before her rippling.

Slade winced and let his head hang. "Quickly," he said, gesturing to her. "Get that door shut, and let's be on our way."

Isara did as she was bidden, kicking the metal door so that it slammed shut and cut off their pursuers. She engaged the lock on the knob. That would buy them a few seconds at least! "We should have anticipated this."

"We did," Slade assured her.

This small room had been an office of some type before the warehouse had been abandoned. Now, it was devoid of furniture or distinguishing features of any kind except for a puddle of flesh that he had left in the middle of the floor.

Slade backed up until he was standing right next to the pool of skin, facing the door with his fists clenched. "This isn't over," he hissed in a breathy whisper. "No, this is only the beginning."

Isara joined him.

Behind him, the puddle rose to form a triangle of veiny skin, standing over seven feet tall with its peak nearly brushing the ceiling. There was a soft humming sound that was drowned out by a harsh pounding.

The door swung open to reveal Dremin Koss standing there with his pistol drawn, a look of shock on his face. He froze for a moment, as if unsure of what he saw, and by the time he thought to act, it was too late.

A bubble surrounded Slade and Isara, making it seem as if their pursuers were all standing under water. A very blurry Dremin Koss lowered his weapon, knowing that it would do no good to shoot at this point.

They were yanked forward into darkness.

When he pushed open the door to the small bedroom Anna had been using, Jack found sunlight streaming in through the small rectangular window, leaving a patch of brightness on the mattress.

Anna stood at the window with her back turned, peering out at a quiet Brooklyn street. "Come to cheer me up?" she asked. "Maybe you're planning to remind me that Raynar's death wasn't my fault."

Grinning like a fool, Jack let his head hang. He scraped a knuckle across his brow. "Am I *that* predictable?" he asked. "Because, you know, I really pride myself on being frustratingly chaotic."

Anna spun around.

She looked up as he approached, her blue eyes glistening. "I'm not so sure you're right this time," she said, her eyebrows rising. "I knew that Slade would find a way to throw us off balance, and I let the kid come along."

Jack scrunched up his face. "I don't accept that," he said, shaking his head. "Anna, you can't be expected to foresee every possible outcome. Raynar proved himself to be an asset in prior engagements."

He sat down on the edge of the mattress with hands on his knees, head hanging as he let out a breath. "The kid was brave," Jack muttered. "I'm going to miss him, but this was *not* your fault."

Anna leaned against the windowsill with her arms folded, turning her face up to the ceiling. "I know," she whispered. "That's the problem. I should be torn up with guilt, but I'm not. So what does that say about me?"

"Nothing."

She barked a laugh.

Turning around with a growl, Anna braced her hands on the windowsill and leaned forward to peer through the pane. "Is this what happens to us, Jack?" she asked. "Do we just get more callous over time?"

Jack closed his eyes, exhaling slowly. "I don't think so," he replied in a soft rasp. "I think that when life forces you to carry the weight we've had to carry, you eventually get used to it."

He tried to sound resolute – for himself as much as for her – but when he studied his friend, Jack had to admit that he could see her point. She was overstating her case, but there was a grain of truth in it.

Was this the same impulsive, headstrong woman who had wandered into his thrift shop all those years ago? That Anna would never have been comfortable leading troops into battle. She had gained confidence in herself, and it made Jack so very proud of her. On the other hand, the Anna of four years ago had laughed a lot more.

Come to think of it, so had he. True, most of his one-liners had been thin veils for the gaping pit of self-loathing that made him second guess his every decision – and Jack was pleased to say that he too was more confident than he had been as a youth – but he didn't laugh as much. Maybe he just didn't feel like laughing.

And that was sad.

He stood.

As if sensing his intentions, Anna turned away from the window and practically stumbled into him, slipping her arms around his back and burrowing against his chest. She trembled with every breath.

Jack returned the hug, and then, by instinct, he began to sway from side to side. Without even thinking, he ran his fingers through her hair. That was the tipping point for both of them. The damn that held back their emotions burst.

"He was just a kid," Anna whimpered.

Jack sniffled, hot tears streaming over his cheeks in rivers. "I know," he whispered, unable to stop his own shivering. "We pulled him out of that hell hole only to throw him head-first into another."

Anna pressed her face into his chest and trembled. Her fingers clutched the back of his shirt. "We should have taken him somewhere else," she said. "Back to Leyria Or...Or I don't know, but *somewhere!*"

There wasn't much they could have done; on a rational

level, Jack knew that. At the time, keeping Raynar close by had been a good idea. After Keli's betrayal, Jena was right to wonder what kind of damage a telepath could do on a world that was not prepared to deal with such power.

Still, there was grief; grief was a good thing. Hell, emotion of any kind was a good thing under circumstances like these. Anna's concerns about being cut off were not totally unfounded. Only then did Jack realize how deeply he had suppressed his sadness, putting it out of his mind so that he could focus on his job. It was a useful skill but not a virtuous one. Not by any means.

Anna must have done the same, and now – with no one else around – it all came pouring out of her. She shook and sniffled and left a big wet spot on his shirt. Not that he minded in the slightest. "It's not your fault."

Anna pulled away, wiping her nose with the back of her hand. "I know." She sat down on the windowsill with a heavy sigh. "Companion have mercy, but I know that. I just feel like it should be."

"Why?"

"Because accepting that it wasn't my fault means accepting that there was nothing I could have done to save him. And that is so much harder to deal with. With all my power, I still couldn't save him."

"Maybe not Raynar," Jack said softly. "But literally thousands of people are alive because of what we did here. I just got the report from Jena. Two Keeper teams raided Slade's warehouse."

"They got him?"

Chewing on his lip, Jack winced and shook his head. "I wish," he said, backing away from her. "Slade escaped through a SlipGate, but they managed to capture the last of his drones and *ziarogati.*"

Anna sat on the bed with hands folded in her lap, staring

down at herself with a frown on her face. "Well, that's something," she murmured. "Now all we have to worry about is your basic, run of the mill psychopath."

"And those are on the run," Jack said. "The teams we have patrolling the city have captured several of Slade's paramilitary cells. We've spotted others fleeing to New Jersey or booking it up the 495. They're scared, Anna."

Jack stood before her with his hands in his pockets, head bowed as he spoke. "It's over," he said softly. "People are going back to work; shops are reopening. This city is back on its feet thanks to you."

Anna looked up to meet his gaze. God, but he could drown in those gorgeous blue eyes. "Thanks to us," she said, nodding once. "Not wanting to point out the obvious here, but you helped."

"I guess I did."

She stood up with a sigh, then hugged him once again. "Thank you," she said. "I guess we better get going. If we're gonna help these people back into their homes, there's a lot of work to do."

The school cafeteria was a trapezoid-shaped room of blue cinder-block walls, lit by windows near the ceiling that allowed sunlight to spill through. In just a few weeks, kids would be sitting in these chairs on the first day of school. That was a certainty now that they had reclaimed the city.

Melissa sat on the edge of one table with her hands in her lap, her legs swinging freely underneath. It was exhausting, carrying the weight of her emotions. Her father had come back from the fighting, as had Jack and Anna. She couldn't be happier about that, but Jena had given her the news a few hours ago.

Raynar wasn't coming back.

She closed her eyes, tears streaming over her face. "They

should call me the kiss of death," she muttered, getting to her feet. "Hey, boys, you wanna make out with Melissa? 'God, no! I want to live!' "

Pressing the heels of her hands to her eye-sockets, she rubbed away the moisture. "You're being stupid," she told herself. "There's no such thing as the kiss of death. Bad things just happen sometimes."

It did nothing to make her feel better; in fact, contemplating the horror of that only made her start crying again. Of course, she understood that life didn't guarantee anyone a happy ending – on some level, she had always known that – but to truly contemplate the enormity of it...

The universe was indifferent to her, uncaring and unfeeling. All her life, Melissa had been a practising Catholic, but now she had to wonder, where was God in all this? She had no illusions about a sagely old man descending from the clouds to protect the righteous and strike down the wicked, but couldn't he tweak the laws of probability just a little? Couldn't he do *something?*

Sniffling, she looked up.

Her father stood in the open doorway, stroking his chin with the tips of his fingers. "It hit you hard, didn't it?" he asked, striding into the room. "I forget how new this must be for you."

Melissa felt a tightness in her face and turned her head so that he wouldn't see. "He was my friend, Dad," she whispered. "I liked him–maybe as more than a friend. I don't know, but he was too damn young to die!"

Harry closed his eyes and let his head hang. A sharp intake of breath betrayed his frustration. "I suspected there might be something..." If Harry started lecturing her about boys, she was going to scream. "Raynar was a good kid, Melissa. Braver than most. And you're right; he was too young."

Melissa crossed her arms, shivering as she let out a ragged breath. "I don't know what else to do," she whispered, stepping closer to her father. "I've tried to focus on my duties, but something just seems wrong."

"Something *is* wrong."

"Then how do we make it right?"

Harry slipped his arms around her, pulling her close. Under normal circumstances, she would be worried about someone coming in to see her hugging her father – she was seventeen, for crying out loud – but today...Today, she accepted the embrace.

It was amazing how he could still make everything better with nothing but a hug and a few kind words. Melissa had been lucky. Not every kid grew up in a loving home. "We don't make it right," Harry said. "Nothing makes this right, Melissa. But we go on, and the wrongness becomes easier to deal with."

Melissa shut her eyes, tears leaking from them to spill onto her father's shirt. "So, this is what it's like to be an adult?" she asked, trembling. "You just keep enduring the pain until you stop caring?"

"You never stop caring," her father said.

Melissa pulled away from him, brushing a tear off her cheek with one finger. "Is there going to be a memorial service?" she asked. "We should probably figure out what Antauran customs would be."

"There will be a memorial service," Harry said. "In a few days, when the current crisis is over."

"I'd like to help plan it."

Harry sat down on one of the tables, heaving out a sigh as he looked down at his own feet. "That's very kind of you," he said, nodding to her. "Maybe I could speak to Dr. Hamilton. With Slade's forces on the run, she won't need so many-"

"No," Melissa insisted. "No. I want to finish my work here."

Her father looked up with a smile. "Seems I raised you right," he mumbled. "The rest of us will be leaving the city once we're sure that key areas are secure. I'm told that people are already returning to their homes."

"Isn't that a little premature?"

Harry shrugged and then sighed as he got to his feet. Melissa knew that look on his face, the one that said someone was doing something foolish and impulsive. "Larani told the mayor not to rush things," he said. "But people want to rebuild."

Her father leaned in to kiss her on the forehead. "You did a good thing here, kid," he whispered. "Finish your work, and then come home. Your mother is probably pulling her hair out worrying about you."

"Thanks, Dad."

She would never be able to explain how much she loved him for moments like this.

Aamani Patel was lying on a bed in the med-bay with the blankets pulled up to just below her chest, her hospital gown rumpled. Her long black hair was in a state of disarray with flyaway strands in all directions.

The right side of her face was still red, but – for the most part – her burns had been healed. In fact, she actually looked content. Jena envied that. Right now, contentedness was the last thing she felt.

Jena was hunched over in a chair with her elbow propped up on her thigh and her chin resting on the knuckles of her face. "Well, this is what I get," she muttered under her breath. "I should have been there."

If she had been, she would have been too busy fighting off battle drones to save one woman from a burning townhouse, but it was a pleasant fiction, telling herself that she would have prevented Raynar's death. He was one of her people in the end, the youngest member of her team.

For all her experience, she had never dealt with something

like this before. The loss of one of her people. Her long career as a Justice Keeper had been a solitary one. She had never had to worry about anyone other than herself.

Aamani's eyes fluttered open, and she stared up at the ceiling for a moment. "How long?" she growled, sitting up. Black hair spilled over her face, but she brushed it away. "How long has it been?"

"Two days," Jena answered.

"Two days?"

With a heavy sigh, Jena got to her feet and stood before the other woman with her eyes closed. "You've been sedated for most of that time," she said, nodding. "They had to perform cellular regeneration."

Aamani touched her face, then winced the instant her fingers made contact, hissing at the sudden spike of pain. "The drone," she muttered. "I remember shooting it, and then the rest is a blank."

"You were trapped in a burning building."

"And?"

At times like this, she felt as if she should have been able to cry, but that wasn't her way. Oh, she could cry. She could cry buckets of tears on her own, but here in public, it just wasn't happening. "Raynar pulled you out," she explained. "Brought you all the way to the barricade…"

Aamani looked up to meet her gaze, and Jena could see it in the woman's face. She had put two and two together. "What happened?"

Gritting her teeth, Jena let her head hang. She hissed like an angry cat, barely able to keep her fury restrained. "He didn't make it," she whispered. "A stray *ziarogat* that we thought was dead…"

"I see."

The other woman was already putting on the mask that every commander had to wear at one point. Jena knew it well.

One night, while they had shared a beer on the roof of the safe house, Anna had remarked that Aamani was cold. The girl didn't understand. Not yet anyway.

When you were the person everyone looked to whenever things got desperate, you eventually learned how to put yourself second. Anna was very free with her emotions – and in some ways, that would serve her well – but sometimes you had to be the steady rock that other people leaned on for support.

Jena had been unprepared for that reality when she had accepted this position. In many ways, she and Aamani were a lot alike. Maybe that was why they had never really gotten along.

"So what now?" Aamani whispered.

"Now we find that damn Key," Jena growled. "And then I put an end to Slade once and for all."

20

Thick clouds made a ceiling of gray across a field of green with a gravel path that gently rounded some pine trees. In the distance, maybe a dozen kids played on a yellow jungle gym, their squeals of delight echoing through the air.

Jack walked up the path.

Dressed in blue jeans and a black windbreaker, he shuffled along with his hands in his pockets. "I figured you might show up," he said, turning. "You know, I was planning to stop by your apartment."

His mother approached in dark jeans and a white t-shirt with frilly sleeves. Waves of honey-blonde hair fell over her shoulders, framing a face with only the faintest signs of middle age. "Your sister told me you wanted to go home one last time," she said. "Of course you'd visit the park where I used to take you."

"You know me well."

"So," Crystal began. "You're going to Leyria."

Jack smiled, then looked down at his own feet. "Yeah," he said nodding. "Good old Leyria: where poverty is a thing of the past, racism is a distant memory and Earthers are essentially cave men."

Crystal chuckled, turning her head to stare into the grassy field. "You'll survive," she said. "You always have. In some ways, I have more faith in your ability to adapt than I do in Lauren's."

Tilting his head back, Jack rolled his eyes at the overcast sky. "That's really great, Mom," he teased. "And you'll be pleased to know that your Machiavellian scheme to pit your children against each other is proceeding unhindered."

In response, his mother spread her arms and waited for him to give the obligatory hug, a request he was more than willing to grant. It was good to see her. In truth, he had hoped that she might stop by; if this was the last time he visited the park where he used to play, it was only fitting that his mother be here.

"So," she murmured, pulling away. "Big changes for Jack."

"Seems like."

"And will Anna be going to Leyria?"

Blushing hard, Jack closed his eyes and nodded to her. "Yes, Anna will be going to Leyria," he explained. "But we won't be working together, and last time I checked, she's still got a boyfriend."

Crystal backed away from him with her arms crossed, smiling down at herself. "At least you'll be together," she said softly. "Forgive me for being Nosy Mother, but it seems to me you've been a lot happier since she came back."

Mopping a hand over his face, Jack ran fingers through his thick brown hair. "Oh, Mom," he grumbled. "You're really going to have to give that up. She's made her choice, and it's not me."

His mother snorted – a response that somehow was more persuasive than the most well-reasoned argument – and then slipped past him and started up the path. Well, what was he supposed to say? Surely, his mother couldn't think it would be a wise idea to confess his feelings to a woman who already had a partner.

He would have said that was that if not for the fact that, somewhere in the back of his mind, Summer felt a touch of irritation and sadness. Apparently his Nassai had started shipping the two of them.

"Don't be silly," Crystal said.

Jack spun around to fall in step beside her, marching along with his head down. "I am not the one being silly," he insisted. "Trust me, trying to make something happen with Anna will only result in badness."

His mother squinted as she stared off into the distance, shaking her head in dismay. "It's like you don't *want* to be happy, Jack." she said. "I'm not suggesting that you go put on your 'Proud to be a Home-Wrecker' t-shirt, but do you really think she's going to settle down with that guy?"

"I try not to think about it."

"Well, maybe you should re-evaluate that inclination," Crystal said softly. "Jack, you're going to Leyria. *She's* going to Leyria. Do you really think this guy is going to uproot his life and follow her?"

"Again with the not thinking about it!"

Christ Almighty! Why was everyone so insistent that he deal with this? First Gabi, and now his mother? He'd been living happily in Denial-Land for the better part of – you know, he really wasn't sure *when* he had started turning a blind eye to his feelings – but the point was that he was fine!

As they came closer to the jungle-gym, he watched the kids playing on the yellow monkey bars. The equipment in this park had been different when he was a little kid. For one thing, it was green back then and a little rusty. Strange how somber he felt, thinking about how the playground he'd loved as a child had changed. Everything changed. Why should this bother him? "You're going to have to face it sooner or later," his mother said softly. "The two of you are in love; you can only hide from that for so long before it bites you in the ass."

Closing his eyes, Jack huffed out a sigh. "Anna's not in love with me." The words came out harshly, but he couldn't help it. "If she were, she'd be with me."

Musical laughter filled the air as Crystal spun to face him with a big grin on her face. "Oh, sweetheart," she said, shaking her head. "It some ways, you've grown beyond your years, but in this..."

"What you're saying doesn't make sense."

"Love very seldom does." Crystal hunched up her shoulders in a shrug, then strode toward him. This close, he seemed to tower over her, and yet she was still a giant in his mind. The woman who scolded him for filching cookies and kissed his forehead whenever he skinned his knees. "Sweetheart, you're at an age when it's hard for people to admit their feelings. Young people are obsessed with independence. It takes a special kind of wisdom to admit that we need other people."

He was at a loss for words.

"I can see it when she looks at you," Crystal went on. "I can see it when *you* look at her. Both of you are thinking it, and neither one of you wants to be the first to open your mouth. But your lives are changing."

Baring his teeth with a hiss, Jack shook his head. "I can't just..." He marched past his mother, into the field, then threw up his hands in frustration. "What am I supposed to do? Just go up to her and say 'An, I fall asleep every night remembering how nice it felt to have you snuggled up in my arms?'"

When he turned, Crystal was watching him with sympathy on his face. "You're just supposed to be honest," she said. "And give Anna a chance to figure out for herself what she wants to do."

"Fine," he muttered. "I'll try."

"Good," Crystal said. "Now, let's go home. We can order a

pizza and watch *The Amazing Spider-Man.*"

"Aw, Mom..."

"What?" she exclaimed. "You used to love that movie as a little kid."

The door to her apartment swung open, allowing her to see the soft light of early evening coming through the living room window, a golden glow that fell upon the sofa and the glass coffee table. Her kitchen – off to her right – was still pristinely clean with the white countertops bare.

The novel she had been reading two weeks ago was still sitting atop the island, turned over to mark the page. Bleakness take her, it was so good to be home! To sleep in her own bed and shower in her own shower. She could even take a bath!

Squeezing her eyes shut, Anna rubbed her forehead with the back of her hand. "Oh, Companion have mercy," she whispered, shutting the door behind her. "No more guerrilla wars, okay?"

Bradley came out of the bedroom door.

He wore a pair of jeans and a black hooded sweatshirt, light glinting off the lenses of his glasses. "You're back!" he exclaimed, crossing the distance between them in two quick strides. "Oh, thank God!"

He wrapped his arms around her and pulled her close, and for a moment, Anna just let herself enjoy the hug. It didn't matter that she was a mess or that her clothes were all rumpled. She was *home.*

Then reality came crashing in.

She pulled away.

Anna smiled, bowing her head to stare down at her own feet. "It's good to see you," she said, nodding. "I, I don't even know where to begin. It was two weeks that felt like two years of endless stress."

Bradley lifted his chin to study her with lips pursed, clearly pondering *something.* "I'm guessing you can't tell me about most of it," he muttered, turning away from her. "I figure it's all classified."

He marched into the living room.

Anna crossed her arms and followed with her head down, letting out a frustrated sigh. "You probably know most of it anyway," she said. "It had to be the only thing the news talked about for weeks."

Her boyfriend stood by the window with his back turned, gazing through the blinds at the buildings in the distance. "It was on the news every night," he said. "But we didn't hear much. The communications blackout..."

She winced, tossing her head back. "I'm so sorry," she whispered, falling into the nearest chair. "That must have been excruciating for you. I wish I didn't have to put you through this, but..."

At the window, Bradley turned to look over his shoulder, his face locked into one of those unreadable expressions that drove her nuts. "I wasn't angry with you, Hon," he said. "Just worried. When we finally did get the reports..."

He laid it all out for her, piece by agonizing piece. Shortly after Jack and Harry had restored communications, journalists had gone into the field to get footage of the war-zone. For the last five days, TV screens had been lit up with images of *ziaro-gati* and even some Keepers performing extraordinary feats.

Bradley even showed her a video depicting the aftermath of their skirmish on the Union Turnpike. She'd texted him, of course, to let him know that she was all right, but that was the first he'd heard from her in almost two weeks. Even before Slade had started jamming their communications, Jena had insisted on radio silence to minimize the chance of Slade's people finding them. At some point, she found herself explaining everything that had happened.

Her boyfriend listened with the usual patience she had

come to expect from him; it was one of the things that made him such a wonderful person. In moments like this, she felt guilty for all those nights she had lain awake, wondering if she really loved him.

"The people of this world are lucky to have you," he said when her story was over. "Would you like to go to dinner?"

Anna shut her eyes, tears leaking from them to run over her cheeks. "No," she said. "Sweetheart, we have to talk. I got some news while I was in New York."

"What kind of news?"

Sinking into the chair with her arms crossed, Anna looked up at the ceiling. "I'll be going back to Leyria when this over," she mumbled. "It's not optional. They want me on a special task force that Larani is setting up to deal with Slade."

Her boyfriend sat on the big blue couch with his legs apart, his hands resting on his knees. "Wait," he said after a moment. "Slade is *here*. Why would you go back to Leyria to deal with him?"

"Do you remember when I told you about the Key?"

"Yes, I do."

"We're close to locating it," Anna explained. "And we think that once it's found, Slade will have no reason to remain on Earth."

Whatever satisfaction she felt in that vanished when she remembered that it would also mean the end of her relationship with Bradley. She watched him for along moment, watched as he studied her through the lenses of those glasses. She could almost see the wheels turning in his head. "Well," he said, "that's good then."

"I don't think you understand what I'm saying."

He stood up with a sigh and slipped his hands into the pouch of his sweatshirt. "I understand what you're *trying* to say," he replied, shuffling over to her. "You think that if you go back to Leyria, it means we're done."

"Doesn't it?"

Bradley sank to his knees in front of her chair, craning his neck to meet her gaze. He really was adorable – or what was that charming Earth phrase? Adorkable? – with his big goofy smiles. "You really think I've never considered this possibility," he said. "I knew your career would eventually take you off world."

Biting her lower lip, Anna squinted at him. "Am I hearing this right?" she asked, shaking her head. "You're saying you want to come with me?"

His face went red, and he lowered his eyes as if to hide his own embarrassment. "Not counting Justice Keepers, 3,217 citizens from this world have migrated to Leyria. I would like to be number 3,218."

"But you have a life here. I'm not worth this much effort."

"It's not just about you," he said. "Anna, your people see space travel as just a fact of life, but my people wouldn't have even thought it possible a few years ago. The chance to live on another world isn't something I would pass up. I've looked into it, and it turns out immigration is fairly simple, at least comparatively speaking. It's kind of sad that it's easier for me to move to another planet than it would be to move to another country on *this* planet."

Anna smiled into her lap, a lock of red hair falling over one eye. She brushed it away with a casual gesture. "So you're saying that you'd move to another planet for me. That's a pretty big gesture."

He looked up at her with one of those cheesy grins that she found so endearing. "Anna Lenai," he said. "Will you move in with me?"

"Yes."

Bradley rose up to gently cup her face in both hands. Then he leaned in close and kissed her on the lips. It was sweet and tender...but...Shouldn't she feel something a little more substantive than gratitude for his kind gesture? Well, there was the growing anxiety that she might be making a mistake.

It was such a big step, moving in with someone; she'd never done it before, unless you counted living with Jack for just over a month. Bleakness take her, Bradley was willing to move across the galaxy for her. Shouldn't she be more excited? And less terrified? But then, this is what people did, right?

Her parents had divorced when she was a girl, and she could remember the many times her father had insisted that relationships took work and effort. No two people got along perfectly. Bradley was a good person; he was kind and attentive; she enjoyed her time with him. Shouldn't that be enough?

Was she selfish for wanting more?

You need to grow up, Anna, she told herself. *Put those silly, childish notions out of your head. You have a good guy here.*

She pulled away with a chuckle, sitting back in the chair. "So," she began. "Let me tell you about some of the places you have to visit when we go to Leyria."

"You should have seen her," Harry said.

His ex-wife sat in a chair at his kitchen table with her legs stretched out beneath it, a beer bottle in one hand as she listened to him tell the story. Truth be told, he was really quite surprised that she hadn't launched into one of her diatribes about putting their kids in danger.

Harry leaned against the kitchen counter with his arms folded, heaving out a sigh. "She was remarkable, Della," he went on. "You might have thought she'd been handling life-or-death crises all her life."

Lifting the beer bottle to her lips, Della closed her eyes and took a sip. "Well, what did you expect, Harry?" she asked, setting her drink on the table with a loud *thunk*. "This is what she wants to do."

Harry winced, shaking his head. "I expected her to be a

teenager," he said, pacing across the narrow aisle between both sets of counters. "Not a seasoned field medic with nerves of steel."

"She gets that from you."

"A compliment, Della?"

His ex looked up at the ceiling and rolled her eyes. "Don't get used to it, Harry," she said. "But it's true. Ever since she was a little girl, Melissa has tried her damnedest to be just like you."

Harry smiled, then let his head hang, suddenly aware of a burning in his cheeks. "Well, I suppose there are worse role-models," he muttered. "But I would have preferred it if she picked someone like Hillary Clinton."

Ignoring the comment, Della slouched in her chair and lifted the beer bottle up to peer through it. "So, have you decided yet?" she asked. "Are we going to let Melissa do her Keeper training on Leyria?"

"Larani Tal says she's willing to make the transfer," he said. "But only if Melissa requests it. I haven't had the chance to ask her directly. You know how these things are. You push too hard, and she'll insist she wants to stay here."

In truth, he'd been avoiding this topic for a while. If Melissa went to Leyria, he was going with her – there was no way he'd let one of his children just fly-off to another solar system without supervision – but that almost certainly meant leaving Claire behind in her mother's care.

Harry wasn't sure how he felt about that. There were days when Della gave him a hard time about the dangers of his career path, but they both knew he was the responsible parent. She got to take the girls from time to time – and though he had initially resisted it, it was good for them to spend some time with their mother – but they lived with him.

Would it be fair to uproot Claire and just transplant her into another society where she knew nothing, not even the language? What about friends? School. Would she be able to adapt to a Leyrian curriculum? Melissa was on the verge of adulthood, Claire was just shy of puberty. His eldest could handle that kind of change, but his youngest?

"What about Claire?" he asked.

A sour expression passed over Della's face before she covered it up with one of her less-threatening scowls. "I know you object to it, but Claire *can* live with me," she said. "I'm not exactly strapped for cash."

"No, just good judgment."

"Says the man who allowed aliens to play with his brain."

Harry pinched the bridge of his nose with thumb and fore-finger, groaning into his own palm. "You're right," he growled. "This kind of fighting gets us nowhere. Have you considered the possibility of letting Claire come with us?"

"You wanna take away both my kids?"

"I want to keep my daughters together." He spun to face her, then shuffled over to the table with a soft sigh. "But I can see why it might not be in Claire's best interest. She might be happier here."

When he looked up, Della was watching him with her lips pressed into a thin line, her eyes focused on him like a pair of laser beams. "Have you considered *asking* Claire what she wants? I'm guessing not so much."

"She's ten years old."

Della put the bottle to her lips and took another long swig. "Ten-year-olds usually have a pretty good idea of what they want, Harry," she muttered. "That's your problem. You're so used to being Mr. Authority, it never occurs to you to ask."

"What the hell are you talking about?"

Leaning back in her chair with hands folded behind her head, Della stared up at the ceiling with an open mouth. "Didn't you ever ask yourself why I left?" she snapped. "Did it never occur to you to wonder?"

Shutting his eyes tight, Harry trembled with a surge of rage.

"You left me because you never finished growing up!" he spat. "Life was just supposed to be one big party. Let the rest of us handle the clean-up."

She turned her head to fix her gaze upon him, blinking as if he'd suddenly started speaking gibberish. "I left because I was tired of you making every decision for me," she said. "You always get to decide the limits of responsible behaviour."

"What does that mean?"

"It means that you think your priorities are universal," she hissed. "Any sensible person would instantly agree with you."

That wasn't true; he knew perfectly well that other people had different priorities, but Claire was a *child*. There was no way a girl her age could understand the magnitude of a decision like this. As her father, it was his duty to figure out what was in her best interest and then do that, only...

Melissa had fought him for months when he opposed her decision to become a Keeper. Ironically, it had been Della's advice that had convinced him to give his eldest a little more latitude. That had done wonders for their relationship. Maybe his ex-wife had a point.

She spared him the burden of having to think about it – in typical Della fashion – by putting her foot down before he'd had a chance to mull it over. "Talk to your daughter, Harry," she said. "If you don't, I will."

Dressed in black pants and a matching top with a round neck, Jena stood before the gray wall of the Science Lab. Her muscles ached, and her nerves were so frayed she was ready to bite someone's head off.

A shower, a hair-cut and a good night's sleep had done very little to ease her stress. She still felt as if she might have to fend off an attack by cybernetic monstrosities or evil robots at any moment. No amount of scrubbing made her feel clean. Her people had all insisted that she stay behind. Generals didn't fight on the battlefield.

Now, Raynar was dead.

It would have played out the same way if you had been there, she told herself. But that was a lie. In all likelihood, things would have been very different, but not necessarily better. There could have been more deaths or greater devastation. Telling herself that did little to ease her guilt.

Jena shut her eyes, trembling as she let out a hissing breath. She turned her face up to the ceiling. "Thank you all for coming," she began. "We just got some very big news from our resident code-breaker."

She turned.

Harry, Jack and Anna stood side by side in the middle of the room, blinking at her like a pack of raccoons who had just witnessed some thoughtless human leaving tasty treats by the roadside.

The hologram of Ven appeared as a vaguely man-shaped being of swirling light – yellow, this time – and lifted its ghostly hand to gesture at the wall. "I have reviewed the data Jack and Harry brought back from their last mission," it said. "I can safely say that I have located the final cipher."

Another hologram appeared before the gray wall, this one depicting a 2D map of North America and slowly zooming in on a spot in the American Mid-West. The white rooftops of tall buildings came into view.

Biting his lip, Jack squinted at the map. "Minneapolis?" he asked, shaking his head. "I don't know, Ven. The last two ciphers were smack dab in the middle of nowhere, not in a major city."

The hologram inclined its ghostly head as if to study the map. "I can assure you that my calculations are quite accurate," it said through the loudspeaker. "This only make sense in light of the fact that Overseer technology attracts humans."

"You mean people," Harry said.

"It would depend on your nomenclature," Ven replied. "I consider myself to be a person, and yet I am unaffected."

Already, Jena was feeling annoyed, and their pointless conversational tangents were only making it worse. Yet another mission she couldn't go on; once again, she had to stay behind and let others do the hard work. What precisely had convinced her that taking a desk job was a good idea?

Clenching her teeth, Jena let her head hang. "This is academic," she said, brushing bangs off her forehead with the back of one fist. "Our first priority should be to recover the cipher. Discussions on personhood can wait."

"You want me and Harry to go?" Jack asked.

"I want you all to go."

She turned away from them, slipping her hands into her pockets and marching back to the wall. "At this point, Slade will be getting desperate," she went on. "I want Harry to have all the protection we can give him."

It was disorienting, tracking them with her spatial awareness. Harry, Jack and Anna were all wispy silhouettes in her mind, but Ven was absent. Her Nassai could only sense matter. The discrepancy between what she knew and what her mind perceived was more than a little unnerving.

"What about Ben?" Anna suggested.

Jena felt her face twist into a haggard expression, then shook her head with a soft sigh. "No, you won't be taking Ben," she said. "I'm sure that you've all been thinking it – Jack most of all – but it must have occurred to all of you."

She turned back to them.

Her three teammates stood there with wide eyes, blinking as if she had suddenly started speaking gibberish. And then there was Ven; the hologram just floated an inch off the floor, watching her.

"Slade has been too good at staying one step ahead of us," she said. "I think he has someone on the inside."

Well, that did a good job sucking the air out of the room. Jack and Anna exchanged glances, and Harry just gave her one of those detective stares that implied he had found a hole in her story. It made her want to snap at him, but Jena managed to keep her irritation under control. She was a professional, Bleakness take her. "So," Jena went on. "We keep this one between us; we get that final cipher, and then we end this."

Ven floated upward, drifting across the room like a leaf on a cool breeze. "I shall forward the coordinates to your multi-tools," he said. "With any luck, we'll be able to do this with minimal bloodshed."

As he sat behind a desk in a dark, cramped little room that had once been a study, Grecken Slade listened to the recording delivered by the bug Isara had planted in the Lab on Station Twelve. So, Jena Morane and her happy little band of misfits had discovered the location of the final cipher.

"I shall forward the coordinates to your multi-tools," that artificial being said through the speaker. "With any luck, we'll be able to do this with minimal bloodshed."

There would be no such luck.

Anger flared within him when he was forced to contemplate the many failures of his subordinates. Arin, who had gotten himself captured while battling Jack Hunter and that ridiculous old police officer, Flagg who was dead at Jena Morane's hands. Valeth who had fled in fear and weakness.

This time, Slade would go himself.

This time, there would be no failures.

His multi-tool beeped when the bug transmitted the coordinates of the third cipher. Jena Morane was correct; the time had come to end this.

21

A single-story house with white aluminum siding and black shingles on its gabled roof stood in the shade of a tall elm tree that grew in the front yard. The grass was that pristine shade of green that only came from consistent watering, and there was even a nice flowerbed under the front window.

In Harry's opinion, it was the kind of house that ought to have belonged to a sweet old lady, and the rest of this quiet suburban street was no different. It was a remnant of a simpler time.

Harry leaned against the driver's side of his rented car with arms folded, ignoring the sweat on his brow. "It's cute," he said, nodding. "You're absolutely certain these are the coordinates Ven specified?"

Why he insisted on wearing a gray suit on a hot day like this was beyond him – he wasn't a detective anymore – but there were times when looking sharp just made him feel that much more confident. In some ways, Harry was also a remnant of another time.

Anna sat on the hood of his car in denim shorts and a light

blue t-shirt, her hair done up in a nubby little ponytail. "Yup. This is the place," she said, checking her multi-tool. "According to Ven, the Overseer device is buried under that house. Address registry says it belongs to a widower named Patrick Osborne."

The house looked so unimposing, nestled between two other cute little homes. He could even see a round wooden table through the front window and paintings hung up on the dining room wall. It was hard to imagine that a human family might be able to have anything resembling a normal life in a house built atop Overseer technology, but then he had bonded the N'Jal several times now with no major side effects. True, he was clearly an exception to the rule, but... Perhaps the device beneath that house was dormant.

On his left, Jack leaned against the car's back end with a distant look on his face. Like Anna, he wore casual clothing – gray jeans and a navy-blue polo shirt – but the kid also wore sunglasses, and that made him at least look like something out of a cop show. "So, what do we do?" he asked. "Ring the bell and casually explain that he might have some alien tech in his basement?"

"We can't do that," Harry said.

Glancing over his shoulder, Jack studied him through those dark lenses. "Well, we better think of something," he said, his eyebrows rising. "Because if Mr. Patrick Osborne comes to the window, I *will* have to lift a boombox over my head."

"Really? You'd Cusak an old man?"

"It's the only thing that turns stalker behaviour into adorable quirkiness."

Anna was hunched over on the hood with her elbows on her thighs, her chin resting on laced fingers. "There's also the issue of digging it up," she said. "I'm betting the house has a concrete foundation."

Jack let his head hang, then used one finger to push his

sunglasses all the way up his nose. "Well those things are pretty powerful," he countered. "The last two tunneled through hard packed dirt and the floor of a cave."

"Digging it up won't be an issue," Harry confirmed. He clasped his hands together behind his back and took a few tentative steps into the middle of the road. "Our problem is secrecy. We're dealing with classified subject matter. Right now, no one outside of our team and Slade's people knows the Key exists."

"We better find some place else to hash this out," Jack suggested. "Come on. I saw a motel a few intersections back."

Lying prone on the roof of a small house, Slade watched the car drive off through a pair of binoculars. A sleek red sedan that drove to the end of the block before its taillights flared at a stop sign. His blood boiled when he saw the back of Lenai's head through the rear window.

He couldn't believe that his enemies would be so pathetically softhearted. The third cipher was right there for the taking! And they hesitated because some miserable old man might balk at the thought of strangers entering his home?

The house with the white aluminum siding was undisturbed on the other side of the street, the elm tree in its front yard sighing as a breeze passed through the branches. Slade could go in there right now – he had no qualms about killing the old man who lived there – but he lacked the technology to extract the cipher from the Inzari device buried beneath the house's basement.

That unnerved him.

The Inzari had not given him the ability to use their technology, but the Fallen Ones had done so for Harry Carlson. Until recently, it would never have occurred to Slade that such a thing was possible.

Was he not worthy enough?

He would simply have to capture Harry Carlson and force him to extract the cipher. That meant killing Hunter and Lenai.

He relished the thought of that.

The sunlight of early evening streamed through the front window of Anna's motel room, illuminating the neatly made bed and the cream-coloured walls. A wooden table in the corner was home to a bunch of pamphlets that boasted the best service in all of Minnesota. And free Wi-Fi! You had to have free Wi-Fi.

Anna sat in a wooden chair with her knees together, a bottle of water in one hand. In the golden light, she looked absolutely stunning, her hair seeming to shimmer. "So he's just going to putter about while he mulls it over?"

Jack sat on the bed with his hands on his knees, head hanging in frustration. "It's Harry's way," he said with a shrug. "The one thing we have in common is a penchant for slipping into Loner Cop Mode."

Anna winced, then pinched the bridge of her nose. "Please, don't remind me," she muttered. "I just don't see any way around it; we're going to have to talk to Patrick Osborne."

"Well, you know Harry and rules."

The glare she gave him could have stripped paint off a car, but she quickly replaced it with a smile and a chuckle. "The two of you..." she said, shaking her head. "You know, there *are* options beyond following the rules to the letter and breaking them outright."

"Like what?"

"Talk to your superiors; explain the need for an exception."

Tilting his head back, Jack felt his brow furrow. "Now, why didn't I think of that?" he murmured to himself. "Oh, yeah! Because it almost never works! People in positions of authority believe that adherence to policy trumps any practical considerations."

Anna lifted the bottle to her lips, then closed her eyes and downed almost half of it. "Even Jena?" she asked. "You seem to trust her."

"Jena's different."

"And me?"

Blushing hard, Jack lowered his eyes to stare into his lap. He rubbed his forehead nervously. "You're different too," he said. "If you told me you needed me to hop on one foot for an hour, I'd start hopping."

When he looked up, she was grinning at him, her eyes full of surprised pleasure. It was the kind of smile he saw every now and then, usually when he said something that made her very happy. He couldn't remember the first time he had seen that smile, but he could remember the first time he had noticed.

That was the smile she had worn right before she kissed him that night while they sat on a bench by the Ottawa River. It was hard to keep himself focused, but he caught it when Anna asked him, "So, why do I deserve so much faith?"

He stood up and tried to find the words to express himself without looking like an ass. "Because," he replied hesitantly. "If you ask me to hop, it can only mean the world is ending, and I can somehow give you the time you need to save the day by making an ass out of myself."

Anna got to her feet.

She stood on her toes to lightly press her lips to his cheek, then pulled back and blinked at him. "That's..." Her face reddened, and she looked away. "That's one of the sweetest things anyone has ever said to me."

He flinched instinctively and turned his head so that she couldn't see his expression. "So, you're going to Leyria to join the new task force," he said. "That'll be good. I was afraid I'd miss you."

Anna stood before him with her hands in her pockets, keeping her eyes downcast. "Yeah," she said. "It's such a mixed bag too. Dealing with the craziness of Earth culture is driving me crazy, but..."

"But?"

"In some ways, I'm gonna miss it here."

Jack crossed his arms and shuffled past her, moving into the warm light spilling through the window. "I know exactly what you mean," he said. "My mom...I can't stop thinking about how much I'm going to miss her."

When he turned, Anna was standing there with her eyes closed, breathing deeply. "There's a lot to miss," she agreed. "But change is good, right? They're always telling me change is good."

"What about Bradley?"

Her face lit up with a warm smile that vanished half a second later. "That's the best part," she said in a shaky voice. "He's coming with me! He surprised me with it last night. Said he wanted to see Leyria."

Those words hit Jack like a kick to the chest. Here he was, making noises about how much he respected Anna, how much he admired her and trusted her judgment. The respectful thing to do would be to keep his damn mouth shut. She was happy. She didn't need an idiot like him gumming up the works.

No, his mother was wrong; Gabi was wrong. Bringing up these stupid feelings of his would only result in heartache for everyone concerned. The past was the past, and it should bloody well *stay* in the past.

"Jack?"

The sound of Anna's voice drew him out of his reverie, and he found her watching him with her head tilted to one side, one eyebrow arched quizzically. "I asked you if you thought it was a good idea."

Chewing on his lip, Jack turned his face up to the ceiling. "A good idea," he said, eyebrows rising. "Well, of course it's a good idea! You two are great together! You love him, don't you?"

Anna frowned and looked down at herself. "Yeah," she said, nodding to him. "I do. He's a great guy."

Something about her tone seemed to invite him to say something, but he wasn't entirely sure *what* to say. Jack was no fool – he had a knack for reading people, and he could sense that she wasn't being entirely honest with him – but if she had chosen to go forward in her relationship with Bradley, she must have done so for a good reason. It was *her* life; he had no business sticking his nose in.

"I'm gonna go for a little walk," Anna said, though he was only half-aware of her saying it. "Lots to think about, you know? I could use a little air."

"Yeah," he whispered.

After she was gone, Jack slid down against the wall until his butt touched the floor. Good God, was he really about to start crying? Not over this, surely. He'd already come to terms with the fact that he and Anna weren't meant to be! He'd cried all his tears over it years ago when she got on that shuttle to leave for Alios. She told him she didn't want a long-distance relationship, and that was the end of it.

So, why was he sniffling now?

Summer was equally unhappy; he could feel her sorrow and her desire to comfort him. In fact, his symbiont was quite eager to talk. He could slip into a trance and let her tell him whatever it was she wanted to tell him, but he decided against it. Right then, he wanted to be alone with his thoughts.

Besides, if he knew Summer, then she would almost certainly urge him to go find Anna and tell her how he really felt; he had avoided direct contact with her for several days for exactly that reason. There was no way in hell that he was gonna make this even *more* awkward.

Damn it, Anna had probably sensed that he was holding back sadness, put two and two together and decided that she needed to be away from him. The last thing he needed to do was burden her with his feelings.

No, for once in his life, Jack Hunter would keep his mouth shut.

The golden rays of the setting sun hit the front wall of the motel, illuminating every scuff in the blue aluminum siding, glinting off the windows that looked into various rooms. Most had curtains drawn for privacy.

The parking lot was nearly empty with only a few cars nestled between two yellow lines. Across the street, she saw a restaurant with a red neon sign that promised the best burger in town. Anna had never questioned eating meat growing up, but after coming to this world and learning that they still killed animals for food...It made her shudder. She had developed a real love of vegetables; she might continue with her new diet once she went back to Leyria.

Anna shuffled along the motel's walkway with her head down, strands of red hair falling over her face. " 'Do you think it's a good idea?' " she mumbled, eyebrows rising. "Come on, Lenai. You can't put him in that position."

When she reached the end of the walkway, she went around the side of the building and continued onward for no particular reason. She just needed to keep moving, and any direction would do.

A narrow road led from the parking lot to an alley behind the motel. That would be private enough, and if anyone caught her skulking...Well, she was a Justice Keeper. There could be something dangerous lurking nearby!

Anna shut her eyes tight, then tossed her head about in disgust. "You're not doing yourself any favours," she muttered under her breath. "If you feel something for him, just bloody well tell him!"

At the end of the road, she found a paved alley between the motel's back wall and a wooden fence that bordered the property. There was a dumpster a little ways off with its lid open to display trash bags inside.

Anna kept walking.

The windows on this side of the building had frosted glass for privacy. It was nice and shady back here, and quiet too. Companion have mercy, the last few weeks had just thrown her life out of whack! She needed some time to think, to reflect. And she wasn't thrilled about the growing cloud of anxiety that seemed to be centred on her boyfriend.

Seth offered comfort as best he could, but there was little a Nassai could say on the topic of human relationships. No, she would just have to sort this one out on her own, and then make the difficult-

Hair stood on the back of her neck.

She sensed it with spatial awareness before turning around to see it with her own eyes. Slade dropped from the motel's rooftop to land crouched in the alley. The former Chief of the Justice Keepers wore black pants and a red coat with gold embroidery, his dark hair blowing in the wind.

"You!" she growled.

He spun to face her with a great big smile, watching her with eyes that practically glittered with murderous intent. "Hello, Anna," he said, taking a step forward. "I really was hoping that you would be first."

Lifting her chin to study him, Anna narrowed her eyes. "The first to kick your ass?" she said, shaking her head. "Because I need to tell you, I usually don't go for virgin boys, but I'll make an exception in your case."

A sly smile appeared on Slade's face, and he bowed his head to her. "I see that you have picked Hunter's talent for witless banter," he said. "He really has been something of a bad influence on you."

"Wait, you think *Jack* taught me how to quip?"

"You are a foolish child, playing with-"

"Because I've been making quips for *years*!" Anna strode toward him with her fists clenched, her head down as she hissed air through her teeth. "I tell you, I get no respect. I was kicking ass across the galaxy all by myself and daunting criminals with a few well-timed puns, followed by a sharp jab to the nose."

Slade was backing away from her, clearly puzzled by her insistence on getting the recognition that was rightfully hers. "I have come here-"

"Yeah, yeah, yeah," she interrupted. "We'll discuss your evil plan and all the ways I'm gonna stop it later. Right now, I'm venting! I mean, really! The instant I get a partner, people are all 'Oh, Jack! He's so funny! He deflates the bad guys with his casual wit and indecipherable pop-culture references!' Hello? Quirky adorableness, right here!

"I'm trying to convey a genuine source of frustration, and here you are, butting in with 'It's time for me to make a villain speech.' Bleakness take me! It's not all about you, you know."

Her tirade died off when she got within three feet of Slade, and suddenly, the urge to demonstrate her wit was replaced by a seething black hatred, a desire to smash his face until she felt the snap of his bones. Anna would've never thought herself capable of such rage. "You killed my friend," she said.

Slade grinned and nodded to her. "I did," he said in tones as cool as a lake in the middle of winter. "I do believe I've killed a lot of people."

Tilting her head back, Anna stared up at him. "Too many," she said, her eyebrows rising. "But if you want to do penance, you've come to the right place. I'm happy to beat the sin out of you."

"Not the words of a Justice Keeper."

"Well, you've been a bad influence."

Spreading his arms wide, Slade looked down at himself. He shook his head ever so slowly. "You don't even want to know why I came here?" The incredulity in his tone gave her pause. "Really, Anna, what's gotten into you? We could have a nice, relaxing chat, but instead you want to fight. All right, let's fight."

Slade began a roundhouse kick.

Anna ducked and felt the man's foot pass right over her head. She rose in time to watch him spin, one arm lashing out for a back-hand strike.

Anna thrust her arm out.

Their wrists collided with the harsh *smack* of bone meeting bone. Anna kicked the man in his side and sent him stumbling away with a sharp gasp. In a heartbeat, he was whirling around to face her.

Anna jumped and snap-kicked.

Her foot slammed into his nose, bringing a spray of blood as Slade's head snapped backward. The evil bastard was still on his feet, still conscious despite a blow that should have knocked him senseless. Anna landed right in front of him.

She threw a punch, but he caught her wrist. His other hand clamped onto her throat, and the next thing Anna knew she was being lifted off the ground. A quick surge of Bent gravity did the rest.

Anna flew sideways until her shoulder crashed into the motel's back wall, rough aluminum siding cutting her skin. Pain flared, but she landed in a crouch, pleading with Seth to heal her quickly.

She turned and found Slade gliding toward her across the width of the alley. The wicked smile on his face promised endless depths of agony once he was through beating her into submission.

Anna charged forward.

She jumped and spread her legs, wrapping them around Slade's waist. Clinging to him like a spider-monkey, she punched his face once, twice, three times. The man winced with every blow.

On her fourth punch, Slade's hand shot up to seize her wrist. He gave a twist and sent a jolt of pain through Anna's body. His other hand covered her face, and then she was being thrown backward.

Anna landed on her ass.

She rolled onto her stomach by instinct, gasping and wheezing. Pushing her hands down on the rough pavement, she flung her body upward to drive both feet into his belly. In her mind's eye, she watched him stumble away.

Anna rolled onto her back.

Curling her legs against her chest, she sprang off the ground and landed upright. "I think I'm starting to get annoyed," she said, wiping her mouth with the back of her hand. "I was hoping to be done in time for a quick supper."

Slade stood by the wooden fence with a hand pressed to his stomach, hunched over as he trembled with laughter. "Do you remember when I sent you after that Nassai Hunter now carries?" he asked. "Such a shame you didn't die in Dead Space."

Baring her teeth with a growl, Anna felt her face burn. "Seems to me it all worked out in the end," she said, striding toward him. "I met my best friend; we made an alliance with Earth, and you got the smackdown."

Anna kicked high.

The man leaned over sideways, evading the blow by inches. He snapped himself upright, then grabbed the back of her shirt as she began a spin. All of a sudden, she was being thrown off balance.

She went face-first into the dumpster, bracing herself by pressing both hands to the metal. This wasn't good. When she turned around, Slade was already closing in for the kill. A lion on the hunt.

He threw a punch.

Anna ducked and felt the man's fist pass right over her head. She threw a series of jabs into his stomach, forcing him backward as her fists pounded him like pistons. Now to finish this.

Anna rose for a hard right-cross.

The man leaned back, catching her wrist in both hands. He gave a sharp twist, and the next thing Anna knew, she was being forced to bend over with her side toward him. A swift kick to the belly drove the wind from her lungs.

Slade lifted his foot above his head and then brought it down like a headsman's ax, striking Anna right between the shoulder-blades. She was forced down onto her stomach, pain surging through her body.

His boot slammed into her rib-cage, the blow augmented with Bent Gravity.

Anna was lifted off the ground and sent tumbling through the air like a log rolling down a hill, flying through the alley until she collided with the dumpster with a painful *clang*. She landed on her belly, trying to push herself up on all fours. That last blow had cracked ribs.

Seth would be able to heal her, of course; with a few hours rest, she'd be running down the street as if nothing had happened. But she wasn't going to get a few hours to rest. She could sense him coming for her.

Slade moved with the elegant of a *zrinthala* dancer, his black hair streaming out in the breeze. His face was serene, carved from stone. This was just business to him. A task to be completed and nothing more.

He stopped when he got within arm's reach.

Bending over, Slade grabbed the back of her collar with one

hand and yanked her to her feet. Another hand clamped onto Anna's throat.

He lifted her clear off the ground.

Anna squeezed her eyes shut, tears running over her cheeks in rivers. "You're five kinds of pathetic," she whispered, ignoring the strength of his grip. "Even with all your power, you're just a petty little man with a vendetta."

In her mind's eye, Slade was nothing but a silhouette, but she could see the misty currents of his face twist in a snarl. "And look at you," he said softly. "Such a tiny thing. A scrawny chicken waiting to be gutted."

"Baby, eat this chicken slow," she hissed. "It's full of all them little bones."

She brought her knee up to strike the underside of Slade's chin, throwing him off balance. He managed to hold on to her, however, and the next thing she felt was a fist colliding with her face.

Everything went dark, and for a moment, she was barely aware of her own body. Then reality came crashing in, every ache and pain more pronounced after a few seconds' reprieve. She dangled from his outstretched hand, squirming but unable to pull free.

Slade pulled her close.

Through tear-blurred vision, she saw his face, his eyes searching, trying to peer into her very soul. His gaze was locked with hers, and though part of her wanted to resist, she found herself transfixed. "It really is a shame, the power of a Nassai wasted on a sad little mouse like you. How you've survived this long, I'll-"

Suddenly, his eyes widened.

The colour drained out of his face, and he stared at her with an open mouth. "No! It isn't possible!" he said, blinking at her. "The Inzari would never allow it!"

He pulled her close until his nose almost touched hers, and then she was drowning in the bottomless pits of his eyes. Sinking into an abyss from which there was no escape. "Impossible!" Slade bellowed. "Again? Again! Will this wretched world give me no rest? *Wǒ de tiān*, Lihua? How many times must I kill you?"

What?

It made no sense; these were the ravings of a mad-man, but while her rational mind recoiled in disgust, something deep within her – something in the very core of her – knew just what to say. "You can't destroy me, Liu," she whispered. "I tried telling you that, but you didn't listen. You never listen."

Slade threw her, applying a Bending.

Anna flew sideways, crashing shoulder-first through the wooden fence, dropping into the grass behind the motel. Her body hit hard, and then she was sprawled out on the ground, aching from head to toe.

Slade came through the hole in the fence, snarling like a feral beast. "I should have known when you defied me," he whispered. "When you flew off, chasing Denario Tarse against my orders."

He stood over her with teeth bared, his face red with rage. "It's time that we ended this, *Anna!*" he hissed, every syllable dripping venom. "And this time, *stay* dead!"

"Break me off a switch, Greck," Jack's voice called out. "I'm gonna have to take you over my knee."

As he strode through the alley behind the motel, Jack struggled to contain his rage. His rage and his fear. The last time he had fought this man, things hadn't exactly gone in his favour, and by the look of it, Slade had just finished pummeling Anna.

The pompous peacock of a man stood with his back turned in a hole in the fence, looking ridiculous in that silly red coat. "Hunter," Slade growled, whirling around. "And I thought I might have a challenging opponent."

Jack grinned, then bowed his head to the other man. "Sorry to disappoint," he said with a shrug of his shoulders. "But, you know, I'm like one of those stress balls. You can pummel me, and I'll just keep coming back."

"More japes."

"Really, Greck?" Jack mocked. "Ever heard the phrase 'Live in the Now?' I mean I'm spouting 90s language, and I'm still more hip to what the kids these days are saying! Should I call you 'bae?' That'll at least bring me into my parents' generation, and I'm told it means 'poop' in Danish; so it kind of fits-"

"Be silent!"

Slade looked up to study Jack. His face darkened considerably, and then he shook his head. "But if she's..." It was like watching a first-grader puzzle out why his father and Santa were never in the same room at the same time. "Then that means you're... Of course, you are! You follow her everywhere!"

Tossing his head back, Jack blinked at the open sky. "Seriously?" he asked, shaking his head. "We can't just beat the crap out of each other? You have to stand there, raving at me like Smeagol on meth?"

Slade started forward.

The man froze after stepping through the hole, his face losing most of its colour. "But the two of you..." His mouth dropped open as he drew in a shuddering breath. "This isn't over! Do you understand?"

To Jack's surprise, Slade leaped right over his head, riding a surge of Bent Gravity to the slanted roof of the motel. He landed there on the black shingles, glancing back over his shoulder. "It isn't over!"

"You're doing it all wrong," Jack called out. "You're supposed to shake your fist and tell me I'll pay for this!"

He ran to Anna, hopping through the hole in the fence, and found her gasping in the grass, staring up at the sky. Her face was red and tear-stained. "He's insane," Anna hissed. "Thought I was...Said I was."

Jack closed his eyes, trying to calm himself. "I know," he said, gently taking her hand. "But right now, we have bigger concerns. We have to get you to a hospital."

22

The sky was deep twilight blue with only a few faint stars visible overhead, leaving the houses on this suburban street as blocky shadows, sentinels that stood watch over a road illuminated by street lamps. A group of teenage boys road past on bicycles, each one intently focused on getting somewhere quickly.

It was a cute little neighbourhood, the picturesque setting that everyone imagined whenever they thought of what had once been called the American Dream. That was why he felt so out of place here.

Harry paced up the sidewalk with his hands in his jacket pocket, his eyes fixed on his shoes. *Can you recall a time when this had been all you wanted out of life?* he asked himself. *It wasn't that long ago.*

That, of course, had been before Denario Tarse had brought alien technology into his city; after that, things had become far more complicated. The simple dreams of the past no longer seemed to make sense in this new age.

And they had never really been *his* dreams. Della was right; he was something of a workaholic, and that may have played a big role in how his family life had played out. It had been so long since he had thought about it.

The small house with white aluminum siding was right there on the far side of the street, a light in its front window allowing him to see into the living room. There was a TV on, tuned to the news.

So, Mr. Osborne was home.

Closing his eyes, Harry let his head hang. "Be certain you want to do this," he told himself, stepping into the street. "Because once this toothpaste is out of the tube, there's no putting it back."

He paused.

It might be wise to be sure he hadn't come here for nothing. Assaulting a man only to discover that the very device they were looking for was not actually here would be nothing short of horrid. If he was going to damn himself, something good should come out of it.

He reached into his pants' pocket, retrieving the curled-up ball of flesh that had all but become an extension of his own body. The N'Jal unfolded the instant his hand made contact, unfolding to become like a second skin that covered his palm, tiny neural fibers bonding with his own nervous system.

He thrust his palm out toward the house.

Finding words for what he did wasn't easy, but in computer terms, it was something like a ping. He scanned the area for Overseer technology, and felt...something. A presence underneath the house. The cipher was here.

Harry winced, shaking his head. "Damn it," he muttered, completing his journey across the street, stepping onto the curb. "You *would* be living right on top of some alien relic, wouldn't you, Mr. Osborne."

He considered summoning the cipher to the street – perhaps it could erupt from the front lawn and spare him the need to go inside – but that would make too much noise and leave people with too many questions.

No, there was only one option.

Pounding on the red front door with his fist, Harry waited for an answer. The door swung inward a moment later, revealing an older man in gray pants and a blue button-up shirt with the collar left open. He was a handsome fellow with a firm jaw, thin white hair and glasses. "Yes?"

"Mr. Osborne."

"Yes..."

Harry crossed his arms with a heavy sigh, then bowed his head to the other man. "I was hoping we could talk," he said, backing away from the door. "We...There might be a problem with your house, sir."

Osborne scrunched up his face as though he'd been sucking on a lemon, then shook his head. "I think you better start by telling me who you are," he replied. "Before I decide to call the police."

"That's funny."

"I'm not laughing."

"No, I mean you calling the police," Harry said, stepping closer. "You see, it just so happens that I'm...Oh, never mind."

He slapped a palm against Osborne's head, the N'jal's neural fibers digging into the old man's skin. Just like that, Harry had control of Osborne's nervous system. He really didn't want to do this, but...

A little oxytocin to make the old man feel a special bond with him, a little gamma-aminobutyric acid to lower his anxiety. Some melatonin to make him sleepy. In less than ten seconds, Osborne was standing there in a daze.

Harry caught the man as he fell forward, slinging one of Osborne's arms around his shoulders. "Come on," he whispered, dragging Osborne into the house, shutting the door behind himself. "We'll find you someplace nice to rest."

He dragged the limp Osborne over to the living room, then eased him down onto the couch. Mercy, but the old man was heavy! Most of his friends these days were Justice Keepers, and they always made feats of strength look easy.

Osborne was curled up on his side with his head on a soft pillow. His eyes drifted shut, and within a few moments, he was breathing slow and steady. Not exactly the best way to gain access to a man's home, but Harry had thought about it for the better part of an hour, and he had come to the conclusion that there were no other options.

He couldn't just tell Osborne the whole damn thing – even with the knowledge of aliens and starships, there was almost no chance the old man would believe him – nor could he go to the city police for some kind of assistance. Making any kind of official record of their trip here would almost certainly alert Slade to their presence. That meant doing something he really didn't want to do.

It meant breaking the law.

Harry thought – or, at least, he hoped – that he had incapacitated Osborne by the gentlest means possible, but that didn't make it any less illegal. However, the illegality of what he had done didn't make it any less necessary.

Once again, his multi-tool buzzed with an incoming call. Harry ignored it. He didn't want to talk to Jack right now; if news of what he had done here made it back to Jena, he didn't want Jack or Anna catching trouble for his decisions.

The foyer just inside the front door led to a small kitchen with linoleum floor tiles and brown wooden cupboards making a ring around the room. In the back corner, he saw a set of stairs that led down to the basement.

He took the steps two by two until he found himself in a drab room with a concrete floor and wooden shelves along two of the four walls. The only light came from a single bulb in the ceiling; it took him half a minute to find the switch.

Sucking on his lower lip, Harry shut his eyes. "You can do this, Carlson," he told himself with a nod. "Besides, it's too late to back out now. You already violated the old man's rights."

He thrust one hand toward the floor, seeking with the N'Jal. What he wanted was down there, all right. Maybe a good fifty feet deep, but it sensed his urgency and began tunneling its way up to the surface.

The room seemed to rumble, tools and knickknacks on the shelves shaking, some falling to the floor. It sounded like an earthquake, but if luck was with him tonight, the neighbours wouldn't notice anything.

Something burst through the floor, spraying chunks of concrete into the air. A thick column of flesh rose out of the hole to form a pillar roughly as tall as Harry's chest with a perfectly flat top.

He stepped forward.

Gritting his teeth with a hiss, Harry shook his head. "How do you get yourself into these messes?" he asked, stopping in front of the humming Overseer device. Right then, he felt disgusted with himself.

Gently, he touched the device with the hand that didn't carry the N'jal, allowing it to interface with his nervous system. Images flashed in his mind: inhuman faces and planets spinning off into the empty night. A sun that might have been his own – there was no way to tell – glowing bright and yellow in the darkness.

There were sounds his mind couldn't process and emotions that felt utterly alien to him. Characters that belonged to no language he had ever read. And there was a hissing that made his flesh crawl.

Harry winced, tears rolling over his cheeks, dripping from his chin. "Come on!" he growled at the device. "Hurry the fuck up! You wanna mind-screw me? Well, get the fuck on with it, already!"

The knowledge flooded his consciousness – so much that he couldn't make sense of it all – but he managed to transfer it all to the N'Jal. Ven could sort it out later. Harry was just the god damn mule.

The vision ended.

Harry stumbled backward, lifting a hand to his eyes and wiping tears away. "Well, wasn't that fun?" he whispered. "The hot new ride they should put in every theme park. Christ, I'm starting to sound like Jack."

He couldn't just leave the pillar here.

This time, he used the hand with the N'Jal when he touched the damn thing, feeding instructions into its nervous system. The pillar screeched in protest – it was alive, after all – but he forced his will upon it.

The pillar let out one final screech, and then it went suddenly, painfully still. The colour drained out of its flesh until it was nothing but a gray husk. Then it blackened and collapsed to a pile of dust.

Anyone else who thought to use that thing to recover the final cipher would find nothing but disappointment in this basement. He couldn't do anything about the hole in the floor, but...Well, his job was done.

He turned and went up the stairs.

A trip to the ER on Earth was a little different from what Anna had grown used to on her world. The last time she visited a hospital on this planet, she had been unconscious and losing blood fast. She never had a chance to really take stock of the experience.

As a girl, she had broken her arm while trying to climb a tree. She had to go at least one branch higher than Devin Sindelo – the boy had honestly believed that since he was bigger, he would have an easier time of it – but Anna had reached that higher branch only to have it snap and drop her a good fifteen feet.

Her mother had been livid.

Sierin Elana had never really understood her youngest daughter's need to outpace the boys in every race, to always climb a little higher, explore a little further. Her people had made enormous strides in gender equality compared to Earth, but it was amazing the kind of ideas that hid in a person's head, passing unnoticed from generation to generation.

Some people still believed that physical size was the determining factor in physical ability, and since women were, on average, smaller...

Anna was used to med-bots when she visited the ER, bots that would scan her and create a report for triage nurses. Her fractured ulna had been repaired by a med-bot under a doctor's supervision. Things were different here.

Jack had rushed her to the ER only to have a triage nurse say that she looked to be in good shape. By the time a doctor had finally seen her, nearly an hour later, Seth had healed the worst of it, leaving her with nothing to fear but pain and exhaustion. They had sent her home with some pain killers.

The view through the window in her motel room showed a nearly empty parking lot under the night sky, but the neon sign from the bar across the street was quite visible. The odd car would rush by every now and then.

Anna sat on the edge of the mattress with her legs together, head hanging from the weight of her fatigue. "You really don't have to do this," she muttered. "I just need some sleep and a hot bath."

Jack dropped to his knees in front of her, looking up to study her with his gorgeous blue eyes. "In a motel bathtub?" he asked, eyebrows rising. "I don't know, An. You really want *another* trip to the hospital?"

She smiled into her lap, ignoring the warmth in her cheeks.

"I *have* endured worse than this, you know," she teased. "One time, I even managed to get shot right through the chest. Now, *that* was touch and go."

"I recall being there for you then too."

"You were."

Jack pressed an ice-pack to her cheek, and she leaned into it, closing her eyes and sighing softly. "Thank you," she whispered, gently placing one hand on his forearm. "I really am glad you're here."

He was smiling, shaking his head with a burst of rueful laughter. "Always willing to help lick your wounds..." Suddenly, he stiffened as if realizing the implication of what he had just said. "And hello to the grossness. Jack Hunter is really the king of suave this evening. Tip your server, folks; it's bound to be a good show."

Tilting her head back, Anna squinted at the ceiling. "You're not the one with cause to feel embarrassed." She heaved out a deep breath. "I figured after I took down Wesley, I would be able to handle him, but-"

"Slade is in another weight class."

Anna squeezed her eyes shut, then shook her head with a growl. "Not the analogy I was looking for," she whispered. "I was just thinking about how people assume that size means you're...Oh, never mind."

Jack got to his feet, crossing his arms and glaring at her like a teacher standing over the desk of a disobedient student. "You *do* realize that Slade hurled me through a wooden beam, right?" he said. "The guy is insanely powerful."

"How is that possible?"

Covering his mouth with three fingers, Jack shut his eyes. "I can only think of one explanation," he muttered under his breath. "Slade has a Nassai, but the Overseers have somehow... enhanced him in other ways."

Wincing hard, Anna groaned. "When he looked in my

eyes..." The experience left her feeling uneasy in ways she couldn't quite express. "There was something..."

Once again, Jack knelt before her, and this time, there was an intensity in the way he looked at her. "He saw the most beautiful thing he'll ever see," Jack whispered. "The spark of defiance in you. That zeal for life."

Just like that, her fear and sadness and shame melted away. The pains in her body were now only a vague memory, barely even noticeable. The only thing she knew in that moment was that her best friend was the most wonderful person she had ever met, and she loved him.

Jack wrapped his arms around her, pulling her into a tender hug. Without thinking, she leaned her cheek against his shoulder and sighed. "How do you do that?" Anna said. "How do you make everything all right like that?"

Instinct kicked in.

She pulled back, blinking at him. "How do you do that?" Gently, she took his face in both hands, and then she kissed him. She full-on kissed him. After a few seconds, it became clear that he was kissing her back.

It was perfect.

Until the moment when she remembered that Jack *wasn't* her boyfriend. All those warm, fuzzy feelings were smothered by a wave of guilt crashing through her like a tsunami wrecking a cute little beach-side village.

Anna pulled away from him, sucking on her lower lip. She looked down into her lap and tried to maintain her composure. "That was wrong," she whispered. "I'm sorry. I shouldn't have done that."

Jack shut his eyes and drew in a deep breath. "You're not the only one who did it," he said, getting to his feet. "And you're not the one who is operating with the benefit of a clear head."

"Don't do that."

"Do what?"

Anna looked up at him with tears on her cheeks, blinking a few times to clear her eyes. "Find a way to make it your fault," she answered hoarsely. "This one is very firmly on both of us."

He backed away from her with his arms crossed, refusing to look up and meet her eyes. "Well, we can play the Reverse Blame Game all night," he said. "Or we can try to answer the more important question: what happens now?"

"I don't know."

"Me neither."

With a heavy sigh, Anna stood up, but her chest felt like it would cave in from the force of the guilt pressing down on it. Making eye-contact wasn't an option. "I think we should both take a little space right now."

"Yeah."

"Good night, Jack," she said. "I'll talk to you tomorrow."

When he was gone, she curled up on the bed and she sobbed. She sobbed despite the aches in her body, despite the flare of pain that accompanied every breath. She sobbed because she knew what she had to do.

And she hated having to break someone's heart.

Jack wandered the parking lot for the better part of an hour, wondering just what to make of everything that had happened. If Ben were here, the other man would probably tell him to be optimistic; somehow, Jack knew better.

Anna's reaction hadn't been that of a woman who had just realized that her true love was right under her nose. No, there was something off, something not right. He couldn't put his finger on it, but he knew.

When he pushed open the door to the room he shared with Harry, he found the other man standing in the space between the two beds with his back turned, staring at something on the back wall. Harry still wore his gray suit, and he seemed to be all right, but something was off here too...

Chewing on his lip, Jack looked down at himself. "Okay then," he said, stepping into the room. "Where the hell have you been for the last three hours? You know, we had a visit from Slade."

Harry's shoulders slumped, but he kept his back turned. It was as if something had drained the life out of him. "Get Anna," he said. "We're checking out and going home. I already have the third cipher."

"Come again?"

"The third cipher."

Jack closed his eyes, suppressing a surge of irritation. "Yeah, I actually picked up on that part," he said, shutting the door behind him. "What I really wanna know is how you managed to get it without arousing suspicion."

Harry whirled around to face him with hands shoved in the suit jacket's pockets, a blank expression on his face. The classic interrogation room stare. "That doesn't matter," he said. "What matters is I have it."

"No, that's not shady at all!"

"We don't have time to argue-"

"Look, I know you're happy you decided to go Section 31 yourself a piece of alien technology," Jack growled. "But there was a time when the squeaky clean Harry Carlson would never get his hands dirty by breaking the rules. So, maybe you'd like to have a seat and tell me exactly what you did?"

The only answer he received was silence and a blank stare from Harry that lasted at least thirty seconds. After that, the man just started fiddling with his multi-tool. As if they didn't have enough problems! It seemed as though the whole team was falling apart.

Dropping into the chair next to the door, Jack set his elbow on his knee and planted his face in his hand. "You see this for what it is, don't you?" He looked up, blinking at the other man. "That thing you carry around with you is twisting your mind."

Harry winced, hissing under his breath. "I feel perfectly fine," he said, sitting on the edge of one mattress. "The N'Jal hasn't made me violent. We needed a way to recover the third cipher, and I found it."

"By killing a man?"

"Killing?"

The other man looked up at him with an open mouth, his cheeks flushed to a deep crimson. "You think I *killed* Patrick Osborne?" Harry protested. "Jesus Christ, Jack! You should know me better than that!"

"Then what *did* you do?"

"I put him to sleep." When Jack opened his mouth to reply, Harry raised both hands and cut him off. "I mean literally! I used the N'Jal to put him into a deep sleep, and then I recovered the third cipher."

Well, at least it wasn't lethal, but it was still assault. It occurred to Jack that this was exactly the kind of case that would fall under Keeper jurisdiction: an assault with a piece of alien technology. So, should he arrest his friend? Haul Harry up to Station Twelve in a pair of handcuffs?

Would he be hesitating if the perpetrator wasn't one of his closest friends? Or was it really that simple? Chances were they needed Harry to...do whatever it was they needed to do when they found the Key. Jack still wasn't entirely clear on that part. Nevertheless, the question of expedience versus justice was a difficult one.

At one point in his youth – a time so long ago, it seemed to be nothing but a foggy memory – Jack had promised himself that he would choose justice every time. So now, was he a failure for being unable to live up to that promise?

"You're a criminal, Harry."

"I know."

Baring his teeth with an angry hiss, Jack shut his eyes. He

touched the tips of his fingers to his forehead. "I don't know where we go from here. But at least we have the cipher."

"We do," the other man replied. "But if Slade is lurking about, we really shouldn't wait around to see if he'll try to take it from us."

"Agreed," Jack said. "I'll get Anna. You get us checked out."

As he left the room, it occurred to him that perhaps he should have reversed those two jobs; Anna probably didn't want to talk to him, right now. Of course, Harry would have wondered why he was the one being sent to collect their spunky strawberry-blonde colleague. There was just no winning. That ought to be the motto for Jack's life.

Ain't no winning here, and there never will be.

23

The "corridors" of an Inzari ship were like passageways through a dark labyrinth of caves: dimly-lit and imposing. Worse yet, each step brought the expectation of hard rock beneath your feet, but instead you felt only the squish of flesh. In fact, Slade wasn't sure this tunnel would have existed if not for his presence. The ship seemed to configure itself to suit his needs.

At the end of the corridor, an open, dome-like chamber was lit only by the reddish glow from the walls. The Inzari was waiting in there; he couldn't see the creature, except for a slight ripple when it moved, but he knew.

He stumbled into the chamber with his hands on his knees, bent over and gasping for breath. "I have failed," Slade whispered. "Lenai and her people have recovered the final cipher. They will soon control the Key."

The Inzari did nothing.

A moment later, Slade became aware of his own doppelganger standing just a few feet away, watching him through dead eyes. "You have the means of tracking them, do you not?" it asked.

Clenching his teeth, Slade shut his eyes and drew in a

hissing breath. "Yes, I do," he confirmed. "But the resources you gave me were expended in New York. What few men I can gather will be no match for a team of Keepers."

The other Slade stood with his arms crossed, a tight frown on his face. "The Fallen Ones and their proxies must not control the Key," he said. "You will serve your function and prevent this outcome."

"And if I cannot?"

"Then you will have become a defective tool."

Slade dropped to his knees, lacing his hands together over the top of his head. He stayed low, making his obeisance. "Hunter and Lenai," he whispered. "Why have you allowed them to come back?"

The other Slade was as still as a statue, contemplating a response. "We know not of what you speak," he said at last. "Hunter and Lenai are not here of our design."

That should not have been possible.

The very thought of it left him feeling sick inside, knocked his world off its axis and left him to scramble desperately for something to hold on to. Could the Fallen Ones be responsible for Lenai's presence? He was wise enough to avoid asking the question. The ways of gods – even fallen gods – were not his to judge.

A tingling flared up in his fingers. Or perhaps he was just more aware of it in the light of his fear. The truth was, his body had been tingling ever since his encounter with Lenai. The girl had dealt him no small amount of damage, and his symbiont was working tirelessly to heal his body.

But the creature was old, and he had pushed it beyond what a normal Nassai could endure many times. Not even Isara and the others were so cavalier with their symbionts, but then, they did not have the Inzari's favour.

"I require rejuvenation," Slade said.

His doppelganger nodded.

The chamber floor began to writhe, a crater forming and then splitting apart to become a deep pool of glowing purple liquid. Its radiance was enough to fill the entire room and reveal the Inzari's silhouette. Slade didn't look too closely. The shape of that thing did not sit well in the human mind.

He disrobed and stepped into the liquid, submerging himself to the very top of his head. It didn't harm his ability to breathe; in fact, he felt the burden of consciousness slip away as he fell into a kind of stasis.

Sometime later, he was curled up naked on the chamber floor, suddenly free of the aches and pains that had plagued his body. A Nassai duplicated its host's cells with near-perfect accuracy, preserving youth well past the point of what would normally be called middle age. But even they could only do so much to halt the inevitable.

In time, when a Keeper's body could no longer sustain its symbiont, the Nassai he carried was returned to its people, and the Keeper was allowed to pass with quiet dignity. Very few Keepers made it far past fifty-five.

Grecken Slade was over two thousand years old.

The Inzari rejuvenated him, repaired his body, strengthened his symbiont and gave him a new lease on life. They were masters of life and death, gods in the truest sense of the word. And he was their humble servant.

Rolling onto his stomach, Slade groaned. He pushed himself up on extended arms, head hanging from the fatigue. "I will secure the Key." His words came out as a hoarse whisper. "And kill Lenai."

His doppelganger stood by the wall with arms folded, watching him with a dull-eyed stare. "Bring the rabble that follow you," he said. "It is time they looked upon the faces of their gods."

"And then?"

"And then we will take away their fear."

He was a criminal.

As he watched his faint reflection in the surface of his coffee table – the ghostly version of himself that stared back at him – Harry felt a powerful sense of shame. What Jack had said was true; he *was* a criminal.

He sat with his knees apart on the couch in his family room, head hanging as he tried to compose himself. "We needed the cipher," he mumbled for his own ears. "It was for the greater good."

Somehow, that tired appeal to utilitarian ethics did nothing to soothe his miserable conscience. True, they did need the cipher, and true, the entire planet might be put at risk if Slade got his hands on the Key. But there were some lines a good man just didn't cross under any circumstances.

He felt sick to his stomach.

The sound of the front door opening made him jump, and for a moment, he half-expected to hear his ex-wife's voice insisting that he was the worst father ever and that the girls were better off without him. Maybe that damn N'Jal really *had* twisted his mind. He didn't *feel* any different, but...

Melissa appeared at the head of the stairs that led up to the kitchen, dressed in a pair of jeans and an old black t-shirt. Her black hair was done up in a bun with just a few flyaway strands. "Dad."

Harry shut his eyes. "Hey, kiddo," he said in a soft voice. "I guess you finished your work in New York. Did Dr. Hamilton send you home?"

Melissa descended the steps with her arms folded, staring down at her feet. "Yeah. Things started picking up once people were free to move about the city." A heavy sigh exploded from her as she paused on the bottom step. "By the second day, we had more nurses than we knew what to do with."

"Well, that's good."

"Dr. Hamilton said I needed the rest."

Harry threw himself back against the couch cushions, breathing deeply. "Don't we all," he muttered. "But at least the worst of it is over."

He waited for some response, but his daughter remained quiet. Out of the corner of his eyes, he saw her at the foot of the stairs, standing stiffly. It was the posture she took on whenever she had something to say but couldn't quite force the words out. Maybe it was about Raynar.

She had taken the kid's death pretty hard. Come to think of it, Harry ought to be a lot more shaken, but this wasn't the first time he had seen someone give his life in the line of duty. Now, his kid was getting her first taste of that life.

"Mom said you wanted to talk to me," Melissa murmured.

Squeezing his eyes shut, Harry groaned. "She won't even give you one night to get settled in," he grumbled. "Yes, Melissa, I was planning to talk to you. I spoke to Larani Tal, and she's willing to let you do your training on Leyria."

Melissa just stood there, blinking at him. Boy oh boy, would he like to give Della a piece of his mind; the woman refused to trust him to handle this in his own good time. "I don't want you to take this the wrong way," Melissa began. "But what made you talk to Larani? I'm not angry, but..."

"Your mother thinks Leyria would be safer."

A low growl escaped the girl as she strode across the room to stand in front of the coffee table. "She *is* aware that I've chosen a career where people will shoot at me, isn't she?" Melissa threw up her hands in frustration.

Harry smiled into his own lap, shaking his head slowly. "Don't be too hard on her," he said, unable to contain his own exasperation. "It's part of being a parent. The urge to protect your kid is hardwired."

"Yeah, well..."

"Well, I *didn't* get an answer to the question," Harry said, deliberately redirecting the conversation. "Do you want to move to Leyria?"

"On my own?"

Harry leaned against the couch cushions with his arms folded, tilting his head back to stare up at the ceiling. "Presumably, I would be going with you," he explained. "They may need me for this anti-Slade task force."

"And Claire?"

"Your mother and I are still working it out."

Tapping her lips with one finger, Melissa shut her eyes. "It's a pretty big change," she said. "I always knew that this career might one day take me away from Earth, but I never thought it would be so soon."

"Well, you better make your decision soon," Harry said. "Jena and the others will be relocating once this immediate crisis is over, and we just retrieved the third cipher. We will be going after the Key any day now."

That made Melissa's eyes bug out, and she stumbled backward until she almost hit the wall. "I need to go with you," she panted. "To the Key. I need to be there."

"No."

Grinding her teeth audibly, Melissa winced and let out a soft hiss. "No, you don't understand," she insisted. "I *have* to be there, Dad. I still remember everything Raynar took from Slade's mind."

"Including what the Key does."

"It's all muddled but…" She pressed the heels of her hands to her eye-sockets and moaned with displeasure. "I don't know. If Raynar were here, he would go, but without him, I'm all you've got."

Melissa stood hunched over, sobbing as tears streamed over her cheeks. "Sorry," she whispered, pressing her back to the wall. "I just…I haven't really had the time to let it all sink in."

Without even thinking, Harry was on his feet and marching

across the room. He wrapped his daughter up in a gentle hug and let her sob against him. Selfish as it was for him to think it, he was comforted by one undeniable reality: no matter how old your kids got, you would always be their rock. "It's all right," Harry whispered. "Everything will be all right."

She cried for a very long time, and when she was finished, she looked up at him with determination in her eyes. "I *have* to go with you to the Key," she insisted. "This is not up for debate."

"Okay."

"Okay?" she mumbled. "Just okay."

Pinching the bridge of his nose, Harry grunted into his own palm. "I can't protect you from this life," he said softly. "I realize that now. I couldn't save you from the pain of losing Raynar, and I can't..."

A shudder went through him, one that made his whole body spasm, but he managed to back away from her with *some* dignity. "If you think you need to go to the Key, then I will be right there with you."

"I love you, Dad."

"I love you too," he said. "Always."

The fogginess receded, allowing Patrick to regain some semblance of conscious thought, but everything was still muddled. He remembered the strange knock on his door, the man who had come to...to what? He remembered the strange sense of euphoria and then drifting off into a deep sleep.

His eyes fluttered open to reveal soft moonlight coming in through his living room window. It was still dark outside, and he was lying on the couch. Why hadn't he gone up to bed? *That man...*What had that man done to him?

He sat up.

And that was when he saw it.

Bathed in cold moonlight that came in through the window,

the silhouette of Death itself stood in the corner of his living room. A cloaked and hooded figure that moved like a wraith as it came toward him. He wanted to scream, but he couldn't. "You will forgive me for this," the apparition said softly.

Death had a woman's voice?

She moved with ghostly dexterity, approaching the couch to stand over him. "It is nothing personal, you understand," she went on. "Once again, I am forced to clean up one of Slade's messes."

"Who...Who are you?"

She leaned forward as if to kiss him.

A gloved finger touched his lips, quieting him. "Shh..." the apparition said in sweet, soothing tones. "This is just a nightmare. You will slip back into a sweet, dreamless sleep and forget that I was ever here."

He saw the gleam of a knife in the moonlight.

The slash across his throat was quick, fierce and decisive. Patrick had to stifle his shock when he felt his own blood pooling in his hands. What? Shouldn't it hurt more? Why was everything so murky?

A hand pushed him down onto his back, and he barely registered a distant voice speaking. "I would have preferred to have avoided this," the woman said. "But we can't have you telling the authorities what our dear friend Harry did."

Who was Harry?

"Rest now," she said. "You have earned a reprieve from the burdens of this world." The last thought of any coherence that raced through his mind was that Death was right. It really was a sweet, dreamless sleep.

24

The Science Lab was abuzz with activity as Ven's hologram floated high above the black-tiled floor with fists on its hips. A spectral being of swirling blue light, it seemed to be fixated on something in the corner.

Dressed in black pants and a matching t-shirt, Jena stood in the middle of the room with arms folded. "So," she said, looking up to fix her gaze upon the hologram. "you said you have something for us."

Ven nodded.

Off to her left, Jack and Melissa stood side by side in clothing identical to her own, both shifting nervously, though she suspected they each had their own reasons for their apprehension. Something had happened between Jack and Anna; she could tell that much by the distance.

Whether they realized it or not, those two usually found a way to be within arm's reach of each other, but today, Anna was on the exact opposite side of the room. Like the others, she was also dressed in black.

The girl sat on the edge of a table with her elbow on her knee, her chin resting on the knuckles of her fist. "Well, don't keep us waiting, Ven," she said. "We got all dressed up. I don't know about you, but I want to go to a party."

In her mind's eye, Jena saw Harry hovering by the entrance with his hands shoved into his pants' pockets. The way he kept casting glances at his daughter. He really didn't want her here, but he had learned not to protest. "Agreed," he said. "Let's get on with this already. Do you know the Key's location?"

Ven's hologram floated with ghostly hands clasped behind its back, running its gaze over the lot of them. "I have analyzed the three ciphers," it said. "When put together, they form what I believe to be the SlipGate equivalent of source code."

Lifting his chin to study the hologram, Jack narrowed his eyes. "Source code," he said, shaking his head. "Source code that does what exactly?"

Ven disappeared.

In his place, what appeared to be a spiderweb of glowing green lines expanded until it stretched from corner to corner across the ceiling. His disembodied voice came through the speaker system. "The SlipGates form a galaxy-wide network that allows for interstellar communication in real time and near-instantaneous travel between any two gates within approximately five light seconds of each other."

When she looked closely, Jena realized that each of those green lines intersected at a glowing green dot. "They are programmed to recognize each other," Ven went on. "But there is not just one SlipGate network; there are two."

A second spiderweb of red lines appeared, overlapping with the first. Together, they formed a beautiful mosaic of light.

Ven's hologram reappeared beneath the glowing spider-webs, descending slowly until he hovered just above the floor tiles. He raised one hand toward the ceiling. "I have analyzed the code over a dozen times."

"And what have you found?" Jena asked.

"I cannot be one hundred percent certain," Ven began, "but

I believe that any Gate that runs the code we have assembled will drop off the primary network and instead join this secondary network."

Harry was leaning against the wall with his hands in his pockets, shaking his head slowly. "What good would that do?" he said. "So, we've tapped into the Overseers private network, but that doesn't give us much."

"If I'm correct, Harry," Ven replied, "there will only be one other SlipGate on this second network. And it will correspond to the Key's location. Consider the enormity of what we have just discovered.

"The Overseers do not know of this second network; if they did, they would have found the Key ages ago. The radicals among them – the ones who wished to preserve the Key for human use – must have designed this second network in secret."

Jena took a moment to let it all sink in. All her life, she had imagined the Overseers as larger-than-life beings. They were a species who could shape planets to suit their needs and scatter thousands of people across the galaxy. Now, she knew something they didn't know. It was humbling–and terrifying.

Jena stood hunched over, tapping her lips as she thought it over. "Okay," she said, taking a few steps forward. "Then what we need is a SlipGate. One that won't be missed after we run the program."

Ven floated up a few feet and watched her with that eyeless stare. "I submit that we already have a SlipGate," he said, gesturing to the corner. "The very one you took from Wesley Pennfield a few months ago."

The puddle of skin that had transported Jack and Anna to a mansion in Hawaii was still sitting undisturbed in the corner. It looked almost like a folded up blanket except for the veins and the slight sheen. The truth was that Jena would have preferred to have forgotten about that damn thing. Everyone had given it a wide birth for the last few months. After all, there was always a chance that it might randomly activate again. "You're saying that we could go now."

"Yes."

Jena closed her eyes, breathing deeply. "Well then," she said with a curt nod. "That was what I wanted to hear. All right, I want everyone geared up and ready to leave in ten minutes. Pack light armaments, ammo and explosives."

Jack stood by the wall with a hand pressed to his stomach, staring down at the floor under his feet. "Explosives?" he said in that mocking tone of his. "You really wanna blow up the ancient piece of alien tech?"

Licking her lips, Jena looked down at herself. "No, I don't," she answered, brushing bangs off her forehead with the back of her hand. "But the fact is that we don't know what this thing does; if we can't control it..."

"Better to destroy it than let Slade have it."

"Exactly."

As if on cue, the double doors slid open, revealing Larani and Ben standing side by side in the hallway. Like everyone else, they were both dressed in black. "Good," Larani said, striding into the room.

The woman squeezed her eyes tight and gave her head a shake. "I was worried we may have missed you." She stopped about five feet from Jena, planted fists on her hips and stood like the statue of a disapproving mother. "I just reviewed the report you sent me an hour ago. You have decoded the ciphers?"

"Yes, ma'am," Jena answered. "And we're going after the Key."

"Then Tanaben and I will be going with you."

"That isn't necessary, ma'am."

Closing her eyes, Larani tilted her head back. She took a deep breath and then let it out slowly. "Jena," she said in mollifying tones. "You're about to unearth one of the most important discoveries in human history. The head of the Justice Keepers should be there."

Jena crossed her arms, backing away from the woman with a heavy sigh. "You're right," she said, nodding her agreement. "I take it you want to command the mission?"

"That's unnecessary," Larani said. "You've been spear-heading the search for this Key for over six months. I'm happy to follow your lead on this one."

"All right then; gear up and be ready to go in ten minutes."

Nine minutes and fifty-five seconds later, they were all standing in a small cluster around the folded sheet of veiny skin in the corner. Ven appeared, hovering over them like an angel. "Are we ready?"

Craning her neck, Jena squinted at the hologram. "We're ready," she said, nodding to him. "Run the program. Let's see what this bloody thing does when we screw around with its firmware."

"Transmitting the code now."

At first, it seemed as though nothing had happened, but then the puddle of flesh lit up for half a moment, glowing blue and bright and forcing Jena to shield her eyes. She wasn't the only one.

Next to her, Harry stumbled backward with a hand raised up in front of his face. "God in Heaven," he muttered, getting his bearings. "Please tell me that we actually did something there. I'd hate to go blind for nothing."

"I am interfacing with the SlipGate," Ven answered.

"Have you found anything?"

Larani stood with her fists on her hips, shaking her head as she stared down at the thing. "Sometimes I wonder," she murmured to herself. "Would we have been better off if we had never found this Overseer tech?"

Clamping a hand over his mouth, Jack shut his eyes.

"Maybe," he muttered into his own palm. "But we wouldn't all be standing here today. We never would have found each other, and that would suck."

Anna let her head hang.

Before Jena could put too much thought into what was going on there, Ven chimed in with his...her...their report. "My suspicions have been confirmed," the AI said. "I am detecting another Gate on the network."

"Where?"

"Tracking coordinates now."

They all turned around to watch a hologram form above the black-tiled floor, the Earth expanding from a point to form a globe nearly six feet tall from pole to pole. Red dots in orbit marked the space stations her people had built.

From one of those red dots, green lines extended–not toward Earth but off into the depths of space. "This is odd," Ven went on. "These coordinates I have received would put the other SlipGate approximately..."

The green lines that extended from Station Twelve intersected at a point, and from that point a second globe expanded. Not a planet but a dried-up ball of gray dust about one quarter the size of Earth.

"The moon?" Jack said. "The Key is on the moon?"

"Roughly thirty kilometres beneath its surface," Ven answered.

Anna stepped forward with her hands in her pockets, her head bowed as if she were fighting off her own exhaustion. "No wonder we couldn't find it," she said. "We scanned the Earth dozens of times–"

"But it was never on Earth," Harry said.

Ven's hologram descended with its arms spread wide, stopping half a foot above the floor and hovering before them. "Your best scans wouldn't have found it anyway," the AI remarked. "Not that far beneath the surface."

"So, are we going then?" Jack inquired.

"Can you confirm a hospitable environment on the other side of the SlipGate?" Jena asked the hologram. Under normal circumstances, SlipGates would not activate if the surrounding area was not compatible with human life. Gates that were underwater or floating in the vacuum of space simply refused to accept a connection.

That was one reason why many people thought the Overseers had designed the SlipGates specifically for human use. Perhaps that was true of the primary network – it stood to reason that the Overseers *wanted* humans to use their technology or they would not have left so much of it behind – but there was no reason to assume this secondary network followed the same rules.

"I suggest we send a probe through," Ven said. "Just to be sure."

The probe was a small box on wheels about the size of Jena's foot; it rolled over to the corner with a high-pitched buzzing sound. It stopped there, one light blinking as it waited for instructions.

Jena stood with her shoulders slumped, watching the damn thing. "All right," she said, her eyebrows rising. "Send it through. Let's see what the Overseers left behind when they moved out."

"Sending now," Ven said.

The puddle of flesh began to writhe, stretching and contorting until it formed a thin triangle of veiny skin. There was a humming sound as the SlipGate began to glow with a cool blue light, and then the probe was caught up in something that looked so very much like a soap bubble.

"Everything looks good," Ven said.

The bubble vanished, taking the probe with it.

Knowing their luck, the probe would reveal that it had been

deposited into a dense atmosphere of fluorine gas, which would require them to wear bulky space suits on top of all their other gear. It wasn't as if they could just decide not to go if the environment turned out to be inhospitable; why she had signed up for this, Jena would never-

"Probe results coming in."

A two dimensional hologram appeared along the lab's back wall, depicting nothing but blackness. Half a second later, the probe's flashlight revealed what appeared to be a cavern floor, but there was no telling how far the darkness extended.

"Well, then," Ven said. "Atmospheric composition 78 percent nitrogen, 21 percent oxygen. Air temperature is a balmy 23 degrees Celsius with pressure holding steady at 100.45 kilopascals."

On the far side of the room, Jack stood with arms folded, watching the hologram. "Everything but mints on the pillows," he said with a shrug of his shoulders. "I'm calling it now; the instant we show up, zombies are rising out of the ground."

"It does seem a little too good to be true," Ben added.

Jena winced and let her head hang. She pinched the bridge of her nose with thumb and forefinger. "We don't get much choice in the matter," she said. "Even if this is a trap, we're still going to walk right into it."

"Admiral Ackbar would be proud," Jack muttered.

"Power up the Gate," Jena said. "Let's get this done."

As he sat behind a wooden desk in his small office, Slade watched code appear on the screen of his computer. The soulless abomination that the Leyrians called an artificial intelligence had transmitted the completed cipher to reconfigure the SlipGate – Slade had listened to their entire conversation – and now the bug Isara had planted was delivering that information to him.

Of course, it would have been easier to have taken the

ciphers directly – that would prevent his enemies from being able to access the Key – but wise men always developed contingency plans. He would kill Hunter, Lenai and the rest and then reclaim the Key for the Inzari. In so doing, he would bring about the End of Days.

He sat hunched over the desk with his elbows on its surface, his chin resting upon laced fingers. "Excellent," he said, looking up at the man who stood on the other side of the room. "Now, it begins."

A tall, handsome fellow with fair skin and a thick golden beard stood just inside the door. Dressed in blue jeans and a hooded-sweater, he looked positively normal except for one thing.

A strip of veiny flesh curled around his right ear and hooked tendrils into the side of his forehead. One of the many gifts of the Inzari. It increased aggression, minimized fear and turned a man into the perfect killing machine.

Slade leaned back in his chair with his hands folded over his chest, staring up at the ceiling. "Gather your men," he said. "We're going to finish this now."

25

When the warp bubble popped, ending their SlipGate trip, Jena found herself total darkness. A darkness so perfect it seemed as if she had been swallowed up by an abyss. Spatial awareness allowed her to see six people standing behind her, and she could make out something that looked like a triangle melting into the floor – the SlipGate returning to its puddle state – but her eyes were useless here.

That changed quickly.

The walls of this cavern began to glow with a soft blue light, exposing a wide, open chamber a little larger than the Science Lab. Of course, it also revealed the fact that these walls were made up of a soft, fleshy substance. They were quite literally inside the belly of the beast, and worst of all...It knew they were here.

Their little probe was just a few feet away, waiting patiently for instructions. That was good; they could use it as a homing beacon to find their way back to this place.

There were three passageways out of this chamber, each one leading deep into the cavern. That only made her more uneasy; now they would *have* to split up.

Jena stood with fists clenched at her sides, trembling as a shiver went through her. "All right," she said, stepping forward. "I don't know about the rest of you, but I'd prefer to get out of the creepy alien cave as soon as possible."

She spun around to face them with arms folded, lifting her chin to study the lot of them. "Jack, Larani," she began. "You two go left. Anna and Ben will go right. Melissa, Harry and I will take the middle path."

It was best to separate Jack and Anna for the time being; she didn't want whatever drama had come between them to keep them off their game. And she wanted Harry and Melissa where she could keep an eye on them. Her boyfriend was far too comfortable with that N'Jal he carried, and his daughter had fragments of Slade's memories floating around her mind. Prudence was essential.

Melissa pushed forward between two other people, approaching her with an open mouth, panting as if she had just run a marathon. "We need to find the Nexus," she said. "It's sort of a control room."

"Any idea of what it would look like?"

"Fleshy and blue?"

Jena winced, hissing as she sucked in a deep breath. "All right then," she said with a nod. "Keep an open comm-line. I want regular check-ins every five minutes, and make sure you report *anything* that seems out of the ordinary."

Jack cleared his throat.

"I'm standing in a weird glowing cave with my bosses, best-friends and the ex-cop who tried to arrest me for liberating an alien symbiont from a downtown skyscraper. The floor is squishy, the walls *glow* – I know I mentioned that already, but really, just let that sink in for a moment – and I'm pretty sure the whole place is watching us."

"Jack..."

"You said anything!"

"Let's move."

A few moments later, she was walking with Harry and Melissa down a long tunnel with glowing blue walls and doing her best to ignore her sense of foreboding. Something was going to go wrong; she knew it.

Closing her eyes, Jena let her head hang. "So," she said, rubbing her forehead with the back of one fist. "About this Nexus...I need to know everything that you can tell me, Melissa. Take a moment and try to remember."

The girl walked with a pistol clutched in both hands, her shoulders hunched up as if she were trying to ignore the cold. "There's not a lot I can say," she muttered, shaking her head. "Raynar wasn't able to figure out what the Key does."

"Any idea where it is?"

"Overseer ships are living organisms," Melissa said. "This place is no different. The Nexus is like a hub."

Harry stood with one hand outstretched, pointing his open palm into the distance. That strange N'Jal seemed to hum. "A hub for what?" he asked. "Are you telling me this place has a brain?"

Melissa shut her eyes tight, breathing deeply through her nose. "Not a brain," she said. "But it does have a nervous system. You might say that the Nexus is the focal point of that nervous system."

"Swell."

Jena couldn't blame him for being uneasy. Being inside another living being was unnerving to say the least. How conscious was this place? It turned on the lights when they arrived, but that could have been an autonomic response to a human presence. So far, she hadn't seen any signs of intelligence.

They came to a large, open chamber similar to the one they had left behind a few minutes ago. This one had only two entrances on opposite sides of the room. There were no fixtures of any kind, just walls, floor and ceiling.

Sliding her finger across the screen of her multi-tool, Jena unmuted the mic so the others could hear her. "Nothing so far," she said. "Just a whole lot of creepy blue tunnels and musty air. What do you have to report?"

"Much the same," Larani replied through the speaker.

"We haven't found anything either," Anna chimed in.

Jena muted the microphone again. It was beginning to seem as though this whole trip was just one gigantic tease. So, the Overseers had built a structure beneath the moon's surface. What exactly did that get them? There was no useful technology here, no secrets of a lost civilization.

Bleakness take her, Jena was beginning to feel tempted to just plant a few explosive charges and reduce this place to rubble. That would keep it out of Slade's hands. It wasn't as if they had much to learn from an empty cave.

As if she sensed Jena's thoughts, Melissa stopped in the middle of the chamber and looked back over her shoulder. "We have to keep looking," she pleaded. "Come on. The Nexus can't be far."

Jena sighed. "You're lucky I can't say no to children."

The glowing tunnel seemed to curve and descend down a gentle slope. Larani knew it was a bad idea, but she couldn't resist the urge to touch the walls. To her surprise, they weren't nearly as slimy as she would have imagined. Of course, there was really no way to predict how Overseer technology might behave. She might very well have set off some kind of security system. "It's not so bad," she said. "This place has a kind of otherworldly beauty, don't you think?"

Behind her, Jack's silhouette stood with one hand on the grip of his holstered pistol, staring off into the distance. "Yeah, it's gorgeous," he said. "You know...In that 'abandon all hope' sort of way."

She spun to face him.

The boy wore a tight frown as he studied her, and his blue eyes seemed to want to drill holes into her skull. "Permission to ask a question, ma'am," he said in a voice that made it clear he resented having to request it.

"Please do."

"Why did you reassign me?"

Crossing her arms, Larani smiled down at herself. "I suppose now is as good a time as any other," she said with a shrug. "From the very moment you joined our ranks, you've been nothing but skeptical about the Justice Keepers."

"Hardly a great resume builder."

"But absolutely vital to me now."

Chewing on his lip, Jack squinted at her. "I get it," he said, nodding once. "Slade's got any number of double agents hiding among us. You're hoping that since I was able to see through Breslan's bullshit, I'll be able to help you find the others."

It was difficult to suppress the urge to laugh; she didn't want him to interpret it as mockery, but it was truly wonderful to watch a keen mind cut right through to the core of the issue. Just one year ago, she would have written Jack Hunter off as a foolish boy who did not appreciate the gifts he had been given.

He had such a frustrating habit of bucking authority, but it was that very habit that allowed him to see what so many of her colleagues unconsciously chose not to notice. A year ago, she would have called Jack's mistrust of Slade paranoia, but he had seen. Even then, he had seen.

Larani spun around.

She started up the tunnel with hands clasped behind her back, smiling down at the floor. "There is much I can teach you, Jack," she said. "Director Morane has always had her own unique way of doing things, but I can show you *why* many of our time-honoured traditions exist."

Jack stepped up beside her with his arms crossed, frowning as he stared off into the distance. "I'm sure that's true," he said cautiously. "But wouldn't you rather have someone like Anna working for you?"

"No. I need you."

"Why?"

Larani felt a grin blossom, then shook her head with a sigh. "Because some of those traditions need to be changed," she admitted. "You're so very much like the Keepers who lived centuries ago."

"They were all obstinate pains in the ass?"

"To the governments and institutions of that time?" she said. "Yes. Very much so. It was something of a mission statement."

History was always one of Larani's passions. There were moments when she half wished she could have lived in the Time of Founding – when the nations of Leyria came together to form a unified government – but the truth was that someone like her would not have lived a happy life in those days.

Back then, her world hadn't been much different from Earth in terms of technology. They had barely even mastered the ability to visit their own moon. The first Bonding of a Nassai and a human had been an accident.

"Four hundred years ago," Larani said, "when my world looked very much as yours does now, things were very different. Racial inequality was still a major issue. Same-sex relationships were still taboo, and there was a lot of violence. The first Keepers played a major role in changing all that."

Jack looked over his shoulder with a curious expression, his blue eyes sparkling in the light of the glowing walls. "How?" he asked, raising one eyebrow. "I didn't think you could solve racism with the ability to Bend space-time."

"It wasn't the abilities the Nassai granted us."

"Then what?"

"It was *who* the Nassai chose as hosts. The first Bonding was sheer accident. After visiting our moon for the first time, we took back a sample of the atmosphere. We didn't know that the organisms within it were sentient until they broke out of their containment unit and Bonded with one of the scientists.

"After that, others volunteered for the joining. The Nassai were very selective with potential candidates. They had none of our prejudices; so when they chose the best and brightest of us, they inadvertently created a truly diverse group of people from all races, genders and orientations. The third Justice Keeper to accept a symbiont was a transgender woman like myself."

Jack blinked.

"You didn't know?"

He went beet-red, then lowered his eyes to stare down at his own feet. "No, ma'am, I didn't," he said softly. "Forgive me, I feel like maybe I should have been more aware of your circumstances."

"It's not something that I speak of often," Larani replied. "The truth is that I sometimes wonder if perhaps I should. I know from my studies of history that there was a time when people like me were ostracized and demonized, but Leyrian society has learned to move past such bigotry.

"Earth, however, is an entirely different story. I sometimes think it would do good for others like me to see that a transgender person can rise to the very top of the Justice Keeper hierarchy. However, my government made a treaty with your United Nations on the understanding that we would not try to sway Earth's political climate toward Leyrian sensibilities. I must walk a fine line."

All of a sudden, Jack stopped and stood in the corridor behind her, heaving out a nervous breath. "I never realized how difficult your job was," he said. "I guess I owe you an apology for being such a pain in the ass."

This time, Larani made no effort to hide her smile or the laughter that followed it. Instead, she spun around and practically beamed at him. "You owe me nothing except the chance to learn from you and to share my knowledge in turn. It's your job to be a pain in the ass, Jack Hunter; don't stop on my account."

"Thank you."

"We need each other," she went on. "And I mean that both in the sense of our two planets needing each other and in the sense of you and I personally having much to learn from one another. Work with me. Help me restore the Justice Keepers to something we can all be proud of."

Jack smiled and bowed his head to her, barely suppressing a snort of laughter. "I appreciate the inspiring speech," he said with a nod. "But you had me at 'Jack Hunter is hereby promoted to the rank of Special Agent and reassigned to the Denabrian Keeper office as the personal attache of Larani Tal.'"

"Well, good," she said. "Now come. Let's find out what secrets this place had to share with us."

"So what's the deal with you and Jack?"

Anna stopped in the middle of the tunnel with hands on her hips, head hanging as she let out a deep breath. "It's hard to explain," she muttered. "And I really don't want to get into it when we're exploring an Overseer base."

There was a soft thumping sound as Ben walked past her and paused to examine the tunnel wall. He still wore his heavy armoured suit, and the scanners on his gauntlet allowed him to examine the structure. Of course, he had been doing that from the very moment they split off from the rest of the team.

Anna winced, shaking her head. "How many scans are you gonna take?" she asked, approaching him. "If you didn't learn anything solid ten minutes ago, I can't comprehend why you think you'd learn anything now."

He looked over his shoulder to study her, blue light glinting off the crimson visor. "Testy," he muttered in tones that made her blood boil. "Whatever's going on with you and Jack, it must be big."

"I don't want to-"

"Did he finally kiss you?"

Crossing her arms with a heavy sigh, she strode past him and did her very best to ignore the comment. The last thing she needed was some emotional outburst that would only stretch out this conversation-

"Companion have mercy, he did!" In her mind's eye, Ben was a misty silhouette of bulky limbs, but he practically jumped up and clapped. "I've been wondering how long it would take! You two have been-"

"I kissed him!" she said, cutting off the man's celebration before it made her want to punch him in the nose. Sweet Mercy, did Ben not grasp the concept of boundaries? She knew he meant well, but this was pushing it. "I kissed Jack. I cheated on my partner, and now I have to have an uncomfortable conversation."

She turned to face him.

Ben just stood there with his arms hanging limp, his gaze fixed on the floor. "I'm sorry," he mumbled after a moment. "I guess I wasn't thinking. I got so wrapped up in the idea of you two being together."

A frown tightened her mouth, but Anna did her best to maintain her composure. She wiped sweat off her brow with one hand. "We're not going to be together," she whispered. "And I don't want to talk about it."

"Okay."

"So...What do the scans say?"

He was tapping at his multi-tool, shaking his head as he

studied the readout on the screen. "Not much," he growled. "It's the same material that makes up every other Overseer installation."

"Any sign of where this Nexus is?"

"You got me."

"So, we should just-"

She cut off when her ears picked up something strange. A rumbling in the distance like the footsteps of an entire platoon of armed soldiers. But they were alone here, weren't they? Who else could be...

Jack spun around when he heard the harsh *crunch, crunch, crunch* of boots on the tunnel floor. By the sound of it there were a lot of them. Perhaps a dozen men and maybe more. "Do you hear that?" he asked Larani.

"I do," she said. "Let's find cover; we're about to have company."

Melissa gasped, covering her mouth with one hand as she backed up and pressed her body to the tunnel wall. "That sounds like a lot of people," she mumbled. "But who else knows we're hear?"

"Slade," Jena growled.

The SlipGate bubbled jerked to a halt, revealing an open space with glowing blue walls that seemed distorted to his eyes. He could already see the blurry images of his men breaking off into one of the three tunnels that led away from this chamber.

The bubble popped.

Grecken Slade stood on the squishy floor in unrelieved black – pants and a simple t-shirt. His long, dark hair hung loose, and his face was as smooth as the finest silk. "Go," he muttered, stepping forward. "Secure the area."

The last of his armoured soldiers – amateurs who couldn't

wait to get their hands on assault rifles, but what else was a man to do – turned their backs and rushed off down the middle corridor, leaving him alone in the SlipGate chamber.

He smiled to himself, shook his head and laughed. "Not long now, Jena," he said. "Not long before I have your ruined carcass to hang on my wall."

26

Ben and Anna found a large, dome-like chamber just a short ways up the tunnel. It was big enough to hold maybe a hundred people, but there was only one entrance, which meant they could force their enemies into a bottleneck. That was really their only chance of survival.

As she took a moment to catch her breath, Anna was surprised to feel nothing more than irritation. Of course Slade would find some way to meddle; the man *always* found a way to meddle. Things *always* went wrong whenever he got involved. But she was quite surprised by her lack of fear. Perhaps she had done this one too many times.

Anna stood with her shoulder pressed to the wall next to the entrance, clutching her pistol in both hands. "They're getting close," she said, looking up at Ben. "Now would be a good time to pull out whatever tricks you have."

He was up against the wall on the other side of the entry-way, clutching his own gun and watching her through that red visor. "By the sound of it, there's at least half a dozen of them," he said. "We're gonna have a hard time."

She peered through the doorway.

A narrow corridor, roughly ten feet long intersected with the main tunnel they had been using. Anyone who came through here would have to do so two-by-two. So, if they could just keep Slade's goons bottled-up here, they'd be okay.

One man appeared in the intersection, carrying an assault rifle in his hands. He was tall, broad-shouldered and dressed in the same gear she had seen these guys carry in New York. "Over here!" he said, glancing in their direction.

He turned toward them.

Anna fired.

A stun-round hit the man's exposed neck, causing him to stumble backward with flailing limbs. But he managed to hold on to his weapon...And he didn't fall down. He just stood in the intersection, lifting his rifle.

Anna ducked around the corner just before a stream of bullets came through the entryway, sped across the room and hit the back wall. An ear-splitting shriek pierced the air. This place was alive, and it didn't like anyone shooting the walls.

Lifting her pistol up in front of her face, Anna shut her eyes tight. "High impact!" she growled. The LEDs on the barrel changed from blue to red.

She aimed around the corner and fired.

The man was halfway up the narrow corridor when a bullet ripped through his vest with a spray of blood. He dropped to his knees only to reveal two more men right behind him, both coming quick.

Ben unclipped something from his belt – a sphere about the size of a golf ball – and tossed it into the corridor. There was a brilliant flash of light that spilled out into the open chamber. Anyone in that narrow tunnel would have been blinded.

Anna looked around the corner.

Two men were standing side by side, both with hands raised up to shield their eyes. Their rifles were sitting discarded on the floor. She wasted no time, aiming for one man's chest and then the other.

A bullet took the one on the right, causing him to stumble backward and spill blood onto the floor. The other one fell down just as quickly only to be replaced with two more armoured men who trampled over their fallen comrades in a mad dash.

Ben stepped in front of the opening, raising a forearm up to shield himself. A wall of flickering electrostatic energy appeared before him, intercepting several bullet. He sent it speeding toward their enemies.

The force-field was like a train rushing through a tunnel, sweeping aside anything in its path. Bodies were thrown back-wards into the intersection. Soldiers dropped to the ground, losing their weapons.

"We can't keep this up forever," Ben said.

"Hopefully we won't have to."

Those footsteps were getting closer.

Jena watched as her boyfriend took two steps forward and stood in the middle of the glowing tunnel with his back to her. He thrust one hand out, pointing the bloody N'Jal at anyone who emerged from the open chamber they had just left behind.

Melissa had her back pressed to the wall, a pistol held in one shaky hand. Her eyes were shut tight, and it was clear that she was muttering a prayer for her safety. Bringing her along had been a bad idea.

Clenching her teeth, Jena let her head hang. She rubbed her eyes with the back of her hand. "No time for self-recrimina-tion," she muttered. "Melissa, snap out of it. You've been training for months. You can handle this."

The girl was jolted out of her reverie.

"You can do this," Jena said.

At that, Melissa stepped into the middle of the corridor to

stand with the pistol held in both hands, a look of determination on her face. "Thank you," she said. "But you have to do something for me. Our first priority is securing the Key. Don't try to protect me if it means putting the mission in danger."

"You're gonna be one damn fine Keeper."

Harry still had his back turned, his arm stretched out like a man who thought he could hold back a tidal wave by sheer force of will. "I will only be able to hold a force-field for several minutes."

Jena closed her eyes, breathing deeply. "That's several more minutes that we would have without you." She set her pistol for high-impact rounds and watched the LEDs turn red. "A standard force-field generator would only give us a few seconds of protection in any event."

Up ahead, two men in black tactical gear emerged from the large chamber and ran into the tunnel. They took about three steps before freezing in place and lifting their rifles for a kill shot.

A rippling curtain of energy appeared in front of Harry, stretching until it was not quite big enough to block the entire tunnel. There were narrow gaps on either side that a stray bullet could get through.

Slugs hit that shimmering wall and bounced off. Thankfully, these guys had to rely on Earth weapons. No chance of EMP rounds that could phase through that force-field. Still, it didn't leave her with much opportunity to counterattack.

As she crept closer, Jena took a quick peek around Harry's body. Through the force-field, she could see the blurry images of men coming closer, firing three-round burst after three-round burst.

"Harry," she said. "Knock them out."

The force-field went barreling up the corridor at blinding speed, slamming into the first pair of men and knocking them backward into their companions. The entire column of soldiers fell like dominoes.

Jena took aim.

The first shot pierced through a man's visor and sent blood spraying out the back of his helmet. Seconds later, the guy next to him tried to get to his feet. That one went down from a shot to the chest.

The next pair of men lifted their weapons.

Just like that, another force-field blocked off the corridor, distorting their images until they seemed to be nothing but blurred smears of blackness. More bullets struck the rippling wall of electrostatic energy. It was clear their plan was to just keep hammering until Harry was to exhausted to maintain the force-field. And it was working.

Tilting his head back, Harry growled as tears streamed over his face. "I can't hold it forever," he choked out, gasping for breath. "Jena, we're going to have to come up with something else."

"I'm open to suggestions."

"Can you cover me?"

"Yes."

She stepped up beside him, close enough that she could touch the force-field with her hands, and the instant that it vanished, she threw up a Bending in its place. The visual shift was subtle; instead of a rippling barrier that made their enemies look like blurry men on the other side of a waterfall, everything became streaks of colour that blended together so that individual shapes were hard to perceive.

Bullets hit the patch of warped space-time, curved off to her right and then drilled themselves into the wall. A high-pitched shriek filled the air. As if she needed yet another reminder that she was inside a living being. "Whatever you're going to do," Jena hissed through gritted teeth. "Do it!"

Harry spun to his right, bracing both hands against the

tunnel wall, pressing hard with the hand that carried the N'Jal. The eerie blue glow flared to a brilliant white, and then something happened on the other side of her Bending.

The black streaks that almost represented men in tactical gear were replaced with blue light similar to that which came from the walls. It took her a moment to realize that bullets were no longer striking her Bending.

She let it drop.

Instead of a tunnel, she found herself face-to-face with a dead end, a glowing wall of veiny skin that seemed to pulse. There were men on the other side. She could hear the sounds of footsteps and muffled voices.

Jena doubled over with hands on her knees, head hanging as she tried to catch her breath. "Can they shoot through that?" she asked, surprised at the roughness in her own voice. "It doesn't look very thick."

Harry had his eyes closed, his head resting against the tunnel wall. "Overseer tech is resilient," he said. "It will heal quickly, but if they hammer away at it for a minute or two, their bullets will start to come through."

"Then let's move."

Despite the tingle in her skin and the fatigue that came from using her powers for more than a few seconds, she turned and ran through the tunnel. Melissa and Harry fell in on either side of her, both gasping.

It wasn't long before she heard an ear-splitting shriek of pain as the creature they now inhabited reacted to the soldiers' attempts to pierce the wall with their guns. Anyone who thought organic technology was a good idea was insane!

Harry spun again, pressing his hand to the wall again. There was a soft, slurping noise as the N'Jal bonded with the creature's nervous system. "What are you doing?" she asked with more than a trace of irritation.

She spun around in time to see another wall forming

behind them, skin growing out of the floor and ceiling until it blended together to make a seamless vertical surface that glowed and hummed. "Companion have mercy…"

"Overseers sculpt flesh to serve their will," Harry muttered.

You are flesh, that dreadful voice echoed in Jena's head. *You will serve our will.* It left her feeling helpless and sick to her stomach. What had they done to her boyfriend? Was he beginning to think like these aliens?

"Come on," Harry said. "I know where the Nexus is."

A man in black tactical gear came around the corner, barreling through the tunnel at full speed. Two others joined him half a moment later, flanking him on either side. They made it about five steps, then jerked to a halt.

All three raised their weapons.

Larani flinched.

Jack leaped in front of her with both hands out, the air before him blurring into a streak of colour. Bullets hit the pulsating barrier, curved off to either side and drove themselves into the tunnel walls, eliciting a scream.

Jack slowly backed up until he was side by side with her. The very instant that he let his Bending drop, Larani put up another one in its place, deflecting incoming fire into the tunnel walls.

Jack kept retreating.

Clenching her teeth, Larani winced and let her head hang. "We can't keep this up very much longer," she said, moving backward. "We're going to have to find some place to mount a counterattack."

In her mind's eye, she saw an intersection of two tunnels just a few paces behind her. Jack already sensed her intentions; his misty silhouette fled around the corner and pressed its back to the wall.

Larani joined him, releasing her Bending.

She pressed her backside to the tunnel wall, then hunched forward with a hand on her chest, panting as she snatched air into her lungs. "They're going to keep coming," she wheezed. "They'll follow us around this corner, and we'll be back where we started."

Bullets zipped through the intersection.

Jack shut his eyes, trembling as he sucked in a breath. "You're right," he said with a nod. "If we stay here, they'll just overwhelm us with superior firepower. We need to find a better place to make our stand."

This second tunnel was much shorter and led to a circular doorway that appeared to look into some larger chamber. Larani could see nothing of value inside – just glowing blue walls – but, if they could get to cover...

She grabbed Jack by the upper arm and pulled him toward the opening. "This will have to do!" Larani shouted. "Maybe we can force them into a bottleneck and take them out one by one."

This new locale was about twice the size of her living room with a dome-shaped ceiling and a lumpy floor. Of course, there was no sign of what the room's purpose might be; she suspected that the Overseers reconfigured each location to fit their specific needs at any given time.

Larani closed her eyes, sweat beading on her forehead. She wiped it away with one hand. "We take positions on opposite sides of the door," she said. "We have to keep them bottled up in the tunnel, so that-"

She cut off when someone stepped into view in the tunnel. Not one of the armoured amateur soldiers that Slade employed to do his dirty work. No, this man wore only black pants and a matching t-shirt.

His hollow-cheeked face was frozen in an expressionless mask, and black hair fell over his shoulders. Not one of Slade's pathetic followers but Slade himself. "Oh, please," he said, striding toward them. "Don't let me interrupt. Let's see; you were devising some strategy that is bound to get you killed."

Baring his teeth in a snarl, Jack shook his head. "Keep talking, asshole," he said, moving toward the door. "It seems to me every time you come up against two Keepers, you run away, and there are two of us here."

Slade lifted his chin to stare down his nose at them. "That eager for another beat-down, are we?" he asked, arching one dark eyebrow. "Yes, Jack, I'm facing two Keepers, but not the right two Keepers."

What does that mean?

Crossing his arms with a heavy sigh, Slade marched through the corridor with his head down. "You pathetic children," he said. "Do you really believe that you can control the tools of your gods?"

"I'm an atheist," Larani said.

The former head of the Justice Keepers looked up at her with dark eyes that blazed, and for just a second, she was tempted to step back. "Then I must question your ability to evaluate the evidence." He paused, spreading his arms wide, gesturing to the walls. "Just look around you."

"I see nothing to indicate divinity."

"No, I suppose you wouldn't."

Slade stepped into the room, clasping hands together behind himself and rocking on the balls of his feet. "So, you're the first two I kill," he said. "It's fitting, really. I've never stopped resenting you, Larani."

Throwing her head back, Larani rolled her eyes. "You betrayed everything that you swore to uphold," she growled, stepping forward. "And somehow it's my fault for taking on the duties you abandoned."

"If you want a fight-" Jack began.

"Yes," Slade whispered. "I would enjoy that. Be honest with me, Jack. You know you're going to die here."

"I'm ready for that-"

Larani jumped, flipping through the air and then uncurling to drop like a pin. She landed between the two men. "No," she said, glancing over her shoulder. "This fight is mine and mine alone."

Jack stared at her with an open mouth, blinking. "You've gotta be kidding," he said, taking one step forward. "You heard about what he did to me right?"

Closing her eyes, Larani let her head hang. She touched two fingers to the bridge of her nose. "Yes, I heard." The words came out as a breathy whisper. "Slade has convinced you that he is something larger than life."

"I believe the term you're looking for is Messiah," Slade hissed.

"I believe the term I'm looking for is 'fraud.' "

That made Slade's face redden, but he smothered a grimace beneath a mountain of self-control. "You truly believe that," he said, pacing a circle around her. "You will learn the truth to your sorrow."

Larani spun to face him with her fists raised in a fighting stance, hissing like a cat. "Stay back, Agent Hunter," she cautioned. "This fight is between me and the man who dishonored everything I stand for."

Slade spun.

His foot whirled around in a wide arc, striking Larani across the cheek and filling her vision with stars. Everything went dark, but she was able to sense her enemy coming around to face her.

The man jumped and kicked out.

Larani's hands shot up, catching his shoe before it made contact with her nose. With a thought, she applied a surge of Bent Gravity.

Slade flew backward over the rubbery cavern floor, hurled a

good twenty paces before the Bending gave out. He dropped to land on his feet with a hand raised up in front of his face.

Larani ran at him.

She jumped and kicked low, driving one boot into the man's stomach, forcing him to double over. The man panted as he stumbled backward. Larani hit the ground and then threw a hard punch.

Crouching down, Slade reached up to grab her wrist with one hand. He clamped the other one onto Larani's throat. The ferocity of his grip was unmistakable. Yes, he truly did loathe her.

Bent Gravity sent them both flying upward, and then Larani grunted when the top of her head hit the ceiling. Even the soft, fleshy surface was still enough to send a jolt of pain through her. Larani fell.

She landed face-down on the floor, groaning on impact. Bleakness take her, she was so dizzy. *You have to focus!* a small voice whispered in the back of her mind. She could feel her Nassai's trepidation. When she looked up, Slade was standing over her.

A boot struck her right between the eyes, blacking out her vision. By instinct, she threw herself into a sideways roll, putting a little distance between herself and the man who wanted to kill her. "Larani!" Jack called out.

"Stay back!" she ordered.

Larani got up.

Perhaps ten paces away, Grecken Slade stood in rumpled clothing, illuminated by the glowing walls, his face glistening with sweat. "It's such a shame, isn't it?" he said in mocking tones. "All that effort for nothing."

Larani strode toward him.

Gritting her teeth with a soft hiss, she squinted at him. "Whatever this bloody thing does," she whispered, shaking her head. "You're not getting your hands on it. So, yes; all your wasted effort *is* a shame."

She ran at him.

Slade drew back his arm for a punch.

Falling backward at the last second, Larani braced herself by slapping both hands down on the floor and brought one foot up. The tip of her boot struck the underside of Slade's chin, forcing his head backward.

She snapped herself upright, then moved in for a hard jab. Her fist connected with Slade's nose, snapping his head back and sending blood flying from his nostrils. *That is for every Keeper you've-*

The man came at her in a full-on bullrush. He wrapped both arms around Larani, lifted her clean off the ground and carried her through the chamber. The crushing force around her chest made it hard to breathe.

Slade threw her with a surge of Bent Gravity.

Larani went flying backward until her spine collided with the cavern wall. She fell to the ground, hunched over and dazed. Pain flared up in her back, but she had no time to indulge it.

Slade charged in for the kill.

Larani jumped, doing the splits in mid-air, allowing him to pass by underneath her. Half a second later, she dropped to the ground to land crouched behind him.

She slammed her hands down on the fleshy floor, lifted her feet off the ground and kicked him right between the shoulder-blades. That was enough to send him face-first into the wall.

When she got up and spun around, her opponent was already facing her with blood staining his bared teeth. A cut on Slade's forehead made it clear that she had done some damage, but he wasn't out of the game yet.

The man spun for a hook-kick.

Larani bent over backward until she was practically folded

in half, watching as a black shoe passed harmlessly over her. With a growl, Slade came out of his spin, whirling around to face her again.

He threw a punch.

Larani's hand shot up, clamping onto his wrist, holding him tight. She straightened and used the other hand to punch him square in the face with enough force to break his nose. Rage filled her until she thought she would burst.

Larani kicked him in the stomach, forcing him back.

Stepping forward, she delivered a back-hand strike that took him across the cheek with a *crunch.* The shout he let out as he staggered backward to the glowing wall was the most satisfying thing she'd heard in a long time. "Impossible..."

"What's the matter, Grecken?" she asked. "Too used to fighting children? Would you prefer an opponent who can't hit back? I'm sure we can find you an adorable puppy to strangle."

"Points for quippage," Jack said.

Slade clutched a hand to his face, groaning as he stumbled away. He braced the other hand against the wall. "You have no idea what you're dealing with," he snapped. "If you will not bow before a messiah, then you will cower before a god!"

He slid one hand into his pants' pocket and pulled out something that looked like a curved knife blade. Only it was made of veiny flesh. The same kind of flesh that coated the walls and ceiling of this cavern.

Slade dropped to one knee, driving the blade of flesh into the floor. It sank all the way down, and then the walls began to hum. Their glow intensified until Larani was surrounded by brilliant white light.

She raised a hand to shield herself.

As the light died down, she saw Grecken Slade leaning against the wall with a cruel grin on his face. "You're too late," he whispered. "I wanted to present your corpses to the Inzari myself, but this will do."

"What was that thing?" Jack demanded.

"Don't you know?" Slade strode forward with his arms swinging freely, ignoring her as he moved into the middle of the room. He took a deep, satisfied breath and let it out again. "It was an Overseer, Jack."

"An Overseer? In your pocket?"

"Merely a vessel to store its consciousness, and now its consciousness has merged with this entire facility." Slade giggled like a school child, covering his mouth with two fingers. "You're all going to die!"

A new opening formed in the walls, leading into a narrow tunnel that hadn't been there before. Slade ran headlong into it, cackling with mad fury. Before she could even think to chase him, the aperture sealed itself shut again.

Jack came stumbling forward with his pistol in both hands, casting fretful glances in all directions. "I think we're in trouble," he whispered. "Big, big nasty trouble with a capital 'Fuck you!' "

"Remain calm," Larani said. "Most situations can be resolved with-"

The original doorway sealed itself shut as well, trapping them in this chamber, and then there was a soft hissing sound like air blowing through a vent. "Multi-tool active!" Larani shouted. "Environmental scan!"

The readout on her multi-tool's screen confirmed her worst fears. The air pressure was slowly dropping as the walls leeched the atmosphere from this room. This place was trying to suffocate them!

27

A wave of light chased them through the twisting tunnel, the walls brightening and brightening until it seemed as if they were running through the corona of a star. Jena had to cover her eyes.

A moment later, it died down.

Splitting her fingers apart to peek through the cracks, Jena turned her head to look for her friends. "Are you guys all right?" she asked in hushed tones. "Harry, do you have any idea what that was?"

Her boyfriend was bent over with a hand pressed to his belly, gasping for breath. "Whatever it is," he wheezed, "I don't think it's anything good. The Nexus is just around the next corner."

Melissa stood with her back pressed to the wall, her eyes shut as she tried to catch her breath. "Can you interface with it, Dad?" she squeaked. "Because I'm pretty sure this place just got a lot more-"

She cut off when a slurping sound drew their attention to skin that rose up from the floor to make a wall that blocked the tunnel. It took only seconds, and now they were at a dead-end, cut off from the Nexus.

Nausea twisted Jena's stomach in knots. A part of her wanted to ask if Harry had been the one to do that, but she knew better. A sudden burst of light and then the whole place started turning itself against them? She knew what that meant. "Quickly," she said. "We'll have to double back and then find-"

Another wall formed behind them, trapping them in a small section of tunnel. Right then she was grateful that she had never been prone to claustrophobia, but that would be of little comfort if-

"What's that hissing sound?" Melissa asked.

Biting her lip, Jena turned her face up to the ceiling. She blinked a few times. "The air," she mumbled. "The walls are sucking up the air! Bleakness take me, those aliens are going to kill us without firing a shot!"

Melissa shielded her face with both hands, stepping away from the wall with a soft groan. "No, no, no!" she squealed. "Not like this! We can't let it end like this!"

"Harry! I need options!"

He was still doubled over and shaking his head in frustration. "I don't know what you want me to do," he barked. "If the walls are turning against us, it can only mean the Overseers have gained control of the Key."

"Think! There has to be something!"

Harry looked up at her, blinking as if he had never seen a woman before. "No, you don't get it!" he insisted. "If the Overseers have control of this place, then that's it. We're done. Situation over."

Jena dropped to her knees before him, grabbing his shirt. She pulled him close until his nose almost touched hers. "I refuse to accept that," she said in tones that made it clear she would not tolerate dissent on this point. "You have the ability to control the walls. So, use it and get us out of here."

"I'd be fighting an Overseer!"

"Would you rather just die?"

He was crying, his body shaking with every sob. "You don't get it, Jen," he began. "We're dealing with beings that terraformed a few dozen planets like it was nothing."

"And you are Harry god damn Carlson!" she growled, borrowing a bit of Earth vernacular. "The best cop in the whole damn city, the best dad on the whole damn planet. That's your daughter over there! Are you just gonna let her die?"

He studied her with tears glistening on his cheeks, and then something changed in his expression. "You're right," he whispered. "I'm sorry."

Harry spun around, clapping his hand against the wall, blending the N'Jal with the organic material that made up this place.

And then he let out a pure, feral howl.

Anna was lying flat on her belly with her face pressed to the floor, gasping as she tried to gulp as much air into her lungs as she could manage. That was getting harder and harder as the air grew thinner and thinner. Somewhere, just a few paces away, Ben was trying to cut through the wall with his nano-blade.

His suit was a self-contained environment that would give him twenty minutes of oxygen before he too started to suffocate. She could hear him muttering, but clearly his efforts were proving fruitless.

They had been holding their own against Slade's pack of minions when a flash of light blinded them and brought a halt to the fighting. Seconds later, the room had sealed itself shut, trapping them in here.

In the back of her mind, Seth was trying to be a comfort, assuring her with warm emotions that everything would be all right. She loved him for that, but she could feel the Nassai's trepidation. He tried to hide it, but it was no use.

Her mind drifted, and she realized that what she wanted more than anything was for Jack to hold her close in these final moments. She loved him. Companion have mercy. How had she not seen it? It didn't matter. She could already feel herself beginning to slip into unconsciousness.

The Overseer fought him at every turn.

With the N'Jal, Harry was able to sense the neural networks that stretched through this entire facility. He tried to stimulate the neural pathways that would reconfigure the walls; the Overseer countermanded his orders. He tried to pump air back into their small section of tunnel; the Overseer blocked that too.

It was impossible; the instant he sent a command, it was already countermanded. He had been afraid that a human using Overseer technology would bring about the alien's wrath, but the creature didn't seem annoyed. It simply responded to his every attempt to take control with appropriate action.

Dimly, he was aware of his own lungs burning. The air was getting thin; he had to find a solution before he passed out or this was all over. Unfortunately, there was little he could do here.

If he got to the Nexus, he would be able to take control of the whole facility, but from here, all he could do was affect the local area. "Keep going," Harry told himself. "You have to keep going."

He tried to open the walls again.

Nothing happened.

It was no use! The Overseer knew this place instinctively. To Harry, the N'Jal was a tool, and through it, the rest of this facility a more elaborate tool. But to the Overseer, this whole place was an extension of its body. There was no way-

Of course!

Harry stimulated every pain receptor in the hallway, eliciting a high-pitched shriek from the walls. He didn't let up; he continued to torture the Overseer, flooding its mind with sensory information; the creature was off balance. He could feel it.

Harry sent a command through the neural networks.

One of the walls blocking the tunnel collapsed, skin melting back into the floor. Air came rushing through the gap, and suddenly he was gasping, trying to fill his lungs with every last particle of it.

He pulled away from the wall.

Melissa was curled up on the floor in the fetal position, hugging her knees and groaning in pain. "Dad," she whispered. "You did it. You did it."

No, he hadn't. Not yet.

Despite his fatigue, Harry got to his feet and stumbled through the tunnel toward the Nexus. He covered his eyes with one hand, moaning in pain. *Can't let that god damn alien gain control again.*

Rounding a corner, he came to a place where the tunnel ended in a circular opening that looked into a wide, open chamber. It looked no different than any of the other ones he had seen on their trek through this place, but he knew through the N'Jal that this was the hub of all the neural networks.

Harry stumbled through the aperture, bending over with his hands on his knees. "You're not gonna win," he whispered, taking a few shaky steps forward. "Strap in for a fight, you bastard! The lab rats are taking control of the maze!"

He thrust a hand out.

At his command, the tissue that covered the floor began to writhe, a lump rising to form a pillar roughly as tall as his stomach. He touched it with the N'Jal, linking the two, and suddenly, he was aware of this entire facility.

The Overseer fought him, of course, trying to take control

of the neural networks, trying to shut him out. But there was one thing the alien hadn't counted on. This place was designed for humans!

The Overseers who had designed it – the ones who saw potential in humanity – had put fail-safes into every system. One of their kind could not activate the Key's primary function without human participation. It was like one of those nuclear submarines where you had to turn both keys to launch the missiles.

It seemed the Overseer renegades had planned for the possibility of their enemies gaining control of this place. There were overrides in every system designed to respond to a human mind. Harry triggered them.

Every room and every tunnel was designed to take in sensory information. There were olfactory systems, pressure sensors, neural networks that responded to light. And through them all, he could sense his friends.

He was aware of Anna gasping for breath in one room while Jack and Larani were both close to passing out on the other side of the facility. With a thought, he opened each of those chambers, allowing air to flow in.

Anna gasped when something that felt very much like a strong wind hit her face, and suddenly her lungs were filling with air. The pressure in her chest seemed to lessen, but she still felt weak.

Through tear-blurred vision, she saw Ben standing with his back turned next to the now open doorway. Had he managed to cut his way out? The wariness in his posture said that wasn't likely.

Pressing a fist to her mouth, Anna winced and coughed. "What did you do?" she asked, struggling to get to her feet. It did no good; she was still too weak. "One of your usual tech miracles?"

Ben stood with fists on his hips, his head tilted back to stare up at the ceiling. "It wasn't me," he mumbled, taking a cautious step backward. "I don't know, An. I think we got very, very lucky."

She looked through the opening to find three men lying dead in the short corridor between this chamber and the main tunnel. Clearly, they had run out of air sooner. Which made sense given the small space they were trapped in. Whatever had tried to kill them was going after humans indiscriminately; it didn't seem to care which side they were on.

Jack was stretched out on his side, barely conscious, and using what mental energy he had left to comfort Summer. The Nassai was amused by his efforts; she thought it was her job to care for him in these final moments. Well, she could just suck it up! If Jack was going to die, then he was going to go out doing some amount of-

His vision was hazy, but he clearly saw the patch of skin that covered the doorway split apart to grant them access to the tunnel. Air came rushing into the room, and he took in a big gulp of it by instinct.

Larani sat up next to him, pressing a hand to her forehead. "It doesn't make sense," she murmured in a strained voice. "Why would the Overseer suddenly give up before it finished the job?"

"Maybe you want to re-evaluate that atheism," Jack panted.

She glared at him.

He rolled onto his back with hands folded over his chest, laughing triumphantly as he stared up at the ceiling. "Look at it this way," he wheezed. "Our luck really isn't that good; fate kept us alive so we could go after Slade."

"Thank you," Larani muttered. "Your cynicism is reassuring."

"Always happy to help."

The Overseer was focused on him now; Harry could feel its attention as it tried to reclaim control of the facility's environmental systems. It did no good, of course; he had blocked access to every single one of them, and in this place, a human mind trumped the will of an Overseer.

He understood the alien's plan the instant it went into effect. Through the facility's sensor networks, he was able to sense the Overseer taking control of some of the organic tissue near his daughter and his girlfriend.

The alien constructed itself a body, forming bone and muscle, skin and nerved in a matter of moment. The organic material that made up this place was incredibly versatile, able to restructure itself on a molecular level.

Harry understood his enemy's intentions.

If it couldn't kill his friends by turning the environment against them, it would settle for beating them to death with its own bare hands – or whatever appendages it decided to construct – and it would start with his daughter. No doubt, this was some attempt to make him leave the Nexus in a fit of paternal instinct, and it might even have worked if not for one little thing. Melissa was currently with the one person who could handle anything the universe threw at her.

Jena.

No, the best thing Harry could do was wait here and maintain control of the Nexus. His presence here wasn't necessary to prevent the Overseer from regaining control of the environmental systems – he knew that much – but he was no Justice Keeper, blessed with enhanced strength, speed and stamina. He was the one person who could use this place to its full potential, and this was where he could do the most-

A figure stepped into the doorway behind him. He sensed it more through contact with the Nexus than he did through his own eyes and ears. In that instant, Harry became aware of a fatal mistake.

He had wanted to spare the men that Slade had sent to kill him and his friends. No one deserved to suffocate. So, he had opened up every tunnel and chamber in this facility. Including the makeshift tunnel the Overseer had created for Grecken Slade.

"Detective Carlson, I presume," Slade purred. "You'll have to step aside now."

Jena watched the creature rise out of the floor with trepidation in her heart, flesh knitting together to form bone and muscle and sinew. It formed a man-like shape with a bald head and a featureless face. Two eye-sockets appeared, blazing with yellow fire.

A pair of bony horns sprouted from its forehead to give the thing a truly demonic appearance. *You begin to aggravate me,* it said without words, striding through the tunnel toward them.

Jena backed up with fists raised in a boxer's stance, ignoring the cold sweat on her face. "Yeah, well, I'm good at that," she breathed out. "I gotta say, of all the bodies you could have chosen, this one is ugliest."

Melissa was sitting against the wall with her legs curled up under her, watching the creature with wide-eyes. Suddenly, the girl took control of herself. "Jena!" she screamed, drawing her pistol from its holster.

She threw it.

Jena caught the grip, feeling strangely empowered with a gun in her hand. Hissing, she drew her own pistol with the other and pointed both at the monster. "Here's the thing about Keepers," she said. "We usually don't use firearms on each other because there's a good chance the bullets will be deflected, but you on the other hand...High Impact!"

Both guns responded.

She fired.

A crater appeared in the creature's chest, thick crimson blood dripping from the wound. Doubling over, the monster braced one hand against the tunnel wall and let out a groan of pain.

Just like that, the wound sealed itself shut, muscle tissue reforming into its proper shape as if no damage had been done. Witnessing that left Jena with anxiety so strong it felt as if her own chest would cave in.

She winced and tossed her head about. "Or you could just do that," she whispered, dropping the pistols. "Okay, big and ugly. Guess we're going to have to settle this one the old-fashioned way."

The hulking creature straightened, standing head and shoulders taller than her. Its fiery eyes were full of menace. *You are nothing but insects,* it said. *A minor irritation and nothing more.*

The Overseer swiped at her in a back-hand strike.

Jena ducked, allowing a meaty fist to pass over her. She delivered a pair of jabs to the stomach, then jumped to throw a hard punch that hit the creature's noseless face. That stunned it for a moment.

Jena kicked, planting a foot in its belly.

She pushed off, back-flipping through the air, landing in a handstand just a few feet away. "Okay," she said, flipping upright. "If we're gonna get it on, then I would prefer to use toys. That good with you?"

She drew her belt knife, holding the gleaming blade extended toward the alien. Of course, that did very little to discourage her opponent. The Overseer tilted its head to the side, watching her with curiosity.

Jena slashed downward.

The alien raised one thick forearm, intercepting the blow. Metal sliced into flesh, but it seemed to have no effect. A four-fingered fist slammed into Jena's face, blacking out her vision.

Luckily, she was still able to sense her opponent. The creature spun.

A back-kick to the chest sent Jena stumbling backward through the tunnel with a sharp gasp. "Not good, not good," she gasped out. "So not good!" She charged at her opponent again.

Dropping to her knees at the last second, she slashed the knife across its belly and spilled its guts onto the floor. *Ignorant insect.* The Overseer bent over in pain, clearly shaken by the wound.

Jena brought the knife up to pierce the underside of its chin, driving the blade all the way to its skull. "Yeah," she replied in a breathy whisper. "We're annoying that way."

Instead of dying like any decent life-form would do, it merely reached up with that ugly, misshapen fist, grabbed the handle of her knife and pulled it free with a squeal. It dropped the weapon to the floor.

Then it came at her.

Jena leaped, flipping over the alien's head. She uncurled to land behind it with a hard grunt. "Okay, let's see how you like this!" She jumped and brought her elbow up to strike the back of its skull.

The creature stumbled.

Jena spun around.

She jumped and wrapped her legs around the creature's midsection, riding it piggy-back. With a growl, she pressed a forearm to the Overseer's throat, trying to cut off its air-supply. Then she remembered that it didn't have a mouth or a nose.

With inhuman strength, the alien reached around behind itself and grabbed the back of Jena's shirt. It pulled her off and tossed her to the tunnel floor. She landed on all-fours, groaning.

The back of a heel slammed into her nose, and then everything went dark, The pain was so intense! For a moment, she wondered if her skull had caved in, but she could still feel her

Nassai working to heal the wounds. That meant she was still alive. That meant she was still in the game.

Jena rolled onto her back.

When her vision cleared, she saw the bottom of a misshapen foot hovering just a few inches above her nose. The creature tried to step on her.

Jena's hands shot up, seizing the thing's ankle and holding it steady with Keeper strength. Sweet Mercy, this alien was strong! Her arms ached from the strain, and worst of all, she was losing this conflict.

"Hey!" Melissa called out. "Ass-butt!"

The Overseer looked over its shoulder.

Jena heard the distinct *BUZZ* of gunfire from a Leyrian weapon, and then the alien stumbled as something pierced its skull, sending bits of gore spattering against the tunnel wall. Jena pushed the meaty leg away.

The Overseer fell over backward, landing hard on the floor just behind her. The fact that it didn't kick or thrash told her that this fight was over. Of course, she really couldn't understand why a bullet to the brain would work when a knife through the skull had done nothing, but Jena wasn't one to be picky about-

The creature's body melted, sinking back into the floor, bony horns disintegrating into a pile of goop that quickly merged with the material that made up the tunnel's floor and walls and ceiling. Something told her this wasn't good.

Further up the tunnel, something stepped out of the wall, organic tissue reforming into a vaguely-human shaped creature with horns that sprouted from its head. It turned its yellow-eyed gaze upon her.

"Oh, fuck me!" Jena shouted.

Harry spun around, putting his back to the pillar and thrusting his hand out to point the N'Jal at Slade. A force-field of rippling energy appeared before him, transforming the other man into a hazy, black-clad figure. "Stay back."

Slade glided into the room with one hand in his pocket. "Honestly, Detective," he said. "You expect to stop me with that."

Closing his eyes, Harry took a deep soothing breath. "You'd be surprised," he said, backing up until his hip touched the pillar. "I brought down one of your freaks with the twisted symbionts."

The other man was pacing a circle around the perimeter of the room, pausing on Harry's left to cast a glance over his shoulder. "An amateur," Slade replied. "Arin wasn't yet fully acquainted with his powers."

Harry spun to face him.

Grecken Slade stood there with hands clasped behind his back, a predatory grin on his face. "You're no match for me," he said, stepping forward. "Relinquish control of the Nexus, and I will allow you and your daughter to live."

"Like hell."

Slapping one hand down upon the pillar, Harry took control of the room's systems. It was a simple matter to stimulate the organic tissue that made up the floor and cause it to grow, wrapping bands around Slade's feet, trapping him.

The other man tried to move forward and stumbled, nearly falling flat on his face. "Impressive," he said, regaining his balance. "You truly have mastered the gift the Fallen Ones bestowed upon you."

Harry pointed the N'Jal at his enemy, creating a force-field that made the air before him shimmer like heat rising off lack pavement. With a single thought, he sent the wall of electro-magnetic energy flying toward Slade.

The force-field hit the cavern wall and fizzled out.

Harry felt his eyes widen. With Slade's feet anchored to the floor, a field traveling that fast should have ripped the man in half and left a bloody mess all over the place, but there was no body, only a pair of scars where the bands holding Slade's feet had been.

In fact, Slade stood a few paces to the right of where he had been, pressing a fist to his mouth. "Heh-hem," he said. "Honestly, Harry, you didn't really think it would be that easy, did you?"

Harry loosed another force-field.

The other man jumped, somersaulting over the shimmering wall of energy and then uncurling to drop to the ground. He landed in a crouch, then stood up slowly. "Sadly, this is becoming tedious," Slade said. "You might notice I haven't counterattacked. I've got no quarrel with you, Harry."

Clenching his teeth, Harry looked down at the floor. "No, of course not," he said, rubbing his forehead with the back of his hand. "You just wanna take control of this thing so you can use it as a weapon of mass destruction."

"Is that what you think?"

"It's what I know."

Crossing his arms with a heavy sigh, Slade marched forward with his eyes closed. "No," he said, shaking his head. "I wish to fulfill the Inzari's purpose, to bring their plans for our species to fruition."

"And if we don't want that?"

"No one resists the will of God, Harry." In one smooth motion, Slade drew a pistol from the holster on his belt and pointed it at Harry's face. The LEDs on the barrel turned white, indicating EMP rounds. "Your force-fields won't protect you from this. You lack a Keeper's ability to deflect incoming fire, and you certainly aren't fast enough to dodge."

All true, though it pained Harry to admit it.

"I am offering you a choice," Slade went on. "Die here defending the Nexus or run to your daughter and do what little you can to help her. If you go now, I will let you both live.

Otherwise, I'll kill you here, turn control of the environmental systems back over to the Inzari and let Melissa suffocate."

Really, there was no choice at all.

Harry ran from the room.

Out in the tunnel, he found a massive horned creature standing with its back turned while Jena launched herself at it. She flew like a wild-woman toward the beast, punching it in the face as she drew near.

The Overseer stumbled backward.

Unfortunately, Jena didn't understand the nature of this conflict. It was clear by the way she fought that she saw this creature as a single discreet enemy. Knock it senseless, and the Overseer would be out of commission.

No, the Overseer's consciousness existed within the neural networks that permeated this entire facility. This hulking monstrosity was just an automaton, a pawn to keep them busy while Slade activated the Key's primary function.

Slade was the real enemy, but Harry couldn't take him out by himself. He needed the others, and that meant he had to put down the Overseer's pet demon. Thankfully, that was easier than it looked.

The horned beast readied itself for a counter-attack.

Harry rushed forward, pressing his palm to the creature's back, allowing the N'Jal's neural fibers to bond with the alien's nervous system. And just like that, he had control of the monster.

He flooded the creature's nervous system with pain signals, drowning out anything it might receive from its master. Its limbs flailed about wildly, and its head jerked from side to side, but Harry kept pushing. *Just a little longer...*

This thing did have a heart and a respiratory system where oxygen was taken in via discreet gills on its neck. Harry stopped them all. The creature spasmed. Then its corpse fell to the floor.

When he looked up, Jena was standing before him with her mouth agape, blinking in confusion. "Well, that works," she said with a shrug. "Now come on; we need to get control of the Nexus before-"

Harry shut his eyes and shook his head. "Slade already has control of the Nexus," he choked out. "And whatever he's going to do, its big. This place...I only got the vaguest sense of its true purpose."

"What can you tell me?"

"I know it connects to other Overseer installations through the SlipGate network," he said. "Hundreds of them across the galaxy. There's no telling how many. If this thing *is* a weapon, we could be looking at the end of the human race."

Baring her teeth with a hiss, Jena looked down at herself. Her face went red, but she took control of her emotions. "All right," she murmured. "Then it's up to the three of us. How do we stop it?"

"Slade is the weak link," Harry explained. "The Key was designed for humans. It needs a human mind to activate its primary function. Kill Slade, and the Overseer will be unable to use it."

"All right. Let's go."

"It's not that simple!" Harry shouted, stepping in front of her with his arms spread wide. Right then, his heart was pounding so hard he thought it might explode in his chest. "With Slade in control of the Nexus, the Overseer will have access to the environmental systems. Now, it will probably take him a few minutes to figure out what he's doing, but once he does, we're right back to suffocating in a sealed off tunnel."

True, Slade had promised to let him and Melissa flee, but Harry had no faith in that man's ability to keep his word. "And let's not forget," he went on. "The instant we walk through that door, the Overseer is going to call up more of those horned creatures."

"You're saying we shouldn't try?" Jena shouted.

Harry stepped around the dead alien's carcass, moving closer to his girlfriend. "I'm saying we don't have time for a long, drawn-out fight," he growled. "It has to be a quick, decisive strike that kills Slade before the Overseer has a chance to react."

For one very long moment, Jena just looked into his eyes. That expression on her face...He knew she was planning something, and he knew he wasn't going to like it. "All right," she said. "Take Melissa, get back to the SlipGate."

"What?"

"Do it, Harry!"

At the mention of her name, Melissa – who had been hanging on the periphery of this conversation – stepped forward and shook her head. "No way," she insisted. "I'm not going to do nothing while Slade just-"

Jena grabbed them both by the shirt and pulled them close so she could whisper. "I don't know what kind of sensors this place has," she explained. "But I am not willing to speak my plan out loud. Trust me, it'll work."

"But-"

"Go!"

Jena started up the tunnel, toward the Nexus, pausing after taking two steps. She let out a deep breath but kept her back turned. "Melissa," she said after a moment. "I need to tell you something."

Melissa went jogging after her, awkwardly moving around the dead alien's corpse. Harry wasn't sure he liked where this was going, but he knew that voicing an objection was definitely a bad idea. Besides, if Jena was about to do something insanely suicidal and stupid, then she probably wanted to give some inspiring words to her protege. Who was he to object to that?

Jena spun around. "You're gonna be an amazing Keeper."

She seized Melissa's face in both hands, and suddenly, Jena's skin began to glow, a white halo that seemed to radiate from every pore. It was as if the sun had come down to wrap itself around his girlfriend. What could...*No,* Harry thought. *No, she wouldn't!*

The halo transferred to Melissa and sank into her skin, pulsing and surging. Harry watched as his daughter stumbled backward to hit the tunnel wall. She sank to her knees, head hanging with exhaustion.

Jena was reeling with a hand on the wall to steady herself, wincing in pain. "Get her out of here," she whispered hoarsely. "The Bonding will have exhausted her. You're going to have to carry her."

"You gave her your symbiont?"

"Go, Harry!"

He stumbled forward, stretching a hand out to his girlfriend, nearly tripping over the dead alien. "We can save you," he pleaded. "Please, Jen, whatever it is you're gonna do, don't do it!"

Jena stood up straight.

A grimace twisted her features, and she shook her head. "I'm already dead, Harry," she said, her voice shaking with every syllable. "Without a symbiont, I've got maybe five minutes before my heart stops. She can't give it back to me, and there's no way to get me back to Station Twelve in time to Bond another."

"But..."

"Go, Harry," she said. "Get out of here."

Numbly, he watched his girlfriend turn away and shuffle up the tunnel as if she had a ball and chain strapped to each ankle. She hobbled around the corner, and then she was gone. *I knew I should have said something.*

Melissa was on her knees next to the wall, bracing herself with one hand pressed to the floor. "Everything dies, baby, that's a fact," she whispered. What the hell? Now was not the time to be quoting the Boss.

Harry went to her.

Dropping to a crouch, he slipped his daughter's arm around his shoulders and then pulled her to her feet. "Come on," he said, starting up the tunnel, away from the Nexus. "We have to get back to the SlipGate chamber."

There was no doubt about it now.

His daughter was a Justice Keeper.

Shoving a blasting cap into the brick of plastic explosive she had pulled from her pocket, Jena shuffled through the tunnel, feet dragging with every step. Her skin tingled, and soon it would be burning. Worse yet, she had no sense of spatial awareness. She had not realized how much she had come to rely on it.

Up ahead, a circular opening looked into a chamber where Slade was hooked into some weird matrix of fleshy tubes that pierced his body. Clearly he hadn't yet learned to control the Nexus, or he would have shut the door to keep her out.

She shuffled through the doorway.

Closing her eyes, Jena felt hot tears on her cheeks. "There are worse ways to go," she whispered, shaking her head. "Did you really want to die in some hospital bed with everybody blubbering about how much they love you?"

In the middle of the room, a tube of glowing blue flesh covered Slade to his waist with smaller tentacles piercing his chest and his arms. Clearly he was naked under there. She could see his clothes discarded on the floor.

His eyes were open, but they seemed to be unfocused, staring dead ahead at nothing at all. "You're too late," he said in a distant voice. "Maybe you're wondering why I didn't take control of the environmental systems."

"The thought crossed my mind."

Evolution

"There wasn't time," Slade whispered. "I did what I came here to do. I began the End of Days. Prepare yourself, Jena."

Jeffery had been working at the Toronto SlipGate terminal for some time now, and if his bosses asked, he would swear up and down that he loved his job. But the truth was that most of the time, he was bored out of his mind.

Stifling a yawn with his fist, Jeffery shut his eyes tight. "Move along, ma'am," he said, waving to the woman who passed through his security checkpoint. "Keep moving. Let's keep the line moving."

"What the hell?"

That woke him up.

He spun around to find the three SlipGates standing side by side on the white tiled floor humming. The sinuous grooves that ran along each triangle's metal surface began to glow with brilliant white light. Three incoming travelers at the same time? That couldn't be right. "Get everyone back!" Jeffery called out. "Back away from the Gates!"

As she climbed the steps from the subway platform, Linara heaved out a sigh of frustration. A tall woman with long blonde hair, she wore a thin black skirt and a white blouse with the top button undone. A sense of style was something of a necessity in her profession. Being the aide to one of the most prominent politicians on Leyria required a certain amount of decorum.

She rounded the corner, into the Denabrian SlipGate terminal.

And she froze.

The four Gates on the far side of the room were all humming, and the grooves that ran along each triangle were glowing ferociously. But how could that be? Gates only lit up when a traveler was coming through. Everyone knew that.

479

"Confirmed," Halina Taros said, tapping away at her control console. The CIC on Station Twelve was a flurry of activity as uniformed technicians scurried about, trying to figure out exactly what was going on while Justice Keepers stood by the door with wary expressions. "The other stations are reporting strange SlipGate activity. As are Moscow, London and Beijing. Further reports coming in."

"What's the cause?" Administrator Sorez demanded.

"Unknown," Halina replied. "Every Gate on the planet seems to be active."

Wahkali scrambled up the mucky hillside with a bow in hand, arrows rattling in his quiver. The tattered pants and tunic he wore had seen better days, and his shoes slipped in the mud. He would come back with a stag, though; he had promised his father that much.

Tall and dark of skin, Wahkali perched on the hilltop, waiting for the opportunity to take his shot. His long, black hair was a mess, tangles clinging to the back of his shirt. If the hunt went well, he would cut it.

Down in the valley below, pine trees rose up to caress the sky with their needles, and beyond that, a stone pyramid rose even higher. The temple of the Sky Spirits. It was said that hunting in sight of the gods would bring misfortune. Wahkali did not know if he believed such tales. Still...

His ancestors had believed that the Sky Spirits brought them to this world for their protection, to save them from certain disasters. No one had seen a Sky Spirit in over ten generations. What the elders believed was-

He froze.

Off in the distance, he could see the strange metal triangle standing at the base of the pyramid. The Symbol of the Covenant, some called it. He had seen it many times – even touched it on one occasion – but today, there was something different.

The grooves on the triangle were glowing.

Had the Sky Spirits returned?

In the depths of space, roughly seventeen lightyears from the Belos Star System, a lone SlipGate floated through the inky blackness. It had once been part of a Wyvern-class troop carrier, but the Overseers had destroyed that ship in an attempt to kill Jena Morane.

The Gate, of course, had survived.

Sinuous grooves on its surface began to glow.

"We're receiving a data burst!" Halina called out, trying to speak over a multitude of voices. Her console began to flicker, accessing star-charts without her consent. A map of the galaxy appeared on the screen, spiral arms swirling around a bright central core.

Tiny red dots appeared on the map, thousands of them scattered across the galactic disk. Some were more concentrated in certain areas. There were plenty here in the Sol System, and even more back home on Leyria. SlipGates? That would make sense in light of the recent activity.

"Disconnect from the network," Administrator Sorez shouted.

"I can't!" someone replied behind her.

Halina was transfixed by the screen. The tiny red dots just kept appearing until it seemed as if someone had scattered crumbs across the galactic disk.

Then something happened that she didn't expect.

A huge red about the size of her thumb appeared on the galaxy map. Then another and another. "What are those?" someone shouted from behind her. Halina was too baffled to answer. More large dots appeared.

And then lines.

Lines that connected the big dots, forming a complex star pattern. Instinct kicked in, and Halina began analyzing the star charts. The closest of those big dots was roughly one thousand lightyears from the Sol System, a journey of six days at high warp. There was another one between Leyrian and Antauran space.

And more on the other side of the galaxy! She counted three large dots scattered throughout the Ragnos Confederacy. What could these be?

"Can we get a message to Leyria?" Sorez asked.

"No, sir; long-range communications are out. Several ships within the system are reporting trouble with their onboard SlipGates. Their consoles seem to be displaying the same navigational data we're seeing here."

What could those big dots be? Halina wondered.

"Of course!" she whispered.

Jena's heart sank when she heard Slade's cruel laughter. The man just hung there, strapped into the tube of flesh, tentacles piercing his skin. He didn't seem to notice the pain. "It's too late," he whispered. "Too late. The end has begun. The first domino falls, and soon the rest will follow."

Jena felt her face crumple, then tossed her head about to clear away the fog. "You could be right," she growled, hobbling closer to Slade. "But I can promise you one thing, Grecken: you won't be here to see it."

She triggered the blasting cap.

Her world ended in fire.

28

The Med-Lab on Station Twelve was a crowded room where doctors in white lab coats scurried about. One young man with a vacant stare sat on the edge of a bed while a nurse in blue scrubs scanned him with some medical device.

Melissa sat on another bed with her hands in her lap, her shoulders hunched up as she tried to make herself as small as possible. "Why did you do it, Jen?" she whispered, trembling as a shiver went through her.

Everything was different now.

In some ways, she was more aware of her environment, aware of everything in this room without having to look. She knew – somehow – that a doctor was coming up behind her, and that in precisely three seconds, he would be close enough for her to turn and grab his collar if she wanted to.

The Nassai that she now carried filled her mind with knowledge. Knowledge of her surroundings, knowledge of her new abilities, and knowledge of pain that wasn't her own. She had cried any number of tears over Raynar, and now she would cry again. Jena had been more than a teacher. She was more than Melissa's father's girlfriend. Over these last nine months, Jena had started to feel like part of the family.

So, Melissa would cry, and this time it would be worse. Because this time, she was crying for two. She could feel her symbiont's pain. It was devastated. It tried to hide that reality from Melissa, but strong emotions flowed freely through their Bond.

A doctor in a white lab coat approached her bed, clearing his throat. He was short but handsome with thick black hair that he wore combed back. "Ms. Carlson," he said. "My name is Doctor Staas. I was sent to look in on you."

Melissa nodded.

The doctor lifted some device that looked very much like a tablet, frowning as he checked the readout. "Your vitals are stable," he said. "There seems to have been no ill-effects from the Bonding."

Shutting her eyes tight, Melissa sniffled. "That's good," she whispered, nodding to the man. "I feel different...Less tired, more...Is it normal to feel like I want to run around the track twenty times?"

He smiled, bowing his head to her. "From what I've been told," he said, eyebrows rising. "You'll get used to the extra energy, the balance, the coordination. What we should really talk about is counseling."

Melissa crossed her arms, doubling over until she was almost bent in half. "I'm not looking for counseling," she hissed, shaking her head. "I just want to work through this on my own."

The man bit his lip as he studied her, nodding slowly. "I understand that," he said, taking a step back. "But, Ms. Carlson, you need to understand that this isn't the first time a Nassai has been passed from one Keeper to another."

"It isn't?"

"No," he replied. "It's happened several times throughout

the last four centuries, and each time, the new host must cope with the symbiont's emotions in addition to her own. It can be quite difficult."

"It feels like a piece of me has been ripped away! It makes no sense, but-"

"Those would be the Nassai's emotions."

"I thought...I mean I was told that the Nassai's emotions wouldn't overwhelm the host. From everything I've read..."

Dr. Staaz sat on the next bed over, resting his tablet in his lap. He looked down at himself and sighed softly. "Under normal circumstances, that's true," he said. "A Nassai's mind is incredibly disciplined, but they develop a very strong connection with their hosts, and a loss such as this can be traumatic."

"So, counseling?"

"It would be my recommendation."

Melissa winced but nodded once in confirmation. "Okay," she said, getting to her feet. "Counseling it is. Can you bring me to my father? He's probably made a trench in the floor with all the pacing he's doing."

She found Harry standing in the drab gray hallway outside the Med-Lab, staring blankly at his own two palms. Of course, her father was still in the black clothing he had worn on their mission, but he had removed his vest, his sidearm and the rest of his gear. And thankfully, the N'Jal was gone too. "So, you're all right," he murmured when he saw her. "No complications from the Bonding."

Complications? Were there complications? Where did she even begin? How about having someone else's emotions in your head? That was new. Or the fact that she carried the symbiont of a woman she had looked up to? Melissa had wanted to be a Keeper for some time now, but she had always assumed that Jena would be there to help her through those first few years at least.

What's more, she wasn't even technically a Justice Keeper.

She had a Nassai, yes, but the rank and the authority only came after years of training. And it was possible for her to fail. A Nassai would never Bond a host that it deemed unworthy. It would perish before allowing its power to be misused; however, most potential Justice Keepers were allowed to Bond a symbiont after their first year of training.

Some were rejected for one reason or another, and they usually went on to pursue other careers. Sometimes, however, a Nassai would Bond with a worthy host who hadn't received any official training; Jack and Anna had both received their symbionts under such circumstances. But worthy in the eyes of a Nassai was not the same as worthy in the eyes of other Justice Keepers. It was possible for her to fail her training and then live out her life with Jena's symbiont doing something else.

Complications?

There were *so* many complications!

"Come on," Melissa said. "Let's find the others."

Jack felt numb inside. Summer, however, was beside herself with white-hot rage that flowed into his mind like water cascading over Niagara Falls. It was hard to provide her with any comfort. Right then, he just wanted to throw himself into his bed with his face in the pillows and shut out the light.

Jena was dead.

He still didn't quite believe it. Shouldn't he be in tears? He remembered seeing his grandfather's open casket at the age of fifteen and wondering why it didn't reduce him to a blubbering mess. He had always been very open with his emotions, but death just did not bring that out in him. Not at first anyway. It just left him numb at first. There would be tears when the shock wore off, when something reminded him that he would never again be able to ask Jena for advice or listen to one of her trademark quips. The world had changed today and not for the better.

Worst of all, no one really understood exactly what the Key had done aside from dumping a bunch of navigational data into their computers and making the SlipGates go all wonky for a few minutes. Some weapon! Of course, he was grateful that there hadn't been any damage, but it seemed as though Jena's valiant attempt to stop Slade before he did–whatever it was he was going to do– had been pointless in the end. His mentor had died for nothing. That pissed Jack off to no end.

He leaned against the corridor wall with his arms folded, staring down at himself. "Nothing's the same anymore, Summer," he whispered. "All the pillars that held up my world are crumbling."

"Jack!"

A quick glance over his shoulder revealed Melissa striding through the hallway in the same black clothes she had been wearing earlier. "I'm glad I found you," she went on. "I need to tell you something."

Jack winced, groaning in frustration. "Hey, kid," he said, stepping away from the wall. "I'm sorry; I've been wrapped up in my own anxieties. This must all be pretty new and scary for you, huh?"

Melissa stopped in front of him, bowing her head to stare down at the floor. "You have *no* idea," she said. "But that's not why I wanted to talk to you."

"What's on your mind?"

The girl looked up at him with big dark eyes, and for a moment he was startled by the intensity in her gaze. "When Jena passed her symbiont to me," she said, "our minds touched for a few seconds. She asked me to give you a message."

"What message is that?"

Pressing a fist to her mouth, Melissa cleared her throat audibly. "Jena asked me to speak these exact words to you. She said that you'd know what they mean. 'Everything dies, baby, that's a fact.' "

Jack closed his eyes, hot tears running over his cheeks. " 'But maybe everything that dies someday comes back,' " he whispered. "I think she was trying to tell us that death is not the end."

"I thought Jena was an atheist."

"She was," Jack said. "But maybe it wasn't about her." He gave Melissa a hug, a tight squeeze that seemed to ease some of her pain. The girl shuddered, and just once, a squeak came through her lips as she sobbed. "It's gonna be okay," Jack whispered. "It's gonna be okay."

After making sure that she was all right, he left her to sort through her own pain. It wasn't as though he was in any place to be offering advice on that topic. Tomorrow was going to be hard, and the next day harder. And then, one day, it would be easier. He didn't want it to be. Easy felt like a betrayal. It was *supposed* to hurt.

On his way to the SlipGate room, he found Anna walking alone through one of the drab gray corridors, ten steps ahead of him. Her back was turned when he came around the corner, but she must have seen him; Keepers had eyes in the backs of their heads.

Jack hurried to catch up with her, stretching one hand out toward her. "An," he said. "I...You must be hurting just as much as-"

She spun around to face him with tears glistening on her cheeks, her red hair in a state of disarray. "I can't really talk right now," she said, shaking her head. "I'm sorry. It's just... things between us are way too complicated, and I can't deal with that and with Jena's death at the same time."

Biting his lower lip, Jack looked down at the floor. "I get that," he said, nodding to her. "But...I mean, is there any chance we can put the soap opera on hiatus while we deal with bigger problems?"

"That's not a good idea."

He was genuinely surprised by that, so surprised that Summer echoed his shock. "But we always deal with tragedy together," he mumbled, barely aware of what he was saying. "It's kind of our thing."

Pressing her lips together, Anna looked up to stare into his eyes. She blinked a few times. "And I'm afraid that's going to have to change." Those words stung worse than a punch to the face. "At least for now."

He let her go without any further protest. There was no point in putting up a fight; when someone decided that they wanted to leave, nothing you could say would change their mind. It was just...Having his worst fears confirmed, knowing that things between him and Anna would never be the same, intensified the pain.

Oh God, where was the numbness? He could deal with the numbness, but this felt like his chest was about to implode. The shock was over then. This was worse than when his grandfather had died. Thomas Hunter had been a man in his late seventies with a heart condition. It was sad, but blah, blah, blah, the circle of life and all that crap.

Jena...

Jena still had many good years left. Most Keepers who managed to survive long enough to reach retirement died in their mid-fifties. Jena was only just past forty. There was still so much for her to do.

He waited a long time before making his way to the Slip-Gate. In part because he needed to focus on his grief, and in part because he wanted to make sure Anna was gone. He really didn't need yet another dash of awkward to enhance the flavour of this already shitty day.

The hallway outside her apartment had green carpets and lamps along the cream-coloured walls that flickered. It almost smelled like lemon-scented cleanser, and the lack of natural light made it seem kind of dingy. Just the same, she was going to miss it. This had been her home for the better part of a year.

Anna stood just outside the door, hunched over with her arms folded. "You can do this," she whispered, shaking her head. "If you keep stringing him along, it's going to be that much worse."

She slid the key into the lock.

When she pushed the door open, she found Bradley standing in the cozy little living room with his back turned, folding one of her shirts and putting it on a pile of laundry he had finished. "You're alive!" he exclaimed.

Anna smiled down at herself. "I am," she said, closing the door behind her. "But..." The dull ache of grief in her chest suddenly became a furious black hole, and it was only going to get that much worse. "Jena didn't make it."

Her boyfriend turned around.

The blank expression on his face as he stood silhouetted by the light that came in through the window told her that he was at a loss for words. Not that she blamed him for that; there were no words. "Anna, I'm so sorry."

Pressing the heels of her hands to her eye-sockets, Anna spasmed as a sob ripped through her. "I can't," she squeaked. "She was like a force of nature, you know? The one person who would outlive all of us."

He came over to her.

Slipping his arms around her, Bradley pulled her close, and she leaned her cheek against his chest. Right then, she wanted nothing more than to accept his comfort and try to forget her misery for a little while. But she couldn't. She knew that.

Anna pulled away, rubbing her nose with the back of her hand. "Listen," she said. "We have to talk."

His expression darkened for a half a second, but he smothered the sudden flash of emotion. "That sentence never means anything good," he said, shaking his head. "So...Is this the part where you break my heart?"

She started crying.

The sobs just ripped their way out of her no matter how hard she tried to suppress them, and the only source of solace she found came from Seth offering sympathy and encouragement. "I'm sorry," Anna whimpered.

There were moments when having a Keeper's ability to see everything around her without having to look was a curse. Turning away from Bradley did no good. He was still there in her mind, watching her like a wounded animal.

She went to the island in her kitchen.

Plunking her elbows down on its surface, Anna rested her chin on the heels of both hands, fingers curled over her cheeks. "I love you, Bradley," she said after a moment. "I really do. You're sweet and kind and wonderful."

Anna winced, shaking her head. "But I don't love you in a way that will make me want to spend my life with you." Forcing those words out was so hard. "You can't come with me to Leyria."

He stood there with his arm hanging limp at his sides, his eyes fixed on the floor. "So, what are you saying?" he whispered. "All this time, and what? You're trying to tell me that you love me as a friend?"

"No."

As she searched for the words to answer him, it dawned on her that her father was wrong. Yes, relationships took work and effort; true, no two people got along perfectly. But it wasn't perfect compatibility that made a relationship endure. There was something else, some missing piece that completed the puzzle. And she knew what that piece was because she felt it every day.

Every time Jack suffered, her heart broke for him. Every time he threw out one of his snarky comments, she felt like he was performing just for her, shining a ray of light into the gloom of whatever crisis had stressed her out. For three years, she had wanted to come back to Earth. Not because she loved this planet, not because she wanted the most high-profile assignment. Because Jack was here.

The part of her that believed in being selfless insisted that her job was to put aside those feelings and honour her commitments, but she realized now that doing so would be so much worse. Bradley deserved better than to have a partner who was always thinking about someone else. He deserved someone who pursued their relationship with conviction, not someone who did it out of a sense of duty.

She had to let him go.

"It's not that simple," she said. "It's more complex than just platonic love versus romantic love. There are degrees of the latter-"

Bradley raised both hands up with palms out, stumbling backward as if she'd just punched him. "Stop!" he growled, cutting her off. "I really don't need to hear this. You don't want to be with me?"

"It's not that simp-"

"Fine!" he barked. "Message received."

He paced to the front door, grabbed the knob and paused there for a moment. Then he yanked the door open and stepped out into the hallway. Grief hit her like a tidal wave the instant he was gone.

She hated herself.

Ben was back in the concrete jungle.

On Leyria, the buildings had a certain elegance; they weren't all narrow rectangles that stretched for the for the sky. In fact many were short, longer buildings that curved as they traced part of the circumference of a circular street, Most were designed to include a spacious interior with ergonomic work-spaces and beautiful indoor gardens.

Here, everything was a glass spire that reached for the heavens where the only real variance was in who stood taller than whom. The skyscrapers of Albert Street rose up on either side of him, blocking the sun's light.

Dressed in black pants and a gray t-shirt, Ben moved up the sidewalk with his head hanging. "You can do this," he whispered to himself for the three hundredth time. "He'll understand what you've been through."

He came to a street-side cafe where round glass tables were spaced out on a patio of red bricks. Most were occupied by men and women in shorts and t-shirts and maybe the odd sundress. But he knew what he would find.

Darrel sat at one table in the corner with a newspaper in one hand, a mug of coffee next to him sending steam wafting up into the atmosphere. The man was as handsome as ever with a face that belonged on a statue and short black hair. If he noticed Ben, he didn't show it. "Darrel?"

The man stiffened.

Ben closed his eyes, taking a deep breath. "You haven't returned my calls," he said, approaching the small fence that bordered the patio. "I wanted to tell you why I've been away for so long."

Darrel remained in his chair, turned so that Ben saw him in profile, and he kept his attention focused on the paper. "I don't care why you've been away so long, Tanaben," he said. "You said you'd come back, and you didn't. That tells me all I need to know."

"I was arrested-"

"For smuggling weapons," Darrel cut in. "I've heard it. One of your friends finally found a few minutes to give me an explanation for why my boyfriend was never coming home. But thank you for coming all the way down here."

Ben swallowed, trying to ignore the heat in his face. "So you know." He grabbed the fence and leaned forward. "Darrel, I would have called or written, but I was forbidden from making any off-world comm-"

The other man looked over his shoulder, squinting at Ben. "You still don't get it, do you?" he asked, shaking his head. "I don't care. For almost four months, I had nothing but my father to tell me what a degenerate you are."

"Your father is-"

"I needed you to be here and prove him wrong," Darrel went on. "And you weren't. But the important question is *why* weren't you here?" Silence stretched on for maybe ten seconds. Ten seconds in which Ben was painfully aware of the other customers looking at him. "You weren't here because you broke the law. And not even for some noble purpose. You gave weapons to people who were intent on fighting a guerrilla war for no god damn reason. You *are* a degenerate, Ben."

It wasn't that simple.

The Colonists on the Fringe Worlds were suffering constant raids from Antauran ships. Leyria's solution had been to just bring everyone home and stave off the conflict a little longer. Sooner or later, the Antaurans would try to expand again. But many of those colonists had lived on Palisa and Alios for several generations. They had a right to defend their homes

Not that he would have any luck explaining that to Darrel. You couldn't argue with someone who didn't care enough to hear your point of view. "I'm sorry," Ben whispered. "I'll leave you alone then."

"Thank you," Darrel said. "But just so we understand each other, let me be clear. I never want to see you again."

Ben said nothing else.

He just walked away with a knife in his heart.

29

A glowing blue tunnel stretched on for maybe fifty feet before its walls went dark. Beyond that, there was nothing but ash and scarred tissue. Men in women in bright red hazmat suits with clear helmets knelt in the ruins of what had once been the Nexus of the Key, all scanning the area with various pieces of equipment.

Dressed in a hazmat suit of his own, Jack stood in the tunnel with his arms folded and looked through the clear mask. "What can you tell me?" he asked through the radio. "Is there any indication of what Slade did?"

One of the men just inside the chamber stood up and spun around to face Jack. "No, sir," he said, shaking his head. "Any neural networks that might give our scientists *some* clue as to how this place works were torched in the explosion."

"I'm sorry," Jack said. "What was your name again?"

"Marc Alenar, sir," the man replied. He shuffled through the large hole in the wall that had once been the entrance to the Nexus, nearly falling flat on his face. "We *have* collected many samples of organic tissue, however," he added. "Most of it is identical to other samples of Overseer technology that we've acquired over the years, but there was human DNA in the mix."

"Whose DNA?" Jack inquired.

The other man shut his eyes behind his mask and heaved out a soft sigh. "A genetic analysis indicates that both Jena Morane's and Grecken Slade's remains are present in the wreckage. They're both dead, sir."

Jack let out a deep breath.

Well, that confirmed it then. Not that he was holding out very much hope for some kind of miracle, but there was always a small part of him that never wanted to give up no matter how slim the odds were. Jena was dead. This time, admitting that brought only a small pang of grief.

At least she had taken Slade with her. Both physically and intellectually, the man was a devastating adversary. Now he was gone for good. One tiny bit of joy in a tempest of pain. "What about the Overseer?" Jack inquired. "Have you seen any indication that it might still be kicking around."

"Unknown, sir," Alenar replied. "Our first team came here in full space suits with oxygen tanks. We've been here almost every day for the past week, and we have seen no indication that the Overseer is still active. Perhaps its consciousness was destroyed in the explosion that destroyed the Nexus. Or perhaps it fled somehow."

And that was quite possibly the thing that bothered him most. They really had no idea what could kill an Overseer. He would have to find out. "Keep up the good work," Jack said, turning away from the other man. "Report anything you find directly to me. No one else. Do you understand?"

"Yes, sir."

Melissa felt out of place at this meeting. The e-mail from Larani Tal requesting her presence wasn't something she could ignore – when the head of the Justice Keepers came calling, even the greenest initiate knew to jump to her feet – but she was surrounded by people who had been working against Slade for months, and she wasn't sure exactly what it was she brought to the table.

It had been different with Jena; deep down, Melissa knew that she had always had Jena's ear. Her symbiont grew solemn and she tried to comfort it. *You need a name,* she told the Nassai. *What would you prefer?*

Larani Tal's office was a modestly decorated room where a desk of SmartGlass sat in front of a window that looked out upon the stars. The head of the Justice Keepers sat primly behind that desk, one leg crossed over the other as she gripped the armrests of her chair. "Report," she said.

Jack stood behind Melissa with his arms folded, his face grim as he studied Larani. "The Key seems to be inactive," he replied. "We still have no idea what the damn thing did, but at least it isn't doing anything else."

At the corner of the desk, Anna sat with her elbow on its surface, her cheek leaned against the palm of her hand. "Well, at least there's that," she muttered. "Engineers have been examining the SlipGates for the better part of a week; they seemed to have returned to normal."

Melissa was cognizant of her father standing with his back pressed to the wall, his gaze fixed on the floor. Whatever Harry was thinking, it was clear that he wasn't really paying attention. In her first counseling session, Dr. Iliathi had suggested that she share this experience with her father, but Harry had been tight-lipped since the day of Jena's passing. She had no idea what he was feeling.

Larani squeezed her eyes shut and sank deeper into her chair. "I believe that we do know what the Key has done," she said. "Ships have been sent to the coordinates that the Key fed into our navigational computers."

"And what did they find there?" Jack asked.

"SlipGates," Larani answered flatly. "SlipGates as large as a space station, capable of hurling a ship across the galaxy in a matter of seconds. They seem to form a network that would allow any warp capable civilization to reach almost any star system in only a few weeks of travel time.

"Each of these new Class-2 SlipGates – or 'SuperGates' as they have been dubbed – orbits a star over ten times the size of Earth's sun. They seem to be drawing energy from the star, though we're not entirely sure how, and they are now broadcasting their location to any ship that passes within twenty lightyears."

"They weren't before?" Melissa asked and then immediately regretted opening her mouth. Her job was to sit, listen and let the experienced professionals have the floor. Not to blather pointlessly.

Swiveling in her chair to face Melissa, Larani replied with a warm smile. "No, they were not," she answered in that cool, crystal-clear voice of hers. "As near as we can tell, these Super-Gates were dormant until Slade used the Key to activate them."

Everyone shuffled uncomfortably.

"I trust you see the problem," Larani said, rising from her chair. She paced a line behind the desk with a heavy sigh. "We have been aware of the Ragnos Confederacy for over two hundred years, but stellar distances prevented them from ever being a threat to us. Now, Ragnosian ships could be on our doorstep in a matter of days."

Behind Melissa, Jack doubled over with his arms crossed, shaking his head. "It's a small galaxy after all," he sang. "That was the Overseers' plan, wasn't it? Keep all those primitive humans apart so they can hate each other from a distance."

Anna leaned back in her chair, then covered her mouth with the tips of her fingers. "And then suddenly provide the means for rapid transit across the galaxy," she breathed. "It's only a matter of time before the shooting starts."

Larani closed her eyes, taking a deep breath. "My plan is to undermine their plan," she said. "Slade may be gone, but the task force is more important than ever. I intend to use whatever political influence I have to convince my government to send peace envoys to both the Antaurans and the Ragnosians."

"And the rest of us?" Harry said.

Pressing her hands to the desk's surface, Larani leaned forward and ran her gaze over everyone present. "Mr. Carlson," she began. "You're not technically a Keeper, but your contributions have been essential to every single one of Director Morane's victories. I would have you with us, if you're willing."

Harry stood against the wall with his hands in his jacket pockets, smiling down at himself. "Not a problem," he said, shaking his head. "But I'll need to put a few things in order, including selling the house."

"The same goes for you, Melissa," Larani said. "I pulled a few strings and got you a spot at the Denabrian Justice Keeper academy. It's yours if you want it."

"I do."

The answer came without a moment of hesitation; she knew, somehow, that going to Leyria was a part of God's plan for her. Now she just had to prove herself worthy of the power she had been given.

Larani stood up straight, clasping hands together behind her back and thrusting her chin out. "Excellent," she replied. "I've already sent Mr. Loranai back to Leyria to begin compiling everything we know about the traitors Slade has positioned among the Justice Keepers. Agent Hunter, you'll be working directly with him."

"Good to know," Jack said.

"The rest of you will continue your efforts to uncover and counter the plans Slade set in motion. You're going to make capturing his lieutenants your number one priority. The masked woman that Anna fought in Tennessee, the woman that Jena fought in New York, any affiliates of Wesley Pennfield: I want them all brought in. The game just got a whole lot bigger, people. Our enemies can hide anywhere in the galaxy; we'll have to be that much better, that much faster. Which brings me to one final point."

Larani tapped a button on her desk.

Melissa twisted in her chair in time to see the door slide open to reveal two people standing side by side in the hallway. The man was tall and athletic with dark skin, a very handsome face and black hair that he wore cut so short it was almost stubble.

The woman...

Melissa had never seen the woman with her own eyes, and yet she recognized her just the same. Raynar's memories filled her mind despite her efforts to push them away. She knew this woman, and she didn't like her.

Keli Armana stood in the doorway with her arms folded, looking very much like a queen in that drab, gray dress. "So," she began, gliding into the room. "I understand you let Slade throw the galaxy into chaos. Well done."

Melissa got out of her chair.

She strode across the room with her arms swinging freely, her teeth bared in a snarl. "What is this monster doing here?" she demanded. "The last person we need on this team is the woman who tortured Raynar every day for years."

In her mind's eye, she saw Anna leaning against the desk with her arms folded. "I'm inclined to agree. The last time we trusted Keli, she assaulted a Keeper, ran amok in Rio and nearly started a war between our people and the Antaurans."

"Always a pleasure to see you too, Lenai."

"Bite me."

Pursing her lips, Keli looked Melissa up and down. "And who might this be?" she asked, raising one eyebrow. "Don't tell me Raynar actually got somebody to fall for his simpering sweet boy act."

It was all Melissa could do not to slap the other woman; her hand actually moved half an inch before she took control of herself. Striking Keli with Keeper strength would not look good in front of her boss.

Keli replied to her barely-restrained anger with a smile so cold it could freeze hot lava. "Temper, temper, little girl," she said. "And a fair warning for future reference; this is why you don't need to read minds to know what someone is thinking."

"Raynar's dead," Melissa growled.

"Is he? I wish I could say I felt bad about that."

"Keli!" the man in the door shouted. "That's enough."

He marched into the room like a general who expected to be obeyed, fixing a dark glare on the back of Keli's head. "You have my apologies, Ms. Carlson," he said. "We've been working on social skills."

"I would like to introduce you all to the newly-promoted Director Jon Andalon," Larani broke in before anyone else could hurl insults around the room. "It seems Jena chose a successor in the event that anything happened to her. Director Andalon will be leading the task force to investigate Slade's activities."

"And Ms. Armana?" Melissa asked with no concern for the venom in her voice. It didn't matter if she pissed off the head of the Justice Keepers. She wasn't going to tolerate the woman who had tormented Raynar for-

"Ms. Armana will be working with you," Larani explained. "She's willing to help, and I believe it will do good to have a telepath on our side. Director Morane recognized the strength in diversity She brought you all together despite different backgrounds, different skill sets, even different powers. I plan to heed her wisdom."

Well, that's just wonderful, Melissa hissed inside her own

head. Of course, it wasn't like she would be spending much time with the team. Keeper training would take up most of her time, but that just meant Keli would have a chance to ingratiate herself with all the others while Melissa was off on the sidelines. Brilliant! Absolutely brilliant.

"In the mean time," Larani said. "I have to check on the ten men we took prisoner on the moon. Make whatever arrangements you need to make. We depart for Leyria in seven days."

How was it that you could be so certain that a decision was the right decision right up until the moment you made it? And then, when it was over, you suddenly began to doubt yourself. You began to wonder if you had acted rashly.

Anna felt like her chest would implode from the pain of this break-up. It was far worse than any of the others she had experienced. Perhaps it was the pain of braking a good man's heart. Or maybe it was the guilt she felt for having such strong feelings for a man who wasn't her partner. She didn't know. She just tried to endure it as best she could. And somehow she knew that this conversation would be much harder than the one she'd had with Bradley.

At the bottom of a gentle slope, a path of black asphalt cut through the grass with tall lampposts standing watch every few dozen feet, and beyond that, the waters of the Ottawa river rippled under a clear blue sky.

Jack was sitting on a bench facing the river, waiting, as he'd promised, for her to arrive. His back was turned, but Keepers didn't need eyes to see the world around them. No point in dragging this out.

She marched down the hillside.

Anna sat down beside him with her elbows on her thighs, lacing her fingers and resting her chin on top of them. "I broke up with Bradley," she said. "He won't be going with me to Leyria."

Her best friend leaned back with his arms folded, heaving out a deep breath. "That's gotta be painful," he replied in a ragged voice. "I'm sorry you had to go through that. But I'm betting that's not why you called me."

Anna squeezed her eyes shut, trembling at the grief in her heart. "It was painful," she whispered. "And no, that isn't why I asked you to come here. We need to talk about what this means for us, Jack."

"Okay," he said. "Big with the listening."

At moments like this, she always paused for half an instant before the words left her mouth. One last chance to decide if she really wanted to go through with it. A quiet voice always whispered that she should turn back, pretend she had come out here to say something else. But no...

She knew that she had to speak these words, and Seth seemed to know it too. Her Nassai was terribly sad, but also proud of her. That was almost enough to make her start crying on the spot.

"I love you, Jack," she began. "But I am so far away from anywhere that might be in the same solar system as ready for a new relationship. Whatever's between us, it's too confusing right now. You deserve someone who can say with conviction that she wants to be with you, not a confused emotional wreck.

"I need to not be around you for a little while. Until I've got my head on straight at least. If you ever need my help – if you find yourself going up against a *ziarogat* – I'll be there in a heartbeat, but aside from emergencies, we can't be in each other's lives."

Jack squinted as he stared off into the distance. "I get that," he said, nodding once. "And please do forgive my insatiable curiosity, but what happens *after* you've got your head on straight?"

"We'll have to see then."

"Okay."

Standing up with a sigh, Anna took a moment to collect herself. On the far side of the river, the buildings of Hull glittered in the afternoon sunlight. It occurred to her that this might be the last time she saw them. It wasn't likely that she would be coming back to Earth any time soon. This chapter of her life was over.

Funny how she was already starting to miss it. For nine months, all she could do was complain about the sexist attitudes of almost every cop she met, the frustrating lack of decent public transit, the pollution and the idiotic monetary system in which there was no harmony between what things cost and what people actually made. But now...This had been her home for a little while.

Anna bent over to press her lips to Jack's forehead, then pulled away, blinking. "I will always care about you, Jack," she whispered. "Never forget that."

Walking away was one of the hardest things she had ever done.

30

Dressed in a gray suit with a black tie, Senator Rick Parsons was a handsome man with chocolate brown skin and short hair that he wore parted to the side. He stood behind a lectern, anxiously eyeing the crowd.

Behind him, a series of flags lined the stage: the New York State Flag next to the stars and stripes of Old Glory and then a silver, four-pointed star on a field of blue. The emblem of the Justice Keepers.

Gripping the sides of the lectern with both hands, Parsons leaned forward to blink at the audience. "We have come here tonight," he began, "through a series of trials. We have passed through the fire together."

The banquet hall was filled with maybe thirty round tables, all with a pressed, lily-white tablecloth and a bouquet of flowers as the centerpiece. Every single one of those tables was occupied by at least half a dozen well-dressed people, and every single one of those people clapped for the introduction of what was bound to be a very rousing speech.

All except Harry.

He didn't feel very much like clapping for anything these

days. Not since his epic failure on the moon. The scene played out over and over again in his mind every time he closed his eyes: Slade stood there with a gun pointed at Harry's face, that mocking smile daring him to put up a fight.

He could have tried.

At the very least, he could have stalled for thirty more seconds. Maybe Jena would have finished off that alien creature and come charging in to help him. That scene played in his mind almost as often as the other.

His girlfriend leaped into the Nexus, doing one of those flashy somersaults of hers. Slade spun around to focus on her instead of Harry, and Jena deflected every last one of his bullets with one of those Bendings.

Then it was a fistfight that would make any martial arts film look tame. Slowly his girlfriend gained the upper hand, pummeling Slade with fists that moved so fast they seemed to blur. Harry seized the opportunity to take control of the Nexus, trapping Slade by turning the very room against him.

Then Jena snapped that bastard's neck.

They shared a kiss before Harry used the Nexus to permanently disable the Key, leaving the Ragnosians stranded on the other side of the galaxy. Melissa went to Leyria for training, eventually receiving a symbiont of her own. Jack and Anna got married. It was over. The horror was finally over. And all because Harry held on for those thirty god damn seconds.

But that wasn't what happened.

Slade had given him a choice, stay and die a pointless death in a fight he couldn't win, or run to help his family. Harry chose his family because the thought of leaving his daughters without a father was too much to bear. Sometimes, he had nightmares about being a ghost, watching Melissa and Claire trying to carry on without him.

Harry chose his family; Harry would *always* choose his

family, and in following that instinct, he had damned the galaxy.

Next to him, Gabi wore an elegant silver dress with a swooping neckline. Her hair was braided and held with a silver clip. "It's all right, Harry," she whispered, patting his arm. Somehow, the woman had sensed his distress.

Harry closed his eyes, nodding to her. "I know," he replied in a voice so soft it was barely audible over the Senator. "I was just thinking about all the people we lost. Raynar and Jena and…"

She patted his arm again.

On the other side of Gabi, Anna was bent over with her arms folded on the table's surface, her head hanging. The girl wore a little black dress that would turn every head in the room, but it was clear that mingling was the last thing on her mind.

Perhaps that was because of the chair next to her.

No one sat in that chair.

The place card in front of an empty plate read "Jena Morane," and everyone who passed by seemed to instinctively give it a wide berth. Even Jack, who sat on the other side of the empty chair seemed to avoid looking at it.

When the senator was finished, they chose to share the names of everyone who had fought to protect New York City. Harry watched as Pedro and several of his officers went on stage to receive a firm handshake from the mayor, a thank you from the Senator and a citation for valour.

Once they finished with the NYPD, it was time to honour the Justice Keepers who put their lives on the line. It was like watching a graduation ceremony that just wouldn't end; Keepers he'd never heard of walked across the stage. There had been teams fighting Slade's minions throughout the city.

Finally, his table was called.

Anna was the first one to receive her citation; she accepted it with a quiet murmur of thanks. Gabi was next, and then Jack. When it was Harry's turn, he had to dig deep to find the willpower to go up there.

The senator shook his hand; they gave him a medal. It was all very dignified. Or it would have been if Harry had been worthy of the honour.

The hardest part came when Pedro gave a speech honouring Jena's memory. The man spoke passionately about how Jena threw herself into harm's way repeatedly, about how she made it her personal mission to protect the people of New York, how she did everything in her power to frustrate Slade's plans.

Harry didn't want to listen to that.

Jena's death was on his conscience.

So Harry did what he always did in situations like this; he followed the rules. He waited for the ceremony to end and then mingled with the other guests. He made small talk with anyone who was willing and shooed away a reporter when she tried to ask him about what had happened on the moon. No way in hell he was discussing that!

Then he went home.

He poured himself a glass of whiskey, reviewed the offer some young couple had made for his house and prepared to emigrate across the galaxy. Hopefully, if he got far enough away, the pain would fade.

Folding a sweater into a neat little square, Jack set it inside his suitcase on top of a pile of clothing. Most of what he owned was now inside that case, which felt weird. The last time he had moved had been over four years ago, when he and Anna had accepted this apartment as compensation from Aamani Patel.

Jack stood over his bed in gray jeans and a black t-shirt with a V-neck, bathed in warm sunlight that came in through the window. "So, are you ready for the trip, Spock?" he asked, eyebrows rising. "Wanna go to a new world?"

The fat orange tabby cat was sprawled out upon the hardwood floor with one paw shielding his eyes from the sun. For the last three days, Spock had insisted on following Jack at all times. The kitty could tell that things were changing, and he didn't like it one bit. Luckily, Jack had been able to book transit on a ship that allowed passengers to bring their pets along with them. There would even be a small habitat where Spock could relax, receive regular meals and chase holograms.

He heard the front door open.

Jack lifted a t-shirt up in front of himself, folded it and dropped it into the suitcase. He wasn't expecting a visitor, but somehow he had a vague idea of who it might be, and he was willing to let his guest surprise him. After all, it was next to impossible to sneak up on a Keeper.

Gabi stepped through his bedroom door in a green sundress with thin straps, her hair pulled back in a long ponytail. "Hi," she said cautiously. "I realized I still have the key you gave me. Thought I should drop it off."

Jack winced, then rubbed his eyes with the back of his hand. "So, that's why you decided to pay me a visit?" he asked in a quiet voice. "Well, my landlord will appreciate having it back."

His ex-girlfriend moved slowly into the bedroom, stopping right behind him and folding her hands over her stomach. "I wanted to see how you were doing," she said. "I figured you might be ready to try being friends."

"I'd like that."

"Really?"

Jack spun around to face her, and though he had seen her in that dress many times, it was still a little odd to be reminded of just how lovely Gabi really was. Even with his talent for projecting colour onto the silhouettes that filled his mind, seeing a woman with your own eyes produced a response that you just didn't get from spatial awareness. His chest felt tight, his palms felt sweaty.

It was probably because his body was hardwired to respond a certain way to visual or auditory stimuli. Spatial awareness, on the other hand, was something that came from Summer. It was knowledge that his mind could use, but his body wasn't programmed to respond to it.

He sat down on the mattress with his hands on his knees, smiling into his own lap. "Yeah," he said, nodding to her. "I'd like to be friends. So, what happens now that you're out of LIS?"

"I'm not sure."

"Well, it's an honest answer."

Gabi crossed her arms, turning her face up to the ceiling. "So, what happens now?" she murmured, arching one eyebrow. "You know, I've always been the kind of girl who likes to plan out everything."

Biting his lower lip, Jack shut his eyes tight. "So I've been told," he replied. "It's a truly horrible vice, one that you should give up immediately. Ten Hail Marys and an Act of Contrition."

"Now, I'm not so sure I want to plan my next move," she said. "I'm thinking maybe I'll take a year off, travel a little, see the planets that I've visited as a tourist and not a spy. Then, maybe I'll settle into a nice analyst job."

"Terrible idea."

"You think so?"

How exactly could he explain this? "You're the kind of person who thrives on social interaction," he said. "Staring at reports, trying to find patterns in the data, that's not you."

He stood up.

Tilting her head back, Gabi stared up at him with those large dark eyes. "I was not aware that you'd become an expert on me," she murmured in that smoky voice that set his blood on fire. "But please, go on."

He turned his back on her and began fussing with the suitcase again, stacking more t-shirts onto the ever-growing pile. Getting the damn thing closed was going to be a pain in the ass, he could tell. "Just calling it like I see it," Jack said. "You don't want my input? I'm happy to keep my mouth shut."

"I'm sorry," she said. "I do want to hear it."

"All right," Jack muttered, noting that he was probably going to regret this. "You are at your best when you're reading people. The subtle cues that tell you what someone is feeling. That's what makes you a good spy."

"You think I'm a good spy?"

"I *know* you're a good spy," he said, spinning around and tossing a rolled up pair of socks at her. Gabi raised her hands up to shield herself and stumbled backward. "You can get information out of pretty much anybody. You learn all the nuances of a new situation in seconds, and – minor, non-essential bonus – you look absolutely gorgeous in a cocktail dress. You put people at ease; you make people want to talk to you, and everything about you makes them want to know you more. The perfect spy."

Gabi was smiling, her cheeks flushed to a deep red. "Thank you," she said softly. "You know, on your world, very few people would believe that someone with my body type could do all the things you just described."

Jack closed his eyes, heaving out a frustrated sigh. "That's true," he said, nodding once in confirmation. "But people on my world are idiots. It's your confidence and your intelligence that make you sexy."

"Not the way I look in this dress?"

"Oh, the dress is definitely a win!" he said quickly. How exactly did one go about explaining this? All his life, Jack had felt that his sexuality was just a little bit different than everyone else's. His high school friends would salivate over pictures of some model on Instagram, but Jack could look at the image of a woman that everyone else called "a perfect ten" and feel nothing at all.

But add confidence, intelligence, wit, and suddenly he would find that exact same woman irresistible. That wasn't to say that physical appearance didn't have *any* effect on him. Gabi in a cute little sundress would always get his attention, but it wasn't the dress itself that mattered.

It was the fact that she *wanted* to look hot. Not for his sake but for herself. He was turned on by the fact that she owned her sexuality and made no apologies for it. "It's not the dress, Gabs," he managed after a moment. "It's the way you wear it."

"That is incredibly sweet."

"Thank you."

"You seem to think very highly of me."

Pressing a fist to his mouth, Jack winced and cleared his throat. "Well, you *are* an amazing person," he said, trying to ignore his own chagrin. "But you could stand to be a little more impulsive."

Gabi stood there for a very long moment, staring at him as if she had never really seen him before. Then, suddenly, she grabbed one of her dress straps and pulled it down over her shoulder. The other strap followed half a second later, and the garment dropped to the floor.

"What are you doing?" Jack stammered.

"Being impulsive." She glided toward him like a goddess who had decided to grace some pitiful mortal with her presence. "We both know that we're not right for each other. But after everything we've been through, I think we've earned a little joy. So, what do you say? One last time?"

Before Jack even realized it, he was pulling his t-shirt over his head and tossing it to the floor. Then he flung the suitcase off of his bed with such force it toppled over and spilled its contents onto the floor. All that noise sent Spock bolting from the room in a fit of panic. Jack would have to repack everything.

He didn't care.

He slipped his arms around Gabi and pulled her close; her skin against his felt *so* good. Gently cupping her face with both hands, he tilted her chin up so that he could kiss her on the lips.

Then he pulled away and started nibbling on the side of her neck. "One condition," he whispered. "I don't think one last time is gonna cut it. We better make it four or five."

The Winnipeg SlipGate terminal was a huge, open room with a high ceiling and arch-shaped windows with metal grating on each wall. Sunlight fell upon people young and old as they made their way toward the four metal triangles that stood side by side near the back wall. "So I guess this is it," Jack said.

He wore black pants and a gray shirt under his brown jacket, the strap of a gym bag over one shoulder, a suitcase in the opposite hand. "I think that I want to go the rest of the way on my own, if you don't mind?"

"So, you'll call?"

He turned.

His mother stood behind him with her arms folded, frowning as if he'd just gotten a D on a spelling test. "I expect you to keep in touch," she said, stepping forward. "I mean, someone has to give me a break from your father and sister."

Jack shut his eyes tight, turning his face up to the ceiling. "I will call," he assured her. "At least once a week, possibly more. Besides, I think you're gonna want to see the new place once I'm settled in."

Crystal bowed her head to him, waves of honey-blonde hair falling over her face. "You know I will," she said, nodding. "And just in case you need a little mom pep talk, you're gonna do great."

"Give my love to everyone?"

"Of course."

He spun to face her, dropping his suitcase to the floor. If the bloody thing popped open, forcing him to pack everything a third time, he really didn't care. Before he knew it, he had his mother in a tight embrace.

Jack felt tears on his cheeks, but he did his best to ignore them. "I'm gonna miss all of you," he said, stepping back. "But I'm only a few days away. Maybe when I'm settled in, you could come for a visit."

"I'd like that."

"Well, I guess this is-"

Crystal silenced him by shaking her head emphatically. "No good-byes," she said, turning her head so that he couldn't get a good look at her expression. Not that he blamed her; no one wanted to be the kind of parent who broke down in front of their kid. "This is just a 'See you soon.'"

"See you soon."

He took his bags and started across the terminal before he got another attack of the feels and found himself thinking that maybe just maybe he was a moron for leaving his old life behind. That wouldn't do. The truth was, he wanted to go somewhere else. He had always been a little disenchanted with this planet, and now he had a chance to start fresh.

Of course, he had to pass through a security checkpoint before he could access the SlipGate. Apparently, that wasn't a thing on Leyria. Gates in secure locations could only be accessed with the right codes, but if you just wanted to travel from one city to another, you could do so freely.

A line of weapons scanners stood side by side, each one comprised of two curved metal plates spaced just far enough apart to let a single person passed through. People formed a queue in front of each one. He chose the shortest.

Moments later, he stepped through the scanner.

Jack closed his eyes as puffs of air hit his body, ruffling his hair. Then there was a soft humming sound that could lull a child to sleep if it was left playing. "You're clear," a gruff voice called out. "Step through, please."

On the other side of the scanner, a desk was occupied by a man in a gray uniform with a black tie, a man who studied the readout on a computer monitor. "Destination?" the guard asked.

"Star-liner *Valeria*."

"ID?"

Jack lifted his forum, activating his multi-tool. The holographic projector displayed an image of his badge and his dossier. "Very good, Agent Hunter," the guard said. "Your destination has been programmed into Gate 3. Please join that line."

He did as he was told, finding himself behind an old man in a Hawaiian shirt and a young boy who stood at his side. "How long are we staying in Florida?" the kid asked in that anxious voice that only a five-year-old could manage.

Jack tuned out the rest of the conversation.

When it was his turn, he approached the SlipGate cautiously. The metal triangle seemed to reflect the lights in the ceiling. The truth was that he felt a little uneasy about the SlipGates after his visit to the moon. He suspected most people did now.

He turned around to find himself staring at a line of people who were waiting their turn. Then a humming noise filled his ears, and a bubble formed around his body, making it seem as if the people were caught in the hazy heat that rose from black pavement.

He was pulled forward.

The bubble slammed to a stop in the middle of a smaller

room with gray walls, but he couldn't make out anything specific. Then it popped.

Chewing on his lip, Jack squeezed his eyes shut. "Never get used to that," he said, shaking his head. "Well, then...Let's just bring out the welcoming committee so that the guy from Earth doesn't get-"

A hologram appeared in the middle of this small room: a tall, slender man in a pair of black pants and a white shirt with a burgundy vest. "Greetings, Agent Hunter," it said through the speaker system. "Would you like to be shown to your cabin?"

"Yes, please," Jack said. "And then to the Rear Observation Deck."

"Right this way, sir.'"

Ten minutes later, he stepped onto a terrace where a large, curved window looked out on the blackness of space. The Earth floated before him with Western Europe still visible under the light of the sun while Asia was now dark.

Round tables were spaced out on the white-tiled floor and a long bench ran along the slanted wall opposite the window, positioned in front of flowerbeds where red tulips grew. It was lovely.

He found Melissa sitting on the bench with her younger sister. The older Carlson girl wore a pair of green skinny jeans and a black t-shirt. And as always, her eyes were downcast. *It takes time to gain confidence,* Jack noted. *You weren't so different, once.*

Claire wore a pair of dark blue jeans and a bright blue t-shirt with the Spider-Man logo. Her hair was pulled back in a pair of braids that fell over her shoulders. "Jack!" she called out when she saw him.

Just like that, she was on her feet and running at him.

Jack dropped to one knee to allow the girl to slam into him. He caught her up in a hug. "Hey! It's good to see you too!" he exclaimed. "So, you guys ready for three days of fun and excitement?"

"I wish Dad was here."

Closing his eyes, Jack took a deep breath. "I know, Sweetie," he said, nodding to the girl. "But he'll be along in a few weeks, and you ladies are gonna stay with me until your new house is ready."

"Yeah, but you're boring."

"Oh, I'm boring, am I?"

Claire pulled away from his embrace, crossing her arms and standing over him like an angry foreman looking down on the assembly line. "Very boring," she said. "You're so old. And you like stuff from like forty years ago."

Jack stood up. "Is that so?" he asked, leading Claire back to the bench with a hand on her back. "Well, then I guess you won't want to join your sister and I for game night. I suppose you could just go to bed."

"Game night? What games?"

"Well, I've got 'em all," he said. "Pictionary, Connect 4, and my personal favourite: Hungry, Hungry Hippos." He had raided his old bedroom closet for stuff he could take on this trip. "How are you, Melissa?"

The girl looked up at him with a big bright smile. "I'm good," she said, nodding. "Scared, but good."

He spun around and sat beside her with his hands on his knees, heaving out a deep breath. "Yeah, that's understand-able," Jack replied. "But you're gonna love it on Leyria. Trust me."

"I do."

Out of the corner of his eye, he saw a woman in an orange dress standing by the window, looking out at the stars. Larani seemed troubled, and he was pretty sure that he should find out what was on his new boss's mind. "Excuse me," he said, getting up. "I'll be right back."

Larani glanced over her shoulder as he approached, raising one dark eyebrow. "The girls seem excited," she murmured. "And a little scared. It reminds me of the first time I went off-world."

"Yeah? What was that like."

"I was twenty," she said softly. "For the first two decades of my life, I never left the planet's surface, never even made it into orbit. Then, suddenly, I'm assigned to a post on Salus Prime, and just like that, I'm whisked away."

Jack stepped up to the window with his arms folded, frowning as he stared through the pane. "Must have been scary," he muttered. "You know, aside from a very brief visit to your world, I've never left Earth."

"Change comes for us all, Agent Hunter."

"That it does."

"Are you looking forward to your new assignment?"

Tapping his lips with one finger, Jack narrowed his eyes. "You know, I think I am," he replied in a quiet voice. "Really, I'm looking forward to a fresh start. Too much pain these last few months."

Larani turned to the window with hands clasped behind her back, breathing deeply. "That's good," she said after a moment. "It's a new chapter for all of us. I suspect there will be many surprises."

"Good afternoon, passengers," a voice said over the speakers. "This is your Captain speaking. We've just received confirmation that our final guests have come on board, and we will be getting underway momentarily. It will take approximately three days and five hours to reach Leyria; during that time, we encourage you to make use of the ship's many amenities. Restaurants and nightly entertainment are available on Deck 4. If you have any questions, please feel free to ask a holographic assistant or contact myself or the crew via the intercom service.

Departure will commence in roughly two minutes. All crew prepare for warp jump."

He waited silently while Claire ran up and took his hand. Melissa joined them half a moment later, looking out at the only world they'd ever really known. Leaving it behind was quite an undertaking. He was nervous, and excited, and he could tell that the girls felt the same way.

The Earth floated in the blackness of space, catching the light of the distant sun. A low hum filled the air as the ship's engines powered up, and then the planet seemed to collapse into streams of blue and green light that flowed around the ship to the front.

They were on their way.

EPILOGUE

Deep in the bowels of an Overseer ship, a large cavernous chamber with reddish walls of veiny skin was filled with a pool of organic goop. It was a room that was used for only one purpose, a room that hadn't been accessed in years.

The molecules within the pool began to swirl, linking together to form chains of carbon atoms, constructing amino acids and then complex proteins. Within minutes, a functioning DNA strand was replicating itself.

It started with a skeletal system, building bones and joints, a skull with teeth and deep eye sockets that looked like pits. Muscle tissue came next, surrounding the bones, laced with veins and capillaries. A nervous system stretched throughout the entire body, sending electrochemical signals that ordered the heart to pump.

Skin formed, covering the tissue with a protective barrier. Black hair sprouted from the skull at an accelerated rate, growing to shoulder length.

A hand broke through the surface of the pool, trails of goop dripping from every finger. It trembled with new sensation as consciousness seeped into the newly-formed brain like water through a hole in the roof.

A face with a gaping mouth emerged, organic matter flowing down the man's throat and making him cough. What was this place? Everything seemed so muddled and foggy. He had been somewhere else before...

The man sat up.

Pressing the heels of his hands to his eye-sockets, he groaned as he tried to get his bearings. "Where..." He looked up, blinking. "Where have you taken me? What have you done to me?"

The memories began to coalesce in his mind, and suddenly he understood. He knew his purpose, the reason he had been created. He remembered it all with perfect, vivid clarity. The loss...The humiliation.

He remembered the look of hatred on Jena Morane's face as she staggered into the Nexus while he just stood there in a euphoric stupor. Bonding with the Key had been an experience unlike any other. It had left him unable to respond, but he had accomplished his task. The Gates were now open.

He remembered dying.

And the abyss beyond this life. A void of endless nothingness where he had been unable to see or hear or touch. Conscious but unable to affect the world in any way. Left with nothing to do but choke on his own hatred. It was a fate worse than the most horrid descriptions of Hell any human mind could imagine, and the Inzari had saved him from it as they had once before.

He climbed out of the pool of goo, naked and shivering, dropping to one knee on the shore. Sensation! Sweet, glorious sensation! He would gladly endure the worst pain over what he had experienced in that place.

"Why?" he whispered.

You have not yet completed your function, the Inzari whispered in his mind. A part of him wanted to insist that he had failed, that he allowed himself to be destroyed, but the Inzari did not see things as humans did. The destruction of his mortal body was nothing more than a minor setback. He had accomplished his task. He had opened the Gates, and so they had rewarded him with a reprieve from the emptiness.

Hunter, Lenai and their allies did not understand. They stood against the Inzari out of sheer ignorance. There was no victory against the Inzari. You could serve or spend an eternity in that empty void. And unlike the priests of every religion, he had the experience to verify his claims. It did not matter. He was himself again, and he remembered all of it.

He was Grecken Slade, and his enemies would pay for what they had done to him.

The End of the Fifth Book of the Justice Keepers Saga.

Dear reader,

We hope you enjoyed reading *Evolution*. Please take a moment to leave a review, even if it's a short one. Your opinion is important to us.

The story continues in *Dirty Mirror*. Read the first chapter for free at https://www.nextchapter.pub/books/dirty-mirror

Discover more books by R.S. Penney at https://www.nextchapter.pub/authors/ontario-author-rs-penney.

Can't get enough of the Justice Keepers Saga? Visit Rich's Patreon for more exclusive content at https://www.patreon.com/richpenney.

Want to know when one of our books is free or discounted? Join the newsletter at http://eepurl.com/bqqB3H.

Best regards,

R.S. Penney and the Next Chapter Team

ABOUT THE AUTHOR

Richard S. Penney is a science-fiction author and futurist from Southern Ontario. He graduated from McMaster University with a degree in mathematics and statistics. Rich knew that he wanted to be a writer ever since he was a child, when he would act out complex stories with his action figures.

He has worked in a number of different fields, including banking, teaching and software QA.

In 2014, Rich published his first novel, *Symbiosis,* the first volume of the Justice Keepers Saga. The story was one that he had been planning to write ever since he was a teenager. The Desa Kincaid novels grew out of a tandem story that Rich started on Theoryland.com, a Wheel of Time discussion site.

Rich has been an environmental activist since his early twenties, and he has given talks on sustainability in Greece and Australia.

CONTACT THE AUTHOR

Follow me on Twitter @Rich_Penney
E-mail me at keeperssaga@gmail.com
You can check out my blog at rspenney.com
You can also visit the Justice Keepers Facebook page
https://www.facebook.com/keeperssaga
Questions, comments and theories are welcome.

BOOKS BY R.S. PENNEY

Symbiosis (Justice Keepers Saga I)

Friction (Justice Keepers Saga II)

Entanglement (Justice Keepers Saga III)

Relativity (Justice Keepers Saga IV)

Evolution (Justice Keepers Saga V)

Dirty Mirror (Justice Keepers Saga VI)

Severed Bonds (Justice Keepers Saga VII)

Dark Designs

Desa Kincaid: Bounty Hunter

Evolution
ISBN: 978-4-86750-421-5

Published by
Next Chapter
1-60-20 Minami-Otsuka
170-0005 Toshima-Ku, Tokyo
+818035793528

18th June 2021

9 784867 504215